THE NECROMANCER'S BONES

Deby Fredericks

To Brandu—
Have a wonderful
holiday and enjoy the
story!
Deby Fredericks

Dragon
Moon

www.dragonmoonpress.com

The Necromancer's Bones

Copyright © 2009 Deby Fredericks

ISBN 10 1-896944-91-4 Print Edition
ISBN 13 978-1-896944-91-3

Dragon Moon Press is an Imprint of Hades Publications Inc.
P.O. Box 1714, Calgary, Alberta, T2P 2L7, Canada

Dragon Moon Press and Hades Publications, Inc. acknowledges the ongoing support of the Canada Council for the Arts and the Alberta Foundation for the Arts for our publishing programme.

The Alberta Foundation for the Arts

COMMITTED TO THE DEVELOPMENT OF CULTURE AND THE ARTS

Canada Council for the Arts   Conseil des Arts du Canada

Printed and bound in Canada or the United States
www.dragonmoonpress.com
www.debyfredericks.com

Dedication

For my parents,
Ann and Eldon Dunn,
and for James C. Glass,
who encouraged me to believe
Shenza's story deserved to be told.

Chapter One

The Chaos Moon

Out in the garden, something flashed. Shenza Waik of Tresmeer looked up as the flare of light caught her eye. Her pen stopped scratching across the scroll of cloth in front of her.

Shenza was kneeling beside a low table in her work room. A teakwood lamp hung above her head. Carved in the shape of a sea-whip, it cast a pool of light around her while the rest of the house lay dark. Shenza gazed through the open sides of the cottage, into a garden hinted by shadows. A light breeze made the treetops whisper like someone calling her name.

The night was warm in Chalsett, City of Gardens. It hummed with songs of crickets and frogs. Another soft breeze stirred the leafy garden and Shenza saw what had caught her attention: instead of stars winking between the branches, a round, shining object rose in the sky.

Which moon was that? Shenza frowned thoughtfully. It was too small to be Prenuse, too pale to be Quaiss, too bright to be Meor. Perhaps it was nothing, yet the tenor of the night had changed. It suddenly felt as brittle and easily shattered as a fallen leaf.

Shenza put down her pen and leaned away from the table, arching her back to ease its stiffness. She rubbed her dark eyes and ran brown fingers through her loose black curls. Then she pushed back the inventory of spell ingredients she had been working on. Shenza was between investigations, an ideal time to replenish the talismans and amulets she had used up, yet she felt too restless to concentrate.

Glad for an excuse to stop, she gathered her purple robe and stood, strolling toward the porch. The mysterious moon was now hidden by trees. Shenza followed a gravel path toward the center of the garden, where she would have a better view. Insects and frogs fell silent as she passed.

The last time she had gone into a garden at night, she had met a stranger—one of the Eleshi, a nature spirit. First in the form of a snake, and then something like a human. It had been like the sea, beautiful and wild and deadly. Shenza shivered, remembering its alien beauty.

That had been the first of several encounters, all of them in darkness or deep shadow. There was no reason to think another spirit was visiting her, yet still she felt tension in the air. She stopped, inhaling lightly. There had been a certain fragrance the spirit carried with it, like blooms of an unearthly flower. She didn't smell it now. A part of her relaxed.

Shenza continued forward, watching her step on the dark path. The cottage behind her was quiet and empty. Shenza shared the dwelling with Master Laraquies, her old teacher. Since her training was finished, she could have returned to her mother's house. Or, since Lord Aspace had chosen Laraquies as his Vizier, he could have claimed a grander residence in the first lord's estate. But the living arrangement was so comfortable, neither one had suggested it. Shenza, at least, benefitted from having access to her teacher's wise advice.

Tonight, Master Laraquies was up at the palace. Lord Aspace didn't entertain as much as his late brother, Lord Anges, but he still had banquets. Laraquies had to be there, observing the byplay of the nobles and sometimes intervening in their squabbles. Shenza had been invited, too, but she had declined. Although her rank as magister was respectable, she still felt like a lowly fisherman's daughter. It was easier to be alone than to deal with the nobles, who resented her intrusion into their elite circle.

Then Shenza smiled at herself for prowling through her garden in the dark. If inventory made her this restless, maybe she should have gone with Master Laraquies. She didn't like the nobles, but Lord Aspace was another story. She could enjoy his company if he ever stopped teasing her.

Not that someone like Shenza could ever have any hope with a man like Aspace. Maybe that was the real reason she avoided the palace. It hurt to like someone so much and know he could never be hers.

Shenza found a clear spot beside the brook that wound through the garden. When she looked up, what she saw threw all her petty complaints out of her mind.

Skall was in the sky. Skall, the moon of chaos! Shenza took a step backward, toward the house. It couldn't be. She felt a sense of unreality, as she had when the Eleshi came to her. Shenza squeezed her eyes tightly shut, then opened them again. The chaos moon was still there.

Now Shenza studied the heavens intently. Inkesh was just rising, its ruby crescent showing in patches through the treetops. Meor rode at its zenith, a gibbous lavender orb. The other two moons weren't visible.

The dim sky made Skall's glow all the brighter. Its face was vivid white marked with darker splotches. Skall was the smallest of the moons. Shenza felt she could pluck it down from the sky and wear it like a bead, but she didn't want to.

Like the other four moons, Skall represented a force in life—chance and change, the whims of fate. While the other moons had regular movements which could be studied and predicted, Skall only appeared rarely. There was never a pattern. It seemed to come and go at its own whim.

Shenza's neck was tight from gazing upward. She shook her head, let out a breath, and forced herself to relax. There was no reason to panic. This was an omen, yes. Skall's appearance foretold an important event, but there was no way to know what it would be. She could only watch, stay alert, and try to prepare.

She took another long look, and then turned back toward the house. Suddenly her inventory seemed much more urgent.

* * *

Morning came to Chalsett-port. Chimi Waik of Tresmeer met it in the market, where she had just opened her fish stall. Though she usually had a ready smile, a frown now marred her smooth brow.

A child was crying. It wasn't the whine of a brat who wanted his way, or the shrill demand of one who felt bored and left out. The low moaning went on without stopping, even through the noise of the busy marketplace.

From the time she was twelve until she turned sixteen, Chimi had spent her days watching the youngsters of her neighborhood. She could tell this was the sound of a child really hurt and afraid. How could any mother ignore such sobs?

"Is there some problem?" asked a woman's impatient voice.

"Oh! No, I'm sorry." Chimi bobbed a quick, apologetic bow to the customer she had been ignoring. She ducked down beneath the counter and straightened with a parcel of fresh fish wrapped in a banana leaf. "I heard a child crying."

"Let his mother worry about him," the woman advised as she turned away.

"Yes, matron," Chimi answered meekly.

The wailing went on. Now that her customer was gone, Chimi looked around for its source. Chimi was a short girl, slightly plump, with brown skin and bright dark eyes. Her hair fell below her shoulders in springy black curls. She would have liked to have it straightened, in the fashionable way, but she knew her mother would never allow it.

Her clothing, however, was as stylish as she could afford. Chimi wore a close-wrapped robe that left her shoulders bare but covered her body to the knees. The bold pattern of blue shells on natural cloth was matched by strands of wooden beads around her wrists and neck. On her head, a neatly wrapped headcloth completed the ensemble.

Still the child cried. It grated on Chimi's nerves.

"Where is it?" she murmured.

Her dark eyes roved, seeking the crying child. And, more importantly, the parents who should have been running to comfort their young one. She couldn't pick them out in the busy scene before her.

It was early morning and the central market was mostly in shadow, but that wouldn't last. Soon the sun would peer over the hills above Chalsett-port. Already the harbor's clear waters sparkled as the first rays struck them. Farther off, beyond the breakwater, the Jewel Sea rolled on without end. A salty breeze made the awning above her head rustle and snap.

The aisle before Chimi was crowded with brown-skinned citizens pushing by on their errands. Their bright robes made the scene a riot of lively colors. On the other side of the aisle, a low wall guarded the short drop to the lower level. Long ships crowded the piers below. Some had tall prows carved like sea-serpents or fishing birds. Crewmen swarmed about them, taking on cargo or unloading merchandise. It wasn't so long ago that the wharves had been closed during the investigation of First Lord Anges' murder. The new ruler, his brother Aspace, was well established by now. The renewed confidence in Chalsett-port meant that business was returning nicely—to Chimi's stall, along with the others.

"Chimi!" whispered another voice.

She turned toward the tenant of the neighboring stall. Nakuri was a large woman, well fleshed, in a robe of bright green with a pattern of yellow lilies. A band of the same fabric held black, curly hair away from her face. A silver ring glinted in one nostril as she jerked her chin down the aisle.

Following her motion, Chimi glimpsed a tall, well-favored young man strolling toward them. She smiled back at Nakuri and made a show of wiping her counter top with a rag. Rellad Offram of Melleen was a regular customer at her booth. He approached so casually now that Chimi knew he was faking. But that was all right. Rellad was the son of a weaver, an apprentice weaver himself. His family was rich. Chimi knew them because her mother, who grew feather-flowers, sold the silken thread to the Melleen workshop.

Not that Rellad was her only regular customer. Chimi had built a good clientele for the fresh mussels and fish she sold. The booth actually belonged to her family's friend, Byben of Cessill. Business had been miserable for the drunken old man, but with a girl as cute as Chimi, the situation had turned around. The old man was sweet, and besides, an elder should be resting, not working to make ends meet.

Usually a girl Chimi's age was kept at home, introduced only to men selected by their fathers or household elders. But Chimi's father was dead, long ago claimed by the sea. The burden of providing for their family fell upon Chimi's mother, but also partly on her older sister and brother. Now Chimi was old enough to work and contribute to the family's income. She ran Byben's stall, while he took her place tending the vines and spinning.

It gave him a chance to get out of his empty, lonely house. Chimi received exactly the same benefit.

Secretly, she reveled in the freedom her job gave her, and in the fact that her careworn mother was too busy to think about finding a wife for Chimi's brother, Sachakeen, let alone husbands for her two daughters.

Chimi was especially excited about Rellad, though. Unlike the others who bought from her, he was attractive, and not too old for her, and he had no senior wives. Not that there was anything wrong with being a secondary wife, but that wasn't the future Chimi wanted for herself.

As Chimi was pretending not to see Rellad, she did see the crying child. The urchin was about four or five, a boy by the cut of his short kilt. His mouth dragged down at the corners, his narrow chest heaved, and tears left gleaming tracks across his cheeks. Water dripped from the bottom of his garment and the curly ends of his wild, tangled hair. He seemed to be coming up from the quays. Had he fallen into the water, then?

Chimi hesitated. She didn't want to miss Rellad, but the little boy's sobbing tore at her heart. Once again she looked around the lively moil of the market. Where were his parents?

She couldn't stand it. "Oh, by the heavens!" she cried.

"What's that?" Nakuri turned in surprise as Chimi raised her counter with an agitated jerk.

"I'll be right back," Chimi said over her shoulder. She slipped through the narrow gap and dropped the counter back in place. "Don't let him leave."

"Where are you going?" Nakuri asked.

"I have to see what's wrong with that boy. Just don't let Rellad leave. Please? I'll be right back!"

"But..." Nakuri's voice faded as Chimi darted after the small, retreating figure.

"Wait!" Chimi called.

No response. The boy kept crying, kept walking. Sandals slapping the cobblestones, Chimi wove through the throng. She called apologies when she didn't quite dodge some passing body.

"Wait for me!" Chimi cried.

The child didn't seem to hear her, but he wasn't moving very fast. Chimi dashed past him and spun, dropping to her knees in front of the boy.

"Wait, I said. What's wrong?" she demanded.

The boy shuffled toward her, bawling as though his heart was broken. Every footstep left a wet blot behind him. To keep the child from walking into her, Chimi grabbed his shoulder.

"Oh!" She drew her hand back with a startled jerk. The bony shoulder was *cold*, cold with the chill of deep sea water. The sensation ran up her arm and left her feeling numb. While she stared at him, the boy finally stopped howling.

"What—" Chimi stammered. She flexed her fingers and rubbed her arm to get the ache out of her shoulder. "Why are you crying?"

"I can't find my mommy." His lips made a trembling line of fear.

So he was lost. As the round, dark eyes fixed on her face, Chimi summoned a smile. "Well, then, we'll find her. Don't worry. Let's go look for her. All right?"

He sniffled, rubbing his eyes with a small brown fist. "I want to find my mommy."

"Of course you do. What's your name?"

"I can't find my mommy."

Chimi sighed. She had forgotten how single-minded children could be at this age. "I know that, little brother, but what's your name? What can I call you?"

He had to think about it. "Yail."

"Good boy," Chimi said, to reassure him. "Now don't you worry, Yail. We'll go find your mommy." She offered her hand, cautiously this time, and was relieved that the cold wasn't as overpowering when his fingers touched hers.

"Chimi," Nakuri called.

Chimi looked around to see Rellad at her counter. He and Nakuri both watched her indulgently.

"Coming!"

She straightened, keeping slightly bent so she wouldn't yank on her companion's arm. "Come with me, Yail. I'll only be a moment."

Yail resisted as she guided him through the crowd to her booth. "I want to find my mommy."

"We will, don't worry. I just need to help my customer. Then we can go."

So saying, she pressed her free hand to her chest and bowed to Rellad. His answering smile warmed the numbness in her shoulders and chest.

"Who's this?" Nakuri asked.

"His name is Yail. He says he's lost," Chimi said. Then she smiled up at Rellad. "Good morning. What can I do for you?"

After a questioning glance at Yail, Rellad replied, "Twenty of the small mussels. My mother really liked them last time."

"Of course," Chimi said. "I always save some for you."

"Lucky me," Rellad smiled back and tossed a mesh bag onto the counter.

Yail whined as Chimi tried to lead him into her booth. The boy would probably wander off if she let go, so Chimi lifted him by the waist and set him on the edge of the counter.

"Stay here for a second," she said, trying to sound more patient than she felt.

"I want to find my mommy!"

"We will," she reassured him. "We will."

More of her attention was on Rellad, who leaned a little closer as she brushed past to get behind her counter. Still smiling at him, she knelt beside the basketry bins, which were woven with magic symbols to keep the food inside from spoiling. With quick fingers she counted twenty of the shellfish in their tight black husks. Her fingers felt clumsy with cold.

On the counter above, Yail began to whimper again.

"I didn't know you like kids," Rellad said.

"Oh, they're great." Chimi wasn't in any hurry to start a family, but she didn't want him to know that just yet. Better if he thought her a likely choice for a wife. "I used to watch them all the time in my neighborhood."

"I'll bet you did a good job."

"It was fun." Chimi straightened and set the bag of mussels on the counter. Since Rellad often purchased the same amount, he had his rukh ready. She glanced at the small squares of copper and swept them into her hand. Not wanting him to leave so soon, she asked, "How is your family?"

Rellad leaned one elbow on the counter. "Doing fine. Father just got a big order in from Amethan, City of Fountains. He'll be needing a few rolls of feather-flower thread."

"Really?" Chimi dropped the coins into a leather pouch hanging from the counter. "I'll be sure to tell my mother."

"You should."

Yail went back to his whining. "Mommy!"

"Oh, don't cry." Chimi leaned over to hug him, trying to ignore the chill as he attempted to climb over the counter into her arms. The boy was heavy, and she struggled momentarily. "We'll find her. Come on, don't cry."

Yail responded by bawling, "I want to find my mommy!"

Nakuri came out of her booth, an odd frown on her face. "Chimi?"

She could hardly hear through the sobs next to her ear.

"All right, all right," Chimi murmured. "We'll go find your mommy."

"My mommy!"

Nakuri reached out to lay her meaty hand across his forehead. She drew it back with a startled expression and blurted, "Chimi, I think he's a ghost!"

"What?" Chimi gasped.

There was a shocked silence. Even Yail stopped crying. Chimi fought the impulse to drop the boy and back away. Rellad, who wasn't encumbered, took a long step backward.

Everyone knew about ghosts. Chimi had never seen one before. Like most people, she hoped not to. She remembered some kind of lessons in general school, but she hadn't paid much attention. Spiritualism didn't interest her. So she stood for a moment, with the dead boy growing heavier and colder in her arms.

"What—what should I do?" she stammered to Nakuri. Rellad's disgusted expression was too hard to face.

"Find a necromancer, and hurry," the older woman said. "They can lay a haunting spirit to rest."

"Right. Can you watch my stall?" Chimi fumbled with the counter and felt a pang as Nakuri, not Rellad, helped her raise it and pass through. The young man didn't even reach for his mussels. Chimi started to hurry away, but quickly turned back. "Where is one?"

"There used to be one..." Nakuri hesitated. "Lelldour. Lelldour of—never mind. He's on the fourth tier, above the ship builders and behind the town shrine. You'll see a red lamp at the gate. Hurry now, and get this little one home."

Take him home—but not the way Chimi had been planning. She had expected a happy reunion with frantic parents. Feeling numb all over, Chimi nodded and turned away. She didn't want to see Rellad shuffling, practically backing up to the sea wall. He didn't meet her gaze, and she felt the cold eating a hole in her heart.

* * *

Sunlight was just beginning to warm the morning air. Chimi's path led her back toward the hills, deeper into shadow. She left the fish market and went under the arbors, which were covered with vines to shade the rest of the market from the full heat of day. There was plenty of foot traffic, and shopkeepers called their wares with loud abandon, but no one spared Chimi a second glance. She wished someone would offer to help her.

Once she started walking, Yail's moaning trailed off. He rested his head on her shoulder, as if he slept. It would have been a touching, trusting gesture except that she couldn't feel him breathing. Chimi had the uncomfortable sense that she was walking away from the normal world, toward some strange land of eternal dusk. Since she didn't want to stay in twilight forever, she went as fast as she could without bouncing him.

It wasn't fair, Chimi thought with gnawing anxiety. A part of her said that Yail was already dead, so there was nothing she could do to help him. She should just put him down and get back to work. Nakuri couldn't handle both shops forever. And she wanted Rellad to smile at her again. Yet she couldn't bring herself to push away the frigid little body next to hers. Alive or dead, he was still a lost child. What kind of person would turn her back on him?

Chimi passed through the center of the marketplace, where a huge fig tree grew in a broad plaza. The terraces of the town rose before her. Marble retaining walls were draped with the lush greenery that gave Chalsett-port its name, City of Gardens.

On the other side of the plaza was the main stairway that gave access to the whole city. The stairs were of marble, pale flights flanked by hand rails and the occasional statue. The white stone looked ghostly against the shadowed hillside. Chimi's legs ached as she climbed the steep risers.

Behind the town shrine, Nakuri had said. That was on the eastern promontory above the harbor. You reached it from the third level. The necromancer, Lelldour, must live on the fourth tier. Chimi turned right after topping two flights of stairs. Her breath came hard as she made her way down the narrow street. The road was paved with large cobblestones. At regular intervals, shallow channels caught water from the island's daily rains and diverted it into household cisterns. On either side, low walls of marble or bamboo screened the homes from prying eyes.

What Chimi could see of them hinted at modest dwellings, round huts topped with roofs of thatch. Occasionally she heard the splash of a fountain or distant voices of families at work or play. A pall of smoke from cooking fires hung in the air. Trees grew everywhere, ferns with shaggy trunks and lacy leaves, conifers with dark needles and pointed tops.

Yail must have lived in this kind of neighborhood. Somewhere, his family must be waiting for him, not knowing what had happened. How could a small child have been left on his own to drown? Chimi hugged her small passenger tighter, ignoring the fatigue in her arms.

She hurried on. The street curved to the right. Confronting a fork in the road, Chimi hesitated.

"Which way?" she asked. Yail didn't answer her.

She took the right hand way and continued on, looking for the red lantern Nakuri had mentioned. She saw a pair of green posts, marking a curomancer's house, but no death-colored ones. Another intersection. The main road curved back west and a lesser way continued east. A gap in the trees showed her the sea, its calm surface studded with tiny coral isles.

The shrine was still farther east, so Chimi went that direction. The road curved sharply, following the shape of the hillside that loomed before them. Her arms throbbed as she continued past a third intersection.

"I hope it's not much farther," Chimi groaned. After some resistance, Yail let her shift him to the other side. While she did that, she nearly missed a bit of dull red on her left.

Even when she stopped and stared, it was hard to see the faded color against a background of vines and shadows. Chimi turned back and approached the gate doubtfully. The wall was of field stones, so covered with moss that she could hardly see their original color. There was a sturdy plinth, and the wooden lantern with its top peaked like the roof of a house. It had been red once, but the paint was mostly gone. Chimi supposed it could have been an advertisement for the necromancer. Maybe it had once given light to visitors. It obviously hadn't been used in a long time. Chimi peered uncertainly into the dusk beneath a dense canopy of trees.

Inside the wall was the most neglected yard she had ever seen. Fallen leaves lay in a thick matt over every surface. As she watched, a single leaf spiraled down to join the rest. Even without going in, she could smell the moldy odor of decayed vegetation. Young trees sprouted from the leaf bed, but they were lanky and pale, starved for light beneath the taller trees.

The round, dark bulk of a house loomed at the end of a level stretch. There must be a walkway under all the leaves. The building had a shaggy look, like thatched construction. She saw no light inside it, nor smoke from a cooking fire.

Maybe the necromancer had gone out for the day? After all, Chimi had never heard of necromancy as a money-making trade. He might have to work for a living. Maybe that was why he had no time for keeping up his yard. Chimi shivered at the thought. Lelldour couldn't be gone. She needed his help. He had to be here!

Jogging anxiously in place, she looked around again. There should have been a bell or gong beside the gate. She didn't see one, though she shifted the vines to look for it. Chimi did glimpse a shadow beneath the foliage. She leaned forward to read the carved letters: Salloo.

That was a clan name, and it seemed right. There weren't many necromancers, even in a city the size of Chalsett-port. Everyone knew their names. Well, people who listened to gossip did, and Chimi listened to gossip. Lelldour of Salloo sounded familiar. Of course, that didn't tell her if he really lived here. Still, there was the lantern.

"Good morning!" Chimi called toward the house. Her voice was shrill in the hush of the street. The neighborhood seemed unusually quiet for this time of day. There weren't even any birds singing, and such big trees should have been full of them. Chimi shivered again and shifted Yail back to her other hip.

"Hello!" It was an emergency, so she yelled more loudly. "Hello! May I come in?"

Chapter Two

Ball and Bone

Still there was no response. Chimi stepped forward anyway. It wasn't nice to go on someone's property without permission, but she was desperate to get rid of Yail. She had to put the responsibility for his life—no, his afterlife—in more capable hands.

Wet leaves squished beneath her sandals. Though she picked her way with care, Chimi felt her feet slip. She took a long step to recover her balance, and heard a distinct splat.

"Ugh!" Chimi cried with disgust as cold water and slippery leaves washed over her toes. A garden stream had gotten clogged with debris and backed up to form a shallow pond. She hadn't seen it under all the floating litter.

It was hard to tell where the water ended and land began, so Chimi stepped carefully. She didn't want to fall in the filthy water. Her clothes would be ruined!

To her relief, the path rose as she got closer to the cottage. Scattered mushrooms poked their heads up from the leaves on all sides. All the trees in the yard were varieties of weeping-wood, she noticed. Their sap could be cooked with brimstone to make rubber. Maybe Lelldour grew the trees for making rubber. In that case, he really should take better care of them.

"Good morning!" Chimi called as she approached the house.

The foundation was of field rocks with thatched walls rising above it. Stone steps led up to a deep porch. Chimi halted at the base, eyeing the dark cavity. The thatch was patchy with neglect, and it had moss growing on it. Like most homes in the humid islands, it had a section of wall open to the garden for ventilation. The interior was dark and still, and she felt a stab of worry. It looked like no one was home.

"Good morning," she repeated loudly. "Is anyone here?"

Chimi bit her lip and jigged with growing dread. *He is here*, she chanted to herself. *He is here, he is here, he has to be here!*

There was a faint noise inside the house. Then a man shuffled slowly onto the porch. He was tall, with a strong frame, but so thin that Chimi thought he must have been seriously ill and hadn't totally recovered yet.

His hair fell to his shoulders in stringy black coils, as if he hadn't combed it in days. His short robe and kilt were blood red, a necromancer's color. In contrast to the faded lamp and neglected yard, the color was vivid and the cloth neatly folded. It looked like he was in his middle years, not yet an elder, but the deep lines and gaunt face gave him an older, sadder look.

Yail shifted in Chimi's arms, looking at the newcomer. Then he let his head drop again. The man's dark eyes regarded Chimi without interest. But she had her goal in sight and she wasn't about to be put off.

"Are you the necromancer Lelldour?" she asked, doing her best to sound cheerful and normal when the situation was anything but ordinary. "I've found a ghost boy, and I'd like you to put him at rest, please. I have to get back to my shop."

"You found him?" A flicker of interest animated Lelldour's features. He was actually almost handsome, although much too old for Chimi, of course.

"Yes. He was in the market, crying," she explained. "I just couldn't ignore him, and when I asked what was wrong he said he couldn't find his mother. Then my friend, in the next stall, she told me he might be a ghost and said I should come to you."

Lelldour looked Chimi over in a way that made her uneasy.

"You," he repeated in a skeptical tone.

"Yes," she said, getting flustered. "So you can take him back to his family. He needs to be laid to rest."

"I can see that, but I'm afraid I can't help you."

Chimi blinked at him, while all the blood drained into her feet and the cold of Yail's body seemed to freeze her limbs.

"But—" she stuttered through chattering teeth. "You are the necromancer, aren't you?"

He nodded. "I was, but no longer. I can't help you."

"What? But—" Half a dozen thoughts chased each other through Chimi's mind. Not a necromancer? He didn't look old enough to retire. And he couldn't refuse to help her. She had to get back to work. She didn't want anything more to do with dead people!

Chimi grasped at the least selfish protest. "But what will happen to him? He has to be laid to rest."

Patiently, as if it should have been obvious, Lelldour told her, "Then you must do it."

This wasn't what she wanted to hear.

"No, no, no," Chimi babbled, resisting the urge to drop the boy and scramble away. "I can't—I don't—Don't know anything about ghosts!"

For some reason, this amused him. "You'll learn," he said.

"No, no, no. I can't!" Necromancy wasn't the kind of thing that interested her. Not even a little bit. It just wasn't feminine! "Please, Master Lelldour, can't you do it? Please."

"No," he answered brusquely. "Do you want my advice, or do you plan to carry the boy around with you all day?"

Chimi felt like crying. Briefly she wondered if that would sway him. Even as she thought about it, Lelldour told her, "Oh, put the boy down. He won't wander off, and you'll accomplish more with your hands free."

She opened her mouth to retort, but then realized he was right. Her shoulders burned with Yail's weight, even as her lungs ached with the cold.

"All right." Chimi bent toward the ground and muttered to her passenger, "Go on, Yail. I know you can stand."

She tried to show the warmth she had felt before, when she hadn't known what he was, and knew she didn't succeed. Still, the boy stood on his own.

Meanwhile, the necromancer sat on the edge of the porch. His long legs easily stretched to the bottom step. In an oddly informal gesture, he patted the worn boards beside him. "Come, boy. Let Big Sister work."

Chimi tensed. It was perfectly polite if Yail called her "big sister," due to the difference in their ages. It was better than calling her "matron," which would make her sound much too old. However, she didn't like Lelldour assigning her the title. It wasn't as if she wanted to be friendly with a dead person.

Yail regarded the necromancer with serious, dark eyes. He finally went to sit on the upper step, where his shoulders were on a level with the necromancer's waist. He didn't look around when the older man patted his arm, but kept his eyes fixed on Chimi.

"I assume you can cast magic spells," Lelldour said.

"Of course," she answered, annoyed that he would think she couldn't. Anyone could do magic. It was a part of the world, as familiar as sun and rain and the green trees around them.

"Then you'll want to look for a red rubber ball. It should be somewhere around here."

Reluctantly, Chimi looked around. She wondered rebelliously why he couldn't get the ball, if it was his, but scant help was better than none. She circled the landing slowly, eyes on the ground, scuffed in the layer of dead leaves, and knelt to peer into the crawl space beneath the house. Glimpsing a round shape in the darkness, she flattered herself to stretch a hand through the bamboo slats, but quickly sat up again as he fingers touched the coarse grain of a stone. Chimi straightened, brushing damp leaves from her clothing, and began to kick through the leaves again.

"Try calling it," Lelldour suggested.

"It's an enchanted ball?"

"Yes. It's a finding ball. Even you should be able to summon it," he added condescendingly.

"You could have said so," Chimi muttered.

Again she struggled with her feelings, her distress at being involved with Yail and her irritation that, instead of using his own skills, Lelldour left the nasty chores for her. To be honest, magic wasn't what Chimi did best. Since her older sister, Shenza, was a professional magician, it had always been easy to ask her for any magic beyond the basics. But Chimi had said she could do this, and now he challenged her to prove it.

Swallowing a lump of self-pity, Chimi squared her shoulders, closed her eyes, and folded her hands at the base of her throat to focus her energy there. The familiar action seemed awkward and strange with them watching her. She took deep breaths and tried to shut out the feeling of their eyes on her.

Power began to build, flowing as much from her agitation as from concentration. A red ball, Lelldour said. She pictured it in her mind. The rubber would have a smooth surface with a dull sheen. If it was enchanted, there would be runes on it. She didn't know what symbols would make the finding spell, so she focused on sensing the substance, resilient yet pliable, that it was made of.

Finding ball, come to me. Chimi thought the words loudly in her mind. *Do your work. Find me!*

There was a feeling of pressure against her temples, and then soft rustling to her right. Chimi opened her eyes. Something twitched beneath the carpet of leaves. She strode to the spot and knelt, pushing the moist covering aside. A small red ball was trying to roll itself over a forked twig. She snatched the ball, expecting it to be slimy from the rotten leaves. To her relief, it was merely cool and a little damp. As she had expected, there were runes drawn on the ball with black ink. The markings were scuffed and worn from use.

"Well done." Lelldour's tone suggested he hadn't really expected Chimi to succeed. As she turned back to him, a measuring expression crossed his face.

"Here." Chimi extended her prize toward him, only to be met by firm denial.

"This isn't my task."

"Then what do I do with it?" she asked impatiently.

"Find." To her annoyance, he actually smirked at her.

"Find what?" Chimi insisted, propping the ball against one hip.

"A restless spirit always has one thing it needs in order to be at rest," Lelldour explained. "Yail told you he's looking for his mother. The finding ball will guide you to her."

"Oh, all right."

He shouldn't lecture as if Chimi was his apprentice. That was the last thing she wanted to be! She cupped the ball in both hands and raised it to the base of her throat. The power flowed more quickly this time. Immediately, she felt a tickle of vibration inside the ball.

Find Yail's mother, she silently commanded.

The ball twitched out of her grip. It fell on the leaf-covered walkway with a soft plop and rolled briskly away. Humps and bumps didn't slow it. When it rolled right into the backed-up stream, Chimi suddenly realized it might not stop.

"Hurry!" She ran to the steps and grabbed Yail's hand. The little boy rose willingly, and Chimi bobbed a quick bow to their host. "Thank you, Master Lelldour."

Smiling, he stayed where he was. "Don't thank me yet."

His words made her hesitate, but Chimi decided she didn't want to know what he meant. If there was any chance to finish this bizarre experience, she wouldn't waste it. Once she got Yail home, that would be the end of it.

"I'll return the ball," Chimi called over her shoulder as she skirted the backed-up stream.

She didn't wait for a reply. The finding ball rolled itself out the gate and into the street. Sandals slapping the pavement, Chimi ran after it. Yail stumbled to keep up as she dragged him behind her.

How could she have let herself get involved in something like this? What would her family say if she didn't get back to work? Grandmother would be furious at her.

Chimi tore her mind away from her worries when the finding ball stopped moving. It had been rolling steadily back the way she came, bobbling occasionally over the paving stones. Now it rocked in place and went still.

Panting, Chimi ran to it. Why had it stopped? It didn't matter. She scooped the ball up and renewed the command, *Find Yail's mother.* She tossed it lightly and was off again, chasing the small emissary that would get her out of this situation.

The sun was over the hilltops at last, and the morning air was warmer. As she ran to keep up with the ball, Chimi wondered why the exertion didn't drive the chill from her lungs. They approached the great stair, where the finding ball made a sharp turn. It plunged down the marble steps and bounced into the crowded plaza.

With sunrise, the market had come fully to life. It was always busy and noisy here. That was what Chimi liked about it. Things were going on, more than one girl's boring, quiet life. At the moment, though, the crowd was a nuisance. She could hardly see the ball through the passing feet.

She and Yail must have looked ridiculous, weaving through the throng after a child's toy. Chimi quickly got tired of apologizing to everyone she bumped into, and ignored the scowls to focus on her quarry. No one seemed to notice Yail. They all glared at Chimi, who was older and allegedly more responsible. Since the whole performance was for Yail's benefit, she thought it was grossly unfair.

Despite her best efforts, Chimi lost sight of the finding ball. She stopped and stared around, feeling panic tighten her stomach. Then she glimpsed a spot of dull crimson between the moving people. The ball had stopped again. Relieved, she pounced on it.

Chimi wondered again what made the enchanted ball stop. Could it only go a certain distance at a time, or had it gotten too far from her? Not that she really cared. Making amulets and talismans was Shenza's job, and she was welcome to it.

This time, Chimi led Yail into a less crowded aisle before she re-activated the charm. They followed the finding ball between rows of stalls where merchants cried for business. There were the metal smiths on one side, booths gleaming with bronze tools and fittings. From the other side came an earthy whiff of clay as the potters spun their wheels. Next were the basket makers, and after them the bamboo shapers. Then the stench of manure and chorus of animal calls from the livestock sellers. Chickens and pigs would be for people to eat, while farmers from the dawn side of the island would buy the gentle swamp cattle for pulling their carts and plows.

Chimi was glad to bypass the weavers, where Rellad's family worked. She couldn't help glancing at the jewelers' aisle, though. She could linger there for hours, but she didn't have time today.

Still the finding ball rolled on. As they came out of the shady aisles, it turned south to follow the border between the market and the warehouses. The noise of the market had faded away, but another commotion rose from the wharves below. Over the low wall, Chimi saw the cheerful pandemonium of ships loading and unloading while captains dickered with port officials. The occasional signal horn pierced the babble. Everywhere was movement, the bobbing of the long seagoing ships, sturdy cranes raising and lowering bales, workers scurrying in every direction.

Since she had barely escaped the market with the boy and the ball, Chimi was glad when the charmed toy bounded past the stair leading down to that level. Someone would kick it into the water for sure, and then where would she be? A strapping peace officer in a dark gold kilt and short mantle stood at the head of the stairs, watching over the chaos below. Chimi knew some of the peace officers, but she didn't recognize this one, so she passed without saying hello.

They had gone by the larger cargo ships, which were moored closest to the market. Now the smaller, rounder fishing vessels passed below. They had their own set of docks, which were much quieter, for the fisherman rowed out at night to harvest the Jewel Sea's bounty. They brought their catch to the market in early morning. Seeing them reminded Chimi that she had been gone from her fish stall much too long.

She wondered how much farther the ball would lead her. They couldn't go much farther on this level. Once again a hill loomed over them. The terrace they were on ended against its steep slope. Stairs led up and down there. Chimi couldn't imagine the ball going up the steps, but there wasn't much below them, either.

Down they went all the same, following a narrow stairway paved with slabs of slate rather than marble. For a moment, Chimi feared the ball would drop into the water, but it did another quick turn and continued east along the lowest level of the town. A boardwalk of rattan logs on tall poles bridged the gap between the main shore and the promontory. Chimi glimpsed the roof of the shrine among the trees.

Ahead of her, the boardwalk curved back to solid land. Chimi was approaching the most sheltered part of the harbor, the work area reserved for boat builders. She could even hear the racket of hammers and chisels. Chimi frowned in confusion. Shipbuilding was a trade reserved exclusively to men. How could she find Yail's mother there?

They had just crossed the inlet when the ball gave a kind of hop and fell off the side of the boardwalk. Chimi yelped in dismay and rushed to the edge. To her relief, the ball had landed on a floating dock and was bobbling back the way they came. She wrenched her hand free of Yail's and nearly fell herself as she clambered down a rickety ladder. The rattan dock dipped under her weight. The much lighter ball skimmed off over the unstable structure. Chimi did her best not to move as Yail came down after her. Hand in hand, they followed the ball.

Chimi had thought she knew Chalsett-port well, but the welter of small boats and barges under the boardwalk was new to her. Lines hung with laundry were strung between the support poles, and smoke from cooking fires drifted over the water.

The ball stopped again near the end of a slimy boarding plank. At the other end, a waterlogged barge barely rode above the water. A crude bamboo shelter had been put up in the center, and a group of children played in front of it. They squabbled and whacked each other with branches from a wood pile under the lean-to. When they saw Chimi, they froze in place.

Chimi thought Yail might go to them, but he stayed at her side. Then the oldest, a gawky girl no more than nine, bolted behind the shelter.

"Mommy!" she screeched as she ran. The barge rocked as the other two pelted after her, yowling just as loudly.

Chimi blinked, watching them go. The smallest one was just a toddler, and the next oldest looked about six. Yail would fit in ages between that boy and the toddler. Suddenly, her throat closed up with tears.

The children gabbled hysterically behind the shelter. The barge listed again as a woman shuffled out from behind the lean-to. Her arms were loaded with threadbare clothing. When she saw Yail, her eyes opened wide and she dropped her burden.

"Yail!" The woman rushed forward, nearly stumbling over the laundry.

Behind her, the other children jumped up and down. The barge rocked wildly with their excitement.

"Yail is back!" they shrieked. "Yail! It's Yail!"

"Mommy!" Yail bawled. He let go of Chimi's hand at last and ran to his mother. "I found you!"

They met in a great, sweeping hug. For a moment, Chimi couldn't see anything but the little boy's dangling legs. Then the mother must have felt the awful cold, just as Chimi had. There was a deep gasp and a terrible silence.

The woman screamed. The children stopped their jumping to jerk around. They stared at their mother without understanding.

"No!" the mother wailed. "No, no! My baby! No, no, no." She sank down, sobbing, still clutching the ghost to her, and then threw back her head to scream again.

Other women dashed in from the neighboring boats. Chimi edged back to let them by. A cold draft blew over her shoulders and across her heart. What was the point of bringing the boy home if it was only for his funeral?

"Is that the boy what run off?" lisped a voice beside her.

"Oh!" Chimi turned with a startled cry. A haggard fellow, missing most of his teeth and barely dressed in greasy rags, had come much too close while she stared.

"Run off?" she repeated, like a fool.

The man nodded, eyes fixed on the stricken family with rapacious interest. Chimi was glad he wasn't looking at her, and that she didn't have anything valuable with her.

"Yah. Hit him, his daddy did. Good and hard." The man grinned ghoulishly. "He run off. Not seen him since. Mama's been looking like mad."

Chimi swallowed heavily. Yail had run off when his father beat him? She didn't want to know any more. And where was the father now? Nowhere nearby, she hoped.

"He's dead, poor boy," she replied absently.

"Dead?" The stranger hissed through the gaps in his teeth. Now he did stare at Chimi, and his gaze made her skin crawl.

Yail's mother was surrounded by the other women, who took up a formal wailing of grief. Chimi couldn't see Yail anymore. She wondered if he had faded away once he achieved his goal and found his mother. Or would the little ghost stay with her until she scraped together materials for a funeral? That could take weeks, for a family this poor.

It was none of Chimi's business, and she felt like an intruder on their loss.

"You don't look like no necromancer I ever seen," the ruffian sneered.

"I'm not," Chimi assured him, babbling in her haste to get away. "I'm not. It was an accident, that's all. Excuse me."

She ran a few steps, then stopped as she realized she had forgotten the finding ball. She had promised to return it. Chimi spun in place and rushed back, trying to ignore the stranger who still leered at her. As she snatched up the rubber ball, something poked her hand. This time she didn't slow down until she was up the ladder, across the boardwalk, and far enough along the wharves that the desolate keening was lost in the babble of commerce.

As Chimi climbed the steps that would take her back to her stall, she finally looked at what was in her hand. Under the worn red ball was a fragment of bone. It was about the length of her thumb, smooth and cylindrical. It looked very white against her brown skin.

A bone? Chimi knew necromancers wore strands of bone around their necks, tied with red cord. But where had this come from?

No, no. Chimi shook her head, determined not to let herself wonder. She would give the bone to Master Lelldour when she returned the ball, and that would be the end of it.

Really.

It would.

* * *

"We've been summoned to the palace," Laraquies said.

Shenza knelt on the sunny garden path, hands poised over a small glass bottle which was half-filled with captured daylight.

"Both of us?" she asked, and glanced up in time to see Laraquies' nod. Shenza's heart fluttered in her chest. She breathed deeply, clinging to the concentration required for her spellcraft.

"Did he say why he wants us?"

"No," Laraquies answered mildly. "Is it our place to question Lord Aspace?"

There was only one answer to that. Shenza sighed and lowered her hands. The brilliant light within her bottle flickered and vanished. She would have to start over again, once she had been to the palace.

Chapter Three

The Lord Commands

A short time later, Shenza followed Master Laraquies out of their house. As they passed along the shaded street, the busy hum of the market came from below, to their left. The summons was ironic, Shenza thought. It was almost as if Lord Aspace knew she had been thinking of him last night. She wondered what task he had for her. Maybe Master Laraquies would know.

"Did you hear anything interesting at the banquet last night?" Shenza asked.

"Of course. Many things," Laraquies answered. "I heard a great deal about Lord Fastu of Kesquin's profits from his shipping fleet. Also, Lord Oriman of Sengool had a good yield from his citrus and banana groves. Sepprith of Kesquin made an unfortunate remark about disease in the orchards, and I had to convince Lord Oriman he hadn't heard right."

Shenza nodded, imagining the scene. It was always something between the Sengools and the Kesquins. Laraquies turned right, up the grand stair, and Shenza followed.

Laraquies chatted on. "Aoress and her troop danced. Excellent, as always. Oh, and Lady Innoshyra of Sengool was there, as lovely and charming as ever." The old man glanced at Shenza with a cunning glint in his dark eyes.

"That's nice," Shenza said.

In Shenza's first investigation, the murder of Lord Anges, Innoshyra had wanted special favors. She had never forgiven Shenza for stopping her scheme to become first lady. Whenever they saw each other, even for a moment, Innoshyra went out of her way to harass Shenza.

She kept her shoulders straight and didn't respond to Laraquies' baiting. Shenza wore her gold mask of office, so her teacher couldn't see her face. She didn't know if she would need it today, but if she didn't, she could always store it in the leather travel case she carried. Meantime, Shenza had her own reasons for wearing the mask, and this was one of them.

Searching for something else to talk about, Shenza glanced upward. The first white clouds dotted the blue arch of sky. Skall rode high, paler in daylight but still plainly visible. Below it, Inkesh was a ruddy sickle. Shenza wondered if Lord Aspace's summons had anything to do with Skall's sudden appearance. Yet she knew that anything could seem like it was connected to Skall. It was just too soon to tell.

A hand fell on her shoulder, and Laraquies warned, "Look out."

Shenza stopped in time to avoid crashing with a cart that two men were pulling across the landing in front of her.

"Thank you," she murmured, glad that no one could see her embarrassment under the serene facade of her mask. "I was thinking about Skall."

"We all are," Laraquies reassured her. "Master Nurune and I had quite an interesting conversation after it rose in the sky." Shenza was surprised, because Nurune and Laraquies got along about as well as Innoshyra and Shenza did. "Try not to worry. There's nothing to be afraid of."

"I'm not," Shenza said, although her instinct disagreed with Laraquies' calm assessment. "I'm just trying to plan for whatever happens." Then she realized something else. "How many times have you seen Skall?"

"Oh, three or four."

After this nonchalant reply, Laraquies said nothing more. Shenza thought that was unfair.

"Did anything happen?" she pressed.

"I don't remember. People make so much of these things," Laraquies said. Then he raised an index finger. "No, I take it back. There was a volcanic eruption one time. The sky went dark, and stones and dust rained from the air. Part of the city burned, too."

The old man smiled with remembered excitement. He didn't seem to realize how intimidating his words were.

"That sounds as bad as when Taisaris flooded our docks," Shenza said. She remembered how helpless she had felt as the monstrous wave roared toward Chalsett.

"It was much worse than that." Laraquies patted Shenza's arm. "This was years ago, on the island of Lappulis. I was only a boy. The mountain had been growling at us for a while, so nobody was surprised."

Shenza nodded. There were many volcanoes scattered around the Jewel Sea, but none close enough to threaten the City of Gardens. Volcanism was one thing she didn't have to worry about.

"Nothing like that is going to happen," Laraquies said, but Shenza heard a strange undertone in his voice. She had the feeling he was reassuring himself as much as her.

There was less traffic as they reached the top of the grand stair and turned left, following the street as it curved with the hillside. On their right was the high wall surrounding Lord Aspace's hilltop estate. A group of peacekeepers stood at the gate, two beside it and two in front of it. They wore bright blue kilts and short robes arranged neatly over their shoulders, with brooches of blue feathers on their headcloths. All four held shields, and the front row barred the way with crossed spears.

An officer stood at the rear, a large scroll tucked under his arm. Shenza knew this one, a middle-aged man with skin so dark it was nearly black. His name was Rakshel, a sub-chief in the city guard before his recent promotion.

Shenza and Laraquies halted at the gate. Rakshel scowled at them anyway.

"State your business," he called.

"I am Laraquies Catteel of Nelnoor, Vizier," Laraquies replied. He placed one hand on his chest and bowed. "This is Shenza Waik of Tresmeer, Magister. We are summoned before my Lord Aspace."

Although the two magicians should have been well known, Rakshel made a show of opening his scroll and scanning its contents.

"You are expected," he bit out. The front two peacekeepers raised their spears, and the back two pulled the gate's grilles wide open.

"Thank you," Laraquies said.

As Shenza and Laraquies walked through, a page stepped forward to meet them. He was a young man, draped in the blue robe of the palace staff.

"Allow me to guide you," he said with a bow.

"Very well," Laraquies said, and they both followed the page.

Like the rest of the island, the first lord's estate was thick with greenery. The grounds were elaborately groomed to reveal something new at every turn. Here was a pond, dotted with lilies. An enormous willow tree trailed its branches in the water. There was a low branch laden with enormous orchids. A light breeze spread their perfume as Shenza passed. A fountain bubbled on one side. On the other was a magnificent pavilion surrounded by green grass. That was where Lord Aspace had his feasts.

Beyond it, a cluster of low buildings stood among the trees. These structures housed bureaucratic offices, yet they were as ornate and carefully placed as anything else in the gardens.

The young page led them through a grove of palm trees. Shenza enjoyed having a respite from the relentless sun, but she still felt sweat beading between her shoulders. She never knew what to expect from Lord Aspace, what his mood would be. Skall's lurking presence only heightened her nervousness.

The page brought them to the base of a steeper slope and bowed to indicate that they could go on without him. Shenza murmured her thanks before following Laraquies. Steps led up to a sunny pavilion on the crown of the hilltop. As they approached it, she had a splendid view of city terraces falling away in graceful curves. Rooftops of tile or thatch peeked between the trees. In the harbor, far below, the shimmering water was dotted with longboats and canoes. From this height, they looked tiny and black, like water-striders on a garden pond.

The pavilion was small and round, its blue-tiled roof supported by spiral columns painted a brilliant green. The low exterior wall was decorated with a mosaic of fishes and corals. It was lovely, but Shenza had already seen something beautiful enough to put mere artwork out of her mind.

Lord Aspace sat on the low wall, his back against one of the columns and arms folded across his chest. One foot was up on the wall, while the other rested on the floor inside. Aspace had a slender frame, neither too thin nor over-muscled. His face was narrow, delicately featured, yet not at all effeminate. Black hair flowed over his shoulders in natural curls. Aspace wore a short mantle and kilt of warm orange-brown with a complex pattern of interlocking white spirals. His headcloth dangled a string of red coral chips, and his sandals were also sewn with coral. His gaze was fixed on some point in the distance, and his expression was shuttered.

Though Aspace seemed unaware of their approach, Shenza felt her heart skip. She paused behind Laraquies when he stopped in the pavilion's arched entrance. Shenza glanced over his shoulder as he bowed. When she saw who else was there, she quickly bowed, too.

"Laraquies Catteel of Nelnoor, coming as my Lord commands," Laraquies said.

"Magister Shenza Waik of Tresmeer also comes." Shenza spoke softly, hoping no one was listening.

First Lady Izmay, Lord Aspace's mother, sat in the center of the shady pavilion. A low table stood before her, dark wood inlaid with mother of pearl. Alceme, the first lord's head housekeeper, knelt beside Izmay, preparing a pot of tea. Izmay's robe was of sheer silk, pale blue painted with a magnificent gold and white heron. She had skin dark as strong tea and wore her silver curls in a coil on her head. With her high cheekbones and heavy-lidded eyes, Izmay reminded Shenza of Lord Anges, Aspace's older brother, whose death had brought Aspace to power. Izmay had the same lazy, feline quality, able to seem completely at ease and yet instantly alert to any change around her.

The fine lines around Izmay's eyes might give away her age, but she didn't let the years slow her. Now she smiled up at Laraquies and patted a cushion on the floor beside her.

"Sit with me," she said.

"As my Lady commands." Laraquies bowed again, and settled himself beside the first lady. Alceme poured tea for both of them.

Shenza, not invited, glanced around for a place to stand. For the first time she noted a stranger opposite Lord Aspace. He was a small man, with a wizened face and dark eyes agleam with cunning. He reminded Shenza of the little monkeys who sometimes did tricks in the marketplace. His robe was full length, pale gray. The only decoration was a pattern of darker gray vines and tiny white flowers stitched along the edges.

Her eyes focused on the last two people in the pavilion, a pair of peacekeepers. Unlike the officers at the gate, they held no weapons. Borleek, the chief peacekeeper, stood slightly apart from the nobles. He was a big man, very muscular, but he seemed uncomfortable, as if he wasn't sure why he was there. Borleek glanced at Shenza and scowled. However, his companion brightened at the sight of her.

"Magister!" he called, smiling broadly.

"Good day," Shenza answered.

Juss Herut of Reiloon came to join her, abandoning his chief without visible regret. He walked with a slight limp, and his brown legs were criscrossed with silvery scars like veins on a leaf. Still, Juss embraced Shenza as a big brother would, with hard thumps on her shoulders.

"It's good to see you," Shenza said, slightly breathless.

"Yeah." Juss glanced around and murmured, "This is like old times."

"Almost," Shenza murmured, thinking of the stranger who watched Izmay and Laraquies chat with open interest. Also, as far as she knew, no one had been murdered this time.

Juss' scars were mementos of their investigation into Lord Anges' death. They hadn't worked together since then. Shenza was always glad to see her friend, but she couldn't help wondering why they had both been summoned.

Her eyes returned to the newcomer among them. To her surprise, he was now looking at her and Juss with the same shrewd expression. He quickly smiled when Shenza faced him. She nodded back, although she felt a prickle at the back of her neck. Shenza was glad when Alceme distracted the man by offering him tea. Who was this person, to stare at everybody?

Then she caught a movement in the corner of her eye and turned. Lord Aspace was also watching Shenza and Juss. His expression was unreadable.

For a long moment Shenza felt caught in his gaze, like a moth in a spider's web. His eyes were green as emeralds, the legacy of a long-ago spirit ancestor. No one else she knew had eyes like that. Even through her mask, she felt he could see her cheeks burning. Her heart thudded against her ribs. Moving with an effort, Shenza broke the spell that bound her. She bowed to her ruler.

"Tea, Magister?" Alceme asked quietly.

"No, thank you," Shenza replied in what she hoped was a natural voice. "Perhaps later."

"Very well. And you, officer?" Alceme looked to Juss.

"Sure."

It was a relief to turn back to Juss, avoiding Lord Aspace's gaze. What she felt was a superficial attraction. She knew that. But Aspace was so beautiful, she couldn't help being drawn to him. Any woman with eyes would be. If Aspace knew how she felt, he didn't seem to care. Yet he was still the first lord. Shenza had to serve under him. It would be harder if she made a fool of herself.

Alceme offered Juss a cup of porcelain so fine that the liquid inside was visible through the sides. The tea was pale amber, spiced with cassia and orange. It smelled wonderful. Except for Lord Aspace's unnerving regard, Shenza might have removed her mask and asked for a cup after all.

"Son, will you introduce our guest?" Izmay indicated the stranger with a slight nod.

"Yes, Mother," Aspace said. His grave humility was undercut by a slight smile.

The first lord of Chalsett-port turned to face them, still leaning against the low wall. He crossed his ankles before him like a child.

"Mother, and Vizier Laraquies," Aspace began, "I present Udama Tocarei of Bosteel, who brings us a request."

"Welcome," Izmay said.

"The lady is kind." Udama's voice was high and quick. Setting his teacup on the wall beside him, he bowed to Izmay and Laraquies in a single fluid motion. "My Lord, Manseen Bosteel of Bosteel, extends his congratulations to Lord Aspace for his ascension. He wishes to visit the lovely City of Gardens and offer his best wishes in person."

From the folds of his robe he drew out a scroll of cloth, tightly rolled and tied with cords of soft gray. Izmay raised her hand, but couldn't reach it. Alceme quickly stepped forward and passed the scroll on to her. Izmay set it aside and kept her dark eyes fixed on Udama.

"I have met Lord Bosteel, briefly," she said. Like Aspace, Izmay had a smooth, honeyed voice that often hid a sting. "It would be delightful to see him again."

"Does Lord Manseen have other business here?" Laraquies inquired.

Shenza, wondered, too. She had heard of the Bosteel clan. Manseen was first lord of Sardony, a bigger island to the north of Chalsett. Udama must stand high in his councils, if he personally carried his lord's messages.

"My Lord would like to open an agricultural exchange with your servant, Lord Oriman of Sengool House," Udama replied smoothly. "My Lord controls many orchards of mango and citrus. He wishes to exchange seeds and cuttings with Lord Oriman, who he has heard grows fine lemon trees."

It sounded innocent enough, but Shenza guessed there must be more. A first lord wouldn't make a personal visit just to trade seeds. She also wondered why Lord Bosteel was approaching Lady Izmay. It didn't make sense.

Izmay might have been wondering the same thing, for she glanced at Laraquies.

"Lord Oriman's orchards are the pride of Chalsett-port," Laraquies said. Shenza was amazed he could exaggerate so much with a straight face.

Udama went on, "My Lord's daughter, Seelit, will accompany him. He would like to introduce her."

Shenza felt the shock wash over her like the coldest waves of deep sea water. Lord Bosteel wanted Lord Aspace to meet his daughter? He wanted to talk about marriage!

"A daughter?" Izmay's elegant brows rose in sly understanding.

It wasn't really a question, but Udama launched into a glowing report. "Seelit is his youngest daughter. She is as gentle as a fawn, as beautiful as jade."

Shenza suddenly discovered an intense interest in the mosaic on the pavilion's floor. Just under her sandals, the design showed a sea-whip wrestling with a crab. At least this explained why Udama was giving Izmay the message. As Aspace's mother, she would have to be the one who consented.

"She sounds fascinating," Aspace agreed. He spoke lightly, as if there was something humorous in the situation, but Shenza couldn't bring herself to look at him.

"Does my Lady know of this family?" Laraquies asked.

"The House of Bosteel," Izmay answered in a considering tone. "Lords of Sardony for many generations. It's a large island with many towns. A prosperous holding. Besides fruit, pepper and cassia grow there..."

"The lady is well informed," Udama put in. "Our soil is indeed productive. My Lord also operates a copper mine."

"That must be profitable," Laraquies observed.

"It is," Udama assured him.

Shenza knew she should be listening, but the words ran together in a blur. She felt like the mosaic crab, helpless in a predator's grip. Of course she had known that Aspace would marry, but so soon? And why did he want her to know about it? She wouldn't have believed he could be so cruel!

Laraquies was asking, "Has my Lord met this young lady, Seelit Bosteel of Bosteel?"

"Never," Aspace replied blithely. "I did work alongside her brother Tenbei for a while, but he never mentioned this jewel."

The sarcasm made Shenza tear her eyes away from the pattern beneath her feet. Aspace's posture was casual, but a slight shadow between his brows made that a lie. Shenza had noticed before that Aspace often played these games, pretending to be bored when he was angry or teasing his mother with feigned humility. She wondered if he was even aware that he did it.

"Lord Tenbei always spoke highly of the lord," Udama answered politely. Shenza spared a moment to pity the messenger, who had to hear his home and family discussed this way.

"It's always wise to seek alliances." Laraquies sounded neutral.

Izmay had opened the scroll, but now looked up from reading it. "It seems he forgives your many faults in light of your improved situation," she teased.

"That must be it," Aspace agreed.

As they bantered, the analytical part of Shenza's mind went to work. Aspace seemed flattered by Lord Bosteel's offer, but that could be just another facade. What did he really feel?

"Will you grant his request?" Laraquies asked.

"Of course," Aspace replied. "I must meet a girl as beautiful as jade."

Though he smiled, Aspace's lips kept a tight line, and his eyes were brilliant with some emotion Shenza couldn't identify. Then his burning gaze came too close to her, and she stared at the tile floor again. She tried to think rationally. The idea of Aspace getting married brought a knot to her throat and Shenza couldn't seem to breathe around it. Yet she didn't understand what he was angry about. An offer of marriage ought to be good news.

Beside her, Juss shifted in his place and then sipped his tea loudly. As if that was a signal, Borleek spoke up.

"What does my Lord need us for?" he rumbled.

"To assure that Lord Bosteel has proper protection," Aspace replied. "Your sub-chief Shamatt might enjoy an assignment like this."

"My Lord will be quite able to provide for himself in that regard," Udama began to argue, very politely.

"As your host, I insist," Aspace replied.

Udama made another nimble bow. It looked like he wanted to argue further, but a little bird made of folded paper glided into the pavilion and circled his head. Someone was sending him a note. Udama plucked it from the air and tucked it into the folds of his robe.

Meanwhile, Borleek tensed. Shenza guessed he didn't like being told how to do his job, but he couldn't argue with Aspace's orders.

"As my Lord commands," Borleek bit out.

The first lord's choice was an interesting one, Shenza thought. Shamatt was a clever investigator. Could Aspace be hinting that he wanted the Bosteels watched?

"Laraquies," Aspace went on, "you and Shenza must also be aware of anything magical surrounding our visitors. I wouldn't want anything to happen to my guests."

Now it was Shenza's turn to hesitate. Again, she felt that Aspace meant more than he was saying. Yet, as magister, she was a lawgiver, not a spy. No matter how much she wanted to please Aspace, she couldn't follow such an order blindly. Laraquies knew it, too. Though he looked on with outward serenity, Shenza felt he was watching her carefully.

Udama tried to hide it, but Shenza caught a flash of real alarm on his face. He protested, "In a time of peace, there is no need for such precautions."

"I Could never insult my Lord's hospitality by intruding into the affairs of his guests," Shenza answered carefully.

"The magister is most wise," Udama murmured. Shenza saw a gleam of satisfaction in his eyes. Too late, she realized she might have given him the impression that Aspace couldn't control his staff.

Indeed, Aspace frowned at Shenza's words. In his annoyance, he looked more beautiful than ever. The urge to bow her apologies was almost overwhelming. Somehow she made herself stand still.

"In that case," Izmay interrupted, "I would be happy to discuss the details with Vizier Laraquies and Udama."

A hint of steel in Izmay's voice suggested she was annoyed about something. Maybe she just wanted to remind her son that Lord Bosteel had actually written to her, not him.

Aspace shifted moods again, bowing with mock humility. "I'll leave it in your hands, Mother."

"I am at the Lady's disposal," Udama said, bowing yet again as he approached Izmay's table.

Aspace stood up from the wall, and the meeting was over. Shenza quickly bowed toward the first lady and backed out of the pavilion. Borleek and Juss were close behind her. She started down the slate steps, trying not to look like she was running away. Aspace was coming, too. He might be angry with her, and she didn't think she could stand it if he snapped at her in front of Borleek. In fact, Shenza didn't want to talk to him at all.

Chapter Four

A Sister's Secret

It was frightening how much time had passed during what should have been a simple errand. The peak sales time was over long before Chimi got back to the market. She had expected that, but it still hurt. The cool morning gave way to a humid afternoon, with clouds building in the sky. Well, Chimi wasn't in the mood to work anymore. Nakuri watched from her stall, obviously bursting with questions, but Chimi didn't want to talk about what had happened.

She accepted her meager earnings with thanks, then avoided talking to her neighbor by tidying her booth with frantic energy. When there was nothing else she could straighten up or clean, she glumly surveyed the unsold merchandise and tried to decide what she could make for dinner. There was sea-whip, flatfish, and a few mussels. But she didn't want to think about food, either. The dismal reunion of Yail with his mother weighed on her. She dragged a sling-backed chair to the far corner of her booth and flopped into it.

It just wasn't right, the squalid poverty of Yail's home and his accidental death. The poor child, beaten by his own father and then a misstep had plunged him into the water. It was wrong, all wrong, and there was nothing she could do about it.

Chimi blinked, and blinked again, and finally wiped at hot tears with the trailing end of her robe. She sniffled irritably. She shouldn't think about Yail. It wasn't like her to worry about someone else's problems. Yet her lungs still ached with cold when she breathed too deeply, and the screeches of seabirds sounded like a woman's mourning cries.

She still had Lelldour's finding ball and the bit of bone. Chimi didn't know what to do with them. They just got in her way while she worked. She jumped up and grabbed a pouch of heavy fabric from under the counter. Usually she carried her wares up from the pier in it. Now she stuffed the unwanted relics into the bag and yanked the drawstring closed.

Above her, someone said, "Excuse me, do you have any sea-whip left?" A customer!

"Of course—ouch!" Chimi stood up too soon and thumped her head on the counter. The girl swallowed her curses. This might be her last chance to make any money today.

Before her stood an elderly woman who had stopped by earlier but left without buying anything. She must have changed her mind.

"Are you all right?" the old woman asked.

"It's nothing." Rubbing her head, Chimi stood up and pasted on a smile that felt as false as a frog's.

"I do have sea-whip," she bubbled. "I've kept it nice and fresh just for you!"

* * *

Hours later, she leaned her elbows on the table and poked at her food. On either side of Chimi, her mother and brother were having an earnest debate about whether to grow yams or beans in their vacant garden plot. They droned on as if nothing in the world was wrong. Maybe, for them, nothing was.

Chimi let her head hang and tried not to listen. Could anything else go wrong today? She hadn't broken even at the fish market after Yail's interruption. Then she'd been so busy frying the noodles that she almost burned the fish. Grandmother's scolding about wastefulness still rang in her ears.

Chimi chewed her scorched flatfish dejectedly. She really had tried to make up for the morning's fiasco. She had stayed in her stall as long as she could, watching the clouds thicken into a solid layer. Eventually they had released their warm rain and Chimi had had to admit the work day was over. She had packed the unsold fish and turned the baskets over to drain. The dripping arbors of the marketplace had echoed her mood perfectly.

Before she went home, Chimi had stopped by Master Lelldour's house to return his finding ball. He hadn't answered her calls from the street, but after the way he had acted, she didn't expect him to. Chimi had marched up to the house and set the ball and bone on the porch. He would see them next time he came out of his dreary den.

As she left, Chimi had soaked her feet again, so she poked around and found a rake. She had dredged some of the leaves from the garden brook. The backed-up pond had gurgled as it drained. She had thought that Lelldour might come out while she worked, but he hadn't. Tired of rain dripping on her shoulders, Chimi had returned the rake to its spot and left. Lelldour had helped her, however grudgingly. Now he couldn't say she hadn't done anything in return.

"All right," Giliatt said crisply. "What's wrong?"

"Yeah," Sachakeen mumbled around a mouthful of food. "You haven't said a word all night."

Chimi froze. She looked up at them, fumbling inside herself for some explanation, but her mother and brother were talking to Shenza.

Shenza didn't answer right away, but her expression matched her somber attire. The older girl was dressed in a plain purple robe and headcloth that marked her as a trained magician. She must have been proud of the uniform; she wore it constantly. Chimi could never have lived with such a limited wardrobe.

A soft humphing noise came from behind Sachakeen, where Grandmother and Byben had a table to themselves. They shared a small keg of nut beer, though Byben no longer drank as much as he once had. Old Myri was the daughter of fishermen on both sides. She resented that her grandson, Sachakeen, wasn't following the family trade. She also thought it was wrong for Giliatt and her daughters to work outside the home. As a young widow, Giliatt had been forced to sell their father's boat to pay his debts. She had turned to growing vegetables, first to eat and later to sell. Then a stroke of luck had allowed them to start planting feather-flower vines. Chimi's work in the fish market was the closest the family came to basing their livelihood on the sea.

Lucrative though the feather-flower trade was, Grandmother couldn't forgive the family for abandoning their heritage. She never missed an opportunity to remind them of her disappointment. Giliatt, who had had years to get used to her mother-in-law's disapproval, pretended not to hear Myri's growling.

"Come, daughter," she said to Shenza. "I can tell when you're upset."

"I'm not." Shenza spoke so quickly that Chimi knew it wasn't true. "It's just something happening up at the palace. It doesn't really concern me..."

"At the palace?" Chimi interrupted. She was always interested in the tidbits of gossip Shenza brought home with her.

Shenza glanced at her, but didn't reply. She often couldn't talk about her work as magister. People might question her integrity. At first, the family had been impressed by Shenza's responsibilities, but Chimi was starting to think her sister just used the cover of official business when she didn't want to talk about something. Like she was doing now.

Sachakeen must have thought the same thing. "What kind of events?"

"Yes, really," Chimi added. Whatever it was had to be more fun than what she had gone through today.

When the three of them kept staring at her, Shenza went on reluctantly. "There's going to be a state visit. Lord Manseen Bosteel of Bosteel will be coming from the island of Sardony."

"Why is that a problem?" Giliatt asked.

"It isn't," Shenza said, but she sounded flustered. "His daughter Seelit will be traveling with him. They're talking about marriage."

"Really?" Chimi shrieked with delight.

Lord Aspace was young, and really good looking, and even though Shenza's business took her to the palace a lot, she never talked about him. It drove Chimi crazy. All her friends were begging for details, and she couldn't give them any.

"A royal wedding." Chimi sighed, imagining the beautiful clothes the bride would wear. Robes sewn with jewels, feathered headcloths, and the feasting, the dancing. It was almost too good to be true.

"As I said," Shenza answered in a strained voice, "it's really none of my business."

Giliatt sat back slightly. She exchanged a look with Sachakeen, who raised one eyebrow. Even Grandmother turned to gaze at Shenza, her dark eyes gleaming.

"I see," Giliatt said. Her expression was sad as she went back to her meal.

Puzzled, Chimi glanced among her family. Something was going on, and she was the only one who didn't know it.

"Come on!" Chimi huffed her annoyance. "Don't just leave it at that. Has Lord Aspace met this girl? What was her name... Seelit? That's pretty."

"Yes, her name is Seelit," Shenza answered. "No, my Lord hasn't met her. He worked with her brother during his time in the High Lord's justice ministry."

"Well, who are these Bosteel people?" Chimi demanded.

With strained patience, Shenza said, "Bosteel is a wealthy house, Lady Izmay says. Remember, this is just a rumor."

That didn't matter. "What is she like?" Chimi persisted.

Shenza sipped her tea, avoiding the question. Then Sachakeen prodded Chimi under the table with his bare toes.

"Let it go, sister."

"But I want to know!"

"Daughter," their mother warned.

"But..."

"Not now!" Sachakeen glowered at Chimi. She glared back at him. He didn't push his authority as older brother very often, so Chimi didn't know whether to take him seriously. Sachakeen jerked his chin toward their sister. Shenza sat quietly, hands folded in her lap and face averted.

"I am sorry, sister," Shenza said in a monotone. "I really don't know any more than that."

Well, why had she even brought Seelit up, Chimi thought angrily, if she didn't want to talk about her? Oh—because Mother had asked.

An uncomfortable silence fell. Chimi returned to her meal, and found it was totally cold. Nothing was going right today. Shenza was upset because of her. Mother and Sachakeen were mad, too. And Yail, Yail was—

"Excuse me, please," Chimi choked out.

Without waiting for permission, she jumped up and banged her knee on the table. The whole table jumped, crockery clattering and liquids sloshing.

"Chimi!" her mother scolded.

And Sachakeen snapped, "What's the matter with you?"

Chimi ignored them, and the pain, and dashed out the open side of the house.

Their cottage was surrounded on all sides by a garden where feather-flower vines snaked up high lattices. It only took her a moment to lose herself there. Voices sounded behind her, a crotchety demand from Grandmother. The path was damp beneath her bare feet. Chimi didn't stop until she found a rattan bench, where she sat with her aching knee tucked up to her chin. Her ragged breathing was the only sound.

The evening rain had dissolved the clouds, revealing a radiant sunset sky. All around her, bright yellow feather-flowers flared open like miniature suns. Every now and then, droplets fell from the leaves with soft pattering.

Chimi felt sheltered among the tall ranks of vines. She couldn't remember a time without the dark foliage and dazzling blossoms. Shenza and Sachakeen did. Sometimes they told scary-tales of the dingy houses the family used to live in. But for Chimi, this house was the only one. She closed her eyes and breathed lightly, savoring the fragrance she had known since childhood. She didn't want anything to change her peaceful life.

Footsteps intruded on her reverie. Sandals slipped on the walkway, nearer, nearer. When they stopped, Chimi opened her eyes to see her sister's concerned face bent over her. She straightened, lowering her knee self-consciously. Shenza sat beside her in a whisper of purple.

"I didn't mean to upset you," the older girl said. "Maybe I shouldn't have come home."

It was just like Shenza to blame herself. Chimi shook her head. "You don't understand. It isn't your fault. It's mine. It's all..."

Her throat closed, keeping the words in. How could she explain? She didn't even want to think about what was really bothering her. And she definitely didn't want her family to know about Yail!

Shenza just watched her. For a moment, Chimi felt pure annoyance. Mother and Sachakeen made such a big deal about Shenza, but they ignored Chimi. Why didn't they ever worry about her?

"What's your fault, sister?" Shenza asked.

Chimi's eyes were hot and wet. The numbness she had felt earlier had gone away during the meal, but now it came back. She couldn't seem to draw a full breath. "It... I..."

Shenza put a warm arm around her shoulders. "Tell me what's troubling you."

Chimi raised a trembling hand to wipe the tears away, but there were too many. She ended by covering her face and sobbing.

I should stop this, she thought. *I have to!* But she couldn't control the sobs shaking her body. Her older sister hugged her, stroking her hair, and waited.

It seemed that Chimi cried forever, yet all too soon her tears eased. While her shoulders still jerked with occasional sobs, Chimi tried to decide what to do. Shenza wouldn't leave without an explanation. It was part of what made her a good magister. Then Chimi remembered that Shenza was a sorceress. Necromancy was a kind of sorcery. Maybe Shenza would know what had happened.

And yet, Chimi desperately didn't want their family to know she had anything to do with necromancy. Could she trust Shenza not to blab?

Despite herself, a sniffle turned into a snort of laughter. Shenza, blabbing? That was ridiculous. Mistress Integrity would never tell tales.

"I'm glad something is funny," Shenza said with gentle irony.

Chimi wiped her eyes with the end of her robe, but she didn't move to leave her sister's embrace. Surely she could trust Shenza. They were sisters. If she couldn't count on Shenza, then who? Her friends? No, she knew better. The story would be all over town within a day, and for all they liked to talk, those girls wouldn't understand a thing. Just like Rellad—but Chimi didn't want to think about him. He would come back to her booth tomorrow. Or the next day.

"You have to promise not to tell anyone," Chimi said at last. "Especially not Grandmother."

"Not tell?" Shenza repeated doubtfully.

"Promise!" Chimi straightened away from her sister. New tears choked her throat as she insisted, "It's important, but you have to promise."

Shenza regarded her seriously. "Have you broken the law?"

Of course, Shenza would think about that. "No, no, no. It's nothing like that. But promise me, Shenza. You can't tell *anyone!*"

Shenza summoned a smile. "Very well, I promise not to repeat what you tell me."

"Oh, thank you!"

Chimi felt the taut energy leave her all at once. She slumped against her sister and started to talk before she could change her mind. Within moments, she was crying again. Things kept getting out of order, but she managed to choke out most of it.

"What is it that upsets you?" Shenza asked at the end of the tale. "That you couldn't help the boy?"

"No! Haven't you been listening? He was *dead!*" Chimi shuddered, remembering the cold strength of Yail's grip. "And he wouldn't let go of me. He just kept staring at me, expecting me to do something for him."

"Well, he was a child," Shenza answered gently. "Young children expect to be taken care of."

"But that isn't my responsibility! His own family has to—"

"He couldn't find them," Shenza pointed out.

Chimi shrugged irritably, though she had to admit Shenza was right. If Yail could have found his mother without help, he would have.

"Don't be upset, sister," Shenza went on. "You should be proud. You did a kind thing."

"Ugh!" Chimi made a dramatic face. Her tears of anguish were giving way to the sense that she had been terribly abused. "I don't like ghosts. And that lazy old man, refusing to help me! I couldn't believe it."

"Yes, that does seem odd," Shenza admitted. "As a magister, I'm obligated to help anyone who calls on me. I believe the curomancers also have that code. Maybe it's different for necromancers."

"Aren't they public servants, too?" Chimi argued.

"I don't know," her sister answered thoughtfully. "Each school of enchantment is different. I don't know much about necromancy."

How could she not know, Chimi wondered angrily. Wasn't she a sorceress?

"I should have found another necromancer, that's all," she grumbled.

"I don't know about that," Shenza said.

"What do you mean?" Chimi asked.

"There is another necromancer in Chalsett-port, but I don't think I would trust her."

"Why not?"

Shenza hesitated before replying. "She's part of a coven that isn't very reliable. They've been accused of malfeasance in the past."

It was Chimi's turn to pause, trying to work out the meaning of this unfamiliar word. "Malfeasance?"

"Dishonorable actions," Shenza explained. "Master Lelldour's advice was enough, wasn't it?"

"He should have taken care of it, not given me advice," Chimi complained.

To her surprise, Shenza laughed and hugged her again. "But sister, don't you see? You did it on your own."

Chimi pushed away irritably. She shouldn't have had to deal with Yail, and it wasn't right that her sister took the side of another magician against her own family.

Silence fell, during which Chimi gnawed on her bitterness. When she glanced back at Shenza, Chimi saw her sister's face turned skyward, her dark eyes restlessly searching. Chimi looked up, too.

Beyond the fiery veil of sunset, the sky was darkening into twilight. The moons were rising across the deep blue dome. A glimmer of lavender hinted at Meor's crescent. Slow-moving Inkesh rose in the east, its gibbous orb flattened on one side. Skall still pulsed above them like a silvery-bright pebble. Chimi glanced at it, and then away. She shivered. Chaos moon, they called it, and Skall the Destroyer. This had been a chaotic day for Chimi, all right. She wanted Skall to go away.

As a magician, Shenza had spent years studying the moons, calculating how their effects would combine. That must be what she was doing now—looking for portents. Chimi rubbed at her aching neck.

"I don't want a forecast," she said.

Shenza smiled indulgently. "If Inkesh was full, I would be more worried."

"I said I don't want a forecast!" Chimi snapped.

"Very well," Shenza said. Then she surprised Chimi by taking her hand. "There is one thing I want to ask you."

She looked so serious, Chimi fought back the impulse to tear her hand away. "What is it?"

"Do you still have your hoka? I think you should wear it for a while."

"My hoka?" Chimi frowned, confused.

The hoka was a special amulet worn by girls during the time of puberty, as a protection against magic and other evil influences. Exactly what the charms protected against, Chimi had never known, but the instructors had been very concerned about it. All the girls in her class had made hokas. The oldest female tutor had taught them how during the last year of general school. There had been a long process of gathering strange materials and preparing them in a very particular way, and only under the influence of the green moon, Prenuse. What Chimi remembered most was how hard it had been to satisfy the tutor's standards. She'd had to re-do part of the weaving three or four times! The pickiness, as much as anything, had crushed Chimi's interest in magic.

"You still have it, don't you?" Shenza prodded.

Chimi had never thrown out anything that might be worn as jewelry. "I think so. But why? I'm a woman now."

"I know." Shenza smiled with a trace of sadness. "I just think it would be prudent for you to wear it again. Death magic is very powerful."

"I don't care what it is," Chimi answered with another shiver. "Death magic, ugh! I don't want it."

"So you said, and that puzzles me," Shenza remarked softly. "You've never been very interested in sorcery. Why should this happen to you?"

Chimi didn't have an answer for that. She didn't care, either, as long as it never happened again.

"I don't have any investigations right now," Shenza went on. "I think I'll ask Master Laraquies a few questions."

"You promised not to tell anyone!" Chimi protested.

"Calm down. I don't have to tell him why I'm asking," her sister said. "I'll know more in a few days. For now, I wish you would wear your hoka."

"But it's what little girls wear," Chimi whined.

"It's just a precaution," Shenza reassured her. "My instinct tells me you should wear it. I wish you would trust me, sister."

Chimi frowned, but before she could answer, their mother's voice called through the twilight. "Girls! It's getting dark."

Surprised, Chimi looked around. The trellises loomed around them, mere dark shapes sprinkled with lighter blots of flowers. Night insects hummed, and from somewhere nearby she heard the hiccups of a frog. The moons showed brightly, purple, red and vivid white among the brilliant shimmer of stars. House lamps of the dead, legend called them.

That reminded Chimi of Yail again. Did he have a little house now, up in the heavens? Her mind veered from that painful question. When she looked down, Shenza was staring urgently at her.

"Please, Chimi."

Giliatt called again, "Shenza? Chimi? Is everything all right?"

"Coming," Chimi called back, and sprang to her feet.

Shenza's gaze hadn't wavered, and Chimi threw up her hands in frustration.

"Oh, all right!" Chimi snapped. "I'll look for it." She hurried off along the gloomy path toward the house. Then she whirled, confronting Shenza as she followed. "But remember your promise!"

Shenza hugged her lightly, serious but still amused. "I won't forget, sister."

* * *

Long into the hot, dark night, Shenza lay awake. Her restless movements made her hammock swing in what should have been a lulling rhythm, but it was no use. Her mind kept replaying the morning's scene, Aspace leaning so casually against the wall while Udama extolled the virtues of Lord Bosteel's daughter. Shenza told herself it wasn't jealousy that kept her from sleeping. The hammock strings cut into her skin, pressing her arms to her sides until she felt like a netted fish. That was what bothered her—not jealousy!

After all, she had nothing but a business relationship with Lord Aspace. True, Aspace didn't ignore Shenza as the other nobles did. He drew her into conversation, even though she said the most inane things. As first lord, Aspace usually accepted her recommendations. He didn't question her abilities, as Borleek often did.

Still, Shenza knew she had no claim on Aspace. How could she? She had always tried to hide her feelings. Revealing herself would only embarrass them both.

No, Shenza wasn't jealous. She couldn't be jealous. But still she lay with eyes open, and felt something gnaw at her heart, like a maggot within a peach, unseen and yet fouling the fruit with its rottenness.

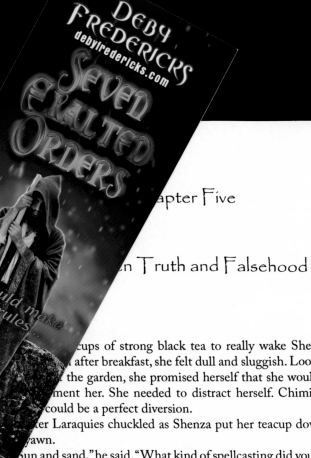

apter Five

n Truth and Falsehood

cups of strong black tea to really wake Shenza the next
after breakfast, she felt dull and sluggish. Looking into the
the garden, she promised herself that she wouldn't let Lord
ment her. She needed to distract herself. Chimi's experience
could be a perfect diversion.

er Laraquies chuckled as Shenza put her teacup down to cover a
yawn.

un and sand," he said. "What kind of spellcasting did you do yesterday,
make you so tired?"

"None," Shenza said, raising the end of her purple robe to blot yawn-tears
from her eyes. She had been too upset yesterday to concentrate on anything.

"What, then?" Laraquies asked. "Is something troubling you?"

He no longer laughed, but spoke gently. Shenza shrugged uncomfortably.
She didn't know if he guessed why she was so tired, but she didn't want to
talk about it. Nothing would change Lord Aspace's plans.

"I was surprised by my Lord's request yesterday," she answered, skirting
the truth. "As magister, I'm the voice of the law. You're the vizier, his chief
advisor. We aren't spies."

"As you say," Laraquies agreed. "Lord Aspace doesn't seem to trust
Lord Bosteel. Maybe he wanted to warn us."

Shenza had to admit that it would have been awkward for Aspace to
say something like that in front of Udama. Yet Aspace had asked for more
than a warning. Before she could say so, a chime's mellow voice rang from
the front of their house.

"I'll get that." Shenza gulped the last of her tea and rose from the table.

"If we're going to have guests, I'll make another pot," Laraquies replied.

Shenza crossed the work room and approached the cottage's main door.
Long strings of beads screened the interior from view, but she already
recognized a familiar bulk at the bottom of the steps.

"Juss?" Shenza pushed the beads aside and touched a graceful rune that
was carved on the inside of the metal bars. "Open," she said, and the gate
swung smoothly outward.

"Good morning," he said as he came up the steps from the street. "Is Laraquies here?"

"Yes, we've just finished eating."

"Good, then I won't be interrupting," Juss said.

Shenza watched, puzzled, as her friend crossed toward the table. It was early for Juss to visit unless something had happened that needed her attention. Yet he didn't seem excited, as he would be if the peacekeepers had sent for her.

"Close," she murmured. The gate swung shut and she trailed after him.

"Good morning," came Laraquies' voice from the kitchen.

"And you." Juss kicked a cushion over to the table and sat down, moving slowly and stiffly.

Shenza went on into the kitchen. "Go ahead and sit down, teacher. I'll take care of this."

"I don't need to be waited on," Laraquies scolded. "You're no longer my apprentice."

"But you're still my teacher," Shenza replied. "If you don't want me to wait on you, we might have to hire a servant."

She pushed at the old man's shoulders. With a chuckle, Master Laraquies strolled back to the breakfast table, where he asked the question that had been foremost in Shenza's mind. "Has something happened? Is Shenza needed?"

"No." Juss seemed surprised by the question. "Lord Aspace told us to work together, is all."

"That he did," Laraquies agreed.

In the kitchen, Shenza listened to water hissing as it heated in a heavy ceramic kettle. She silently rolled her eyes. She loved the old man, but he was obviously going to insist on talking about the one thing she least wanted to discuss. She busied herself pumping water to rinse the teapot.

"What does Chief Borleek think?" Laraquies asked, proving Shenza right.

"We shouldn't let this Lord Manseen on the island," Juss grunted, imitating his chief. "It's nothing but a lot of extra work."

It was probably the first time Shenza had ever agreed with Borleek. She called over her shoulder, "I could always close the port. That would keep him out."

Juss whooped with laughter. Shenza heard dishes rattle as he pounded the tabletop with his fist. Laraquies laughed, too. Months ago, Shenza's first act as magister had been to close Chalsett's harbor in order to trap a murderer. Although the tactic had been successful, Borleek had hated her for doing it. That, too, had created extra work.

Even Shenza smiled at the joke while she gathered dry tea leaves into a twist of cloth and placed it in the pot. The water on the stove was already boiling, so she poured the steaming liquid into the teapot and set it on a tray, along with a clean cup for Juss.

The two men were still chuckling as Shenza brought the tray to the table. Clearly, if she wanted to talk about something besides Lord Aspace's possible wedding, she would have to change the subject herself.

"There's something else I wanted to ask you, Master." Shenza knelt to place the tray on the table and chose a cushion for herself, tucking her robe neatly behind her knees. "I've had a complaint against one of the necromancers. What do you know about their customs?"

"A necromancer?" Juss' broad features twisted in an expression that mirrored Chimi's feelings the night before.

"Was it Vesswan Sanguri of Zeell?" Laraquies asked with a trace of sharpness.

"A necromancer, yes," Shenza replied. "Vesswan of Zeell, no. It was Lelldour Mokseem of Salloo."

Laraquies' brows rose like white birds taking flight. "I thought Lelldour was reliable."

"A woman encountered a ghost in the market," Shenza explained, hoping he wouldn't press for details. "She took the ghost to Lelldour, but he refused to lay the spirit. He made her do it herself."

"Really? That does sound odd," Laraquies said. He lifted the lid on the teapot and peered inside, then shut it again to let the tea steep longer.

"I thought only necromancers could lay a spirit to rest," Juss put in.

"I thought so, too," Shenza said. "Necromancy isn't like our spellcraft."

"Necromancy isn't like any other specialty," Laraquies said. "They don't have a hierarchy, as we magisters do. There is a minister of justice who serves High Lord Kinojen in Porphery, but there is no ministry of death. As I understand, necromancers don't answer to the living at all. They claim to serve the dead directly."

Juss shuddered again. "What a job."

"Someone has to do it," Laraquies reasoned. "No one can force Lelldour to help a restless spirit, but it surprises me that he wouldn't want to."

Shenza propped her chin on her hand and considered that. She had always thought of necromancers as serving people—heirs who needed clarification of an inheritance or families who wanted to settle a feud. If Laraquies was right, Lelldour should have wanted to help Yail. Why had he refused to step in?

While she pondered, Laraquies poured tea for the three of them. Shenza savored its fragrance as he placed a steaming cup before her.

"Can necromancers retire?" she asked after a warming sip.

"Who would tell them they can't?" Laraquies retorted with humor.

"That's true," Juss added. "I've never heard of one being fired."

"If no one hires them, nobody can get rid of them, either," Shenza said.

She and Laraquies shared a wry glance. Laraquies had once tried to get Vesswan of Zeell banished from Chalsett-port, but the vulture was still here. That fact raised a point against Laraquies: Vesswan didn't serve the dead. She would hold any seance if she was paid well enough—and the dead didn't pay with silver.

Before Shenza could follow that thought, the door chime rang again. Sandals slipped softly over the wooden floor as she returned to the cottage door.

"Open." The gate swung wide and she pushed through the beads to the porch. "Good morning."

A stranger waited for her this time. He was a stout fellow in his middle years, belly straining against the folds of a short brown robe. From the faint odor surrounding him, Shenza guessed he worked with livestock. His face was round, the brown skin dark with temper, and he breathed heavily as if he had been running. The man slapped one hand to his chest and bowed with a jerk.

"Magister, I need your help," he puffed. Beads of sweat glittered in the black curls receding from his forehead. "One of my piglets has been stolen. A little sow, just weaned and ready for market. Taken right from her pen."

"Of course, I'll come. Just a moment, please." Shenza's interest quickened at the prospect of a puzzle to solve. She called across the workroom, "Juss, are you on duty?"

"I could be."

"If you don't mind."

"All right." Juss gulped his tea and stood up.

"I know who did it," the pig farmer went on with angry certainty. "My neighbor, Attali Moreet of Shoma, she's always hanging around. Pinching the piglets when she thinks I don't see."

"One moment," Shenza interrupted. "I must gather my materials before I can take your testimony."

She left the man grumbling and hurried into the workroom. Shenza had wanted a distraction from her feelings about Lord Aspace. A real investigation would be even better than trying to analyze Chimi's problem.

* * *

Chimi stood in her small room, pouting into a bronze hand mirror. Her reflection had no pity. There was just no way to make the hoka look like anything but a hoka.

To think, she had once been proud of this monstrosity! She'd worn it constantly when it was new. The palm-sized basket was woven of red bamboo strips. It held a green feather, a white shell, and a blue stone. The hoka was supposed to stop evil influences from affecting her, but it was too big to make a proper pendant. Even several strands of wooden beads couldn't hide it. Chimi sighed, exasperated.

In the three days since her encounter with Yail, she had tried to put the whole thing behind her. She worked extra hard to make up her loss, and the money she earned did offer its own consolation. In the evenings, she cleaned the house from the crawl space to the roof beams. Not only did the work make her tired enough to sleep without dreaming, but it kept her away from her family and their questions.

Every fifth day was Chimi's day of rest. That was today. She was aching to tell her friends Shenza's news about the first lord. That, and her spending money, should help her forget her troubles.

If only the hoka would let her hide it!

But it was obvious that trying to hide the hoka only made it look like she was hiding it. Maybe she was making too much of nothing. Her friends might not even care. Irritably, Chimi yanked off most of the beads and hung them on their wall pegs. Then she straightened her headcloth and put the annoying mirror away.

In the main room, Mother and Grandmother were at the work table, shucking feather-flower pods. With Sachakeen out on his own errands and Byben at the marketplace, the house was quiet. Chimi was sure she had heard voices earlier, but now the dry crackle of pods was the only sound.

"I'm going, Mother," Chimi announced as she walked through. Her cheerful voice was loud in the silence.

Mother's back was to her, but Chimi saw her shoulders tense. Grandmother was giving Mother a beady-eyed stare.

Giliatt cleared her throat. "Just a moment. Let me look at you."

Something was definitely wrong, Chimi thought as she saw Giliatt's serious face. She hoped they hadn't found out about Yail.

"Oh, Mother." Smiling, as if at a game, Chimi stopped with her arms outstretched and did a full turn, showing off her outfit.

There shouldn't have been anything to complain about. Chimi was dressed in a full-length sheath, bright pink, and over it a short robe splashed with yellow and green flowers. Her headcloth dangled a spray of beads that matched the ones around her neck. Chimi even lifted a corner of her robe to show the silver anklet resting above her sandals.

Mother reached out to tuck a stray curl into Chimi's headcloth, but her dark eyes focused on the hoka. Chimi kept smiling, although she felt her teeth might crack.

"Come," Mother said. Chimi felt the weight of Grandmother's eyes as they left the work room.

"Mother, what's wrong?" Chimi whispered as they stepped onto the porch that circled the house.

"I was hoping you could tell me," Giliatt replied. Her voice was soft, but her gaze was strong. "Is something going on?"

"What—no, no, no!" Chimi's tongue tripped over itself as she rushed to reassure her mother. "There's nothing, nothing going on. Nothing. I'm going to meet Winomi and the others."

The two women walked toward the path that led to the gate. Blooming vines passed on their left, and the wind made them rustle like whispering gossips.

"You've always done a good job with the cleaning, but it isn't like you to work so hard," Giliatt said with gentle humor. After a moment taut with hidden feelings, she asked, "Is there a young man you've met?"

Only Rellad, and he hadn't been back to her booth since the day of Yail's visit.

"No," Chimi answered, her voice strained. "I wouldn't try to make my own match, Mother. Come on, you know me."

Giliatt nodded, but she looked sad. "I haven't been able to find you a husband yet, I know. I keep hoping to save enough for a dowry, but... Well, you know."

Chimi did know. Giliatt earned enough money to feed and shelter her family, but nothing extra. Neither of her daughters would have a good dowry. Besides, Mother couldn't be left to care for Grandmother by herself. Chimi had always assumed that she wouldn't leave until Sachakeen got married. Then his wife could take over the responsibility.

"Nothing like that is happening," Chimi protested. "There's lots of time. I'm not in a hurry."

They had reached the front gate. Giliatt stopped, staring at Chimi wistfully.

"Mother, don't look at me like that," Chimi said.

Giliatt leaned over to kiss her cheek. "Just be patient."

Chimi watched her mother walk back toward the house. In a way, she was glad Giliatt had jumped to the wrong conclusion. She wouldn't have to worry about them finding out about Yail.

Still, she wished her mother had believed her.

* * *

Chimi ran down the last few steps to the plaza. The angle of the sun behind gauzy clouds told her she was late. She hoped her friends hadn't started shopping without her.

The grand fig tree was a popular meeting place, and she couldn't pick out the girls among the crowd. Breathing hard, Chimi circled the area. It was a warm morning and the scent of ripening figs was heavy in the air.

"Chimi!" A distant call tickled her ears. She turned, dark eyes seeking. "Chimi!"

There—kneeling backward on a bench, waving madly—was Winomi Igola of Kesquin. Their other friends were clustered nearby in the tree's deep shade. Chimi waved back and trotted toward them.

As Chimi got closer, Winomi was saying, "See? I told you she would be here." Straightening her headcloth, the plump girl sat on the bench.

"Thanks, Nomi," Chimi panted. She bent forward with her hands braced on her knees. "Sorry I'm late, everyone."

The sisters, Jeruki and Lukita Morro of Gavant, turned with welcoming smiles, but the fifth girl, Azma Lusheel of Kesquin, scowled at her.

"You made us wait long enough," she sniffed. Azma wore a floor-length robe of feather-flower silk, pale green with orange and black fishes. The fine strands shimmered as she moved. Azma's black hair had been artificially straightened and cut in a sharp line above her frowning brows. Behind her, it fell though arcs of silver chain to another severe, straight line.

"I said I was sorry," was Chimi's breezy reply. Azma always seemed to be put out lately. She did her best to ignore it.

"What kept you?" Lukita asked. Her hair was also long, but it fell over her shoulders in natural curls. The soft yellow of her robe brought out the amber in her eyes. It was decorated with a pattern of scarlet trumpet flowers, and she had a pair of real flowers tucked into her headcloth.

"We've been waiting a long time," Jeruki argued. Her garment was just like her older sister's, but reversed, red with yellow trumpet flowers.

"My mother had to look me over before I could leave the house," Chimi complained.

Winomi rolled her eyes. "Mine, too."

She was wearing a blue-green robe with a pattern of feather-flower silk that shimmered like waves on the sea. It didn't look good on her because it emphasized her weight. Of course, it was all right for a girl to have some flesh on her bones—it showed good health—but Winomi had too much. Chimi would never hurt her friend's feelings by saying that, though.

"Anyway, I'll make it up to you." There wasn't much room between Azma and Jeruki, but Chimi wiggled her way in. "Wait 'til you hear this!"

"Hear what?" The others clustered around her. Even Azma turned to look.

"Well," Chimi began, enjoying their attention, "my sister, you know, the magister... She says that Master Laraquies, you know, the vizier—"

"We know," Jeruki interrupted. "You keep telling us."

"You don't need to brag," Azma added.

Chimi sat back, folding her arms across her chest with playful indignation. "Well, if you don't want to hear about the first lord's visitor..."

Four pairs of brown eyes fixed on her, all of them wide with excitement.

"The first lord?" Lukita repeated eagerly.

"What kind of visitor?" Winomi wanted to know.

"Lord Manseen Bosteel of Bosteel," Chimi reported with relish. "Nakuri says he's the ruler of Sardony, City of Fountains. Guess who's coming with him?" She didn't wait for an answer before telling them, "His daughter! She's going to meet Lord Aspace."

"What?" the other girls squealed.

"They might even get married," Chimi crowed.

"Married!"

"You're making this up!"

"I don't need to make things up," Chimi answered smugly.

"I hadn't heard anything about this," Azma snapped. As a child of the local nobility, she liked to act like an expert in their affairs.

"I have inside information," Chimi retorted.

"Are you sure?" Jeruki asked, taking Azma's side.

"Yes, I'm sure," Chimi preened. "Shenza told me, and she was there when Lord Aspace announced it."

"When?" Winomi begged to know.

"Shenza didn't know. But isn't it exciting?" Chimi grinned. "A royal wedding!"

"Maybe you'll get to meet her," Lukita told Winomi. "Azma, too."

"I've been wanting an excuse to buy a new robe," Winomi giggled.

"What's her name?"

"How old is she?"

"Is she pretty?"

"Her name is Seelit." Chimi interrupted the chorus of questions. "That's all I know. Shenza didn't find out anything else about her!"

The girls fell to talking, but Azma remained silent. Chimi turned, saying, "You should tell your father."

The words died on her lips as she saw the hard look in her friend's eyes. Why was Azma so angry?

"Well, anyway," Azma asked mockingly, "did your mother dress you herself today?"

Chimi blinked, startled by her brittle tone. "No, I—"

"Then what's that?"

Chimi stopped as she realized Azma's gaze was fixed on her chest. No, on the hoka. Chimi felt her cheeks tingle with embarrassment.

"Chimi," Lukita gasped, concerned. "Are you ill?"

"No, no, no! It's nothing like that. It's just—" Chimi fumbled for an excuse. "Well, my sister, you know, she's a sorceress. She made me wear it. Some kind of a bad influence from Skall, or something. I don't understand all that magic stuff, but she insisted."

"Oh, is that it?" Azma's mocking smile implied something else.

Winomi quickly reassured Chimi, "You look fine."

"We all wear them sometimes," Lukita said.

"Hmmm." Her sister eyed Chimi suspiciously.

"And how's business been, Chimi?" Azma asked. Chimi bit her lip. Azma knew a lot of people, and she always had interesting stories to tell. That was why Chimi liked being with her. This time the story seemed to be about Chimi, and she didn't like that at all.

"It's great," she insisted. "I made almost seventy rukh yesterday, and I got keep some of it for myself."

"Great? That's not what I heard," Azma taunted.

"What do you mean?" Jeruki asked eagerly.

"Yes, what?" Chimi demanded.

"I just heard that Rellad hasn't been by to see you much, that's what."

"Oh..." cried Lukita with instant sympathy. Winomi laid her hand on Chimi's shoulder.

"That? It doesn't mean anything." Chimi made herself shrug carelessly. "His family's workshop is really busy. They just got in a big order. I'm sure you knew that, too."

From Azma's expression, she hadn't known. Still, her lips curved in a smirk. "Well, you've been babbling about this boy for months. We thought you were practically engaged."

Chimi tried to think of something to say that would stop Azma without making herself look stupid. "We're not," she said after an awkward pause.

"I guess not," Azma sneered.

"I'm sure he'll be back to see you soon," Lukita said softly, trying to break the tension.

"Of course he will," Winomi added.

Chimi smiled, but she couldn't meet anyone's gaze. Her shock gave way to hurt. Why was Azma acting like this? There was no ignoring the dark gleam in the girl's eyes as she enjoyed Chimi's embarrassment. The twine holding the hoka made Chimi's neck itch, and she rubbed the spot irritably.

Then her gaze came into focus, and what she saw threw Azma's pettiness right out of her mind. Leaning against the fig tree's massive trunk—it was that man, the nasty-looking one with no teeth, who had witnessed Yail's tragic reunion with his mother. He was staring right at Chimi!

Chapter Six

Dead Eyes Watching

Chimi jumped to her feet, muffling a gasp with both hands. She couldn't let her friends see a man like that near her. The other girls looked up, startled. A worried frown creased Winomi's brows.

Before they could ask any questions, Chimi exclaimed, "Well, that's enough talking about me. Let's go! I have money to spend, you know."

Winomi jumped up at once. "What are we waiting for?"

Their voices were both a bit too cheerful, but Chimi didn't resist when her friend took her hand. She held on tightly and wouldn't let herself look at that dreadful man.

"What's your hurry?" Jeruki retorted, but she and Lukita rose, too. Azma came last, and the cruelty of her smile made Chimi's stomach churn. It was weird that Azma and Mother both mentioned marriage on the same day, and Chimi wasn't in the mood for any more coincidences.

"Don't listen to her," Winomi whispered.

"I'm not." Chimi covered her anxiety with breezy assurance.

Winomi and Azma were cousins, from different lines within the House of Kesquin. Sometimes it was hard to believe they were related.

Well, Chimi had set out to have fun today, and by the heavens, she was going to! She pulled Winomi across the busy square—away from the toothless man—as fast as she could.

The crowd closed around them like a comforting blanket. Chimi loved to go through the market with money in her sash. There were so many pretty things to see. She savored the babble of voices and the smells of vine flowers and of food roasting over open coals.

The five girls moved together, though Chimi sensed Winomi and Lukita were trying to keep Azma away from her. She could tell Winomi wanted to know what was bothering her, too, but her friend didn't pry. Chimi was glad to leave it at that.

She had been planning to get a necklace and earrings, maybe amber or copper instead of cheap shells and painted wood. She had to be sensible, though. They browsed in several booths, but nothing satisfied Chimi. Winomi found a stall that had strands of red and white coral. There were earrings, necklaces in two lengths, bracelets and anklets. Chimi liked them, but she paused as another thought came to her.

"Don't you want them?" Winomi asked over her shoulder.

"I do," Chimi answered, "but just a minute."

She stepped aside, taking out the pouch that hung from a sash concealed beneath her robe. She opened it and stirred the flat copper squares with her fingers, counting rukh and sekh.

"I think maybe I'll look for a new robe," she said. "At the House of Melleen."

"Oh." Winomi nodded knowingly.

The House of Melleen had a large shop to sell the fabric their weavers made. Chimi didn't expect to see Rellad there, but she knew word of her visit was likely to reach him.

Winomi looked around, then asked in a low voice, "As an apology?"

"What? No!" Chimi protested. "There's nothing to apologize for, Nomi. It's more like, you know, just to say I'm thinking of him."

"You flirt," her friend giggled.

Chimi couldn't help smiling with her. "He's been buying from my shop for a while now. It's only fair to repay him."

Winomi glanced around again. "Well, we don't have to wait for them," she murmured.

Following her gaze, Chimi saw Azma deeply involved in barter with the jeweler. She hesitated. She hated to leave after making everyone wait for her. They had all known each other since general school. Though Azma and Winomi were of higher rank, their status had never been an issue before. At least, Chimi hadn't thought it was.

Something had happened in the past few weeks to sour Azma so much. Chimi tried to be pleasant. She just couldn't understand why Azma didn't like her any more. Lukita and Winomi were still good companions, but Jeruki was too eager to please Azma. It was getting harder to stay friends.

"Yes, let's go," Chimi decided reluctantly. She passed the coral necklace she had been holding back to the dealer. Whatever Azma's problem was, Chimi didn't have to take her abuse.

"Kita," Winomi called. Lukita turned. "We'll be at the House of Melleen. Meet us there?"

The older girl nodded, and Chimi saw sadness in her eyes. Azma turned sharply, but Chimi waved and walked away. She couldn't help sighing. Her fun day wasn't turning out to be so much fun.

"Don't let her bring you down," Winomi said as they wove their way through the crowd.

"I don't understand," Chimi complained. "We're supposed to be friends. Azma didn't even want to hear about Lady Seelit."

Winomi didn't answer, but Chimi glimpsed a shadow of guilt in her brown eyes.

"What?" she demanded.

"I'm not sure, either," Winomi confessed. "She's been saying some unkind things, Chimi."

"Like what?"

"Mostly what you heard." Winomi's eyes veered away, and Chimi knew there must be more. Had Azma found out about Yail? How could she know? Had Nakuri told someone else?

"Why is she—oh!" Chimi yelped as she bumped someone going the other way. She whirled to apologize to an elderly woman, who seemed dazed by the impact. "I'm so sorry. I didn't see you."

Chimi trailed off as she recognized the intense, throbbing cold where their shoulders had touched. It couldn't be!

"I'm sorry," Chimi stammered as she backed away.

The old woman stared after her. Chimi had an impression of deep-set, sad eyes in a face lined with care, and a beautiful dark blue robe sewn with silver beads. Then she whirled and fled.

"Chimi, what's wrong?" Winomi cried as Chimi dragged her blindly through the crowd.

"Nothing!"

"Let go. You're hurting me!" Winomi pulled against her grip.

Chimi did slow down, but only because she had raised enough sweat to drive the chill from her lungs.

"It'll be all right," Winomi soothed her. "Azma won't stay mad. You'll see."

She didn't know what she was talking about, Chimi thought with a kind of lucid terror. She hadn't seen the ghost. How could there be another wandering spirit? Chalsett-port wasn't a very big town. There weren't that many ghosts, were there?

As her panic faded, Chimi realized she was in danger of spoiling her own plans. The girls were coming up on the cloth sellers' aisle.

"Chimi, slow down," Winomi said. "You're pinching my hand."

"Sorry." Chimi let go. She was surprised to find their skin had stuck together with sweat. She flexed her fingers to ease the cramping. "It's just, this whole day, everything has been going wrong, and I—"

Once again misinterpreting Chimi's problem, Winomi gave her a quick hug. "Don't worry. You're cute, they'll like you. Just be yourself."

Chimi nodded, though her conscience pricked her. She had promised Mother she wouldn't try to find her own husband, and here she was, approaching a boy's family. It was too late for second thoughts as Winomi urged her around the corner.

The House of Melleen ran a large shop, occupying four stalls together.

Row upon row of racks were draped with fabric in every color imaginable. The arbor above was hung with smaller swatches for headcloths. Almost everything was feather-flower silk, and most of the fabrics were embellished with beads or embroidery.

"This is my favorite shop," Winomi said as they entered.

"How pretty." Chimi sighed with bliss as she stroked a length of pure silk. It was sheer and soft as a cloud. Still, she couldn't help wondering if she was out of her depth here. She had forgotten that the House of Melleen catered to elite clients. The money she had might not be enough after all.

"Good day, ladies," a pleasant voice said.

They turned to see a woman draped in a stunning silk robe, the color fading from the green of new leaves to pale gold like the sky at dawn. Butterflies were embroidered on it, with sparkling beads among the threads. Her hair was tightly wrapped in a pale green headcloth with its own flight of butterflies. Even her heavy eyelids shimmered with a vivid green cosmetic. She assessed them with a cool, amused indulgence.

"Tuseeva!" Winomi greeted her with a delighted cry. "Oh, I hoped you would be here."

Meanwhile, Chimi bit her lip. Tuseeva Hasapai of Melleen was one of Rellad's aunts. According to Azma, she personally oversaw the sales staff. Chimi hadn't expected to have such an important person wait on her.

"It's a pleasure to see you again, Lady Winomi." Tuseeva placed both hands on her chest and bowed gracefully.

"This is Chimi Waik of Tresmeer," Winomi went on. "Chimi's family grows feather-flowers, you know."

Chimi felt her cheeks glow. She could have kicked Winomi for saying her name like that.

"Welcome." Tuseeva bowed her head, one hand touching her chest. "I've heard of your family. My brothers speak well of the House of Tresmeer."

"Oh, thank you!" Chimi gushed. "I see the raw floss all the time, but it's wonderful to know where it ends up. Your robes are so beautiful!"

Tuseeva accepted her flattery with aplomb, but the twine holding Chimi's hoka was itching again. With an effort, she kept from rubbing her neck. Chimi pretended to admire a length of pale blue silk painted with creamy yellow starfishes. A while ago, when the hoka had bothered her, that toothless fellow had been staring at her. She turned to another rack, darting wary glances around her. If he was following her, she was going to call a peacekeeper!

Her gaze met the piercing dark eyes of the old woman she had bumped earlier. She stood in the shade of the arbor just outside the Melleen stall. The sun shone brightly behind her, and a light breeze rifled the leaves on the vines. The old woman stood as still as the post beside her. The wind didn't touch her.

Chimi felt slightly sick, and her shoulder ached with chill. She jerked back toward Winomi and Tuseeva, running a trembling hand over a piece of silk without really seeing it.

"Do you prefer that one?" Tuseeva asked politely.

"What?" Chimi blinked, distracted. Her hand was resting on a length of deep red silk with large white flowers. That was the kind of thing you'd wear to a funeral. She shook her head vigorously.

"No, no, that's much too dark. This would be better, I think." She shifted the red robe to expose a fabric similar to Tuseeva's, but shaded from pink to orange to yellow.

"It is a becoming color," Tuseeva agreed. Too late, Chimi realized it was a lot like what she was already wearing. Tuseeva must think she was a fool.

Once again, Winomi intervened. "Well, let's look at some others. You have lots of choices, and there's no hurry."

"Oh, yes, let's look around," Chimi babbled, eager to get farther away from the old woman who watched her.

It was hard to concentrate on what she was doing, though. Chimi kept hoping the old woman would move on if she ignored her. She didn't. Any time Chimi looked around, the old woman was still there, still staring. What was wrong with her!

"Chimi?"

Once again, the sound of her name startled her. Winomi and Tuseeva were looking at her, obviously waiting for an answer. A gorgeous deep blue robe was draped over her arm. Pale green stitchery and copper beads made it shimmer.

"It's beautiful, but, really..." Chimi hesitated. She didn't want to say it, but she could never afford a robe like that.

"Maybe something more modest?" Winomi put in.

"Can you suggest something?" Chimi asked with a winning smile.

"Ah." Tuseeva nodded, and carefully replaced the garment she had been holding. To Chimi's relief, she showed no disdain as she ushered them off. "We offer a range of products for those of varying means who want to look their best. This way, ladies."

She led them to the last of the four booths. Chimi immediately knew when they left the realm of feather-flower for that of common cloth. Hemp was plentiful and easy to grow, used in a variety of products from stout rope to fabrics that could be nearly as nice as silk. It didn't have the sheen and distinctive texture, however.

"Perhaps something like this?" Tuseeva drew out a length of gauzy stuff dyed in the graduated shakes of pink and orange that Chimi liked so much. She nodded wistfully. This was a new style, so pretty, and she knew hemp was better for daily wear than silk.

"Yes, I'd like that." Gathering her courage, she asked, "What are you asking for it?"

Tuseeva eyed her, as if gauging her seriousness. "Twenty-five rukh, I think, for work like this."

The price made Chimi gulp. Twenty-five! Even in a shop like this, she would expect to pay that much for pure silk! Besides, she barely had eighteen rukh. She looked around for Winomi, but her friend had strolled off discreetly to give her privacy for the negotiations. Chimi didn't want to look cheap by objecting to the price, but she didn't want to play the fool by paying too much, either. Tuseeva's bland expression offered no help.

Chimi put on an innocent face. "I thought this was hemp, not feather-flower. Was I wrong?"

"That's right."

"Then I couldn't possibly go higher than thirteen." Chimi tried to match Tuseeva's indifferent air.

The lady merchant smiled slightly, and Chimi realized Tuseeva had been testing her. Was she trying to show off in front of Winomi? If so, was she desperate enough to overpay?

"It takes great care to get the fine gradient," Tuseeva countered. Still, she started folding the cloth as if it was already sold. "Our dyers worked hard. Perhaps twenty-three?"

"I suppose I might, if it had some silk in it," Chimi replied. "Fifteen rukh, five sekh."

Now the bargaining began in earnest. The price came down with reassuring speed, and she even forgot for a moment that the old woman's ghost was there. Chimi finally settled for seventeen rukh and eight sekh, which was almost all the money she had.

"Come back again soon." Bowing, Tuseeva presented the folded bundle.

"Thank you very much. I will." Chimi summoned her sweetest smile as she received her prize.

Her triumph was crushed when she turned to look for Winomi and saw the old woman watching with patient, dead eyes. Chimi's chest tightened, choking her, and her ears rang with the force of her heart's pounding.

A voice in her ear startled her. "That's a really nice robe. I think she likes you." Winomi practically danced with glee.

Chimi whirled to her friend, away from the ghost's accusing eyes.

"She probably thinks I'm stupid," Chimi moaned. Clutching her soft burden to her chest, she walked off. She had to get away from the ghost before Winomi noticed it.

"No, I'm sure she doesn't," Winomi soothed.

Abruptly Chimi whirled away from her. "I'm sorry. I have to go."

"But the others haven't come yet," Winomi protested.

"We've been here a long time, Nomi. I don't think they're coming," Chimi snapped. Her friend looked hurt, and she immediately felt bad.

"Anyway," she murmured, beckoning Winomi closer, "I don't have any money left."

"It's still fun to look," Winomi said. "And I'll buy your lunch, you know that."

"I'm not hungry." In fact, Chimi was feeling nauseous again. She couldn't bear to stay here with the ghost just standing there, staring at her.

"I understand," Winomi said softly. "You don't have to explain. But when I see Azma again, I'm going to give her a piece of my mind!"

Chimi looked up with a jerk. "No, no, no. It isn't her. It's just—" Her vision blurred. She buried her face in her new robe, blotting up the tears.

"She can't treat you that way." Winomi's eyes flashed indignantly.

"Nomi, don't!" Chimi mumbled through the cloth. "It isn't like that. You shouldn't fight about me."

"Then why?"

The noonday heat pressed in on Chimi, stifling her. A cloud passed over the sun, darkening the area, and the ghost was right behind Winomi. Chimi could see the wrinkles around her eyes and mouth, the silver mist of her hair. The old woman didn't cry the way Yail had, but she was obviously waiting for Chimi. Wanting her to do something. And she couldn't. She wouldn't!

"It's just..." Chimi stammered. "Azma isn't... Ooh, I have to go!"

She turned and ran, bumping and weaving through the crowd. Chimi knew Winomi was sensitive and her feelings would be hurt, but she couldn't help it. She couldn't stand still another second. She had to get away from the old lady and her awful staring!

*   *   *

When Chimi arrived at Lelldour's gate a short time later, she was panting and sweating and too upset to care about manners. She charged right into his overgrown yard.

"Master Lelldour!" she cried.

The sun was high in a sky full of huge white clouds. It was very hot out in the street, but it felt cold under the shade of Lelldour's trees. The dense foliage seemed to absorb her voice the way thirsty plants drink water. Chimi pitched her voice higher and strode toward the darkened house.

"Master Lelldour!" In her hurry, she didn't notice that the stream had backed up again. "Oh!" Chimi ground her teeth in annoyance as her feet got wet. Her fear had been turning to anger as she came, and this was the insult that sparked her fury.

"Master Lelldour!" she yelled as she approached the shaggy overhang of his porch. A new layer of fallen leaves crackled beneath her feet.

A red-robed, lanky figure wandered out onto the porch. His sluggish pace and lack of curiosity fueled her outrage.

"So there you are." Chimi stopped with her new robe bunched up in an angry knot at her hip.

"And here you are," he replied.

At his feet, the ball and bone lay where she had left them. He hadn't bothered to pick them up! Chimi tore her eyes from the objects with a feeling almost like guilt.

"You've got to do something," she snapped up at Lelldour. Her voice echoed slightly in the space beneath the eaves. "It's your responsibility."

Infuriatingly, Lelldour didn't seem to know what she was talking about. "I beg your pardon?"

"The ghosts!" Chimi shrieked. "There's another one following me. She's been staring at me all morning. I won't stand for it!"

"Why is it my problem if the ghost has been following you?" he retorted. "Ask her what she wants."

"I won't!" Chimi restrained herself from stamping her feet like an angry child. "I won't—I'm not the necromancer. You are! It's your job, not mine."

With a sigh, Lelldour said, "As I've already told you—"

"And I'm telling you—do something!" Chimi interrupted with more force than she had ever thought she would use in speaking to an adult man.

Softly, regretfully, he said, "I can't do what you want."

"Don't say that," she snarled. "You were the necromancer for a long time. You can't just forget all you knew."

"I haven't, I assure you," Lelldour told her, "but there are rules you aren't aware of. May I make a suggestion?"

"What?" Chimi sulked.

"The red lamp at my gate. Did you see it?"

"Of course! I'm not blind," she retorted.

Ignoring her disrespect, he continued, "If the lamp was lit, the ghosts would be drawn here."

Chimi liked that idea. Lelldour would have to do something if the ghosts were hanging around, staring at him.

His next words dashed that hope. "Then they would wait here for you to help them, rather than following you. I would have to show you how the oil is enchanted, of course."

"I don't want to help them," Chimi wailed. "I just want them to leave me alone!"

The retired necromancer stared at her impatiently. "Then you'd better get used to being followed."

"Stop it!" Chimi clenched her fists at her sides. The beads on her headcloth rattled with her fury. "I'm not going to do this."

"You have to do it," he answered implacably.

"But—"

"Let me explain something to you," Lelldour interrupted. "There are two kinds of necromancer: those who accept their duty to serve the helpless, and those who serve only themselves. They view our sacred calling as a way to make money." He spoke of the second kind with such contempt, she didn't have to wonder what kind he was.

"I didn't choose this," Chimi protested. "I don't know much about magic, really, and I don't like ghosts."

"But you did choose," he said firmly. "You helped a little boy who needed you. Was that the wrong thing to do?"

She only did it to impress Rellad, Chimi thought rebelliously.

"Nobody told me what it meant," she said. "You didn't tell me. You didn't say there would be others. I only wanted to help once." She faltered, hearing how selfish she sounded.

"Life is full of unexpected events," Lelldour said. "Some choose and some are chosen."

The seriousness of his tone made Chimi shiver in the dense shade. She clung to the heat of her anger as an antidote to her dread.

"You can't make me do this."

"I don't think you can refuse," Lelldour said in a strange, flat voice. As if he didn't care, but he was determined that she should. "The ghosts won't let you."

"Oh, yes I can," Chimi argued.

"It isn't like farming, where you can just put down your tools and sell your land," Lelldour insisted. "Not every deed can be undone. If you did refuse, the consequences—"

"I don't care about that!" Chimi was yelling again, she couldn't stop herself. "I said I won't be a necromancer!"

Lelldour smiled with surprising malice. "I suggest you tell her that."

Chimi looked where he was pointing. She cringed when she saw the old woman standing nearby. Chimi wondered how much the ghost had heard, but she showed no anger.

"I just need someone to cook," she said in a bewildered voice.

Cooking sounded simple enough, and Chimi was good at it. But Yail's request had seemed easy, too.

The old woman went on, "It's my husband, my Tevo. He hasn't been eating a thing. He's gotten so thin. I want to make a meal he likes, so he'll eat and feel better."

Despite herself, Chimi's anger yielded to pity. And confusion. It sounded like the old woman had come back from the heavens out of concern for her family. She hadn't known someone could do that. She'd thought wandering spirits were people like Yail who hadn't had funerals.

"Can you cook?" the old woman repeated plaintively.

A wave of self-pity rolled over Chimi, but she found herself nodding. "Yes, Grandmother, I can cook." She turned back to Lelldour with tears of rage in her eyes. "But this is the last time!"

"I wouldn't be so sure."

Chimi had started to walk off, but when she heard Lelldour's smug response, she whirled to confront him again.

"I mean it!" she shrilled up at him. "You're not the only necromancer in Chalsett-port. If you won't do your job, I'll find someone who will!"

Lelldour drew up his gaunt frame as if she had struck him. "If you do that, you're even more stupid than I thought."

Chimi was glad of his anger. Finally, she had hurt him as much as he was hurting her.

"Then maybe you'd better start doing your job!" she snapped.

This time when Chimi turned away, she didn't look back.

Chapter Seven

The Patience of the Dead

After her last visit to Lord Aspace's palace, Shenza wasn't happy to be back. She hurried through the first lord's garden, feeling as much a fugitive as the thieves she had helped capture. The path ran beside a rocky stream bed. Shenza told herself to slow down, calm down. She only had to report on the stolen piglet. Since Laraquies wasn't home, she knew she would find him here.

Her path wound through a cluster of small buildings. It crossed the dry stream on a stone bridge and she saw her teacher ahead of her. As vizier, Laraquies had been given one of the cottages for his office. Many of the courtiers had them if they needed to be available for Lord Aspace. So far, Shenza had managed to avoid being assigned one. She felt more comfortable in her own home, farther away from Aspace.

Laraquies was sitting under a row of fern trees, in a tiny courtyard paved with gray stone slabs. Before him, a low table held a game board and many carved ivory tiles. Behind him, steps ran up to his office. Seated opposite Laraquies, Lady Izmay studied the game board. She was wearing a cream colored robe with a pattern of pale green leaves. Silvery curls fell loose over her shoulders, held in check by a clasp in the shape of a dragonfly with iridescent shell for its wings.

Suddenly, Izmay leaned forward. "Ha!" she cried. "Try to get out of this." White teeth flashed in her brown face as she slapped down one tile and scooped up another.

Shenza had never seen the first lady react with such energy. It wasn't very ladylike, and yet it was genuine. Shenza was surprised because she didn't often see true emotion among the courtiers, who were so trained in measured words and dignity.

Laraquies smiled with regret. "The game is yours," he acknowledged. Looking past Izmay, he nodded to Shenza. "Come along, we've just finished."

"Sit down, child," Izmay added. Her dark eyes still sparkled with pleasure in her victory.

"I'm sorry to interrupt," Shenza apologized. She pressed her right hand to her chest and bowed before sinking to her knees beside the table. "I have the day's report, Master Laraquies."

"Did you retrieve the piglet?" Laraquies asked.

"Yes, teacher. However, the farmer, Jubai Conoor of Onari, wasn't completely honest with me. His neighbor, Attali, didn't steal the piglet. She purchased it, but—" Shenza frowned "—she brought along a bottle of rice wine to smooth the bargaining."

"Oh?" Laraquies chuckled. "To smooth the bargaining. I see."

"So she said," Shenza replied with asperity. As a sorceress, she never drank alcohol because it might interfere with her magic. Every time she saw a case like this, she was glad to avoid the nuisance. "Once Jubai recovered his senses, he realized how one-sided the bargain had been."

"And then he brought his complaint," Laraquies finished for her.

"Correct." Shenza opened her travel case and drew out a scroll of cloth. She set it on the table beside the game board. "The details are here."

Izmay, who had been gathering the tiles into neat stacks, glanced up at Shenza. "What was your judgment?"

Although she seemed at ease, Shenza remembered that this was Lord Aspace's mother. Anything she said could be repeated to him.

"I could have fined Jubai for wasting my time," Shenza admitted. "That seemed unfair, though, since he had already been taken advantage of. I ordered Attali to return the animal, and Jubai to return her payment."

"If they're neighbors, how do you know they won't keep feuding?" Izmay asked.

"I told them I'll fine the next person who makes a false report," Shenza said. "And I meant it."

"If they aren't afraid of the law, maybe they're afraid of losing money." Laraquies chuckled again.

"I'm sure of that," Izmay agreed wryly. She glanced at Shenza again, and her dark eyes gleamed. "It seems a valid judgment. My son was right about you."

Shenza had felt her heart lift at the first lady's praise, but it fell just as quickly. Aspace talked about her? She cleared her throat.

"It is my honor if my Lord speaks my name," she murmured.

Izmay turned to Laraquies. Her eyes crinkled at the corners with amusement. Laraquies smiled sweetly in return and lifted his shoulders in a shrug. No words were spoken, yet Shenza felt like they were talking about her, too. Her cheeks tingled with warmth.

"She's a good girl." Laraquies patted her shoulder. Shenza stared at the travel case propped open against her knees. She closed it abruptly.

"There's no need to worry," Izmay said. "He speaks well of you."

Shenza ran her fingers over the stitching on her travel case and tried not to squirm. She did want Izmay to like her. "Lord Aspace has been kind."

"He has good judgement, like his mother," Laraquies added, his voice a silken purr.

"Listen to you," Izmay countered, smiling. "A few weeks as vizier and you're a flatterer like all the rest." Still, she didn't seem to mind his compliment.

Izmay went on, "I was impressed, Magister, when you wouldn't agree to spy for my son. So many young women just do as they're told, especially for a man as good-looking as Aspace. He needs to know that not every girl will fall at his feet."

"It was my duty," Shenza protested, though the first lady's approval did raise her spirits again.

"We were both caught by surprise," Laraquies put in. "Do you have any idea why he would ask us to do this?"

"He hasn't told me," Izmay replied. Clearly, she didn't like it. Shenza reflected that Aspace might not be the only one who was used to having people fall at his feet. "It should be interesting when Bosteel arrives. You'll both be there, of course."

Shenza wanted to protest, but Laraquies answered first. "Of course. When will they arrive?"

"Master Udama thought ten days or so, if the tides are right."

Ten days! Shenza felt a sudden pinch at the back of her neck as tension gripped her. All at once, she couldn't sit still. Her fingers closed over the handle of her travel case and she rose, pushing against the table.

"Excuse me," she murmured.

"Is something wrong?" Izmay asked, surprised.

"Not at all," Shenza answered over a dry lump in her throat. "Now that I've given Master Laraquies my report, there's another case I'm investigating." Shenza backed off a step and bowed again. "It was good to speak with my Lady. Master, I'll see you tonight."

Shenza turned and hurried off, before her misery could show. Behind her, Lady Izmay's voice murmured a question. Now Shenza was sure they were talking about her.

* * *

Chimi didn't slow down until she was well down the street. Great clumps of clouds did little to block the sun's heat. Under the merciless rays, she felt emotionally limp, unable to summon her fury any more.

Why is this happening to me? she wondered miserably. *And how dare that man try to make me his apprentice? By the heavens, I won't do it!*

Then came the cold presence at her side, making her vow a lie. Chimi knew she was lucky the old woman wasn't angry. Grandmother Myri would have been biting Chimi in half for showing Lelldour so much disrespect. But the ghost didn't scold or complain. She just followed, watching Chimi with the patience of the dead.

Sighing, Chimi stopped. The old woman stopped, too. Making a try at good manners, Chimi offered her arm to the shorter woman.

"I'm Chimi Waik of Tresmeer, Grandmother. And you?"

The ghost paused, as if she couldn't remember. Well, elders could be forgetful. Although, now that Chimi thought about it, Yail had had trouble with his name, too.

"Hawadi Seltees of Calloon," the old woman finally said.

"Well, shall we go to the kitchen, Grandmother Hawadi?" Chimi suggested, resigned.

"Oh, no." The old woman looked surprised. "He doesn't have any decent food in the house. We have to go to the market first."

"The market?" Chimi gulped. She had just left the market. Her friends might still be there. What would Winomi think if she saw Chimi shopping with some stranger? Chimi's mind raced, looking for a way out.

"Grandmother, I don't have any money to buy food," she said. Would Hawadi follow her everywhere until she saved enough money to buy the food? No, she couldn't stand it! Unless she could convince Hawadi to cook fish.

Hawadi patted her arm. Her chilly hand felt almost pleasant in the day's heat.

"You just come with me. I'll show you my hiding place."

Reluctantly, Chimi let Hawadi guide her through the town. The old woman must have been a pretty girl once, but that was a long time ago. Chimi knew she shouldn't take an interest in a life that was already over. She had learned that from Yail. Chimi had to think of herself. She had a reputation to protect. Chimi didn't plan to let this stranger—a dead stranger—ruin her life.

Still, Hawadi seemed like such a normal old lady. She moved slowly, leaning on Chimi so that Chimi had to hold herself back from dragging her along. Chimi did her best not to fume. The ghost hadn't had any trouble keeping up on the way to Lelldour's.

Brooding, she didn't pay much attention to where Hawadi took her. She vaguely noted a staircase from the fourth to the sixth levels and a turn back toward the town center. Then they passed beneath an arched stone gateway into a small, sunny yard.

Low mounds of foliage covered with tiny blossoms surrounded a stone cottage with a thatched roof. A brook trickled down to a pond, which they crossed on a bridge made of thick bamboo logs. The water was green with algae. White and gold fishes crowded to the top of the pond, kissing the surface as if they hadn't been fed in a long time. Chimi couldn't help noticing that only one shadow fell on the jade-green water.

So this had been Hawadi's home? Chimi glanced at her and saw no emotion on the wizened brown face. That seemed odd. And where was this husband she was so worried about? Shouldn't he notice a trespasser coming into his yard? Yet there was no sound as they approached the house. Maybe he was napping, she thought with an inner shrug. Byben took a lot of naps.

To Chimi's surprise, they didn't go into the house. Instead, Hawadi took her farther along the gravel path, which curved around the side. They drifted to a stop where the open porch blended into the back wall. Hawadi looked at Chimi expectantly.

"Well, where's this hiding place of yours?" Chimi demanded.

"Underneath." Hawadi gestured at the porch.

Chimi groaned, but dutifully knelt with one hand on the porch for balance. Cool air bathed her face as she peered into the shadows under the cottage. Like most buildings in rainy Chalsett, the house had a hollow foundation for air flow and to prevent flooding.

Blood running into her head made her ears pound. Chimi straightened, rubbing her temples.

"I hope your roach-repellent spells are working," she said. "And spiders?"

"Of course. My house is very clean," Hawadi replied.

Her patience only made Chimi feel more sorry for herself. "Where is it, underneath?"

"In the outer wall, to your right. There is a large white stone. Put your hand on it and say 'open'."

Open? How very original. Chimi closed her lips on the sarcastic words and carefully set her new robe on the porch, out of the way. Her headcloth had felt loose when she bent over, so she yanked out the brooch holding it on. Sighing over the time she had wasted getting dressed this morning, Chimi shrugged off her outer robe as well.

Another thought struck her and she smiled. That was it! If she changed clothes, her friends might not recognize her. Winomi was the only one who had seen her new robe, and she wouldn't expect Chimi to be wearing it yet. It was a perfect plan!

Much more cheerfully, Chimi put her outer robe and headcloth on the porch. She lowered herself onto her back and reached above her head to grip the rim of the opening in the foundation. Pulling against the cold rocks and kicking with her feet, she wriggled into the gap.

Her body blocked the light from outside, making the crawl space even darker, but she waited, and blinked, and the outlines of bamboo slats emerged from the blackness above her. It smelled dusty. Chimi was relieved to see and hear no sign of insects. However, the chilly dampness under her shoulders hurried her about her work.

She reached to her right, groping toward a lighter blot in the gloom. The rough texture of stone made her fingertips tingle. Then she felt a straight edge. Squinting, she made out a large, squarish stone with the shadows of a symbol cut into its face. It was a stretch, but she managed to press her palm to the sigil.

Concentrating, she said, "Open."

There was a soft grinding noise. The stone face came away, bruising her hand as it fell. Muffling a pained curse, Chimi shook her throbbing fingers. She groped in the exposed cavity until her fingers touched something soft and slack with harder objects inside. A money pouch? She grabbed it and squirmed her way back out.

"Is this it?" Daylight stung Chimi's eyes as she held the fabric bag up for Hawadi's inspection.

"Yes."

"Thank the heavens."

Chimi stood up, brushing grit off her shoulders. Turning left and right, she tried to see her back. Damp patches showed up against the bright pink, but it wasn't too bad.

"I'll just be a moment, Grandmother," Chimi said.

She shook out her new robe and gathered it into a long, loose band. This she draped over her shoulders, crossing her chest in front, and joined it in a knot at the back. She twisted, making sure the trailing ends would cover the wet spots on her back. Then she pulled the loose fabric up over her bare shoulders.

Hawadi watched patiently as Chimi gathered her hair, twisting the dark curls into a knot on top of her head. She re-wrapped her headcloth over that. It wasn't much of a disguise, but she hoped it was different enough from what she had been wearing that her friends wouldn't recognize her if they saw her.

"All right, Grandmother," Chimi sighed. "What was it you wanted to buy?"

✳ ✳ ✳

Shenza brooded over Izmay's words all the way down to the fourth level. It was bad enough that she had to watch while Lord Aspace courted another woman. She had taken some comfort from knowing it would all take place at some vague future time. But ten days? That was just too soon.

Now the cruel truth tore her illusions away. Whatever lay ahead, she had ten days to prepare herself. She also had that long to get some answers about Chimi's mysterious encounter with the ghost boy. Once Lord Bosteel and his daughter arrived, she wouldn't have time to think about anything else.

A patch of dull crimson caught Shenza's eye. This must be the necromancer's lamp Chimi had told her about. She approached the gate, taking in details of the low stone wall, the moss on its mortar and vines creeping over from the other side. The faded, flaking paint was just as Chimi had described it.

Shenza stopped between the two gateposts and called, "Hello!"

She was struck by the gloom and musty odor. Chalsett was a forested island, and trees were encouraged to grow where they shaded the houses. Shenza was used to the gentle cycle of leaves dropping and returning to the soil, but there were too many here, layer upon layer in a shroud of decay. It was a kind of hell, a place of death without renewal.

"Good afternoon," Shenza called again. "I am the magister. May I come in?"

Again she waited, studying the neglected property. Did the necromancer's presence interfere with nature's way somehow? She had never heard any legends about that. It seemed like something only nature spirits could do. But Shenza was well aware how little she knew. Her last contact with a ghost had been a fraud. Makko of Kiliwair had tried to deceive her with the illusion of a ghost.

Her lack of knowledge was really becoming frustrating. Obviously, Shenza could ask the other necromancer. But she didn't trust Vesswan of Zeell, no matter how accurate her information was. The woman was too closely associated with Nurune of Sengool, another of Shenza's past adversaries.

Shenza tried again. "Good afternoon! Is anyone home? I'm the magister. I need to speak with you!"

A slight breeze rustled the treetops. That was the only reply. No light or movement showed in the dark house. Not even birds called in the branches.

Shenza looked around the edge of the pond Chimi had told her about. Water had backed up over the stepping stones. The leaves at the edge were slightly trampled. By someone walking? The track was so faint, it couldn't have been more than one person. Maybe Lelldour had stepped out on some errand.

Even so, Shenza could see why Chimi hadn't liked this place. Something wasn't right. Unfortunately, even though she was the magister, she still needed permission to come on Lelldour's property. Unless she had some reason to believe he had committed a crime, of course, but there was nothing to make her think that.

Reluctantly, she turned away. Chimi's complaint had to go beyond negligence before Shenza crossed that line. She would have to come back later if she wanted to know what line had been crossed, and by whom.

* * *

Despite Chimi's best efforts, the afternoon was as maddening as the morning had been. Hawadi insisted on going with her to the market. She wouldn't even consider staying to talk with her husband while Chimi did the shopping. She wanted to choose everything personally and nothing less would satisfy her.

Chimi escorted Hawadi to the marketplace with gritted teeth. She used side stairs to get there, avoiding anywhere her friends might be. Inspecting the produce took forever. Hawadi's standards were ridiculously high. The only thing she let Chimi do was bargain. Even then, it was lucky Hawadi's cache held enough coin to pay for the best. Chimi was in a hurry, and she paid top prices.

She did all the carrying, too. Chimi's arms were soon groaning with a bag of millet, fresh redroots and seaweed, a string of salted fishes, and a pair of chili peppers whose scent made her eyes burn. At least Hawadi hadn't had her heart set on a whole piglet or roast goose. It would have been worse if she made Chimi do the butchering, too. So Chimi told herself while Hawadi gave her a long and detailed description of her husband's favorite meal.

By the time they got back to Hawadi's house, the clouds were swollen and tinged with gray. The afternoon rains were coming. Chimi was afraid she would be late getting back home.

"Excuse me!" She called as she strode across the bridge over Hawadi's pond.

There was no reply. Well, Chimi couldn't cook Hawadi's precious meal without going inside. She had to use the kitchen.

"Hello, I'm coming in!" she yelled as she stomped up the steps to the porch.

"What's going on?" a peevish voice answered. "Who's there?"

An old man appeared in the door. His body was bent into a permanent stoop, and his brown face was shrunken like over-ripe fruit. A long, thin moustache trickled down his chin. Skin drooped around his belly and under his arms, as if he had recently lost a lot of weight.

Small as he was, the man was blocking Chimi's way and she nearly crashed into him. She did her best to smile as she lurched to a stop.

"Good afternoon, Grandfather," Chimi chirped as brightly as a bird. "Someone has come to visit you."

The old man stared past Chimi's shoulder as if she wasn't even there. "Wife," he breathed.

"Husband," Hawadi answered with more tenderness than Chimi had ever heard in a single word.

Chimi wasn't used to being ignored, even by old men. Gritting her teeth, she went on, "Yes, I'm here because of Grandmother Hawadi. She told me—"

"Wife!"

The old man shoved past Chimi, surprising her with the strength of his wizened arms. She tottered, scrambling to keep hold of her parcels. Chimi ended up leaning on the door frame, watching as the couple embraced.

"Wife, wife," he repeated. He was clearly weeping. "My wife."

Embarrassed, Chimi backed into the house and looked around, blinking to clear the mist from her eyes.

The old man obviously hadn't been taking any better care of the house than he was of himself. Anything dropped or put down had been left where it lay, and the dishes hadn't been washed in days. Chimi piled her burdens on the nearest counter. Hoping she wouldn't be called on for cleaning services, too, she started poking into bins and drawers for pots and utensils.

When she had scavenged enough to work with, she drew water and put it on the stove. It was a very nice stove, a heavy stone disc with sigils carved into it. Not like at home, where they had to burn wood. Chimi touched one of the symbols and concentrated.

"Heat," she commanded, and quickly lifted her hand as warmth radiated from the magic symbol.

She started on the millet first, then the vegetables. She chopped seaweed and redroots; the peppers had to be seeded before she could slice them into rings. Her eyes burned with the fumes, and she was careful not to rub her nose or eyes. Touching another symbol, she started a porcelain teapot as well. In a third pot, she heated the dried fishes in water. While they simmered lightly, she squeezed a lime to make sauce.

Hawadi and her husband, whose name was Tevo, had moved their reunion into the main room, which was separated from the kitchen by a painted screen and a low wall. The counter along the wall was the only clean cutting surface Chimi could find. She made sure to chop the vegetables as loudly as possible, so she wouldn't hear what they said.

It was hard to miss some things, though. Tevo had given up on himself in the months since Hawadi died. The old woman was trying to convince him to sell their property or let one of their sons' families move in and take care of him. Tevo said he didn't want to be fussed over. Watching him enjoy Hawadi's fussing over him, Chimi held back a snort at his hypocrisy.

The meal was coming along nicely. Chimi's stomach growled as appealing odors filled the house. At the same time, her nerves stretched thin. Clouds were dimming the sky outside. Even on a day out with her friends, she should be home by now. With Mother already acting strange, Chimi didn't want to give her anything else to wonder about.

While she fretted, the pot of millet nearly boiled over. Chimi stirred frantically to rescue it. The vegetables went into the pot with the grain. While those cooked together, she sliced a small melon in half and scooped out the seeds. A few deep cuts, and the sections fanned out like a creamy golden flower. Then she grated a ginger root and mixed it with fish sauce and lime juice. A bit of rice flour thickened it. In each step she followed Hawadi's instructions faithfully. If she had to re-do anything, Chimi thought she would scream.

Finally, it was all ready. She scooped the millet mixture into a bowl, leaving a slight depression on top, which she filled with sauce. She laid the fishes in a graceful arc on top. That should be good enough for Hawadi. It certainly made Chimi hungry to look at it.

She quickly loaded the food, teapot and utensils onto a lacquered tray and carried it into the main room. Hawadi and Tevo sat beside a low table. Chimi bowed from the waist as she approached, and set the tray on the floor. A few swipes of a damp rag cleaned the table, and she set the meal there with a flourish.

Tevo watched with mute surprise, as he couldn't remember seeing her before, but Hawadi's sad eyes lit at the sight of the food.

"Eat now, husband," the old woman said softly. "I want you to be healthy."

Chimi added cheerfully, "You should listen to Grandmother Hawadi. All of this is very fresh, and it's good for you." She poured tea into a porcelain cup and pushed it across the table toward him.

Slowly Tevo reached for it. "I always listen to her," he said tremulously.

"Good for you. Now don't let it get cold!"

With a parting bow, Chimi scurried back to the kitchen. Neither of them seemed to notice her leaving. She quickly checked that the spells heating the stove were off and that the bag with the rest of the money was in plain sight. Chimi didn't like to leave so many dirty dishes, but she really had no more time. Anyway, Hawadi hadn't asked her to clean, only cook.

Her spare robe was on the porch where she had left it. With hasty jerks, she shook off her new garment and reached for the other one. As she straightened, shaking it out, something rattled away across the wooden porch. Without thinking, she slapped her hand down to catch it.

Chimi regretted it when she saw the narrow cylinder of bone lying stark across her fingers. Another of these? Torn between curiosity and irritation, Chimi turned it over in her hand. Now that she thought of it, necromancers wore strands of bones like this around their necks, tied together with scarlet cord.

A shiver tickled her back and her fist clenched over the bone. She lifted her hand to throw it, but something stopped her. Even if she didn't want to be a necromancer, this seemed important. Much as she wanted to drop the bone into Hawadi's pond, she couldn't.

But that didn't mean she had to keep looking at it. Chimi poked the narrow sliver of bone into her hoka, jiggling until it slipped inside the loosely woven basket. That settled, she swirled her old robe around her. Thunder rolled softly overhead, and the wind stirring the treetops was scented with rain. Though Chimi's hands shook with stress, she managed to re-wrap her headcloth. The first fat raindrops splatted around her as she finished.

As Chimi walked away, she could see the couple inside the house. Tevo was eating at last. Hawadi sat very still, her back toward Chimi. They looked like an ordinary couple, devoted in their old age. You would never have guessed that one of them was dead.

Should she say good-bye? Hawadi might want to thank her. No, it didn't matter. The rain was falling harder from those gloomy clouds, and Chimi was seriously late. What was there to say? Hawadi was still dead, and Tevo was lost without her. Chimi didn't think one meal would cure his grief.

A hard lump closed her throat as she scurried away. At least this time no one was screaming as she left.

Rain fell on the hot pavement, raising wisps of steam that gave the town a clammy feeling. Chimi ran most of the way home and got thoroughly wet despite her efforts to stay under the cover of trees. Her headcloth had shaken loose again. As she rounded the curve just before Mother's house, she paused to adjust the twisted fabric.

When she started forward again, Chimi heard a noise. Her sandals weren't the only ones slapping the wet stones. A robe that wasn't hers rustled heavily with damp. Chimi glanced over her shoulder. She saw nothing, yet there was the rasp of someone breathing close behind her. Shoulders hunched protectively, she quickened her steps. The pillars of her mother's gate were just ahead, behind a neighbor's hibiscus bush that stuck out into the street. She walked even faster, her spare robe a crumpled wad against her chest.

Once she had reached the safety of her mother's gate, Chimi spun around. Again, the street seemed deserted. The prickle as hairs rose along her arms told her it wasn't true.

"Who's there?" she demanded in a voice shrill with fear. "Show yourself!"

With a lazy shuffle, a man's figure rounded the hibiscus. Toothless! Chimi stepped back and bumped into a gate post. The tension and anxiety of the day paralyzed her, until she felt only the wild beating of her heart in her throat.

The stranger's lips split in a smile, baring the ragged stumps of his teeth, but his eyes were empty, dead.

"Don't you want to know what I want?" he lisped.

"Stay away from me!" Chimi shook free of her terror and bolted down the path between the feather-flower vines.

"Chimi!" Sachakeen raced around the nearest trellis. She shrieked again as they crashed into each other. "Sister, what's wrong?"

"There's a... a man..." she sobbed. "He's following me!"

"What?" Sachakeen demanded. "Where?"

Her brother's indignation would have been gratifying, if Chimi hadn't been so scared. The tears she had been holding in all day broke loose. Their salt made her tongue burn.

Sachakeen left her only for a moment. He strode to the gate and looked angrily up and down the street.

"There's no one there," he said.

Chapter Eight

Penance

The day was sultry beneath a cloudy sky, but that wasn't what made Chimi sweat. Grandmother's stare did that.

Despite the fact that no strangers had been found near their house, Mother had insisted Chimi be chaperoned ever since. For the first two days, Sachakeen had come to work with her, watching while she inspected fish and tended the counter. When he got bored, Chimi had thought she would be set free.

But the alternative to her brother's presence was even worse: Grandmother Myri came to the market with her. The old woman had declared that Chimi was dressed provocatively and insisted on choosing her clothes. Now she sweltered in full-length robes the color of beach sand, a headcloth that totally covered her hair, and no jewelry except the hoka. Chimi felt like she was doing penance at the town shrine for some crime against the spirits. For two long days, the old woman had been sitting at the back of the booth, criticizing her every move. Her feet ached, and Grandmother had the only chair, but Chimi didn't dare complain. The old tyrant might make her change more than her clothes.

It wasn't easy to keep the business going without her usual flirtations to smooth the road. Grandmother scowled at the customers as if each one of them might be Chimi's stalker. Her dour presence drove some people off without any sales at all. Chimi hadn't seen Rellad for two hands of days. Disappointment only made her feel worse.

If only she could have told Nakuri about the second ghost. Nakuri was always nice to her. She had helped Chimi find Lelldour, for all the good it did. Chimi was desperate to find out who the other necromancer was, and Nakuri probably knew, but Chimi couldn't ask while Grandmother might hear.

Meanwhile, Winomi wouldn't let her alone, either. She had come to see Chimi twice. Winomi seemed to feel guilty over Azma's gossip, determined to make up for things that weren't her fault. Since she couldn't tell Winomi the truth, Chimi tried to reassure her with vague mumbles about her family worrying when she got home late. It hadn't worked.

Glancing down the aisle, Chimi could see Winomi coming. Jeruki and Lukita were with her. Compared to their colorful robes, Chimi felt as drab as a mud hen in Grandmother's dreary robes.

"Good morning," Lukita looked concerned when Grandmother scowled at her. She quickly joined Winomi in a respectful bow.

"Hello," Chimi sighed.

Jeruki looked from Chimi to Grandmother with a cruel smile. They might as well have brought Azma along, Chimi thought sourly. She could picture Azma's smirk when Jeruki told her that Chimi's family had taken her in hand.

"Is business good today?" Winomi asked with false cheer.

And Lukita asked gently, "How are you feeling?"

Chimi shrugged. The air felt stifling, heavy with things she couldn't say. Leaning forward, she murmured, "*Old*. I hate these clothes. They make me look so—"

Winomi and Lukita were startled into laughter. "You look fine," Winomi assured her. "Even in that."

But Jeruki eyed Chimi mockingly. "They really must be mad. What did you do, stay out all night?"

She didn't bother to lower her voice. Chimi felt her throat tighten with fury at the insulting suggestion, but Lukita spoke first.

"Sister!" she scolded. Turning to Chimi, she went on soothingly, "It's only for a while. They can't stay angry much longer."

"That's right," said Winomi. "Can you come visit tomorrow? Everyone will be at our house. If you're not working..."

Chimi shook her head. She knew better than to even ask for another excursion so soon. When Grandmother let her choose her own clothes, she might try it.

"I'd love to, Nomi, but we're starting our next crop and I have to help."

"Oh," Winomi pouted.

"I'm sorry," Chimi said. "I wish I could go, you know I do." There was nothing more fun than trying on things from Winomi's wardrobe. She reached across the counter to squeeze her friend's hand. "Thanks for inviting me."

"We'll miss you," Lukita said in her soft, slow way. Jeruki's lips twitched as she held in laughter. Chimi wanted to slap her.

Then the hateful smirk fell away. Lukita and Winomi tugged on each other's robes. Chimi turned to follow their gaze and swallowed a gasp. Rellad! Her heart leapt with joy and then fell like a stone in her stomach.

"Look, look!" Winomi jerked on Chimi's hands excitedly.

"I know," Chimi hissed, and wrenched away.

Rellad was coming. Coming here. Where he would be glared at by

Grandmother Myri. And Chimi was wearing these awful clothes!

"We should get going," Lukita said loudly. "Our mother is expecting us." She backed away, pulling on her younger sister's arm.

Jeruki pulled back, protesting. "No way! I've *got* to see this!"

Winomi took her other arm. "See you soon, Chimi!" she called as she helped Lukita drag Jeruki around the corner, back into the marketplace.

Amid the noise and hurry of the fish market, Chimi was left feeling completely alone. She pretended to look out over the harbor, but she could hear the slip of Rellad's sandals coming closer as if it was the only sound. Chimi's gaze briefly focused on a group of men nearby. One was small, wearing gray robes, and a pair of paper butterflies hovered near him. He was talking to an older man in sorcerer's purple, while a pair of soldiers in Sengool orange stood watch.

Even that interesting sight couldn't keep Chimi's attention. Her heart fluttered like the butterflies. What did Rellad think of her? Was he afraid Yail was still there? When he got closer, she dared a glance.

His face was just as always, sure of her attention, though his confidence wavered as he glimpsed Grandmother in the back of the stall. A shadow appeared between his brows as he saw Chimi's plain attire. Her chest felt so tight, she could hardly get a breath to speak.

"Good day to you." Chimi made herself say it as if he was a stranger, no one special. "We have sea-whip or mussels for sale, and today's special item is crab. What would you like?"

"Mussels, of course." Rellad sounded faintly puzzled by the question. Then he leaned on the counter and smiled at her. "The special ones you keep just for me."

Chimi gulped at his words, and he frowned again.

"Very good, sir." She knelt to get the shellfish from beneath the counter. It helped to hide her face for a moment. He had to be crazy, saying that in front of Grandmother. There was no way the old woman could have missed his familiarity. With shaking hands, Chimi grabbed the usual number of mussels before rising to accept the usual amount of coin.

"Here you go. Will there be anything else?"

This time he couldn't pretend to ignore her cool tone. Still, he didn't lift his elbow from her counter.

"What's the matter with you?"

"Nothing at all, sir." It tore Chimi's heart to mouth the words, *I can't talk to you now.*

Rellad shrugged with an annoyed jerk. "Too bad. I was going to ask if you wanted to go for a walk later."

He swept up his bag of mussels and turned away, leaving Chimi speechless. He wanted to see her? And she had been so abrupt! Even though Grandmother might punish her later, Chimi called after him, "Come back again soon!"

Rellad didn't acknowledge her. She watched his back with despair until he was out of sight. He strutted, she suddenly realized. Chimi was surprised to feel a burst of resentment. Rellad had seen Yail. He had seen Grandmother. How could he act like nothing was wrong? Chimi had been trying to get out of her predicament for days and he, one of the few people who knew about it, pretended it had never happened.

From behind her, Grandmother said, "So that's the young man."

Chimi froze. She said nothing until Myri commanded, "Come here, grand-daughter. Sit with me."

Eyes downcast, Chimi shuffled to the rear of the booth and sank to her knees beside the old woman's chair. She hoped her meek air disguised her terror. Chimi's mind beat with the frantic energy of a caged bird as she tried to invent the right story. If Grandmother thought she was doing something wrong with her customers, she might lose her job and all her precious freedoms.

But really, there was nothing going on, and now it looked like nothing ever would. What was there for her to lie about?

"Well?" Grandmother pressed. "Who is he?"

"His father is one of Mother's customers," Chimi answered defensively. "I have to be nice to him."

"Mm." A wordless sound conveyed the old woman's disbelief.

"That's how I sell so much, by being nice to people," Chimi insisted. She followed with a proverb, "Good will greases all the wheels."

"Mm."

Despite herself, Chimi burst out, "Grandmother, I haven't done anything! Why do you even think that I would?"

The old woman stared back at her. Chimi saw a flicker of emotion in her eyes. Before Myri could answer, a new voice interrupted.

"Excuse me?" Another customer had come to the booth.

"Coming!" Relieved by the interruption, Chimi jumped up and ran to the counter. And that was where she stayed for the rest of a very long afternoon.

* * *

"Is this the right place?" Juss' broad face wore a doubtful expression.

"Yes." Shenza didn't blame Juss for asking. Lelldour's property looked just as gloomy as it had before. She had come by three times in the past two days, choosing different times in hopes of meeting the elusive necromancer. Each time, no one was home. Each time, she felt more uneasy.

That was why she had asked Juss to come with her this time. Since Lelldour didn't answer her calls, she had to take bolder action—and she might need Juss' strong arms to do it.

"Lelldour of Salloo," Shenza called as loudly as she could. "I am the magister. I'm going to come in!"

"Are you sure you want to?" Juss muttered, eyeing the dismal yard.

Shenza chuckled, but she told him, "I have to."

She no longer expected Lelldour to reply, so it wasn't a surprise when ringing silence followed her words.

"I'm coming in!" she cried one last time.

Then she stepped past the overgrown gateposts, into the deep shadow of the trees. Juss followed, walking softly and warily. The leaves' musty odor rose around them. The path of flat stones was obvious, but the trail of footsteps Shenza had glimpsed two days before had vanished beneath more fallen leaves.

"Not much of a gardener," Juss said.

"Watch your step," Shenza murmured as they came to the flooded part of the path. It felt wrong to speak too loudly in this place.

"I'll go first," Juss said.

Thick leaves rustled as he brushed past Shenza without waiting for permission. He took a long step over the water, then turned and offered his hand to steady her.

"Thank you." Shenza let him help her across the pool and took the lead again as they approached the house.

As she had guessed, it was all thatch, although another coating of leaves made it hard to see the roof. The interior was dark, yielding just a glimpse of sparse furniture. There was no scent of lamp oil or a cookfire. Shenza could hardly believe Chimi had found Lelldour here.

Cautiously, she called, "Good morning. Is anyone home?"

"What's that?" Juss asked, jabbing a finger at the porch.

A small rubber ball and a bit of bone lay on the top step. The bone showed stark white against the darker wood of the porch.

"I think it's a finding ball," Shenza said. She recalled Chimi saying she had left the ball and bone for Lelldour to find. Apparently, he hadn't bothered to retrieve them. Shenza leaned closer, studying the bone with interest. She wondered if it would be an intrusion on the necromancer's art if she put on her mask and looked for magic symbols.

Something else caught her eye—a black, moving speck. Shenza frowned as her eyes followed a trail of ants marching over the porch, up one of the posts, and into the thatch. Noting her interest, Juss leaned closer, too.

"He's got a pest control problem," the peacekeeper said.

"Yes," Shenza agreed.

Ants were always a problem in tropical Chalsett. Thatch roofs made convenient nesting places for them, and they were incorrigible raiders once established. Most houses had spells specifically to keep ants away. The magic was very easy to do.

It seemed a minor thing, yet Shenza felt the chill seep into her body through the fabric of her robe. Why would Lelldour let his pest controls lapse?

Juss, being himself, stated the obvious: "I don't think anyone lives here."

"Lelldour has been seen," Shenza said, although her common sense agreed with Juss.

He shrugged, accepting her word. "I guess we'd better look around. I'll check the back, if you want to try inside."

"All right." Shenza bent to take the bone and ball so she wouldn't step on them. She tucked them into a fold of her robe and went up the steps, announcing yet again, "I'm coming in!"

She stepped into eerie silence, under the porch and through the open wall. The main room was a workshop, dimly lit by sunlight filtering in from outside. A plain, round lamp hung in the center of the room. Shenza focused her will on it.

"Light," she commanded. She felt her power connect. There was a slight sizzle, but nothing else happened. "That's odd."

As her eyes adjusted to the half-light, Shenza noted a row of wooden buckets along one wall. Those must be used to collect sap from the weeping-wood trees on the property. A large granite stone in the center of the chamber was carved with sigils to provide heat for boiling the sap. A nearby table held stacks of molds for shaping the finished rubber. It was all very tidy, except that she felt a layer of fine grit when she ran her hand over the cold stone.

The slight grating of her sandals sounded too loud as she went on. There was a bedroom in the back of the house. The hammock had been rolled up and pegged to the wall. Beside it was a window screened with strips of woven bamboo. Shenza heard movement on the other side—Juss prowled by outside. Beneath the window was a small chest, which she opened to reveal several folded robes. They were all deep red, a necromancer's uniforms.

In the kitchen, breakfast dishes were propped on the counter beside the sink. When Shenza lifted a corner of the dish towel, it was completely dry. She set her travel case on the counter and knelt to look underneath, where a row of basketry bins should hold foodstuffs. Shenza chose one at random and lifted the lid.

Something invisible and sticky brushed against her hand. Shenza jerked back. An equally startled spider dropped to the floor and scuttled behind the bin.

"Ugh," she grumbled, but quietly. If Juss thought she was in trouble, he would come running.

Shenza straightened, wiping the spider web off her hand. She reached for her travel case. "Open."

As the magical seal released, Shenza took out her bottle of sunlight from its pouch. She lifted it and looked up, noting flickers of shadow. The high corners of the room were thick with cobwebs. First ants and now spiders. How could a house look so clean, and yet be so dirty?

From the main room, Juss called, "Magister?"

"Here," she answered. Boards creaked slightly as Juss came to join her. Shenza kept looking around. Her overall impression was that someone had cleaned this place carefully, and then left. Permanently.

"The bath house is totally dry," Juss reported. "Did you find anything?"

"Only spiders," she admitted.

"This place is abandoned," Juss said bluntly.

"It does look that way," Shenza said. Yet Chimi had no reason to lie about Lelldour being here. Brown fingers drummed on the counter. Then she replaced her vial of sunlight in its pouch. As an afterthought, she tucked the finding ball and bit of bone into a separate pouch. As she folded her case closed, she said, "He isn't here now. But he was seen—"

"When?" Juss interrupted.

"About six days ago." Which didn't fit with the evidence here, either. From the condition of Lelldour's house, he had been gone a lot longer than six days. "Maybe one of his neighbors knows something. We'll have to ask around," Shenza decided.

"Fine, as long as we get out of here." Juss rubbed his arms against the persistent chill in the room. "I want to go stand in the sun for a while."

* * *

Rain droned outside the house, falling from the thatched eaves with a noisy chatter. Chimi was in the kitchen. It hadn't been easy, but she had managed to get Grandmother home before the rain started. She had to rush, because the ghosts could have appeared at any time. Chimi couldn't let Grandmother see them, or she might have realized Chimi's stalker wasn't just a man. The ghosts didn't seem to like daylight. Chimi only saw them when dark clouds blotted out the sun. Sometimes she wondered what they did during the bright, sunny days. Mostly, she tried not to wonder about those details. She didn't want to know the answers, anyway.

At the moment, Chimi was trying not to think about anything except cooking. Chopped chilies and greens lay in mounds on the counter, while a big pot of water steamed on the stove. Grandmother sat with Byben at their usual table, playing a game with colored tiles. At the other table, Sachakeen helped Mother sort feather-flower seeds for tomorrow's planting. No one was talking much. Chimi thought gloomily that she would be seeing a lot of these quiet domestic scenes, because Grandmother wasn't going to let her out of the house again until she was as old and feeble as Byben.

"Hello, I'm home," a voice called faintly from the direction of the street.

There was a lengthening silence as the family looked among themselves to see who would answer the door. It was Shenza's voice, but Chimi hesitated. She had food cooking here. It wasn't that she didn't want to see her sister. She just didn't want to face the ghosts who waited at the gate. Just as Mother sighed and got to her feet, Chimi realized that was exactly what she needed to talk to Shenza about.

"I'll go!" Chimi dropped her knife and bolted past Mother.

A moment later, she splashed through shallow puddles in the garden. As expected, Shenza was at the gate, her robe as somber as the rainy sky. She didn't seem to notice the three ghosts who stood around her. There was the skinny one Chimi called Toothless, and Scarface, a brawny thug with a lurid wound over one eye. Just yesterday, the Drowned Girl had joined them. Lank hair covered that ghost's face and released a constant, slow drip of seawater.

The ghosts didn't acknowledge Shenza or each other. They didn't look like the kind of people who would have waited their turn when they were alive, but now they lined up along the fence and stared at her. For some reason, they could neither come in nor go away, no matter how much Chimi wished they would.

Chimi got as close as she could stand to. For the benefit of her family, who might be listening, she exclaimed, "Hello, big sister!"

Shenza looked puzzled by the distance, or maybe by Chimi's drab attire. "How have you been?" Shenza stepped forward and greeted her sister with a quick kiss on the cheek.

All at once, Chimi swallowed to keep back tears. She grabbed her sister's robe and wailed, as softly as she could, "Horrible!"

"Are you still seeing ghosts?" A frown drew Shenza's brows together.

"Yes, can't you?" Chimi made a cautious gesture toward the ghoulish lineup. "They're right over there."

Shenza turned, following her motion. "I don't see..." she began, but then broke off. "Sun and sand," she murmured. To Chimi's disgust, Shenza actually moved back toward the gate.

"Don't talk to them," she snapped, dragging at Shenza's robe. The air smelled faintly steamy as rain fell on warm pavement, yet Chimi shivered as droplets chilled her bare shoulders.

"How long have they been here?"

"Too long." Chimi's sense of grievance grew. "They stay there all the time. You see why I can't stand it."

Shenza stood in silence, studying the ghosts intently, until Chimi pulled on her arm again.

"Let's go. I can't talk to you with them staring at me."

"All right," Shenza said, but she came away slowly, looking behind them as they went.

Chimi guided her sister to the left, between two rows of fully grown vines, where they were shielded from both the ghosts and the house. Unfortunately, they were still out in the rain.

"This must be awkward for you," Shenza began.

"It's worse than awkward!" Words burst from Chimi almost too fast to choke them out. "There was another one, an old lady. I couldn't get away from her. I had to cook dinner for her. She made me late, and then one of those ones was following me! Now Mother and Grandmother think I'm sneaking off to see a boy or something."

"Did..." Shenza began, but Chimi whined on.

"They won't let me out of the house without an escort. And Grandmother's making me dress like I'm older than her. It's been so awful! Now these ones are hanging around. What if somebody sees them?"

"If they haven't yet, I don't think they will." Shenza hugged her again, and Chimi was momentarily comforted by her good sense. "Have you been wearing your hoka?"

"Yes, yes." Chimi grimaced. "And it isn't helping me, you know. My girlfriends think I've lost my virginity because I'm wearing it!"

Shenza gasped, and then chuckled. "I hadn't thought of that."

"It's not funny," Chimi insisted. "That's probably where Grandmother got her ideas, too. Honestly, that Lelldour is worse than useless. I should just find the other necromancer."

Shenza turned very serious. "Chimi, no. She can't be trusted. She only works for pay, and her price is too high."

That made Chimi pause, knowing how little money she made with Grandmother as a chaperone. Besides, she was sure Lelldour had said something about necromancers who took money for their services. Of course, she no longer cared what Lelldour thought about anything.

Chimi lifted her chin. "I can get money."

"No!" Shenza repeated. "Chimi, Vesswan of Zeell summons spirits and forces them to say what she wants. The last time I heard of her, she tried to trick a dead man's family into giving all his property to one creditor, instead of dividing it between his children. Can you imagine that—trying to bankrupt a grieving family?" Shenza shook her head. "There must be a better way."

"Then what is it?" Chimi demanded. The rain was seeping through her clothing, and that made her cross. "All you do is tell me what I can't do. How can I get rid of the ghosts?"

For a moment Shenza stood dumb, and Chimi knew exactly what she would say.

"I'm sorry, but I don't know. Necromancy is a specialized craft, like curomancy and magistry. There aren't any records in the libraries I have access to. I've looked. I can't even find out how they choose new apprentices. There must be some sort of evaluation, but..."

"Well, what about Master Laraquies? You said you would ask him." Perversely, it felt good to push the momentum of her anger.

"It isn't that easy, sister," Shenza said. "I can't ask too many questions without him wanting to know why."

"You haven't even asked him," Chimi accused.

"Of course I did!" Shenza sounded hurt. "He said he'd never heard of ghosts following someone who wasn't a necromancer. Hauntings aren't very common."

"Not common? I've seen five in just a few weeks!" Again, Chimi felt the cold rain soaking through her clothing. If Master Laraquies couldn't explain what was happening, what could she do?

"I am sorry," Shenza said with real regret. "I don't understand either. Why don't you just tell Mother the truth?"

"No!" Chimi sniffled angrily, hugging herself against the rain's chill. "If they're this worried now, what would they think then?"

"They already know something is going on," Shenza reasoned. "You're letting them think the worst."

"Me?" Chimi cried, shocked that her sister would blame her.

"Hey, what are you two whispering about?" Sachakeen's voice held a bored challenge. From the rhythmic plodding, he was on the porch, coming toward them.

"Nothing!" Chimi called back. To Shenza she hissed, "Remember what you promised."

Shenza seemed to sigh, but she hugged Chimi again. "I won't forget, little sister." Together they walked around the vines, and Shenza adopted a lighter tone. "It's just girl talk, brother."

"Right." Hands on hips, Sachakeen watched suspiciously as they stepped up to the porch. Chimi crossed her eyes and made a face at him. She might have to accept this questioning from Grandmother, but not from him. Her brother responded with a sneer of his own.

"Shenza's come for dinner," Chimi called as they entered the main room. She tried to act like she was happy about it.

Byben looked up from his game with a smile. "Welcome home."

"If the food doesn't burn," Grandmother interrupted in the same severe tone she had been using all day.

With a yelp, Chimi dashed into the kitchen, where the pot of noodles was boiling furiously.

Shenza said, "Good evening, Grandmother, Byben." She kissed Mother's cheek and then suggested, "Maybe I should help Chimi."

"She needs all the help she can get," Sachakeen muttered.

Chimi bit her lower lip to keep back angry words. Grabbing two pads woven with symbols to protect against burning, she lifted the boiling pot down to a flat spot on the side of the stove, where it could cool.

Silence fell over the house, a stifling shroud. Shenza and Chimi worked shoulder to shoulder, draining the noodles and frying them with the greens, chilies, and some crab meat left over from the day's business. Chimi was keenly aware of Grandmother watching from the other room. Adding to her annoyance, Sachakeen strolled over to lean his elbows on the low wall between the kitchen and the work room.

"So, sister, what's the news?" he said to Shenza.

A shadow fell over her face. "It looks like Lord Manseen will be here in a few days."

"Really?" Chimi cried, startled out of her brooding. Her hand jerked as she spoke, and a drop of hot oil splashed her. "Ouch!"

"Careful," Shenza said, too late.

"What's wrong?" Mother asked from the other room.

Hand in mouth, Chimi mumbled, "'M all right."

Ignoring her pain, Sachakeen said, "When is all this going to happen?"

"Have you heard any more about Lord Manseen's daughter?" Chimi demanded. She wouldn't tell Azma or Jeruki, but Winomi deserved to know the details.

"The messenger said they're riding the current of coral waves," Shenza replied in a dull voice. "If the seas are calm, they should get here in another few days."

"Will you get to meet them?" Mother asked.

Shenza nodded. "It's none of my business, but Lord Aspace has commanded me and Master Laraquies to attend."

Mother and Sachakeen exchanged a silent look. Chimi snorted, annoyed.

"What are you so worried about? And why does Laraquies keep telling you these things, if you aren't included?"

Shenza paused, maybe irritated by the criticism of her beloved mentor. Her answer sounded strained. "I'm sure he's just keeping me informed."

Her words made Chimi laugh out loud. "Oh, come on. You want to meet her, too. You're just too proud to say so."

Shenza didn't answer that.

"Quiet." Sachakeen glared at Chimi.

With a sigh in her voice, Mother asked, "Isn't that food ready yet?"

"Almost," Chimi said. She seized a stack of bowls and a handful of bamboo utensils from their bins and shoved them across the counter to her brother. "Do something helpful."

"Huh," Sachakeen grunted, but he did set out the dishes while Mother put away the baskets of seeds.

Meanwhile, Shenza was slicing a golden pineapple and putting the sections on a platter. Glancing at her somber face, Chimi realized she had been wrong. Shenza didn't want to meet Lord Manseen and his daughter. She wasn't happy about them coming. Because it might mean a change up at the palace? No, it seemed like more than that.

Chimi thought about it as she divided the meal into two bowls, a large one for the main table and a smaller one for Byben and Grandmother. Social things were so important to Chimi. She didn't understand how Shenza could not be interested.

No answers came to her as she scooped hot-and-sour sauce into dipping bowls. Her hand stung where the oil had burned her, but not as much as her jealousy. Shenza had everything Chimi wanted—freedom to move around, access to the palace—and she refused to take advantage of it. Meanwhile, Chimi was treated like a criminal, or maybe a child. It just wasn't fair!

"I wish I could go," she muttered.

She hadn't meant Shenza to hear, but she did. "Maybe you could," Shenza said as she carried her platter to the table.

"Can I?" Chimi swept up the larger bowl of noodles and scrambled after her sister.

Shenza said, "It would be nice if I wasn't alone. I don't have many friends among the nobles. Half of them still resent Master Laraquies for replacing Nurune of Sengool as vizier, and I'm Laraquies' student."

"Maybe because you both have the first lord's confidence," Sachakeen suggested.

Shenza shrugged. Before she could continue her meandering explanation, Chimi exploded with glee.

"Yes! Oh, please, can I go?" She all but dropped the steaming bowl on the table and threw herself on the floor at Giliatt's knees. "Please, please! I'll be good forever!"

"I don't know," Mother said doubtfully. Grandmother frowned, too. Shenza quietly set the smaller bowl on the elders' table and returned to sit beside Sachakeen.

Their brother eyed Chimi with fresh annoyance. "Get up, would you?"

Chimi kissed her mother's hand, as if she were a supplicant before the first lord. "Can I go? Please? I'll be with Shenza. I won't leave her for a minute. Or Winomi. You remember her, a very nice girl, properly brought up. Nothing could possibly happen."

"Winomi of House Kesquin?" Shenza asked.

Chimi knew she was grasping at straws, but she would say anything to break away from her miserable existence and see the spectacle of a royal courtship.

"You'll like her. Even if you don't like the nobles, Nomi is a friend to everyone. Maybe she'd even put in a word for you with her family."

Shenza seemed to like that idea. The older girl turned to Giliatt. "Mother, what do you think?"

Giliatt didn't reply, but gazed at her daughters thoughtfully. The only sound was soft tapping as Sachakeen, ignoring Chimi's dramatics, served himself from the main bowl.

Shenza turned to Myri. "Grandmother?"

Chimi's heart sank, because Grandmother's stern expression made it clear what her answer would be.

Unexpectedly, Byben patted Grandmother's hand. "She's been a good girl." To Chimi's amazement and delight, Grandmother didn't pull away.

Chimi clasped her mother's hand and whined, "Please?"

"Say yes," Sachakeen mumbled around a mouthful of food, "or we'll never hear the end of it."

Chimi stared at Giliatt, heart beating in her throat, but Giliatt reached for the utensils.

"I'll think about it," she said. "Let's eat before it gets cold."

There was a moment of quiet, the whole family waiting for Chimi's reaction. She wanted to scream and burst into tears, but she knew she would have a better chance of getting what she wanted if she cooperated. Chimi let out a trembling breath.

"Yes, Mother."

As if she had released them, the rest of the family started to move again. Mother served herself from the steaming bowl. Shenza tilted the teapot, and dark liquid purled into their cups. Chimi ate, too, although she barely tasted the fried noodles. Her mind was too full of chaotic emotions.

She couldn't bear being trapped like this. She'd done her best to help others, even when she didn't want to. There was nothing wrong with that and she wouldn't accept being punished for it. Shenza was no more help than that lazy Lelldour. Neither was her precious Master Laraquies.

If that was how it was, then Chimi would have to help herself.

The royal consultation would give her a good excuse to get out of the house. Now that Chimi knew Vesswan's name, it should be easy to find her. Nakuri would help. With the visitors distracting her, Shenza would never know where Chimi went. It was a perfect plan, if only Mother would let her out for an hour!

And Shenza's own personality gave her an easy answer. Chimi lifted her head with an urgent expression. "Sister, what will you wear?"

"What?" Shenza asked.

"When Lord Manseen gets here, what will you wear?" Chimi gestured at Shenza's damp-darkened robe. "You can't wear *that*."

"I wouldn't," her sister replied, defensively enough that Chimi suspected it was exactly what she had been planning to do.

Turning to Mother, Chimi said, "At least let me go shopping with Shenza. She has to look perfect in front of the nobles." Remembering Grandmother's pride, Chimi wheedled, "It would shame our house if she attended a royal reception in her work clothes."

"You just want a new robe for yourself," Sachakeen said.

Now Chimi was glad of her visit to the House of Melleen. It allowed her to retort, "I already got one. This is for Shenza, not me."

Her brother snorted, but Chimi turned to Shenza. "You have a salary, right? So you have some money to spend."

"I suppose I do," Shenza admitted.

"You have to get something beautiful," Chimi urged. "Show those nobles you're just as good as they are."

"I don't think it's that easy," Shenza answered softly. She stared at her bowl, where the food lay nearly untouched.

"I said, I'll think about it," Mother interrupted.

From her tone, Chimi knew Giliatt would give in. Buoyed by the thought, Chimi nudged Shenza and whispered, "Let's eat."

Outside the house, the rain was slackening off. Sunlight filtered through breaks in the clouds, adding light and warmth to the wet world. Finally, Chimi had a way out of the trap she was in. If she could get rid of the ghosts and see Lady Seelit's arrival, even digging up the garden tomorrow would be worth it.

Chapter Nine

Under the Red Lantern

Shenza woke amid a steady roaring, like the pounding of sea waves. Her hammock swayed wildly as she sat up. It was deep night. Only a hint of the moons' light penetrated the darkness of her room. Discordant jangling filtered in from outside. Then a heavy thump came from nearby.

Confused, she rolled out of her hammock. As her bare feet touched the floor, Shenza felt a powerful vibration. The floor was shaking! The trembling went from her soles right up to her chest and sat there like a frightened animal.

Fear quickly cleared the sleep from her head. Shenza stood and listened, one hand clutching the door frame for balance. The silvery jangling came from a wind chime on the porch outside and the hissing was tree branches shaking. But already the vibration slowed and ceased. The earthquake seemed to be over.

"Master Laraquies?" she called anxiously. The old man had been out at another of Lord Aspace's banquets last night. She hadn't heard him come home.

"Light," Shenza commanded. She blinked as the lamp in the work room flared into life. A glance into Master Laraquies' chamber told her he wasn't there. That wasn't unusual; he often slept at the palace. Still, she wished she didn't have to be alone just now.

Cautiously Shenza padded in the direction of the loudest noise. A large ceramic pot had fallen over in the kitchen. She checked it for cracks, then set it back upright. Dark as it was, she couldn't tell if there was any damage outside the house.

Shenza put out the light and went back to bed, but she didn't sleep right away. She couldn't remember ever experiencing an earthquake in Chalsett-port. Was this what Skall had warned them of? The wandering moon had already vanished as mysteriously as it came, but Shenza fancied she could still feel its presence, haunting Chalsett-port like one of Chimi's ghosts.

The darkness held no answers. Eventually Shenza slept again, though she didn't rest easily. Master Laraquies never did come home. Shenza missed him as she prepared a breakfast of cold rice balls, tea and fruit. She would have liked to hear what he thought about last night's tremor.

She knew that couldn't be her first priority, though. Shenza had only a few more days to unravel Chimi's puzzle, and she wanted to do everything she could. She knew how it felt to be shadowed by Grandmother's disapproval. She had faced it for years, after her apprenticeship took her away from home, marriage and the other expected duties of a female child. Besides, what was the good of being a magister if she couldn't help the people she loved?

There was no sign of Master Laraquies by the time she finished, so Shenza packed her travel case and put on her magister's mask. Wrapping an extra robe around her shoulders against the morning chill, she left the house and ordered the gate to lock itself behind her.

The first rays of sunlight touched the treetops as Shenza set off. She saw no one else on the street, although a distant murmur told Shenza the market was coming to life. She had been to Lelldour's so often that it seemed only a moment before she was back at his gate. No light gleamed in Lelldour's cottage, so she didn't bother calling out. On her way, she had heard voices in the cottage next door. She turned back to it, hoping someone there had seen Lelldour.

As she got closer, Shenza realized the voices belonged to children. A boy and a girl were on the porch, arguing passionately over whose turn it was to feed their pet goose. The goose itself stood in a patch of gravel beside the thatched house, stretching out its gray neck and honking to urge them on. Somewhere inside, a baby was wailing.

Shenza hesitated. Children weren't good witnesses. Then again, she wouldn't learn anything just standing in the road.

The two youngsters ran along the porch, still screaming at each other. The grinning boy held a shallow basket away from his sister, who looked ready to knock him flat despite her lesser height. They were dangerously close to the edge of the porch. Shenza decided to speak up before one of them got hurt.

"Excuse me," she called.

The two children stumbled to a halt. The boy let the basket sag, and a stream of grain pattered down on the porch. The goose flapped up to snatch it, while both siblings stared at Shenza.

"We didn't do anything!" the boy blurted.

"I'm sure you haven't." Shenza did her best not to laugh at his guilty face. "Is your father or mother home?"

"Our mommy is here," the girl said.

"I'll go get her." The lad shoved the basket into his sister's hands, as if he hadn't been doing everything in his power to keep it away from her just a moment before, and ran into the house.

His little sister immediately started tossing out more grain with a very self-satisfied air.

"This is my goose," she explained. "Daneel says it's his, but I found the egg. I'm Sujah. My goose is Bonta."

Shenza answered, "I am Shenza," and bowed as if greeting an equal. Sujah giggled and bowed back, spilling yet more grain. She straightened the basket with a startled jerk.

The baby's crying got louder. Obviously, Daneel had found his mother. He ran out of the house a moment later.

"She's coming."

Shenza nodded. Daneel edged toward Sujah, possibly hoping to reclaim the basket. Then a young woman appeared from inside the cottage, rubbing at puffy eyes while she held the crying infant against her hip. She was only a little older than Chimi, and very thin. When she saw Shenza, her face took on a frightened expression.

"Magister?" The woman bowed hastily. "I am Rumia Polleth of Bentei." She shifted the baby to her shoulder and started to pat its back, swaying from side the side.

"Forgive my interruption." Shenza felt her heart go out to the harried mother. She pitched her voice up to be heard over the wailing. "I need information about one of your neighbors."

The patting seemed to help, for the infant's angry shrieks subsided. Still, Rumia shook her head wearily.

"I'm only a tenant, Magister. I don't know the neighbors."

Disappointed, Shenza asked, "You've never met Lelldour of Salloo?" She gestured toward the gloomy yard next door.

"No, Magister. I've never seen anyone over there. Have you?" She looked to her children, who shook their heads.

"It stinks over there," Sujah added.

Shenza nodded. She supposed that boiling rubber might create an odor.

"Don't say that." Daneel scowled at his sister's audacity.

"Well, it did when we got here." Sujah seemed pleased to annoy her brother.

"Both of you, hush," their mother scolded.

"How long has your family lived here?" Shenza asked.

"Two months," Rumia replied. Then, like her daughter, she seemed unable to restrain her curiosity. "Has he done something wrong?"

"Not at all," Shenza said. She mentally calculated two months against the amount of neglect in Lelldour's house and decided that Rumia couldn't have any useful information.

The baby started to whimper again. Shenza knew she'd better go if she wanted to escape the crying.

"I can see that you're busy." She bowed and stepped away.

"It's no trouble," Rumia said, still patting the baby's back.

After retreating, Shenza looked at the other houses on the street. There was a smaller dwelling directly across from Lelldour's. Its low fence was covered in trumpet-flower vines. A bronze chime hung at the end of a neatly swept path, and a large stone tiger crouched beside it.

Shenza approached, noting a very tidy cottage at the end of the path. It was of pale gray stones, with a roof of darker tiles. No moss had been permitted to grow on the stonework. A row of lime trees bloomed along the porch, screening the interior of the house. Shenza caught a faint whiff of their fragrance. It was all very pleasant and bright, especially compared to Lelldour's overgrown property. Shenza tapped on the chime with a wooden mallet.

A tiny old woman scurried out of the house. She was dressed as neatly as her yard was trimmed, in a bright blue robe with an intricate geometric design. Her headcloth was wrapped so tightly that not one hair escaped it. She crossed her hands on her chest and bowed.

"Magister, welcome!" Silver bangles chimed sweetly as the old woman moved. "How can I serve you?"

Shenza bowed in return. "I'm merely seeking information. Are you a permanent resident?"

"Why, yes. My husband and I have lived here for more than twenty-five years." The woman's voice and smile were perfectly composed. Shenza wondered who she was trying so hard to impress. "I am Sussani Akaneer of Quasill."

"What can you tell me of your neighbor, Lelldour of Salloo?" Shenza asked.

"I do know him." Sussani frowned. "He is a quiet neighbor, considering his profession of necromancy. However, Wallass and I do wish he would take better care of his property."

Shenza nodded. Sussani's immaculate garden made Lelldour's look even more disheveled.

"We work hard to improve our property," Sussani went on. Her dark eyes gleamed with resentment. "It reflects badly on the whole neighborhood when one of us lets his place go."

"Have you filed a complaint with the city?" Proud as Sussani seemed to be, it wouldn't have surprised Shenza.

"No, I spoke to him directly. He said he hadn't been feeling well. I suppose, if he has been ill, we must make allowances."

So Lelldour had been sick? Chimi hadn't mentioned that.

"When did you last see him?" Shenza asked.

Sussani paused, thinking. "I'm not sure, Magister," she admitted. "It must be three months or more. I've called at his gate, but he doesn't answer. As you can see, the place is looking worse every day," she concluded resentfully.

"I've been trying to reach him, too," Shenza said. "He never seems to be home. Did he tell you he would be traveling?"

"No, he didn't say anything about that."

If Sussani was always this fussy, it didn't surprise Shenza that Lelldour would avoid her.

"Thank you," she said. "What you've told me is very helpful."

"Anything to help, Magister."

The two women bowed in farewell, and Shenza retreated to the street. She thought that she'd better start making notes before she forgot something. As Shenza looked around for a place to sit, a man came out of the gate on the far side of Lelldour's house. Seeing Shenza, he waved and trotted toward her. Curiously, she walked to meet him.

"Good morning," Shenza said when he was close enough.

"Good day to you," he panted. This neighbor was a man of middle years, with streaks of silver in his loose, wavy hair. Small eyes were set in a fleshy face, and his unshaven jowls glinted with silvery stubble.

"Do you need me?"

"Not at all, not at all." The fellow bowed with a jerk. "I saw you at Lelldour's before, and now you're talking to all the neighbors. I just wonder what's going on."

"I'm looking for Necromancer Lelldour," Shenza explained.

"Oh, I know him, I do," the man answered. His little eyes were keen with interest.

Shenza hesitated. She didn't like his prying manner. Still, if this was one of Lelldour's neighbors, there was no reason not to question him.

"May I have your name?" she asked.

"It's Groad," he said. "Groad Corneen of Yalloe."

"Have you seen Lelldour recently?" Shenza asked, hoping against hope.

"Sorry, sorry, but I haven't. Not for some while," Groad said. "Come to think, it's been pretty quiet over there. Not like a few years ago."

"What do you mean?" Shenza asked.

"Oh, they always argued over there, always," Groad answered with a smirk. Shenza had the feeling he enjoyed showing off what he knew. "Him and his apprentice, I mean. Pretty girl, that Vesswan, but they were fighting, fighting all the time. I could hear it clear over at my house."

Shenza nodded politely. She could imagine the man lurking near the low stone wall around Lelldour's property, greedily taking in every word. She asked, "What did they argue about?"

"Oh, the business." Groad rocked back on his heels, obviously enjoying her attention. "Seems they disagreed on how much to charge. He kicked her out last year, or maybe the one before. I remember that fight," he grinned.

Shenza regarded Groad for a moment, struck by an important fact. Carefully, she asked, "He threw Vesswan out? She never finished her apprenticeship?"

"Must have found another master." He shrugged, far less interested in Vesswan than Lelldour. "She's been practicing the trade, I hear."

"Yes," Shenza murmured.

What Groad said only made sense if you didn't know much about sorcerers. A student who had been dismissed by his master usually couldn't find another teacher.

"So what did Lelldour do?" Groad asked eagerly.

"Nothing," Shenza said, trying not to resent how he had interrupted her thoughts. "I just need to ask him something."

"Ah." Groad sounded disappointed that she didn't say what she wanted to ask Lelldour about. Even so, she could fairly see his mind playing with the news that Chalsett's magister needed information from a necromancer.

"Magister!" a familiar voice called out. Shenza turned, glad of the excuse to avoid Groad's snooping. Juss came toward her at a fast limp.

"Excuse me." Shenza made a brief bow and strode to meet her friend.

"Find out anything useful?" Juss asked, stopping at her side.

"I'm not sure," Shenza answered. After three interviews, her fingers itched with the need to write it all down. She rubbed her hands against her outer robe.

"I hate to do this," Juss said, "but Chief Borleek wants you. He and Shamatt want to talk about safeguards for Lord Bosteel's visit."

"That's all right," Shenza assured him. In the corner of her eye, she saw Groad still standing in the road, watching. Juss seemed aware of him, too, for he scowled and turned slightly in that direction. Shenza tapped the big man's shoulder.

"Never mind him," she said. "Let's go."

✳ ✳ ✳

"Shouldn't you wait for Shenza?" Giliatt asked.

"We're getting together at her house," Chimi answered. "It's closer to the market. Don't worry, I'll stay with her the whole time."

Chimi hugged her mother and breezed out the door. If Giliatt had any last cautions, Chimi didn't hear them. She was already dashing down the path to the street.

Things were finally looking better. Grandmother had fallen asleep in her chair yesterday, giving Chimi a chance to talk to Nakuri. As she had hoped, Nakuri knew how to find the other necromancer, Vesswan Sanguri of Zeell. Now Chimi was free. She knew exactly where to go, and she had just enough time to get there and back before Shenza would expect her. It had all worked out perfectly. She didn't like lying to Mother, but what was happening now was so much worse, Chimi hardly noticed.

As usual, the ghosts were waiting for her at the gate. There was another new one, a younger man who wore the blue robes of a palace servant and an air of sour superiority. Even in the shade of the big hibiscus bush, the ghosts looked faded, like fabric left out in the sun too long. Four pairs of dead eyes stared as Chimi approached. Her chest tightened with horror as she hurried past with her face turned away.

Staring, always staring! A self-pitying shudder rolled down her back. Maybe it was because she hadn't actually touched them, as she had Yail and Hawadi, but it seemed the ghosts could only follow and watch her. Well, that was bad enough. If she wanted to get rid of them for good, she had no time to waste.

Chimi walked down the street, trying to act calm in case Grandmother was watching. She headed downward, as if she was going to Shenza's house, but turned off at the level below and followed the terrace to a side stair. Then she went up three flights. With every step, she felt that someone was watching her. It was probably just the ghosts. Chimi stayed in the sun as much as she could. That way, they would have to keep a distance.

On the sixth tier landing she paused and looked back, but no one she knew was in sight. Despite that, her stomach fluttered as she ran up the stairs, higher and higher, until she came to the eighth tier. Panting, pressing a hand to her side, Chimi leaned against the rail.

This wasn't the very top of the town. That sat just above her, on the three hilltops where the wealthy clans lived in their walled estates. In fact, Chimi could see the main gate to the Sengool estate right up the stairs. The highest peak and the first lord's palace were behind her. The Kesquin estate was farther over, across a low saddle of rock. Chimi didn't look at it. She hadn't forgotten that Winomi had invited her over today.

Depression settled on her like a physical weight. The Kesquin house was so beautiful, especially the lotus blossoms in their main pond. If only things could stay the way they had been. Chimi hated this whole situation! She would rather be with her friends, not sneaking around the town.

Then a chilly draft blew past. It reminded her why the sneaking was necessary. She scurried on her way, looking for a tall gate with a red lantern hanging down.

The houses in this area mostly belonged to people associated with the Sengool family. They weren't as grand as the noble estates, but they were still impressive compared to Chimi's house. Nobody here had a crooked fence or uneven walkway. They didn't grow vegetables in their yards, either.

How Chimi longed to live in a place like this!

The street narrowed and angled downward. Chimi hadn't noticed any red lanterns yet. She stopped, looked back, and then rushed on. Finally she rounded a curve and saw a spot of red. Chimi hurried toward it.

The property was small, enclosed by a high marble wall which showed the polish of careful maintenance. The peak of a tile roof showed over the wall. Fern and palm trees stood like sentinels beside the high arch of the gate. Crimson tiles set in the stonework spelled out, "I can help." The lantern hung below that. It was intricately carved and painted bright red, but it wasn't lit.

Chimi rang the chime beside the gate, enjoying its sweet, bright tone. A female servant soon came out, dressed in muted orange. It wasn't quite the official Sengool color, but close. Chimi was impressed. She hadn't realized Vesswan was part of that clan.

"Can I talk to the necromancer? It's an emergency." Chimi told her.

The servant looked at her for a moment. Chimi felt her stomach drop as she realized that everyone who came to see a necromancer must think their problem was an emergency. But hers was!

"This way," the woman answered in a soft, neutral voice.

"Oh, thank you. I really appreciate it," Chimi said, willing to grasp at even this faint invitation.

"Of course," murmured the serving woman.

Chimi followed her under the arch and along a gravel path. A tall hedge on their right screened the house. On the left was a small pond where dragonflies darted among the reeds. The dark water gleamed like polished jet. The hillside slanted sharply upward, and just at its base was a tiny pavilion. Its pillars and beams were ornately and painted in jewel tones of amethyst, sapphire and gold. It was so charming, Chimi almost didn't notice the three people inside it.

One was an older man, dressed in magician's robes finer than any Chimi had ever seen. His purple robes and headcloth were sewn with copper beads that winked in the pavilion's shade. A smaller man in drab gray stood near him. They looked familiar, though Chimi couldn't remember where she had seen them before. As the servant led her closer, she heard a woman's voice.

"Rest assured, my Lords will hear the moment there is any..."

The little man glanced around warily as Chimi and the servant approached. His eyes were bright and black. He cleared his throat, and the woman fell silent.

This must be Vesswan, Chimi realized. To her surprise, the necromancer was a young woman, just a little older than Shenza. She was tall and very thin, with a long neck and arched eyebrows. Her black hair was pulled up high and braided into many narrow strands. Her robe was scarlet, of course, with loops of a necklace made from tiny bones.

"Welcome," Vesswan said to Chimi. "Can you wait, child? I'll be a bit longer here."

"I don't mind," Chimi started to apologize, but the sorcerer cut her off.

"No, we'll be going." His voice was deep and mellow, supple as suede. Sharp lines puckered his forehead as he told Vesswan, "If you can do no more on our project, then we must wait."

"But if my Lords..." Vesswan began.

"It's better to take care now," the smaller man said with an easy smile. "My Lord will tolerate no errors, and haste is an open door to mistakes."

"We'll call on you again, Vesswan."

The sorcerer strode down the stairs, with his companion following closely. With a bow, the female servant stepped back. Chimi did, too. They seemed to expect it, and besides, it was never a good idea to annoy a magician. As the two men swept past her, Chimi wondered who they were. She hoped the sorcerer wasn't someone who knew her sister. What if he told Shenza where he had seen her?

"Now, child," Vesswan said, "what can I do for you?"

The necromancer glided to the top of the stairs, moving with an elegant grace that reminded Chimi of a pretty little vine snake. Her lips curved in a permanent smile, just like a snake's, the kind that kept you from knowing exactly what she was thinking.

Chimi mounted the steps hesitantly. She didn't want to be called "child" all day, but there wasn't a polite way to say so. She took a deep breath and blurted, "Some ghosts have been following me. I want them to stop!"

"That must be awful." Vesswan took her arm and guided her toward a small table. "Come, sit down and tell me about it."

The table stood on narrow, curved legs. It held a bowl of dates, an ink well, pen and scroll of cloth. There were three crimson pillows for seating. Chimi sank down on the nearest one. Inside, she felt the tightness of many days' frustration begin to relax. Finally, someone was going to listen to her!

"Can I offer you anything?" Vesswan suggested. "Tea?"

Chimi shook her head, and Vesswan dismissed her servant with a wave. "Are the ghosts here now?" she asked kindly.

"Over there." Chimi darted a quick gesture toward the back of the pavilion. The ghosts loitered just beyond the rail, where the building's shadow fell up the slope. Chimi didn't have to look to know they were there. She could feel them watching.

Vesswan did look, for a long, thoughtful moment. She clucked her tongue with sympathy.

"You poor dear." She patted Chimi's shoulder with a cool, soft hand. "I can see why you're so upset."

"They won't go away!" Words burst from Chimi in a desperate wail. "They follow me everywhere—please, you have to do something!"

"Of course I will," Vesswan reassured her. "But ghosts don't usually follow random strangers. When did you first notice them?"

"I heard the first one crying in the market," Chimi began. She launched into her story and found the telling easy. Vesswan was so comforting and understanding. It was almost like talking to Shenza. No, better—Vesswan didn't try to push the responsibility back on Chimi.

"Just a moment," Vesswan interrupted when Chimi got to her first encounter with Lelldour. Her eyes were keen. "Are you sure it was Lelldour himself?"

"Yes." Chimi nodded, puzzled. "Nakuri, my friend, she told me his name and I asked if it was him. He said it was."

"I believe you, child." Vesswan sat back, easing away whatever emotion she felt. "Please, do go on."

And Chimi did. Vesswan was a wonderful listener. Chimi couldn't see why Shenza didn't like her. Vesswan chuckled when Chimi described the trouble that had come from wearing her hoka.

"You can take it off," Vesswan said. "It has nothing to do with ghosts."

"Oh, thank goodness!" Chimi sagged against the table, rubbing at the itch where the hoka's cord hung around her neck. "My sister, she's the magister, you know..."

"Oh, yes. I remember her," Vesswan said with a trace of irony. "But that's not important. Believe me, you don't need a hoka. Now, what happened with the old woman?"

Chimi went on, describing how Lelldour had refused to lift a finger for Hawadi. It made her angry all over again.

"He wouldn't do anything to help me. It was like he thought he could make me his apprentice—but I won't do it! Nobody can make me!"

Vesswan nodded to herself. "Yes, I suppose he would want that." She sounded annoyed, too. "Did he force you to help with any other ghosts?"

"No. I made sure not to touch any of them." Chimi described how the Toothless ghost had started following her, joined every day or two by another lost soul. When she finished, Vesswan sat silent. Her dark eyes were fixed on the table top with a hooded expression.

"You can help me, can't you?" Chimi asked. "Make them go away, or..."

"Of course." Vesswan was all reassurance again. "I have a lamp of my own, and I can light it to draw the restless dead here. Since these ones have already fixed on you, I'll need something of yours. A strand or two of hair, I think. And, of course, a small fee for other materials."

Chimi hesitated. She seemed to remember from classes that it could be dangerous to let someone have your hair. But Vesswan was so nice, Chimi quickly put that out of her mind. The money could be a problem, though.

"How much?" she asked. Chimi was afraid to barter, as she would in the market. She couldn't risk making the necromancer angry.

"Five rukh should be enough," Vesswan said. "I have to do it right or it won't work, and then where would you be?"

"Still stuck." Chimi summoned a smile. Once again, this would take all her money. It would be worth it, though, to get rid of those horrible, staring ghosts! "I agree to five rukh."

"Excellent. I know you won't be disappointed."

Vesswan sat for a moment, still smiling, until Chimi realized what she was waiting for and reached into the folds of her robe for her coin pouch. While Chimi counted the money, Vesswan studied the four ghosts speculatively. Once the coins were on the table, Vesswan swept them into the shadow of the date bowl without really looking at them.

"If you would remove your headcloth for a moment," she directed. Cool air tickled Chimi's scalp as she obeyed. Vesswan rolled out a blank writing scroll. "I don't have a comb here, but this will do. Bend forward, child."

The necromancer ran her cool fingers through Chimi's hair. A few loose strands fell on the pale cloth in black coils.

"Just one more, to be sure," Vesswan murmured. Chimi felt a brief, sharp pain. "There, all done."

Vesswan carefully placed a single curly hair on the cloth and rolled up the scroll, trapping the hairs.

"Let me help with that," Vesswan said, and she helped Chimi re-wrap her headcloth. "You should know that the herbs must be gathered during an hour when only Inkesh is in the sky. That will be late at night, so my spell won't take effect until tomorrow. Can you be brave a little longer?"

"Yes," Chimi said, although she did feel a twinge of disappointment. Another day of dead eyes staring at her? She supposed she would have to put up with it.

"Come." Vesswan walked Chimi back to her gate.

"I appreciate your help," Chimi said. "You have no idea what it's been like, seeing things no one else does and not being able to talk about it."

Vesswan chuckled. Chimi realized she was babbling again. Of course Vesswan knew how she felt. As a necromancer, she must see ghosts all the time.

"It's no trouble," Vesswan said. "In fact, this should be an interesting challenge. Do call on me again, if there's anything else you need."

They had reached the street. Chimi bowed farewell. Just for a moment, she looked into the necromancer's dark eyes and had the feeling that Vesswan was laughing at her. She couldn't think why.

Chapter Ten

What She Must See

"Sorry I'm late," Chimi cried as she ran up the steps to Shenza's cottage. "It's all right," Shenza answered softly.

Even with Chimi's company, she wasn't looking forward to this excursion. She still had no solution to her sister's problem with the ghosts, and the recent earthquake had only put her more on edge. It didn't help that they would be shopping to dress her for Lord Aspace's courtship.

Panting, Chimi leaned against the porch rail. Necklaces dangled, swaying as she caught her breath, and her headcloth was loose over disheveled hair.

"It isn't so important that you had to run all the way here." Shenza was surprised at how sulky her words came out.

"Of course it is!" Chimi straightened, face flushed and eyes brilliant with emotion. "It got me away from Grandmother, didn't it?"

"I guess so," Shenza said.

"Anyway, it's important for you, too," Chimi went on, a little sharply. "You're always saying how you don't fit in at the palace—but your clothes are so old, you don't even look like you're trying."

"I do try," Shenza protested, stung by the lecture.

"You can't go to state banquets dressed like a beggar, sister," Chimi said. "They probably think you're scolding their extravagance. Nobody likes to be scolded."

"I don't scold them."

Chimi waved her words aside with a skeptical smile. "Now, the main thing is, how much can you spend?"

"I didn't count," Shenza said. She had been saving some of her salary for several months, in case of emergency. Getting new clothes wasn't what she'd had in mind.

"Let me see." Chimi held out her hand imperiously.

Shenza reached into the sash beneath her robe and drew out a leather pouch sewn with magic sigils. A muffled clink sounded as she passed it to her sister. Chimi tugged at the cords, but they remained knotted.

"Is there a spell on this?" Chimi frowned.

"Oh, I guess there is." Shenza laughed awkwardly. Chimi handed the pouch back, and Shenza concentrated. Power flowed through her hands. "Release."

She passed the pouch to Chimi again. This time the cords slipped loose. Chimi poured the coins out into her palm. Some were silver-bright, others tarnished by use. She stirred the pile with a finger, dark eyes moving as she counted.

"Well!" Chimi smiled approvingly, then poured the rukh coins back into the pouch with a sing-song sound. "We might be able to get more than one."

Shenza started to protest that she might need the money later, for something really important. Then she saw the glint of challenge in her sister's eyes.

"We'll see," she demurred.

"Come on!" Chimi grabbed Shenza's arm and tugged her down the steps to the street.

"All right, don't pull," Shenza protested. Chimi's fingers seemed cold compared to the warmth of the day. Over her shoulder, she called, "I'll be back later, Master!"

If her teacher answered, she couldn't tell. Shenza let Chimi draw her along the street, watching her step over the cobblestones. It felt odd to be dragged along, drab in her sorcerer's purple, just the way Grandmother had been dragging Chimi around in colorless robes. Despite her worries, Shenza chuckled at the image.

"What?" Chimi asked at once.

"Nothing."

In a way, it was a relief that Chimi was so focused on shopping. It kept her from asking about Lelldour, at least so far. Shenza hoped that would last.

"Where should we go first?" Chimi asked happily.

"I don't know," Shenza answered honestly. Chimi knew the market better than she did. Her sister darted an exasperated glance at her. "You go shopping with the Kesquin girls, don't you? Where would they buy a new robe?"

Shenza had thought the reminder would cheer her sister up. Instead, Chimi looked flustered.

"The House of Melleen. You know, Mother's customer. They're the best place, but I don't want to go there."

The words came out in a rush, and Shenza looked at her sister curiously. Why wouldn't Chimi want to go to the best place, when she had just been telling Shenza to make a better impression on the nobles?

"Why not?" She had to ask.

"I bought my last robe there," Chimi answered, speaking a little too quickly. "We should spread the wealth around. Let's just browse and see where we end up."

"All right," Shenza agreed.

The part of her mind that was magister-trained noted the pattern of Chimi's hesitation and response. Was something wrong with the House of Melleen? Or maybe she'd had a fight with the Kesquin girls. Then Shenza scolded herself for imagining things. Chimi was under a lot of stress, that was all.

The two women walked in silence for a while. Something else Chimi had said stuck in Shenza's mind. Their family had never had the money to keep up with nobles, even if there had been some reason to try. It had never occurred to her that the aristocrats might take her forced moderation as a rebuke of their extravagances.

Even if Chimi was right, what could Shenza do about it? She refused to take up gossip and gambling just to "fit in." Nobody had expected Master Laraquies to change when he became vizier. Why should Shenza be singled out?

A louder babble of voices drew her out of her thoughts as they descended the grand stair. The sky above the harbor was very blue, dotted with puffs of cloud so perfect that they looked like they had been painted by a master artisan.

As they approached the giant fig tree in the central square, Chimi grabbed Shenza's hand again and pulled her into a sunny aisle. Shenza's trained senses alerted her again. Chimi acted like she was trying to avoid someone. Realizing that it was probably a ghost, Shenza closed her mouth on her questions.

Still, she couldn't help thinking as she followed her sister between booths full of gleaming porcelain in the potters' aisle. During her last visit home, Chimi had confronted her the moment she arrived. Today didn't she mention the ghosts. Why?

They had nearly reached the cloth merchants' aisle. Shenza felt a slight stickiness of sweat in the bends of her elbows as they turned a corner.

Chimi paused dramatically. "Sister, your paradise awaits," she said with a sweeping gesture.

Shenza hardly knew where to look first. Displays of fabric covered both sides of the aisle in front of them. Cloth of every shade imaginable flowed in drapes from counters and racks. Geometric patterns, floral patterns, sea life and more were printed or woven into the cloth. The very air seemed to glow with color. In a nearby stall, she glimpsed a young women bent over an embroidery frame. Farther down, a merchant helped a woman pin a feathered brooch just so.

Mistaking Shenza's confusion for interest, the shopkeeper bustled out from the booth she was in front of.

"Welcome!" His words were smooth as oil. "What would you like—

perhaps this? Perfect for such a lovely young lady and enchantress."

White teeth flashed in his dark face, emphasizing the compliment. The man pressed a folded cloth into her hands. Shenza looked at it distractedly. Dark blue and yellow stripes, sea monsters interwoven. It wasn't well made, and Shenza felt the coarse texture of common cloth under her fingers. Before she had a chance to respond, her sister interrupted.

"Not that!" Chimi thrust the offending garment back at the vendor and yanked on Shenza's elbow.

"We have many other choices," the merchant protested, but his voice was soon lost in the babble of the marketplace.

"You don't want hemp," Chimi scolded. "It has to be feather-flower. That's what all the nobles wear. You should know that, sister."

"He said I was lovely," Shenza told her, baffled.

"Well? You are," Chimi answered, as if this should be obvious. "You can still do better. They have the prettiest blended shades now. If you want something stylish, that's what we're looking for."

"If you say so," Shenza murmured. In her heart, she couldn't believe the shopkeeper's compliments. He had just been flattering her, hoping to win her business. Shenza didn't think she was attractive at all.

Chimi answered with a loud sigh. It was a relief to Shenza when she eased her fierce, cold grip. They strolled along the aisle together, stopping occasionally to look at something more closely. Shenza saw several fabrics she liked, including a turquoise silk with a subtle pattern like rippling water.

"There are hangings like that in the audience chamber," she said. "A darker blue, I think."

"You don't want to look like a tapestry," Chimi scolded.

They stopped at a tiny stall where the robes were adorned with silver or copper beads. An advertisement of wealth, Shenza supposed. She couldn't help wondering how you washed them without tarnishing the beads. Chimi spent a long time in that booth, but eventually Shenza drew her away.

As they moved along, Shenza noticed graduated fabrics hanging in several of the stalls. This must be the fad Chimi had told her about. In the largest shop, one of those caught her eye. It was a creamy shell pink shaded into soft lavender. She crossed the aisle for a closer look, then ran her hand over the silken fabric. Tiny shells had been sewn to it, white spirals against the lavender.

"Would this do?" Shenza asked.

"Does it have to be purple, sister?" Chimi teased.

"It isn't a true sorcerer's purple," Shenza countered. "It's mostly pink."

"How about this one," Chimi suggested, drawing out a light blue shading into green. "Or this?" Yellow birds with fanciful crests flitted among bright red hibiscus blossoms. It was a very traditional pattern, yet rendered with exquisite skill.

"That's looks like something you would wear," Shenza said.

"If only I could," Chimi replied with a trace of bitterness. "I don't have anything to spend on myself these days."

Shenza barely heard her complaint. She stretched out the lavender and pink robe, folding the fabric to see both colors against her skin. She couldn't help wondering if Lord Aspace would approve. Would he think she was lovely?

"I wonder if he'll like it," she mused.

"Lord Manseen?" Chimi asked.

"Any of them," Shenza answered quickly. She hadn't meant to speak aloud. Even though Chimi was her sister, Shenza knew how she loved to gossip. She held up the robe again. "Really, what do you think, sister?"

A different voice answered, "It's an excellent choice for you."

Startled, Shenza turned to face the shopkeeper, a lovely older woman wearing an elegant robe of pale gold with reddish streaks that reminded her of coral branches. Bands of coral held the waves of her hair away from her face, and more coral crusted the golden hoops in her ears.

"Oh, Tuseeva! I didn't know if you would be here," Chimi chattered. To Shenza's ear, it sounded as if she was barely containing her panic.

"Miss Chimi." Tuseeva bowed her head with an indulgent smile. "It's good to have you back so soon. And you must be..." She trailed off, looking to Shenza.

"Oh!" Chimi cried. "This is my older sister, Shenza Waik of Tresmeer."

Again Shenza heard the tremor in Chimi's voice. Too late, she understood that this must be the House of Melleen—exactly where Chimi didn't want to be.

"Sister, this is Tuseeva Hasappai of Melleen," Chimi went on.

"Magister." Tuseeva executed a full bow, both hands pressed to her chest. "You honor our humble shop."

"Good morning." Shenza bowed in return. Remembering Chimi's lecture, she realized that her tepid reply might be taken as a snub. She quickly added, "I can see whose good taste is responsible for your shop's reputation. Now, I do like this one. Is there also a headcloth to go with it?"

"Certainly. One moment." Tuseeva beckoned to one of her assistants. The girl began probing among the rainbow of fabrics in the rafters with a long pole.

Meanwhile, Chimi beamed her approval of the niceties. She whispered, "See? It isn't so hard."

"No," Shenza answered, though she felt awkward delivering such overt flattery.

"Will it be just the pair?" Tuseeva asked.

Chimi lifted her chin with a trace of defiance. "We might consider others, if I can bargain for the lot."

"Come right this way." From the twinkle in Tuseeva's eye, Shenza wondered if Chimi had impressed her or walked into a salesman's trap.

Whatever the reason, Chimi seemed to shake off her doubts. She threw herself into the task of acquiring what she considered decent attire for Shenza with energy and focus. There were a few moments when Shenza felt sightly left out while Chimi and Tuseeva debated the merits of a darker pink or compared natural fabrics with ones that had been enchanted to brighten the colors. Still, Tuseeva did seem to care about finding things that looked good on Shenza, not just selling something. That was as reassuring as Chimi's enthusiasm when they all agreed on a second robe, turquoise painted with silvery-white orchids. Here and there, clear glass beads glittered like droplets of water after a rain.

Tuseeva asked again, "Will there be anything else?"

"Not today," Shenza quickly answered. Beautiful as the new robes were, she was already dreading the price Tuseeva would name.

"All right, then," Chimi said. "Let's talk this over."

"Shouldn't I?" Shenza began. After all, it was her money.

"No," Chimi said. She glanced at Tuseeva, who watched them with amusement, then took Shenza's arm to pull her aside. Chimi hissed into Shenza's ear, "If you want anything left over, let me do it!"

"All right," Shenza said reluctantly.

"Go wait over there," Chimi waved her toward the aisle, "and think about what we should have for lunch. I'm hungry."

So Shenza stood in the aisle, feeling both embarrassed and relieved, while her little sister bartered with Tuseeva. Chimi dickered with energy and confidence, the stray ghosts apparently gone from her mind. Shenza was glad to see her acting more like herself.

Her stomach rumbled, and she remembered that she was supposed to be thinking about food. Shenza breathed lightly, sampling odors on the air. She smelled roast yams and some kind of marinated meat. Her stomach rumbled more loudly.

Chimi looked smug and happy when she came to join Shenza. A mesh bag bulging with fabric swung from one hand. With the other, she pressed a much lighter money pouch into Shenza's waiting hand.

"Well?" Shenza asked nervously as they strolled toward the food stalls.

Chimi leaned closer as they wove through the crowd. "I got them both for fifty-five rukh! Can you believe it? She wanted seventy, but I talked her down."

Shenza swallowed a gasp. That was a lot of money, although it was a fair price for such fine workmanship. It was amazing she had anything left in her pouch at all.

"She must like you," Shenza said.

"I guess so." Suddenly Chimi's smile held a trace of sorrow. "Anyway, I told her I'll be bringing her more business later."

"What do you mean?" Shenza asked. She wouldn't be buying any more clothing—not at those prices.

"I was just thinking, when we've met Lady Seelit, she might want to go shopping with Winomi and me," Chimi said.

"Chimi!" Shenza scolded. She didn't even want to meet Seelit of Bosteel, and her little sister wanted to use the girl to make herself feel more important.

"Well, she might," Chimi argued. "Do you think she'll want to sit in the palace all day with a lot of people she doesn't know?"

"She doesn't know you, either," Shenza shot back.

"We still need to show her our town," Chimi protested. She added with a grumble, "You're no fun."

Shenza sighed. Maybe Chimi was right about welcoming Seelit, who might be first lady soon. Maybe she was right about the nobles, too. Shenza just didn't want Chimi taking advantage of Seelit.

The silence dragged between them until Chimi cleared her throat. "What's for lunch?"

They found the meat Shenza had smelled cooking, strips of chicken glazed with ginger and honey. With bananas and chunks of roast yam, it filled their stomachs nicely. Shenza felt better after eating, maybe because the shopping was mostly done. It shouldn't be so hard to buy things for herself, but it was. She felt as if she had taken money from her own mother's hands.

When they were finished, Chimi grabbed the bag and jumped to her feet. "Let's go look at jewelry!" she cried.

Chimi knew the baubles even better than the fabric. She spotted a silver necklace with chunks of turquoise and earrings to match. They also found shell jewelry that nearly matched the ones sewn on the lavender-and-pink robe.

By this time, clouds obscured the sun and the wind puffed a warning of rain. Shenza noticed Chimi looking past her again, then frowning and looking away. The younger sister rubbed at her neck, where her hoka's twine rested. The ghosts must be nearby—lost souls only Chimi could see.

"My feet hurt," Chimi said abruptly.

"Let's go home, then," Shenza replied. "The market will be closing soon, anyway."

The two of them gathered their parcels and walked toward the fig tree. Shenza debated telling Chimi that she had reached a blank wall in her search for information about Lelldour and the ghosts. She felt like a liar, keeping it secret. After all, if she was brave enough to shop for court robes, she should be brave enough to tell her sister the truth. It was just so frustrating, not being able to question Lelldour. Chimi had found him, so why couldn't she?

All at once Shenza stopped, ignoring the townsfolk who bustled past her. She stared at Chimi's retreating back and wondered how she could have missed something so obvious.

* * *

Being a magister had ruined Shenza, Chimi grumbled to herself. Shenza took the responsibility *so* seriously. She had hardly smiled all day, just shuffled around looking pinched and sad. You'd think it hurt her to have fun. Honestly, when a girl couldn't enjoy shopping, there was something really wrong with her. And then she'd tried to discourage Chimi from making friends with Lady Seelit! Chimi had to wonder where her loyalties lay.

Her big sister's shortcomings seemed painfully obvious now that Chimi had met the lovely and gracious necromancer, Vesswan. That woman was proof that a sorceress didn't have to be a shriveled-up old maid. Chimi just didn't understand why Shenza insisted on making herself out so plain and glum.

She sighed to herself as they wove their way through the crowds. After all Chimi had been through, putting up with the ghosts and sneaking away to see Vesswan, she thought she deserved to have a little fun. Yet even the triumph of bartering Tuseeva down sat uneasily in Chimi's stomach.

That was sort of funny, in a sad way. Tuseeva would probably tell Rellad's parents that Chimi had been looking for him again. He might come back to her booth, but she didn't want to see him anymore. Chimi wasn't sure what she did want, except maybe to hug Winomi and have a good cry.

She caught herself sniffling, and straightened her shoulders irritably. Things would be better after today. Vesswan would get rid of the ghosts. Chimi would meet Lady Seelit and make friends, and if Shenza didn't like it, she could just choke. Azma, too.

Speaking of Shenza, she was being pretty quiet. Chimi glanced toward her, then stopped. Where was Shenza? Chimi turned and spotted her sister about ten feet behind her. Shenza's haunted expression had been replaced by piercing intensity.

"What's wrong?" Chimi asked. For a moment, she was afraid Shenza had figured out that she'd met with Vesswan. But that was impossible.

"Come with me." Shenza swept forward, carrying herself with more confidence than she had shown all day.

"I have been." Chimi tried to laugh, but her heart jumped in her chest as she remembered how Shenza had warned her to stay away from Vesswan. Guilt pricked at her. She tried to brush it aside. If Shenza had helped her, even a little, she wouldn't have needed Vesswan. Chimi lagged behind as Shenza went back to the cottage she shared with her teacher.

"Master Laraquies? Are you home?" Shenza called as she ran up the steps. Chimi didn't hear an answer. "He must have gone back up the hill," she murmured.

Shenza strode across the porch and opened the grille. To Chimi's dismay, she dropped all her parcels just inside the door and hurried into the workshop. She jerked open one of the cabinet doors.

"What are you doing?" Chimi demanded.

"I need to pick up a few things." Shenza's voice came muffled from inside the cabinet.

"I didn't barter for new clothes so you could ruin them," Chimi chided. "This is delicate fabric. You have to treat it right!"

She carefully retrieved the abandoned bag. Luckily, nothing had snagged. Chimi folded the robes, savoring their silken softness, and put them away in Shenza's bedroom.

When she came back to the workshop, Shenza was pressing a stylus and scroll into her travel case and folding it shut. "Seal," she murmured.

"What's going on?" Chimi asked warily.

"I've just thought of something," Shenza said. Her dark eyes were intent on Chimi's face. "Something important. I need you to help me with an experiment."

"I thought we were going home for dinner," Chimi said. "I need to start cooking soon."

"This won't wait," Shenza answered. "Come on." She strode out of the workshop without even looking to see if her sister would follow her.

Chimi did, grudgingly. Her frustration boiled again, a hot tide against the afternoon's gloom. That was Shenza all over, making people guess what she meant. No wonder the courtiers didn't like her. Chimi slouched after her sister, up stairs and along shady streets. She didn't pay much attention to where they were until a familiar shape caught her eye: a faded red lantern.

"What are we doing here?" Chimi all but shrieked as she recognized Lelldour's overgrown yard.

"I need to talk to Master Lelldour." Shenza watched Chimi over her shoulder with a penetrating stare. "Will you call him for me?"

Chimi backed away, rubbing her arms nervously. Was this a trap?

Maybe that was why Shenza had been so quiet all day.

"I don't want to talk to him."

"But I do." Still Shenza pinned her with that unnerving stare. "Come in here. Quick, before the neighbors see you."

Someone might be watching? Chimi ran into Lelldour's yard as if there was a scorpion in the street.

"This isn't fair," she complained, and dragged her feet through the leaves along the path. The stream was overflowing again and the house stood in deep shade, as desolate as ever.

"Now call him," Shenza ordered.

"I don't like him," Chimi snapped, frightened by Shenza's insistence. She folded her arms across her chest. "Do it yourself."

Shenza's lips tightened, her eyes narrowed with anger. Then her expression changed as suddenly as the sun rising over the sea.

"I can't do it," Shenza said gently. "He won't answer me, little sister."

Her response startled Chimi. She had expected to be scolded for her defiance.

"What are you talking about?" she scoffed. "Of course he…"

"He will only come to you," Shenza interrupted, "because you are a necromancer and he is a ghost."

Chapter Eleven

The Power of Balance

"No," Chimi breathed in horror.

"I didn't understand it myself until just now," Shenza went on. She still spoke softly, as if to a child. "Lelldour doesn't come when I call, but I must talk to him. Not just for you, but for…"

She kept talking, rationalizing and explaining, words without meaning. Her voice faded into the deathly silence of Chimi's fears. Cold shadows closed in, squeezing her chest like a snake crushing its prey. Chimi sucked in a long breath, until her lungs felt fit to burst.

"No!" She wailed the denial with all her heart. "This can't be true, it can't!"

Startled, Shenza stopped talking. Then she said, "It's the only thing that makes sense. Remember how you told me that you saw the old woman's spirit, but Winomi didn't? So far, you're the only one who's spoken to Lelldour. Logically…"

"Nakuri saw Yail," Chimi interrupted, desperate to prove Shenza wrong. "So did Rellad."

"You were touching him," Shenza said. "You wanted them to see him, just like you wanted me to see the ghosts at home."

"That doesn't mean anything!" Chimi crossed her arms over her chest and rubbed her shoulders, trying to warm herself. But her hands were cold, so cold, and her lungs ached with every breath.

"Maybe the magic is erratic because it's new to you." Shenza reached out to hug her. Chimi whirled away, feeling only the brief warmth of her sister's fingers brushing her skin.

"Hold still," Shenza ordered, frowning. She stepped closer and rested her hand on Chimi's shoulder. After a moment she shifted her hand to feel her sister's back beneath the drape of her robe.

"Stop that. It tickles!" Chimi jerked away again. Her voice was thick with tears.

"You're cold," Shenza said accusingly.

"I'm fine," Chimi snapped.

"You're cold as a fish from the deep sea," Shenza corrected her. "It's a wonder Mother hasn't noticed."

"I said I'm fine." Chimi hugged herself again with chilly hands, but her eyes started to sting. The world blurred around her. She sniffled, "You're wrong. I can't be a necromancer."

Tears overflowed and ran down her cheeks. Even they were cold. She wiped at them with the trailing end of her robe.

"Don't cry," Shenza said. "There's nothing wrong with it. Necromancy is an honorable..."

"It's grotesque!" Chimi cried. "I hate it! I won't do it!"

"Well," Shenza said, slowly and carefully, "we could ask Lelldour if he's really a ghost, but only if we can find him."

"I told you, he's useless," Chimi said.

"I still need to ask him some questions," Shenza said. "I don't know how he died, or..."

"You don't know that he's dead," Chimi cut in.

"All right, I don't know *if* he's dead," Shenza corrected herself. "I can check the town archive, but I doubt there's any record of his passing. For one thing, Master Laraquies knows all the magicians in town. He would have told me if Lelldour was dead. So I have to report this, but I need to know exactly what happened."

Chimi's eyes smarted with more tears, and the sting of betrayal—or truth, she no longer knew which. How could Shenza be so self-righteous when Chimi's world was tottering around her? She glared at her sister, tears turning to cold rage.

"I'm not going to summon him, because I can't. I am not a necromancer."

Despite her vow, Chimi felt a kind of tightness in her forehead. The pressure built, and suddenly eased. Perversely, the missing necromancer chose that moment to appear. He didn't walk out of the darkened house; if he had, Chimi would have seen him coming. Lelldour was just *there*.

Shenza must have seen the shock in Chimi's face, for she whirled.

"Oh," she gasped, looking up at the tall, red-robed figure on the porch.

"Where have you been?" Chimi demanded, before Shenza got the chance to gloat.

"I could ask you the same," Lelldour replied with some irritation. "We were supposed to enchant lamp oil, I believe."

"Tell her you're not dead," Chimi demanded, waving in Shenza's direction. "Tell her!"

Lelldour glanced toward Shenza without curiosity. The older girl bowed with a hasty jerk.

"Necromancer Lelldour?" she asked uncertainly. "I am Shenza Waik of Tresmeer, the magister. I have been here before and called for you. Did you hear me?"

Shenza had been here looking for Lelldour? Chimi frowned. No one had been spending so much time up at the palace recently. At least she would have plenty of time to write out her notes and think things over.

To her surprise, Shenza saw light inside her cottage. Golden lampglow came to her through the silvery curtain of rain, and she caught a faint whiff of something cooking. Her stomach rumbled. Shenza hurried up the steps from the street, eager to get out of the wet weather.

"Open," she murmured. The gate swung free, and she pushed through the strands of shells just inside it. "Master Laraquies?" she called through their clatter.

Shenza stopped, surprised by the scene before her. Lady Izmay sat across the table from Master Laraquies, who was pouring tea for her. He turned with a start. As Izmay caught sight of Shenza, her coy smile vanished, smoothed away into polite greeting. In the center of the table were a small bowl of fresh dates and a vase of orchids. The flowers looked like tiny faces with exaggerated moustaches.

"Excuse me." Shenza quickly bowed, all too aware of her damp robe and wet hair. Although it was her house, she had to ask, "Have I interrupted?"

"Certainly not," Izmay replied, so calmly that it was hard to believe she had been taken by surprise. "The palace is so noisy most nights, and it's peaceful here."

"You're just in time to eat," Laraquies added. His smile betrayed just a trace of chagrin. "But I thought you planned to go shopping with Chimi, and then eat at home."

"It didn't go well," Shenza said.

"How could shopping go wrong?" Izmay asked with genuine curiosity.

"It wasn't the shopping," Shenza said, though the reminder did nothing to settle her confused feelings. "In fact, maybe later I can show you what we got and see what you think."

"I would love to," Izmay murmured over the rim of her teacup.

Master Laraquies was looking at Shenza thoughtfully. He could always tell when something was bothering her.

"I have other bad news," Shenza began, because she had to say something.

"Go get dry." He waved cheerfully toward her bedroom. "Tell me while we're eating."

"All right."

Gratefully, Shenza retreated. Once she had reached the safety of her own room, she raised both hands to cover a giggle at the memory of Laraquies' expression when she first came into the house. She had never seen him embarrassed before. He must have arranged this private supper, expecting Shenza to be gone all evening. Izmay had been flirting with him, too. Shenza didn't know why it surprised her. They were of equal ages, both widowed. There was no reason for them to be old and alone, to use Chimi's hysterical words.

Shenza changed into a dry robe, pink and lavender flowers on a pale yellow background. The fibers caught against her fingertips, and she felt keenly aware of its coarseness compared to the silk she had handled earlier. Meanwhile, her thoughts ran in circles. Shenza wanted Master Laraquies' advice, but what could she say without betraying Chimi's confidence? Or did the changed circumstances finally allow her to tell the truth?

Once she was dressed, Shenza went into the kitchen. "Can I help with anything?"

"Oh, no," Laraquies answered, stirring a pot of mustard sauce. "Go sit down. It's almost ready."

Shenza glanced around the kitchen, spying a bowl of steamed millet, fish rolls wrapped in seaweed, and shrimp like ruddy half-moons sizzling on skewers. As she had thought, a meal for two.

"You sit, Master Laraquies. I'll be your handmaiden tonight." Shenza plucked the whisk from his hand and pointed toward where Izmay sat, just out of sight in the main room.

"You don't have to," Laraquies protested, but Shenza knew he was pleased.

"I thought you had to tell us something." Izmay's voice drifted around the partition.

"I'll be a talkative handmaiden," Shenza called back. She smiled at Master Laraquies and pushed his shoulder gently. "Go on. Elders should be taken care of properly."

"I like her attitude," Izmay joked as Laraquies joined her.

Shenza got to work on the food. There might not be enough to satisfy all of them, since Master Laraquies hadn't planned for her being there. She peeked into the bins, looking for a good addition. There might be breadfruit on the tree in the garden, but she didn't have time to roast it. Her best hope was a pineapple, fruit to add sweetness to the meal.

The skewers of shrimp were sizzling vigorously. Shenza moved them off the heat and set to work on the pineapple, coring and slicing the fruit before placing the wedges in a graceful pattern on the platter. The murmur of voices came from the other room, but she was too busy to listen. Izmay laughed often, but in a relaxed way, not forcing mirth as the courtiers did at the palace.

Shenza looked the food over, and it still didn't seem like enough. She chopped greens and cooked them in the oil left from the shrimp skewers. When they were just wilted she mixed them with the steaming millet.

Now Shenza was afraid the food would get cold, so she took out the fruit tray, and then the millet in small bowls with the skewers of shrimp

Picking scrolls at random, Shenza found formulas for processing weeping-wood sap into rubber and Lelldour's household ledgers. Scanning the dates, she found the most recent one and tucked it into her travel case. She also found several scrolls of meditative verse. Strangely, there was nothing about necromancy. Maybe Lelldour had memorized his spells so perfectly that he didn't need instructions, but Shenza doubted it. He had rubber recipes, and he must have known that job just as well. Besides, his apprentice would have needed materials to study.

The empty spaces seemed very suspicious. She looked down, searching the dusty floor for signs of disturbance. The only footprints were her own.

Outside, she could hear Juss' rake scratching at the pavement. The noise sounded as if it came from another world. Shenza tried to concentrate on her goals. Not only had the necromancer's body been moved, but his library had been raided. Had that been the motive for murder? Looking around the modest house, Shenza couldn't see much else that would be worth killing for.

Frowning, she glanced into the kitchen, where the dishes lay on the counter. The bedroom was just as neat as she remembered. Too neat, she now thought. Someone had cleaned Lelldour's house—probably not out of kindness.

Footsteps sounded in the workroom and Shenza turned to see Juss coming in. "Find anything?" he asked.

"Not yet," Shenza answered. Gesturing to take in the tidy bedroom, she said, "Here's what doesn't make sense: Lelldour said he went to sleep and couldn't get up the next day, so this is where his body should be. Even if ants cleaned his bones..."

"Ugh." Juss made a disgusted face.

Shenza nodded. "Obviously, they've been removed and everything nicely put away."

"It looks pretty normal," Juss agreed. "As a trick, I guess. You think he was murdered?"

"Why else would someone hide his body?" Shenza asked back. "It has to be nearby. You couldn't take something like that through the city streets without being seen. Unless it was at night?" She glanced a question at her companion.

"There are watchmen," he said.

"But someone could avoid the patrols if they were patient and watched the routine," Shenza said.

Juss shrugged. "Can't you use past-sight? That's what you did when you were looking for Makko."

"It's been too long," Shenza answered with real regret. "With Lord Anges, it had been less than a day, so I could see very clearly. The more time passes, the harder it is, and Lelldour wasn't even sure how long he's been dead."

"Too bad," Juss sighed.

"Yes," Shenza said. His idea would have made things easier.

She walked back to the porch with Juss beside her. They both looked out on the overgrown property. There were lots of potential hiding places.

"The killer might not have needed to move him very far," she observed.

"A body would be heavy, too," Juss agreed. "Let's search around the house. I've got the rake."

"There should be a broom in the kitchen," Shenza said. She soon found one, a simple bundle of rushes tied to a bamboo pole.

She took it back to the porch. Juss was kneeling beside the foundation, but he straightened as she approached.

"Nothing in the crawl space," he said, wiping his hands against his kilt. "So we're looking for bones?"

"Or someplace where the soil was disturbed. He could have been buried," Shenza told him.

"They didn't even give him a funeral?" Juss grumbled. "No wonder he can't rest in peace."

"You couldn't burn a pyre in here," Shenza pointed out. "The neighbors would be sure to notice. Anyway, a killer wouldn't care about respect for the dead."

Slowly they walked around the stone foundation. Shenza brushed away the dry upper leaves, and Juss scraped at the soggy layers beneath. The chill of damp earth seemed to cling to Shenza's feet.

"Where now?" Juss asked when they had circled the whole house with no success.

Shenza leaned on her broom, scanning the yard. It would help if she even knew when Lelldour had died. Then she straightened.

"It stinks over there!" she exclaimed.

"What?" Juss demanded, confused.

"The little girl, what was her name, Rumia's daughter," Shenza said. "Sujah, that's it. She said, 'It stinks over there.' I thought she meant Lelldour boiling rubber. How could I be so dense?"

Shenza turned toward the side of the property that faced Rumia's house. Beyond a thick screen of bushes, she heard children's voices.

"Let's try over there."

Juss smiled ironically and gestured for her to lead the way. With much swishing and crackling, they slogged through the calf-deep leaves. Tiny creatures rustled away from them under cover of the litter. Bits of leaves clung to Shenza's damp legs, increasing her discomfort. She tried to ignore that and concentrate on the terrain around them.

There was a flat area where buckets for collecting sap were stacked. Forest debris covered them. Behind that was a row of thorny bushes, which would give berries in the dry season. Shenza slipped between them, tugging at her robe when it snagged. Juss cursed softly behind her.

"It's nothing," he said when she glanced back, looking for spiders.

Beyond the thorns was a relatively clear patch along the wall. Lizards darted up tree trunks as they forced their way into the opening. It was dark under the trees. Shenza was glad of her enchanted mask, which helped her see. Then she stumbled over a hidden rock.

"Ouch!"

Juss grabbed her arm to steady her. "Are you okay?"

"Nothing's hurt but my pride." Shenza tried to laugh, though her toes throbbed. She bent forward, keeping her weight on the other foot, and scanned the ground ahead of them.

If she was hiding a body, Shenza decided, she would want to put it on this side of the berry bushes, where the thorns would discourage searchers. She couldn't just leave it lying out, though. The wall was only waist height, of round gray stones with a thick growth of lichen. Someone in Rumia's yard would be able to spot a corpse where Shenza was standing.

She could easily see into Rumia's property, where Bonta the goose dabbled in a shallow pond. Sujah stood on the porch, yelling Daneel's name over and over, while the boy crept between rows of bean vines, obviously hiding from her.

Shenza watched them for a moment, then pulled herself back to her work. Sujah had said she smelled something. The body might have been placed right up against the wall, perhaps covered with leaves. Shenza edged forward, probing with her broom handle for anything that felt like another rock—or a set of hidden bones.

"Let's start here," she murmured when they were within arm's reach of the wall.

"Right."

Once again they worked as a team, Shenza carefully sweeping off the loose leaves and Juss dragging the lower layers aside. They made a lot of noise, so Shenza wasn't surprised when Sujah stopped yelling and stared at them.

A moment later, the girl rushed toward the wall. Daneel gave up hiding and pelted after her. Sujah seemed to know the race was on, for she stretched out her bare arms and grinned with delight when she was first to touch the wall.

"I winned!" she shouted happily.

"Won," Daneel snapped, trying to look as if correcting her was more important than losing the race. He scowled up at Shenza. "I know you."

"Good morning." Shenza paused to greet them. Then she cautioned, "Stay where you are, please."

"What are you doing?" asked Sujah. The child was so short that only her bright brown eyes and curly black mop of hair showed over the top of the wall.

"Looking for something," Shenza said as she worked. They had already cleared a stretch beside the wall and not found anything.

Daneel slapped both hands on top of the wall and pulled himself up. Sujah jumped in place, trying to do the same. Her brother made no move to help her, but sat with his skinny brown knees dangling over the wall.

"I can't see," Sujah whined.

She bumped Daneel, who wailed, "Watch out, you baby!"

Shenza had a terrible mental image of the two children tumbling off the wall and landing in a spray of leaf-litter and bones.

"Juss," she sighed, "help her up before someone gets hurt."

"Sure." Juss handed Shenza his rake and leaned over the wall. "Up you come." He lifted the little girl and set her beside her brother with the amiable warning, "Now remember, you keep out of our way."

The children nodded solemnly and Shenza gave Juss the rake back. They returned to their dirty, noisy work. Daneel sneezed several times as dust drifted his way, but he and his sister followed along the wall like two little brown birds. It was nerve-wracking to watch them and also search. Then she had another idea.

"Sujah," she asked, still sweeping, "do you remember how you told me it was stinky over here?"

Sujah nodded importantly.

"Where was the smelliest part of the yard?"

"Down there." Sujah pointed, wrinkling her nose. Her gesture took in the back corner of the yard, where it came up against the base of the fifth tier.

"You can't smell anything now," Daneel argued, as if that erased Sujah's contribution.

"Will you show me?" Shenza asked Sujah.

"Okay!" Sujah spun in place and dropped down on the other side. She trotted along the wall, weaving between shrubs. Daneel also jumped down. He pushed past Sujah to race into the back corner of the yard.

"Daneel!" Sujah wailed. "It's my job! I'm doing it!"

"Over here!" Daneel waved and grinned.

"Daneel!" Sujah shrieked with sudden fury. She rushed at her brother. Daneel retreated, but Sujah chased him all the way into the bean vines. Catching the excitement, the goose swam to the center of the pond and honked loudly.

"Are you sure she knows what she's saying?" Juss asked as he and Shenza waded through the leaves after Sujah.

Shenza shrugged. "She smelled something rotting. I'm sure she didn't realize what it was."

The siblings' quarreling reminded Shenza of Chimi and Sachakeen, years ago. There had always been something to their arguments, however slight. She hoped there would be a kernel of truth in Sujah's claim, too.

In the back corner, they set to work again. The children soon returned, although Daneel kept a certain distance from his sister.

Almost at once, Shenza heard a difference in the squishy-scrape of Juss' rake. She turned, even as Juss said, "This might be it."

Something pale and round lay amid the sodden leaf-mould.

"What is it?" Sujah demanded, crowding close to her brother. For once, he didn't push her away.

"A skull," Daneel breathed with fascinated horror.

"Bones, too," Sujah squealed as Juss' rake revealed an arched row of ribs. She didn't seem at all put off by the grisly discovery. "There's lots of them!"

"That's what we were looking for," Shenza said.

"Looks like little sister had it right," Juss said. He worked carefully, pulling matted leaves away from the grave site.

The bones gleamed softly against the dank ground. As Shenza had suspected, the body had been thoroughly cleaned by ants and other insect scavengers. There was no odor except the earthy waft of dead leaves. She didn't see any churning of the soil to suggest that the body had ever been buried. The skull seemed to stare at her with hollow eye sockets half-buried in leafy debris. Its expression was bewildered and helpless.

"Where did they come from?" Sujah asked.

"From inside someone's body," Daneel answered with utmost disdain.

"But where did it come from?" Sujah persisted.

"That's what we're investigating," Shenza replied. "Now please be quiet so we can concentrate."

The children fell silent, although only for a moment. They watched, commenting eagerly as Juss uncovered the arm, hip and leg bones. The sight of a human skeleton didn't seem to bother them. If they could face it, Shenza thought, then so could she. Lelldour's remains were actually quite sanitary compared to the charred corpse of Lord Anges during her first investigation.

"Well, there he is," Juss said when the last foot bones had been laid bare. "What do we do next?"

"Normally, we would send for a necromancer." Shenza smiled wryly. Juss groaned, acknowledging the irony. "Or we would notify the family to claim the bones and let them hold the funeral. However, Lelldour has no family here."

"Wouldn't do much good anyway," Juss said. "He told you he can't rest until he has a successor."

"True," Shenza said. Then she frowned, staring at the skeleton and seeing what wasn't there. "You didn't pull off anything but leaves, did you?"

"No," he answered. "Why?"

"There's no clothing. And I don't see his bone necklace, either."

"Could the cloth have rotted away?" Juss asked.

"I'm sure it would have started to," Shenza replied, "but there should be something left. The ants won't have wanted it. Besides, even if the cord had decomposed, the necklace should still be here."

"All the other bones are," Juss agreed. "Well, if you're going to keep the skeleton until his family claims it, I'll get a litter from the ward."

"All right." Shenza wasn't sure where to take the bones, but she couldn't just leave them here. It was bad enough Lelldour's body had been dumped naked in the brush. She wouldn't add any more disrespect.

"I'll be back!" Juss crashed off through the leaf cover, leaving Shenza with the skeleton and her thoughts. She glanced at the wall, where Daneel and Sujah were starting to fidget.

"There won't be anything else to see," Shenza told them.

"It's okay," Daneel said, but Sujah dropped down and wandered toward her house.

While she waited, Shenza decided to make a sketch of the skeleton. She rustled back to Lelldour's cottage for her travel case, and also borrowed one of his robes from the bedroom. That would do to wrap the bones in.

Returning to the wall, she found that Daneel had deserted his post as well. Relieved, she opened her case and took out ink, a stylus and a scroll of cloth. Leaning on the wall, she began to draw.

As she worked, Shenza noted many details of what she was seeing. The skeleton's right hand was pinned beneath its hip bones, and the legs were slightly skewed to the left. This would fit with Juss' theory that the body had been dragged outside and dropped. The skeleton seemed complete, although she still wanted to have a curomancer examine it.

The bones looked straight, but there were many subtle curves to them. Shenza knelt for a closer look, and was surprised when her mask revealed a purple glow on the outside of the right arm. Spell residue? The mark was faint but clear, an irregular blot on the bone just above the elbow.

Puzzled, she leaned back against the wall. Spell residue meant that powerful magic had touched that place. It would usually appear on something that had been enchanted, like a talisman or charm. There was no sign of any wood or shell left over from a charm. Anyway, that kind of magic shouldn't leave a mark on someone's body. And people wore charms around the neck or wrist, not on their elbows.

Shenza put out a hand, hesitated, and then rubbed her fingertips over the mysterious mark. To her relief, the bone felt cool and slightly coarse, not at all slimy. She couldn't feel the tingle of active magic, but she hadn't expected it. The stain was too weak. Shenza crouched a moment longer, mulling this discovery, before carefully marking it on her sketch.

With her task complete, she sat on the wall and held her scroll open to dry. She looked again at the area around her. This hiding place didn't strike her as a panicked response to an unexpected situation. Like the tidying up inside, it hinted that the killer had known the area and planned the crime in advance.

Her mind went back to Groad, the nosy neighbor who seemed to know everyone's habits. Yet, as far as she could tell, Groad wasn't a magician. He would have no use for a necromancer's bones and spell books. Neither would Sussani, who only wanted Lelldour's property to look better. Rumia's family hadn't even moved in until after Lelldour died.

Could there be an angry client who wanted revenge on him? That didn't make sense if his true customers were the ghosts.

On the other hand, Vesswan Sanguri of Zeell might want Lelldour's things. If she had lived there, she would have known the area. Shenza considered that as she waited for Juss. Groad claimed Lelldour had thrown Vesswan out. A rejected apprentice might hold a grudge. On the other hand, Vesswan and Lelldour had been working in Chalsett-port for some time, as direct competitors. Shenza hadn't heard of any open disputes between them. Something would have had to happen to escalate an old argument to murder.

There was no evidence to implicate Vesswan, except what Shenza knew of her business practices. Come to that, Vesswan was mostly in Shenza's mind now because of Chimi's situation. It wasn't fair to blame her. Vesswan of Zeell had nothing to do with Chimi, and that was how Shenza wanted it to stay.

When Juss returned with the litter, Shenza told him she wanted to take the bones to a curomancer. He shrugged.

"Whatever you think."

They spread the necromancer's robe over the litter and carefully transferred the bones onto it. There was more sinew left than Shenza had expected, so they were able to move the head and torso in one section, the hips and legs in another. The delicate hand and foot bones had to be picked up individually. Shenza counted to herself, making sure the sets of fingers and toes matched.

With the skeleton arranged, they folded the robe over it so that nothing would come loose during transit. Then they lifted the litter together. Although not heavy, it was a bit awkward. Shenza struggled for a moment before finding the best way to hold its handles and her travel case at the same time. Once that was done, they set out for the curomancers' clinic.

It was a relief to leave Lelldour's overgrown property. Shenza felt as if she had been in a cave all day. She longed for warmth and light to revive her.

They moved along the street to the grand staircase, then down three flights to the central square. Shenza caught many curious glances from passers-by and remembered how she had told Juss that someone couldn't carry a body through town without being noticed. The sight of a peacekeeper and the magister carrying a funeral bier was certainly attracting attention.

They angled right at the giant fig tree, passing the rounded bulk of the peacekeepers' ward and the smaller port offices. The docks were on their left, and beyond them the busy harbor. Feathery clouds drifted in the heavens. Shenza would have looked to the five moons for portents, but Juss turned right again, and she had to watch her footing.

They entered a small courtyard screened by tall clumps of bamboo, where patients could nurse their injuries in private while they waited for a curomancer. The clinic itself was farther back, a long building shaded by palm trees. Stone benches stood empty. The apprentice on duty, a young man in a green and white striped robe, jumped to his feet when he saw them.

"Officer, Magister." He pressed both hands to his chest and bowed. With a trace of doubt, he asked, "Do you need healing?"

"Good day, Meersatta." Shenza leaned slightly to her left to see past Juss' broad shoulders. "We need to consult Mistress Kafseet. Is she available?"

"She's with someone," Meersatta apologized. "Will you wait for her, or would you like another curomancer?"

"We'll wait," Shenza said.

"There's no hurry," Juss added with a chuckle.

"Come this way," Meersatta began, but Shenza heard loud voices approaching behind them. She glanced over her shoulder to see a group of seamen in brown kilts entering the courtyard. Two men supported a third, who hopped on one foot and held the other out before him. A pained grimace twisted his face.

"Healer!" one of the men bellowed.

"I'll send someone right out," the apprentice called. He beckoned to Juss and Shenza.

"Hurry," the injured man groaned. "I think it's broken!"

Meersatta led them beside the clinic, where folding screens made a series of small rooms. Shenza thought she heard Kafseet's voice behind one of them.

"Bring it in here." Meersatta gestured to indicate an open room.

"This will be fine," Shenza assured him as she and Juss entered. "Go on, if you need to see that man."

"Thank you, Magister." The apprentice bowed again, backing away. "Mistress Kafseet will be with you shortly."

The makeshift chamber contained a low table, just the right size for a person to lie on. Juss and Shenza lowered the litter onto it. As Shenza straightened, flexing her stiff fingers, Juss dragged two chairs over to the entrance. She sat in one, took off her mask, and tucked it into her travel case.

They waited, resting in the cool shade while small birds swooped and darted over a pond on the other side of the path. At last, Shenza heard voices nearby.

"Drink this tea in the morning and at night for two hands of days," Kafseet directed crisply. "Strong tea, or it won't do any good. If your stomach still hurts, come back to me."

"I will," an anonymous woman murmured. "Thank you, curomancer."

"Not at all." Kafseet's voice sounded closer, and Shenza was not surprised when her friend swept around the partition.

Kafseet Ikarys of Hei was a tall woman of middle years, with the quick movements and slender frame of a sandpiper. Her hair was woven into a neat crown. Pearls gleamed against its blackness. More strands of pearls rested against the green of her curomancer's robe.

"Nice to see you, Shenza," Kafseet said. "Juss, how are you?"

"Good," he answered. Shenza merely smiled.

Kafseet took in the red-wrapped bundle on the table. "Have you brought me a patient?"

"A puzzle. Please take a look," Shenza said.

Kafseet flipped the robe open, revealing the skeleton. She glanced over it and said, "An adult man. How did he die?"

"A spider bite, the ghost said," Shenza told her.

"But you have questions?" Kafseet glanced up at her with a keen eye. "I do, too. From a spider's bite there should be pain and swelling, but I wouldn't expect it to be fatal. Some shallow-water fishes, now, or a sea snake—that would be different. A human is too big for most spiders to do permanent harm."

"Yet, as you see, he did die," Shenza said.

"Anyone I know?" Kafseet asked.

"Did you know Lelldour of Salloo?" Shenza asked.

Kafseet tilted her head, thinking. "I've heard the name, but I don't think we ever met."

"You won't," Juss said.

"That's enough," Shenza said. The joking was a habit of his, but this wasn't the time for it. "Since you know more anatomy, I was hoping you would examine the skeleton. I want to be sure we didn't leave any pieces behind."

"Of course." Kafseet nodded firmly.

"I also noticed a strange mark, here, on his arm." Shenza bent forward, pointing. "I was hoping for your insight."

"I don't see anything," Kafseet said, frowning.

"You'll need a spellfinder," Shenza answered.

"I'll be happy to take a look," Kafseet said. "If you can just leave this? I'll have to work on it between patients, but I'll send word when I learn anything."

"That's all I ask," Shenza said.

Chapter Thirteen

Tales Not Told

Chimi leaned on her counter, savoring a sea breeze and the sun's warmth. No ghosts at the gate when she left the house. No empty eyes staring under the fig tree. No cold draft on her shoulders. Vesswan had been as good as her word. The ghosts were gone.

Better yet, Grandmother was already dozing in her chair. Even if Chimi was stuck wearing these terrible clothes, it didn't matter. For the first time in days, she could relax and be herself.

No ghosts, she gloated to herself. She had gotten rid of them. Despite Shenza's interference, Chimi had her life back. She felt as light as a bit of feather-flower silk drifting on the breeze. She could hardly wait to see Winomi again. Or—she covered her mouth so Grandmother wouldn't hear her giggle—maybe even Rellad, if she decided he was worth her time.

With no ghosts to complicate things, Grandmother would soon forget Chimi's supposed offenses. She would be able to go where she wanted, do what she wanted, shop or flirt or give that sour Azma her own snubs back. It was going to be a wonderful day.

* * *

"What's next?" Juss asked as they left Kafseet's clinic.

With the skeleton delivered, Shenza had the rest of the day before her. She just wasn't sure what to do with it.

"You can go back to the ward," she said. "I don't want to annoy the chief by keeping you for no reason."

"Are you sure you won't need me?" Juss asked, as she had known he would.

"Do they make you work so hard?" Shenza teased. Juss grinned. She added, "I'm finished for today. I need to think about my next step. Can you meet me at the fig tree tomorrow?"

"I'll see you then," Juss said. Then he warned, "Just don't go off by yourself. Remember what happened last time."

"I promise." Shenza folded her hands across her chest and bowed as if to an elder.

With a snort of laughter, Juss limped off toward the peacekeepers' ward. It wasn't fair of him to remind her, Shenza thought. In a city as small as Chalsett, people seldom attacked someone like a magister. There had been no reason for her to expect that Makko, her nemesis, would try to poison her. That investigation still nagged at her because it hadn't been fully resolved, but there was no reason to dwell on it.

Shenza strolled aimlessly into the marketplace. She paused when she found that her feet had carried her toward the fish sellers. Chimi's harsh words echoed in her memory. Maybe it wasn't a good idea to talk to her so soon. Other shoppers brushed past Shenza. She stepped to the rail above the docks to let them get by.

Peering down the aisle, Shenza saw her sister at the counter. Her customer was a man about Shenza's age. Chimi looked up at him with a teasing smile that reminded Shenza of Izmay's coyness the night before.

Shenza was surprised to feel a burst of irrational fury. She spun in place and stalked away, sandals slapping the pavement. What was Chimi doing, flirting with that man? The ghosts needed her, and anyway, a girl her age shouldn't be smirking at men that way! After she had complained so much about being restricted, too. It would serve her right if Shenza told Mother everything.

Shenza passed a shady nook with a small fountain and benches. She turned aside, sank onto one of the benches, and sipped from a bamboo dipper. The purl of flowing water soothed her irritation. Shenza let go a sigh. She had promised not to betray Chimi's secret. Although she was starting to wonder how long she could keep her word, it wasn't time to give up yet.

Still, she did want to go home. Shenza had been looking forward to seeing everyone yesterday, and Chimi had taken that away from her. It wasn't fair.

She sipped again from the dipper and went back into the market. This time she sought the fruit stands. Within a few minutes, she headed up the stairs with her travel case in one hand and a small bag of oranges in the other. These were one of Mother's favorite treats.

She walked south along the third tier, into a poor quarter where thatched huts were cramped close together, then up an angled stairway to reach the next level. Her family's home was behind a fence of bamboo poles, which stood up straight after being rebuilt recently. Shenza glanced aside as she passed the area where Chimi had shown her the ghosts during her last visit. Of course, she saw nothing. She rang the gong at the gate.

"Coming!" Her brother's voice came from somewhere in the yard. Shenza heard rustling to her left. A moment later, Sachakeen pushed between two trellises of father-flower vines to lean over the chest-high fence. "Oh, sister. Come on in."

"Thank you." Shenza stepped onto the path that led to the house. Sachakeen came to meet her with a brisk, slapping hug.

"Mother, Shenza's here!" he called, and then more quietly, "We missed you yesterday. Chimi said a case came up?"

So that was how Chimi had explained Shenza not coming yesterday? She didn't know how lucky she was to be right. Still, something in Sachakeen's voice made Shenza look at him twice. Did he doubt Chimi's word?

"I spent the morning uncovering a body." Shenza gave the hem of her robe a shake. Dust and bits of broken leaves swirled around her ankles.

"You did?" Sachakeen stepped back to give her room.

"A body?" Shenza turned as her mother came onto the porch. They embraced, and Giliatt quickly kissed her cheek before accepting the oranges.

"Just the skeleton," Shenza explained. "He had been dead for a few months."

"Do you want to use our bath?" Giliatt asked. She glanced a silent question at Sachakeen. He answered with a tiny nod and Giliatt's tired face relaxed. She was relieved, Shenza guessed. But why?

"It's all right," Shenza said, although a warm bath would have helped get the grit and chill off her feet. "I really just wanted to see you. May I join you for lunch?"

"Of course." Giliatt brightened.

"How has everyone been?" Shenza asked as the three of them strolled into the cottage's main room.

"Oh, we're all fine," Giliatt replied, but Shenza caught a worried undertone in her voice.

Shenza had expected to see Grandmother and Byben sorting floss at the low table, but the workroom was empty. Looking toward their sunny garden, she saw a hammock suspended between two of the porch support posts. Byben lay stretched out in it, apparently napping.

"Grandmother's at the market with Chimi?" Shenza guessed, keeping her voice low to avoid disturbing the old man.

Giliatt nodded as she carried the oranges into the kitchen, but Shenza saw that her shoulders were stiff with tension.

"Let me help," Shenza offered, following her into the kitchen. "I'll make the tea."

Giliatt nodded, and Shenza ladled water into the kettle from a large earthenware jug.

"She's been so restless," Giliatt sighed, bending to reach into a basket under the counter.

"Chimi has?" Shenza guessed. Giliatt nodded.

"We never know whether to believe her," Sachakeen added. Standing in the workroom, he propped both elbows on the counter. "Most of the time, I don't think even she knows what she's saying."

"I see." Shenza could understand why Chimi would have been distracted during the past weeks. However, she didn't want to feed the natural antipathy between brother and sister.

"Is something wrong?" Giliatt asked as Shenza finished filling the kettle.

"Well," Shenza murmured, searching for a way to dance around Chimi's problem yet again. She put the kettle on the stove and bent to add a few sticks to the fire. Heat rose around her, perhaps not from just the stove. Speaking in such low voices, she felt as if she was conspiring against her own sister.

"I did have this investigation yesterday," she finally admitted, "but we had a fight, too."

"You?" Sachakeen gasped with mock horror. "A fight?"

Giliatt, who had been peeling an orange, turned a worried look on her daughter. "What did you fight about?"

Shenza shrugged awkwardly as she crumbled tea leaves into a plain brown teapot. "What you'd expect. That nobody understands her and everyone is persecuting her."

"Oh, right!" Sachakeen slapped the counter top irritably. "It's all our fault."

"Shh," Giliatt cautioned, glancing toward Byben's sleeping form. She added to Shenza, "I hoped Chimi would tell you what's going on."

She had, but Shenza couldn't admit it.

"Grandmother says there's a boy she's been making eyes at," Giliatt continued.

"A boy?" Shenza gazed at both of them, confused. This had nothing to do with ghosts. And there she had thought Chimi told her everything. "She didn't mention any boys."

On the other hand, Shenza remembered how Chimi had been flirting with her customer earlier in the day. Grandmother might have good reason to be concerned.

"Maybe Grandma's thinking about *her* life," Sachakeen smirked.

"Son," Giliatt interrupted with a stern look.

Sachakeen didn't say any more, but there was a mischievous gleam in his eyes. The kettle began to hiss loudly. Shenza took it off the heat and poured steaming water into the teapot, but she felt even more puzzled. What did Sachakeen mean about Grandmother's life? What did that have to do with Chimi?

"Did you at least go shopping?" Giliatt asked when the silence grew too long.

"Oh, yes. She enjoyed that part." Shenza smiled at them with humorous irony. "In fact, I saw Lady Izmay later on, and she said Chimi has excellent taste."

"Good thing she didn't stick around to hear that," Sachakeen snorted. "She'd be bragging about it for weeks."

Shenza and Giliatt both smiled, but Shenza couldn't help feeling a trace of sadness. Chimi would have been thrilled to know that Laraquies and Izmay were seeing each other, but Shenza couldn't share the tidbit even if her sister had been talking to her. A woman like Izmay wouldn't want to be the topic of rumors.

Giliatt arranged the orange slices on a tray along with dried fish and cheese, while Shenza took teacups and plates to the table. Byben showed no sign of waking, so the three of them sat down and ate in silence.

"It's too bad, Shenza," Giliatt murmured after a while. "This is the second death you've had to investigate. Sometimes I wonder what the world is coming to."

"And that man was following Chimi, too," Sachakeen said.

"This case is different," Shenza told them, although it was true that Lord Anges' spectacular murder had only happened a few months ago. It was true that Master Laraquies had never investigated so many deaths during his years as magister. A part of Shenza wondered what she was doing wrong.

Still, Lord Anges' death wasn't like Lelldour's. For one thing, nobody was looking over her shoulder, telling her how to handle the inquest.

"It'll be okay," Sachakeen said, comforting Giliatt.

"I know," she murmured around a mouthful of orange. "I just feel... I don't know. Chimi has me on edge, the way she's been acting. That's all it is."

Sachakeen seemed satisfied, but Shenza wondered if Giliatt had been sensing the dark energy within Chimi. Giliatt might have gifts she didn't realize, or had never learned to use. Both her daughters had strong magic, and they must have inherited it from somewhere.

Then Shenza realized she was feeling something, too. There was a prickle in the air, like spider-feet running up her arms, and a distant rumble, growing louder.

"Do you hear that?" she asked.

Even as she spoke, Shenza felt the first vibrations through her knees. Then the whole house moved around them. The tray and its contents rattled on the table. The tremors grew stronger. Tea sloshed out of cups and something in the kitchen fell with a crash.

"Another earthquake," Giliatt cried, her voice broken up by the shaking. "Everyone get outside!"

The family jumped to their feet and ran for the porch, reeling as the floor shuddered beneath them. Shenza fought back her fear that it could be just as dangerous outside as it was here. What if a tree fell on them?

"Help! What's going on?" Byben sat up, clinging to the sides of his wildly rocking hammock.

"I'll get him," Sachakeen called, and he stumbled toward the hammock. Shenza and Giliatt continued past him, half-falling down the steps into a rain of leaves shaken out of the treetops. The rumbling seemed to come from everywhere at once.

They turned to look back. Sachakeen dragged the old man out of his bed and tried to carry him down the steps. He lost his footing and fell sideways. The two women jumped forward. Shenza reached out to support her brother, while Giliatt helped catch Byben. The four of them backed away from the house, holding each other for balance as the ground heaved under their feet.

After a final spasm, the earth's growling faded. The tremors subsided into a restless flutter. The family stood breathless, poised for more danger.

"That was the worst one yet." Sachakeen spoke in a low voice, as if he feared to start the shaking again.

"I know." Shenza's heart still pounded in her chest. This tremor had definitely been longer and stronger than the others.

"What could be causing all these earthquakes?" Giliatt fanned herself with one hand, a nervous gesture.

Byben, who still leaned on Sachakeen's shoulder, raised a trembling hand. "Maybe that?" he quavered.

Shenza looked where he was pointing and gasped. From this part of the family's yard she could see the waters around Chalsett-port. The shallow sea was dotted with coral isles, like pearls among the shimmering waves. But one of those islands was simply gone, replaced by shoals and foaming, boiling water. A column of smoke and steam rose steadily higher, like a tea stain on the fine fabric of the sky.

"Oh, no," Shenza murmured. She knew that isle. It was a sacred place of the sea spirits. She often went there with Master Laraquies to gather materials for their spellcasting. They always made sure to drop offerings into the sea before they went ashore. It was impossible to recognize the place with churned-up silt fouling the water and fumes polluting the air.

"That's a volcano, isn't it?" Giliatt asked.

"I think so," Shenza said.

As they watched, flickers of fire lit the vapors from within. The shaking hadn't completely stopped, either. She could still feel tiny vibrations through her feet. It really was a volcano, Shenza realized with increasing dread. And very close to the city.

"Is it going to keep growing?" Sachakeen asked.

"Who can tell?" Giliatt replied.

"Is it safe to stay here?" Byben asked.

"Where else can we go?" Sachakeen retorted. "This is our home!"

Shenza had no answers to the questions swirling around her. Logically, she knew that this wasn't her fault. It was beyond her control. But as a sorceress and magister, she had to do something. She was one of Chalsett's defenders. She had to save her family and her city.

"I'd better find Master Laraquies." Shenza was surprised at how calm her voice sounded. A few quick steps took her back into the house, where her travel case was waiting.

"Let us know what he says," Giliatt called after her.

* * *

Grandmother jerked awake from her nap. "What's that?" she demanded.

"I don't know," Chimi answered carelessly.

"Don't just stand there!" the old woman scolded. She grabbed her walking stick and started to get up from her chair.

To keep her calm, Chimi dutifully looked around. Now she did hear something—a kind of rumble, like moth wings beating in the dark. She looked for the source of the noise and saw a line of swell coming across the harbor, right toward the town.

She just had time to think that this wasn't normal. The next instant, the ground bucked beneath her feet. A roar was all around them, like wild wind and pounding surf. Grandmother gave a startled cry. She might have fallen over, but Chimi didn't turn to look. She just clung to her counter for balance.

The noise was all around them as everything shook. Rattan booths rattled in place and boats bashed against the docks. There was a loud crack followed by a crash somewhere nearby. At last the roaring died away and the vibrations smoothed out into stillness.

Chimi's heart was still jumping, as if the shaking within her wasn't quite over. There sure had been a lot of earthquakes lately.

"Well, that was exciting," she managed to joke.

"Don't be a fool," Grandmother snapped.

The old woman really had fallen, though her attitude didn't make Chimi feel very sorry for her. She looked all right. In the next booth, Nakuri hadn't fared so well. The support poles had given way, dumping her canopy and dried fishes onto the ground. All down the line of booths, merchandise lay scattered and awnings billowed loose. Chimi's booth had been one of the few to stand up to the tremor.

"Nakuri?" Chimi called as she stepped over to give Grandmother a hand up.

"I'm all right."

Chimi heard Nakuri's voice, but she couldn't see her. Something was moving around under the fallen canopy. A stunned silence had followed the earthquake, but now Chimi heard terrified wails rising over the marketplace.

"Hang on, I'm coming," Chimi called to Nakuri. To Grandmother, she asked, "Were you hurt?"

"I'm fine," Myri said, although her voice sounded as wobbly as some of the booths. Chimi steadied her for a moment, then hooked the chair leg with her foot.

"Why don't you sit and catch your breath," Chimi suggested as she dragged the chair over to them. "I'll see who else needs help."

Grandmother nodded. "Go." As Chimi went to help Nakuri, she heard the old woman mutter, "It'll be the first kind thing you've done in days."

Chimi scowled and yanked at the canopy that had fallen over Nakuri's booth. Nothing she did was ever good enough! Why did Grandmother have to be so mean?

* * *

Shenza hurried along the street that led to the marketplace. She could guess some things without Master Laraquies' help.

There had never been any sign of a volcano near Chalsett before. The only power great enough to raise one belonged to the nature spirits. Someone must have really offended them, to make them destroy a sacred place. The obvious solution was to go to the spirits. Maybe she could find out what was wrong and try to placate them.

She went back to the market looking for an offering. Not surprisingly, there was a lot of damage from the latest tremor. The ground around the giant fig tree was covered with loose figs. All kinds of merchandise lay on the ground—vegetables, flowers, tools, baskets. She saw a flock of chickens flapping madly, pursued by shouting shopkeepers.

While the vendors tried to clean up, the market was emptying rapidly. Shoppers talked anxiously among themselves about the noise, the shaking, the ominous cloud growing offshore. Shenza hadn't thought anything could be frightening enough to close the market. Now she knew better.

She considered going to the fish market, to see if Chimi and Grandmother were all right, but then she remembered how Chimi had been acting. If Chimi needed help, she could recruit one of her handsome customers. All the girl seemed to care about was men.

Shenza walked away, but her resolve only held for a few steps before she sighed and turned around. Chimi was her sister, no matter how difficult she was being. Shenza quickened her steps when she saw that almost a whole row of fish stalls had collapsed, but then she glimpsed her sister bustling around, helping Nakuri gather her wares off the ground. Chimi was all right.

Satisfied, Shenza continued on her way. She bought a handful of cassia bark from a distracted shopkeeper and hurried up to the fourth terrace. The town shrine was an ancient building, marble walls topped by a roof of weathered tiles. Tall support pillars were carved with plant, sea and cloud motifs. A shallow pool lay in the center, with jutting rocks to symbolize the many islands of the Jewel Sea.

One side of the building was open on a wide view of the town and the sea beyond. The new volcano was clearly visible. Its vapor cloud was spreading toward Chalsett-port, creeping over the water like some faceless beast.

Three bronze statues stood on low pedestals under the sheltering roof. Each statue had a brazier before it. The coals winked and flared as townsfolk made their offerings. A woman dropped a handful of silver coins into one brazier, begging aloud for the sea spirits to let her family get away from Chalsett. Nearby, a man poured wine into the fire. He leaned forward as steam billowed out, whispering his prayer into the rising fumes.

A short line of people waited. As Shenza joined the queue, she studied the idols. Legend said there were three kinds of nature spirits. Eleshi, which she had personally seen, controlled animals, plants and fertility. Eleshouri were masters of the sea and the fishes within it. Elitheri, lords of the sky, controlled the weather and all flying creatures. These beings were represented as humans, standing with hands open both to give blessings and receive offerings. Graceful as the statues were, they didn't capture the alien beauty of the spirits as Shenza remembered it. But then, no mere human craftsman could.

No one seemed to be wasting any time. They prayed quickly and hurried off. Shenza wondered how many of the residents were planning to flee, like the woman with the coins. As the last supplicant scurried away, she found herself alone. Shenza stepped forward, bowing to all three statues before she took her offering to the altar of the Eleshouri. She scattered the incense on the brazier and bowed again.

"Lords of the waves, have mercy," she began. Flames crackled around her offering, and its heady fragrance flowed upward with the smoke. "Your servant is foolish and ignorant, but even such a fool can see that you are angry. Your wrath has made the earth tremble and the waters shake. Your loyal servant begs you to say what has been done to displease you. Let her know whatever small thing she can to do to restore your favor."

Shenza's voice seemed to echo strangely inside the shrine. The building darkened around her, and for the second time that day an invisible draft raised the hairs along her arms. Weird gurgles came from behind her, almost like words of a foreign tongue. With a thrill of dread, she realized that her prayer had been heard.

Fear made her knees stiff and slow to respond, but she forced herself to turn. The shrine was dark because the volcanic vapors had reached it. Pale tendrils filled the sanctuary, bringing with them damp heat and a foul, sulphurous odor. The water in the reflecting pool churned. Shenza choked back a cry of fear as a column of spray abruptly rose toward the sky.

Just as suddenly, it contracted into a humanlike form. She had the impression of an unnaturally tall, gangly frame, translucent skin, eyes bright and hard as pearls. Its mouth was a sharp beak, like a fish's. On its head, something more like a sea-whip's tentacles than hair flowed down to merge with swirling liquid robes. As with the spirit Shenza remembered, this being was neither male nor female. It had narrow, masculine hips and small breasts with no nipples. Some part of it always seemed to be moving, watery drips and curls that mingled and separated at random.

Shenza crossed her hands on her chest and bowed deeply. "Lord of the Waves, you honor this unworthy servant."

"We hear you, human," came a voice like rushing water. "Now hear us."

She fell silent, her throat dry. Along with its alien beauty, she had forgotten the powerful presence of the nature spirits. Between that and the choking fumes, Shenza could hardly breathe.

"One of you creatures has stolen from us," the Eleshouri announced with angry scorn. "Our punishment shall be swift. The blood that flows from our wounds shall overwhelm your puny village and burn your kind from our sea."

Shenza had seen the wrath of the spirits before. She remembered all too well how the legendary monster, Taisaris, had patrolled the harbor entrance and sent a great wave smashing into the town. She couldn't let that happen again.

"Your unworthy servant begs for mercy," she said, although she was afraid to offend the spirit even more by interrupting. When it didn't turn on her, she hurried on. "Please give your servant a chance to return what was taken. This is her duty as magister."

"We gave you warnings," the spirit replied, "though you were slow to perceive them."

Shenza bowed, fighting her panic. She had been right all along. The earthquakes had been a warning of the spirits' anger.

"My people are weak," Shenza began to apologize, but the Eleshouri interrupted her.

"A hole was made," it said, tendril hair twitching in sharp jerks to emphasize its anger. "Our sand was taken, the stuff of our own body.

Imagine, human, if you slept and found that your flesh had been cut away in the night."

"My only desire is to right this wrong," Shenza said. She couldn't help shuddering at the image in her mind. "Only tell your servant how to find this person."

"The thief was hidden from us," it said.

"How is it possible that the mighty lords should be deceived?" Shenza asked.

"The thief came at noontime, when the sun steals our power." Silvery-pearl eyes narrowed, as if the Eleshouri resented having to admit any weakness. "Even we know nothing more."

Shenza was silent, daunted by the knowledge that she was expected to find a criminal when the most powerful beings in the world couldn't do it.

"You have been touched by our kind before," the spirit went on. "Thus we give you this one chance to redeem yourself. Return what was stolen and deliver the thief to us. But be swift, for the blood still flows from our wound. You tiny creatures, who have forgotten your place, may yet suffer our vengeance."

With a sound between a gurgle and a growl, the Eleshouri sank into the ripples of the pool. Before Shenza could protest, it was gone.

Chapter Fourteen

Too Much Honor

The last ripples smoothed away on the pond and volcanic fog cleared with magical speed. Shenza blinked as daylight filtered into the shrine. She felt as if she had fallen asleep on her feet and was just waking up. Fear of the Eleshouri's threats clung to her like the remnant of a nightmare.

Faint voices told her that more people were coming to pray. She hurried out of the building, terrified that someone would ask her about what had just happened. She didn't know where to go or what to do, but she couldn't stand still. As her head cleared, she realized there was only one possibility. She would have to go to the palace. Lord Aspace and Master Laraquies needed to know what the Eleshouri had said.

Then she looked down at herself. Her purple robe was dusty up to the knees, and a faint odor of rotten leaves clung to its folds. Chimi's voice scolded in her mind that this wasn't how a young lady should present herself to her lord. Not if she wanted to fit in.

Just thinking of her sister irritated Shenza all over again. Chimi had always been the pretty one, never needing to worry about her looks. Still, respect for her own position as magister was enough to make her go home. Laraquies wasn't there, but she hadn't expected him to be. Shenza hurried to the small bath house behind their cottage. Water trickled in from the garden, warmed by magic symbols glazed into the ceramic basin. She sat on its edge to wash the grit from her feet and hands.

As she cleaned up, Shenza repeated her encounter with the spirits in her mind. She remembered the Eleshouri's odd proportions, and especially the weird angles of its face. The Eleshi she had met hadn't looked like that. Its human shape had been both beautiful and natural. Now that she was calmer, the analytical side of her wondered if the Eleshouri were less skilled at taking human form because they were beings of the elements and had less of the beast within them.

Once dry, she smoothed on fragrant oil. Dressed in a clean robe, headcloth neatly tucked in, she set off again, ordering the gate to lock itself behind her. Clouds hung thick overhead, threatening rain at any moment, but the pavement stayed dry as she climbed the central stair. A familiar nervous flutter started in her chest as she approached the palace gate.

Two officers of the palace guard stood with spears crossed, barring the way. Rakshel was their captain, as usual.

"State your business," he called, though he had to know who Shenza was.

"Magister Shenza, seeking Vizier Laraquies," she answered.

"You may enter." Rakshel sounded faintly bored. The two guards raised their spears.

"Good day," Shenza murmured as she walked between them.

A young page in a blue kilt sprang up from a bench just inside the gate. "Master Laraquies is attending my Lord Aspace in the Peridot Court. May I guide you?"

"Very well," Shenza replied, although she could have found her own way.

She followed the page, who strutted ahead with childish importance. Shenza barely noticed as they passed a pond whose surface was drab with the reflection of clouds. Lord Aspace wouldn't be pleased by what she had to say. He hadn't liked it when the Eleshi claimed kinship with him. Now the Eleshouri threatened his city with volcanic fire. No one who lived there was safe from their wrath.

Shenza's breath caught in her throat as she realized what she had been thinking. It would be hard enough to protect the people of Chalsett from the spirits' wrath, let alone a group of visitors. Hope flickered in her breast. Considering the danger, maybe Lord Aspace would cancel Lord Manseen's visit. That would be wonderful! Shenza tried to push the idea from her mind. It wasn't her decision to make.

The pathway curved, climbed a set of stone steps, and brought them to the Peridot Court. It was a small plaza ringed by a low marble wall. Thick moss grew over half-sunken paving stones. Honeysuckle vines covered the wall with yellow blossoms and perfumed the air. Wooden benches formed an arc near the center of the pavement. Lord Aspace and Master Laraquies sat on two of these, facing a man who stood at the center of the arc. The man's voice was a low rumble of words that she couldn't distinguish.

They wouldn't have mattered anyway. Shenza's eyes caught on Lord Aspace, leaving all else a blur. He lounged, as always, with one arm thrown over the back of his bench and a jeweled goblet held carelessly against his knee. Disappointment and longing swirled within her. Shenza reminded herself that she had no chance to be with Aspace. There was no point in looking, but she couldn't seem to turn away.

The page didn't stop when Shenza did. He went ahead, ready to announce her presence. Shenza leaned forward and caught his shoulder.

"I'll wait here," she whispered to the boy.

He retreated with a crestfallen air. Shenza sucked in a breath of relief as she focused her attention on what was happening.

"Are you sure it's the same island?" Laraquies was asking.

"When the fishermen first reported it, I went to see for myself," the man replied. As he spoke, Shenza recognized Harbormaster Arze. He was an older man with a grizzled head and features toned dark by the sun. He wore a plain brown kilt and a short robe, for Arze worked shoulder to shoulder with shipmasters and crewmen rather than wearing fine robes and staying in a comfortable office.

"Someone has been to the sacred isles," Arze confirmed. "I saw marks of a small boat up on the beach, and footprints around it."

"How many people?" Laraquies inquired.

"Just one set of tracks, Vizier. Farther up, a hole had been dug, perhaps this size." Arza extended his arms, making a basket in the air before him. "It was too far from the water for digging clams, and anyway, no one takes just one clam. They dug something up, though I can't guess what."

"And you saw this on the morning after the first earthquake?" Aspace asked.

"My Lord is correct."

The sacred isles? Shenza's heart gave a lurch. Arze might have seen evidence of the robbery the Eleshouri had told her about.

"I thought sorcerers often gathered materials from those islands," Aspace said.

"Small items," Laraquies agreed. "A few leaves or a stalk of bamboo. Those things the spirits touch have special potence. You only need a little. No one should dig a hole there. Such presumption would offend the spirits."

Shenza knew Lord Aspace was skeptical about the spirits, and his expression showed it. He asked, "What do you think they took?"

"I saw a hole," Arze said, "but no piles of sand."

"Could they have taken the sand itself?" Laraquies asked.

"Why would they want sand?" Aspace nearly laughed with scorn. "There's plenty here in Chalsett-port. We dredge the harbor often enough."

Shenza shifted uneasily, and her sandals scraped the pavement. Everyone looked around at the unexpected noise. Lord Aspace frowned slightly. Shenza bowed at once. She felt terribly exposed without her mask to conceal her feelings.

"I beg my Lord's pardon," she murmured.

Aspace eyed Shenza irritably, but then seemed to relax. Laraquies smiled and patted the bench beside him, but there was little point in sitting down.

"I also have information on what Master Arze observed," Shenza said. She walked stiffly to stand beside the much taller harbormaster. Laraquies raised one eyebrow in gentle curiosity.

"Go ahead." Aspace waved at her lazily.

"The spirits have spoken to me," Shenza began. She nodded slightly to Arze, trying to sound as calm as Master Laraquies did when he spoke before the court. "The harbormaster is correct. The sand is what was stolen. Or, as the Eleshouri said, the flesh of its body was taken."

"The spirits spoke to you?" Aspace interrupted.

Shenza bowed again. "Forgive your servant for saying that which upsets you."

He surprised her by shrugging. "If you say it was the spirits, I believe you."

"My Lord honors me," Shenza stammered. It was hard to tell if he really meant that. "After the latest tremor, your servant went to the town shrine to pray for mercy. An Eleshouri came to me there."

Arze took a half step away, as if distance could protect him from the spirits' anger. As for Aspace, he swirled his goblet idly and stared into its depths with narrowed eyes.

Laraquies asked, "What else did the spirit say?"

"They want justice," she said. "The tremors we've felt are their shudders of pain, and the volcano that rises come from the sea is the blood that flows from their wounds."

"Spirits want justice from humans?" Aspace asked sharply.

"Or revenge," she answered. "As to my Lord's question, all things touched by the spirits contain great power, just as Master Laraquies says. Whoever stole the sand took a big risk that the spirits would punish them. They must plan to use it for some kind of magic, and it has to be important or it wouldn't be worth the risk."

She glanced at her teacher, but the old man shook his head. "I don't know of any enchantments like that, although I can certainly look into it."

"It will be interesting to see if someone suddenly starts showing more power than they used to have," Aspace said.

"True," Shenza murmured. That could be one way of finding out who had desecrated the sacred isles. Unfortunately, they might find out too late to stop whatever the thief had planned.

She cleared her throat and added, "Forgive your servant for speaking out of turn, but should my Lord have a group of guests now? As long as the volcano grows, everyone here is in danger."

Again, she tried to sound calm, not as if she was trying to shape the first lord's policy. Aspace's eyes blazed, but he smiled at her, a dazzling and dagger-edged smile. Shenza felt her cheeks warming.

"I won't be driven from my home," he said pleasantly, "by the spirits or anyone else."

"As my Lord says." Shenza was sorry she hadn't sat down when Laraquies suggested it. Before she could say any more, something cool touched her shoulder. Raindrops struck the paving stones with heavy splats that came loud in the stillness.

Lord Aspace glanced skyward. He looked annoyed, as if the rain had come at this moment just to bother him. Then he stood up. "We'll have to discuss this. Come."

Laraquies and Shenza both bowed, preparing to follow him, but Arze looked uncertain. "What would my Lord have me do?"

"For now, nothing," Aspace said, sounding more like himself. "It's good that you brought me this information, Harbormaster. I'll let you know if there's anything else. Only..." He paused, then seemed to come to a decision. "If people want to leave, don't stop them."

That was a courageous choice, Shenza thought, since it might leave Aspace as lord of an empty town.

"If my Lord permits," Laraquies interposed. At Aspace's nod, he said, "Don't let our guardsmen go, even if their families do. We'll need them to keep order if we have to evacuate."

"As my Lord commands." Arze crossed both hands over his chest and bowed before walking away.

A gravel path angled up the hillside behind the Peridot Court, where a lone cottage stood behind a screen of flowering trees. Aspace went up the path without looking to see if anyone else was coming. Shenza and Master Laraquies had no choice but to follow.

Raindrops chased them up the steps and a warm wind tugged at their robes. Dust stung Shenza's eyes, making her blink. Lord Aspace paused just beneath the overhanging roof. He raised his hands, and Shenza felt the prickle of magic in the air. Lamp light flowed out of the house, like a hostess eager to meet them.

"Come in." Aspace said as Shenza followed Laraquies onto the porch. "Sit down."

Laraquies bowed briefly and stepped inside. Lord Aspace quickly lowered a set of fabric screens, cutting the wind from outside. Shenza felt a moment's surprise that no servants waited to do it for him. She hesitated, realizing she was about to enter Aspace's personal quarters. Then the habit of obedience won out and she followed her teacher inside.

It wasn't the luxurious mansion she had expected. Shenza had seen his brother's house during the murder investigation. Lord Anges' decorating had been lavish and complicated, some wonder of fabric or carving revealed wherever she looked. Most of it had favored the brilliant royal blue, a boast of Anges' exalted position.

By contrast, Lord Aspace's home was small and simple. The main floor was open for entertaining, with an upper level accessible by a few steps. Silk screens, painted with jungle scenes, shielded his private room from view. From one side, a huge red ape gazed like a sad old man. A river-bear lurked on the opposite side. The cushions and hangings were all in muted greens. Porcelain lamps shaped like huge white hibiscus blossoms glowed on the walls. Shenza joined Master Laraquies beside a low table, teak inlaid with ivory.

"Do you want anything?" Aspace asked as he joined them. "Tea? Fruit?"

"My Lord is kind, but your servant isn't hungry," Shenza answered quickly. Even if she hadn't eaten with her family, her stomach felt tight with nervousness.

"Nor I," Laraquies said. "If my Lord recalls, Lady Izmay is expecting me. I can't stay long."

"I do remember." Aspace's lips quirked in a smile as he settled on another cushion across the table from Shenza. It sounded as though he knew how much time Laraquies and Izmay were spending together. She wondered how he felt about seeing another man court his mother.

Although they had been invited in, Shenza still felt like an intruder. She cast about for something to say.

"I meant to tell you," she said, turning to Master Laraquies, "we did find Lelldour's body this morning."

Laraquies nodded somberly. "I hoped you wouldn't."

"So did I."

"Mother told me about that," Aspace cut in. "So it was his ghost you saw?"

"I'm afraid so," Shenza said. It took a moment to remember that Lady Izmay had said she would tell her son about Lelldour's disappearance. "His family is supposed to live on the dawn side of the island. I'll have to find some way to let them know what's happened."

"First ghosts and now spirits," Aspace mused. He angled his head to eye her with droll mockery. "You do have the most interesting friends."

Shenza faltered, momentarily confused. How did he know about Chimi? No, now she remembered. He was referring to Makko's illusion, which had pretended to be the ghost of Lord Anges.

"If my Lord recalls," she said, "that was a phantasm, not a true ghost." Then she stopped, suddenly struck by something. The two men waited. Shenza couldn't concentrate with Aspace watching her. She closed her eyes, mentally counting hands of days.

"What is it?" Laraquies prompted.

"Something Mother said." Shenza opened her eyes and saw Aspace still looking at her with wry humor. "I'm guessing that Lelldour died a little more than two months ago. I'll have to review my records, but it seems like my Lord Anges died at nearly the same time."

"You think the deaths are related?" Laraquies asked.

"It could be coincidence," Shenza answered quickly. "There's nothing to make me think so except the timing, and I'm not sure of that."

There was a silence. Aspace stared at Shenza, his green eyes strangely brilliant but his expression inscrutable. Shenza wondered what he saw when he looked at her that way, or if he truly saw her at all. She cleared her throat, prepared to apologize if his brother's death still upset him.

"When did you say Lelldour died?" Laraquies asked.

"He didn't know," Shenza said, glad to look away from her lord's intense gaze.

"Then how can you say he died at the same time as Anges?" Aspace demanded.

"From the condition of the remains," Shenza told him. "We found his body in a thicket, covered by leaves. The ants had stripped it down to the bones, and that takes time. Also—"

"Who's we?" Aspace interrupted.

"Myself and Juss Battour of Reiloon," Shenza said. "You remember him." Aspace nodded. "Go on."

"Well, I'm speculating that Lelldour died a little more than two months ago, because his neighbors moved in around that time and the children noticed an odor in the yard. Lelldour must already have been dead then."

"The smell can't have been very strong," Laraquies remarked.

"Maybe," Shenza said. "The adults might have ignored the children's complaints, but they would have moved if the odor was enough to bother them, too. It must have been longer than two months. Say, three months. But I don't know how that matches with my Lord Anges' death."

"I can tell you that," Aspace said.

He sprang to his feet and jogged up the steps to his chamber. Aspace soon returned, carrying a scroll tied with shiny blue cord. He dropped back onto his cushion and pulled at the cord. Shenza caught a glimpse of elegant script as he opened the scroll. His green eyes moved, scanning the document.

"Here it is." Aspace turned the scroll toward Laraquies and Shenza.

The scroll was Aspace's own journal. Shenza fought back a twinge of embarrassment as she leaned forward to read. Aspace held the scroll to reveal only one entry. It began with *"Coronation today,"* but the date took Shenza's mind off the rest of his words.

She sat back, counting backward in her head. When she looked up, Aspace was watching her with that intense, dispassionate gaze. As their eyes met, Shenza felt a shiver tickle her spine.

"They may have died on the same day," Laraquies' thoughtful voice shattered the moment. Aspace turned toward him, and Shenza felt instant relief.

"So it seems." The first lord re-rolled his scroll, tying the cord with quick jerks. "Anges died, what, seven days before the coronation?"

"And he got all the attention." Shenza took up the tale, pleased that her voice was steady. "Because of his position, or perhaps because his murder was so much more..." She hesitated, groping for the right word.

"Spectacular? Grandiose?" Aspace suggested with a bite in his tone. "Everything he did was like that, even his death."

Laraquies shrugged, deflecting the hostility. "While everyone was focused on Lord Anges, the necromancer died quietly, unnoticed."

Something in his soft voice made Shenza's stomach tighten again. A part of her, her cautious and didactic self, reminded her that she had no evidence of any link between the two deaths. The sorceress in her, trained to sense the unseen, had no doubt of it. Yet she couldn't believe Lord Anges' murder had been nothing but a diversion. It was too drastic an action, unless the stakes were very high.

The cottage was quiet as each of them thought about what they were learning. A faint flicker of lightning came from outside, and then a distant growl of thunder. The rain came down harder.

"I didn't want to mention it in front of Harbormaster Arze," Laraquies said quietly, "but it does seem to me that I once heard a story where sand was used in a spell."

"What kind of spell?" Aspace asked.

And Shenza said, "Why didn't you want Arze to know?"

"It does no good to start rumors," Laraquies told her. "I can't remember all the details, but it was something about a necromancer who aspired to be as powerful as the spirits. He created a golem, a creature neither living nor dead. No human could stand against its power. No sorcery could touch it. Not even the spirits could affect it."

"He made it with sand?" Shenza's hands tightened in her lap as she considered how many people would like to have that kind of magical servant.

"And other things." Her teacher nodded. As always, his weathered face was serene and untouched by the fear Shenza felt.

"But..?" Aspace prompted.

"In time, his creation turned against him. They were both destroyed," Laraquies replied. "At least, I think that was the tale. It's been many years."

"Would you please try to find someone else who knows that story?" Aspace asked with another of his knife-edged smiles. "I'd like to hear it all the way through."

"As my Lord commands." Laraquies bowed from the waist. As he straightened, he added, "I should go. With my Lord's permission?"

"Go ahead." Aspace waved negligently.

Laraquies stood up, backed a step away, and bowed again. Turning, he tugged on the ties that fastened the shades. Shenza felt a burst of panic as he let himself out. She ought to leave, too. It wasn't right for a young woman to be alone with a man.

"Did your mother have any other ideas?" Aspace asked with a sweet sting.

"I'm afraid not." Shenza wished he wouldn't tease her. It made her feel things that would only hurt her in the end. A little defensively, she added, "I assure you, I don't discuss the details of investigations with my family."

"I never said so." Aspace looked pleased to have provoked her.

Shenza tried to be annoyed with him, as he deserved, but it was hard. "Does my Lord require anything else?" she asked.

"Is it always about what I require?" he asked back at her. Aspace used a casual tone, but she had the feeling he was irritated with her. "Is my company so disagreeable?"

"No," Shenza said. It seemed an inadequate response.

In her mind, she heard Chimi saying she would be insane to leave now. Lord Aspace was single, and she liked him so much. She had seen, as Laraquies left, that the rain was slowing to a light patter. The air felt heavy and humid. Shenza had to admit that there was a certain guilty excitement in doing what she shouldn't. Where was the harm in a few minutes together on a rainy afternoon?

"Good," Aspace said, interrupting her internal dialogue. "If we'll be working together, I want to know you better."

He leaned back, swirling his cup idly. Gems winked as it moved. Shenza thought she heard a familiar undertone. It was his pretending-not-to-care voice. Which implied that he did care about something—she didn't know what—enough that he was afraid of being embarrassed.

Shenza studied the ivory inlay of the table top and thought about it. Her heart leapt like a netted fish. Did Aspace really want to spend time with her? But what was the point? They couldn't be together.

Now Shenza wished she had accepted when he offered her tea. It would have given her something to do with her hands. She searched for a different subject to talk about. The only thing they had in common was troublesome siblings. Maybe Aspace could even suggest what to do about Chimi.

"May I ask..." she began.

"That depends what you want to ask," he countered, playfully intrigued. Shenza wondered why he always played these games.

Shenza tried again, "My Lord once told me..."

"Stop." Aspace raised his hand, suddenly irritated again. "I've told you before, it's tiresome being my-lorded all the time. Just say you and me."

Shenza met his gaze for a moment, then looked away as her cheeks began to burn. Could she be misreading his intentions? Maybe this wasn't what it felt like.

"As long as it's in private conversation," she finally said. "I can't be so familiar in public. People would talk."

"Propriety." He sighed with mock despair. "I suppose I must allow you that. So..?" He trailed off, inviting her question.

Shenza swallowed, trying to keep her back straight while his smile made her feel weak all over. She fumbled to remember what her question had been.

"My... Uh, you once said that you didn't get along with my Lord Anges," she said.

Aspace nodded, his expression intense. Shenza chose her words carefully.

"You said he would harass you when my Lord Asbel wasn't paying attention. Did he ever do something, something wrong, that you knew about but your parents didn't?"

Aspace sat back slightly, leaning one elbow on the table. "Once or twice," he said, but his droll tone implied it had been much more often than that.

"What did you do?" Shenza asked.

"Nothing, usually." Aspace's green eyes darkened with some memory. "We were natural rivals, I suppose. Anges didn't like to share, even though he was the oldest and got first chance at everything. He took anything I did as a threat. So, of course, whatever I said would have been dismissed as jealousy."

"Then you didn't tell what he had done?" Shenza wondered if this gave her permission to keep Chimi's secret.

"Sometimes I did, if it was important," he said. "If someone got hurt, especially, then I told Mother and she would tell Father. After a while, our nursemaids knew to keep us apart."

Shenza nodded, feeling sympathy for a man whose childhood had been warped by politics and jealousy. Aspace tilted his head slyly.

"Does this have to do with anyone I know?" he asked, again with that feigned casualness.

"No," Shenza answered. Although Chimi had been presented to the first lord once, that didn't really count as knowing him.

"I can rest easy, then." Aspace touched his brow with exaggerated relief. Shenza couldn't help smiling in return.

He quickly sobered. "It's interesting that you mention Anges. I've never been satisfied with the explanation for his death."

As he spoke, another tremor shook the house. They both tensed, waiting to see how bad it would get. When the sound and shaking had faded, Shenza's happiness had evaporated like a puddle in the sunshine.

"I'm sorry that I failed my... failed you," she murmured.

"Did I say that?" Aspace asked back at her. "I didn't like Anges, but he was my brother. Someone hired Makko to burn him alive. I want to find out who it was."

"As I do," Shenza tried not to sound defensive.

"I think you'll have the chance." Aspace was brooding now, swirling his cup idly.

When he didn't go on, Shenza prodded, "My Lord?"

He looked over at her piercing green eyes. "Four months ago, I was vying with Tenbei Bosteel of Bosteel to be Justice Minister Ittaht's chief aide. Everyone knew Bosteel's main qualification was his family connections. And there was more—odd purchases, secretive meetings. I never got the chance to figure out what they were up to, because my brother suddenly died. I had to leave Porphery and take his place here. Now that man's father wants to call on me."

"You were investigating them?" Shenza asked. But that didn't change the painful facts. "And his daughter..."

"Who Tenbei never mentioned to me," Aspace interrupted. "It doesn't make sense. Not unless the introductions are just a ploy to cover up something else. Such as maybe finding out why Makko isn't responding to communications. But even if it doesn't have anything to do with Anges, I still want to know what interests them about my town."

No wonder Aspace had wanted her to spy on Lord Manseen. Shenza dared to ask, "Have you told my Lady Izmay what you suspect?"

Aspace shook his head. "Mother is retired. She deserves to enjoy herself."

That was an interesting perspective on Izmay's apparent romance with Laraquies. But Shenza felt compelled to say, "I can't help feeling that she would want to know who ordered her son's murder."

"I'll tell mother when I think it's necessary," Aspace retorted.

It was unmistakably a warning. "I understand," Shenza said. Then, "Lord Bosteel commands a powerful house."

"Here, I have the advantage," Aspace said. "As long as he's in my town, I can deal with him as a first lord. No visitor can match that." He spoke with a familiar snap, as a ruler giving orders to his servant. "You can go on investigating the necromancer's death, but it would be best if you finished before my guests arrive. I'll be counting on you and Juss while they're here."

"I'll do my best." Shenza bowed slightly across the table. Defying convention did have its attraction, but she was glad to be back on a normal footing.

"I know you will," Aspace said with a ruler's casual arrogance. Then he added, "Laraquies boasts about you, did you know? Nurune can't stand it."

"No, I didn't know that." Shenza felt her cheeks coloring.

"Every time I talk to you, I understand why."

Aspace's eyes were strangely gentle, but Shenza ducked her head to avoid his gaze. The compliment seemed too good to be true. A shiver ran down her spine. The sultry afternoon was one with his nearness, both wonderful and unbearable. Shenza groped under the table for her travel case, as if it could shield her from the chaos of her own emotions.

"You honor me too much," she managed to whisper. "I must go."

"If you must." Aspace sounded resigned, and faintly bored. That was never a good sign.

Moments later, Shenza hurried down the steps. She let the last of the rain cool her face. This, she thought, was exactly the reason that young women weren't left alone with men.

Chapter Fifteen

Questions Not Answered

Another tremor rattled through the house. Nothing broke this time, and Chimi hardly noticed it. She was in the kitchen, trying to act busy so she could listen to the conversation in the workroom.

"What should we do?" Sachakeen asked. He had joined Giliatt, Grandmother and Byben at the work table. They were talking about the volcano, of course. Since this morning, it was all anyone wanted to talk about.

"What can we do?" Giliatt replied. It was a logical question, but she still sounded worried.

"We can't control the elements," Byben said. "We must be patient." The old man knelt at the table between Grandmother and Giliatt, counting the day's receipts. They had been pathetically small after the earthquake scared everyone so much.

"Toaran's family is packing to leave," Sachakeen said, naming a friend two houses down. "They're going to stay with relatives in Amethan-port."

Chimi scowled to herself. Sachakeen wasn't that much older than she was. Just because he was a boy, he got to be part of the conversation. It wasn't fair.

"We can't leave Chalsett," Grandmother said sternly. "Our ancestors were born here. This is our home."

That wasn't exactly true. The family didn't own the house. They just rented it. Glancing around, Chimi saw the sparse furnishings as if for the first time. There really wasn't anything they couldn't leave behind. It felt strange to admit that.

Then Chimi caught a hard glance from Grandmother. She concentrated on slicing the leftover fish from the booth and slipping it into broth to simmer. With all the shoppers scared away, there were a lot of extras today. You'd think Grandmother would be in a better mood, since she'd had a nap during the afternoon. Chimi hid a smirk, remembering how Winomi had come by with steamed buns. They had both had a good laugh at Grandmother drooling in her sleep.

That reminded Chimi of something. The furniture might not be worth much, but all her friends were here. She couldn't leave Chalsett-port. She would miss them too much, especially Winomi.

Giliatt sighed. "We just started a new crop. We won't have any money until it comes in."

"We still have some seed," Sachakeen argued. "If it's not safe here, we can take them with us. Didn't you say you already fell once today, Grandma?"

"You fell?" Byben gasped with immediate concern.

"It was nothing," the old woman said, though she looked gratified by his attention. "Just the earthquake."

"You have to be careful," Byben cautioned.

Chimi lifted a pot lid to see how the steamed greens were coming. Now that she thought about it, Byben himself might be one of the things they had to leave behind. He was a good friend, but he wasn't family. If Sachakeen got his way, would they say good-bye to Byben? That was a horrible idea! And it would be nice if someone asked Chimi what she wanted to do.

"We don't have to decide now," Giliatt was saying. "Maybe the volcano will stop and everything will be fine."

"Maybe," Sachakeen muttered. Then he looked at Chimi. With an edge, he said, "By the way, sister, I wanted to tell you. Remember that investigation Shenza had?"

He paused dramatically, waiting until Chimi was forced to answer him.

"What about it?" she asked warily.

"She and Juss found his body today," Sachakeen announced.

"Ooh," Chimi shuddered. Then she demanded, "How do you know?"

"Shenza had lunch with us today," Mother said. "Right before the big earthquake."

"That's nice," Chimi said, though panic fluttered in her chest. She stirred the fish furiously. Why couldn't Shenza just leave things alone? It wasn't like Lelldour had been anyone important.

Her feelings must have shown on her face, because Sachakeen snorted, "Calm down. It doesn't have anything to do with you."

If only he knew. Her brother was still looking at her, as if he knew something he wasn't saying. No—as if he expected her to say something else. Well, she wasn't going to fall for it.

In a way, Chimi was surprised that Shenza hadn't told them about her escapades with the ghosts. Then she felt ashamed to think that. Shenza was *so* upright and dependable. Of course she hadn't told.

There was no reason for Chimi to worry. Nobody knew her secret, but they might find out if she gave herself away. She had to be careful.

Now Mother was looking at her, too, an unspoken question in her dark eyes. Chimi quickly ladled fish and broth over rice and steamed greens.

"Is anyone hungry?" she asked with all the sweetness she could summon. "Dinner's ready. Let's not let it get cold!"

She pushed bowls across the counter and quickly turned back to check on the wood stove. All this guessing and wondering hardly left her with any appetite. As she slouched in her place, Chimi saw the small stack of coins Byben had left for her. Immediately, her tension vanished.

Turning toward the elders' table, Chimi saw Byben nod with a twinkle in his eye. Sometimes she thought he was the only one who cared about her at all.

* * *

Two days passed in pleasant boredom. No ghosts bothered Chimi, and Shenza didn't try to tell her her duty. Jeruki did drop by with news that Azma's parents were considering an offer of marriage from a young man of Sengool House, but Chimi refused to let it bother her. Even Grandmother seemed to be tired of harping at her. The old woman had let Chimi choose her own jewelry this morning, and she hadn't had to beg at all.

Only the frequent earthquakes still darkened her days. The market stalls were back up, but business wasn't what it had been. The shaking kept everyone on edge. The new volcano grew like an unsightly wart on the face of the sea. Sometimes, as now, the wind carried its fumes toward Chalsettport. It made the whole town smell as if something had died.

Chimi wrinkled her nose, waiting for the noxious plume to blow off. A muffled snore at the back of the booth told her that Grandmother was napping again. That was what she did most days. Chimi supposed that the considerate thing would have been to bring a parasol, so her elder could have a bit of shade. Unfortunately for Grandmother, Chimi wasn't interested in consideration anymore. Where had it gotten her?

She glanced aside, and was surprised to see Rellad of Melleen coming her way. He scurried anxiously instead of sauntering the way he usually did. Chimi felt a moment's disappointment. She would rather have seen Ginro of Keerith, her current favorite customer. He was a jeweler's apprentice, and very handsome. Chimi's mouth watered just thinking about the presents she might get from him.

Still, Rellad would be someone to talk to. Chimi smoothed her robe and glanced over her shoulder to be sure Grandmother was really asleep. Satisfied, she turned back just as Rellad's shadow touched her counter.

"Good day to you," Chimi chirped up at him.

"Do you have any mussels? My mother was asking for some." Rellad spoke warily, and Chimi saw him glance past her. He seemed to relax when he saw Grandmother sleeping.

"Of course," Chimi answered. "Let me get them."

As she knelt beneath the counter, Chimi wondered if it had been Rellad's own idea to come here, or if his parents had made him do it. Chimi had brought Shenza to the House of Melleen. That meant not only money, but prestige for their shop. Shenza didn't seem to understand how important that was, but Chimi did. Not that she cared about the House of Melleen anymore.

"Here you go," Chimi said, straightening up to lay the bag of shellfish on the counter. His money was already there. She toyed with the idea of asking for more, but then just swept it into her pouch. To pass the time, she asked, "How are things?"

"We've been really busy," he answered, and Chimi could almost hear a trace of apology. "Father has us weaving from dawn until dusk. He heard a rumor that some nobles will be visiting from Sardony, and he wants to be ready."

"Really?" Chimi asked innocently. She would have bet the rumor came from Jeruki. She was so anxious to get Rellad's attention, it was pathetic.

"Yes." Rellad whined a little now, playing for sympathy. "He's moved us under the pavilion so we don't even have to stop working when it rains."

Chimi, who always did chores after work, held in a sarcastic retort. "I'm surprised they let you out today," she said.

"We ran out of thread," Rellad said. "We had to give the spinners a chance to catch up with us."

"Well, I'm glad you got away," Chimi fluttered up at him.

"Me, too. I missed seeing you." Rellad's words came in a nervous rush. "Can you go for a walk later? We could get a cup of tea."

Chimi suppressed a burst of irritation at his thick-headedness. Wasn't the answer obvious?

"I have to ask first." She glanced over her shoulder, then spread her hands in a display of helplessness. Feeling spiteful, she added, "Maybe Grandmother would let you help us take down our booth when it starts to rain. Then you could walk home with us."

Chimi expected Rellad to say no, since he was already complaining about having too much work to do. To her surprise, he seemed to think about it.

"If you want me to." He glanced around the booth in confusion. "There isn't much to carry, though."

That wasn't the point. "Unless you count Grandmother," Chimi giggled.

Rellad's eyes focused on the back of the booth, and he frowned slightly. "What happened, anyway? How did you get in trouble?"

"It was totally not my fault," Chimi said. Rellad actually sounded concerned, so she decided it was her turn to whine. "They made a big deal out of nothing."

Rellad leaned back a little. In a way, he was as bad as Azma and Jeruki. Did he really not remember Yail? Had he even thought about what it meant?

"Chimi!" Nakuri called from the neighboring stall. "Take a look at that!"

Nakuri was pointing toward the harbor. They both turned to look, and Chimi gasped with delight.

A pair of ships glided into the harbor through a gap in the breakwater. They were long and narrow, tall prows carved into snake heads and painted with bright colors. Ranks of oars flashed, throwing up lines of spray that glittered in the afternoon sunlight. A low structure extended down the center of each one, providing cover for passengers or goods. Rich fabrics wafting on the sea air told Chimi who the passengers might be.

"That's him," Chimi murmured, half to Nakuri and half to herself. "It must be Lord Manseen!"

"Lord who?" Rellad asked. Chimi had forgotten he was there.

"Manseen Bosteel of Bosteel, from Sardony," Chimi snapped. "You know, the noble visitors from another island?"

She turned her eyes back to the harbor. Those were deep sea ships, much larger than the local canoes and fishing boats which scattered to get out of their way. Chimi knew most of the regular merchant ships. She saw them row in and out from her booth. A few of them were this large, but none were decorated like that.

"Can you see anyone?" Chimi moved so she could see around Rellad. The ships were still too far away to pick out many details.

The magnificent vessels back-paddled, drifting to a halt near the center of the harbor. Giving everyone a chance to stare, Chimi guessed. Glancing down the row of piers, she thought they might also have to wait for other ships to move before there was enough room for them to tie up. She did see a peacekeeper patrol boat skimming toward the newcomers.

"Ooh, this is so exciting!" Chimi cried, turning to grin at Nakuri. "I can't believe she's finally here."

Across the counter, Chimi was barely aware when Rellad picked up his bag of mussels.

"Maybe I'll see you later," he said. Chimi watched him hurry away and wondered what he was so disappointed about. Then a slight snuffle behind her warned that Grandmother might be waking up.

"Come again soon," she called dutifully.

Actually, Chimi didn't care if Rellad came back. He was such a fool. She couldn't remember why she had liked him in the first place. Once again, she wished that Ginro would come by. It might be good for him to know that Chimi had other suitors.

"Chimi!" Nakuri's gentle scolding drew her attention away from the harbor. "He was trying to talk to you, and you ignored him."

"There are plenty of others," Chimi retorted, and she turned her eyes back to the Bosteel ships. Rellad was nothing to her, less than a bit of feather-flower fluff. But this... This was important!

* * *

"It's a good thing we're healthy," Juss grumbled.

Shenza chuckled along with him, although exertion made her legs ache and her heart beat faster. The climb to the hilltops above the town seemed especially long today. She had hoped to have word from Kafseet by now. Shenza reminded herself that Kafseet had other patients whose needs had to come first. Still, the lack of news was disappointing. It left her with no one else to question except Necromancer Vesswan.

"Nice place." Juss' voice drew Shenza out of her thoughts. They were approaching the gaudy arch that marked Vesswan's dwelling. Juss read, "'I can help.' Likes to brag, does she?"

Shenza shrugged. This wasn't the same house Vesswan had lived in when Master Laraquies had interviewed her a year ago. That one had been farther down the hill, in more modest surroundings. Seeing the gracious residence the necromancer now occupied, Shenza felt a twinge of envy. Vesswan had moved up quickly thanks to her association with the Sengool coven.

Well, Shenza had moved up, too. She rang the gong with a firm hand. A few minutes later, she and Juss followed a female servant toward a small pavilion tucked against the hillside. Vesswan glided to meet them.

"This is an honor, Magister," she said, so smoothly that Shenza knew she didn't mean it. "May I offer you something? Tea?"

"No, thank you," Shenza answered.

"Then please make yourselves comfortable."

Vesswan dismissed her servant with a gesture and motioned them to join her at a small table. The necromancer was lovely in her scarlet robes, though her necklace of bones made a chilling counterpoint. She was graceful and assured, Shenza's opposite in every way. Maybe that was why Shenza had never liked her.

"Allow me to congratulate you on your elevation to magister." Vesswan's voice was sweet as honey. Without giving Shenza a chance to reply, she continued, "What brings you to me?"

"It is bad news, I fear." Through the eye holes of her mask, Shenza watched

Vesswan carefully. "Lelldour Mokseem of Salloo has been found dead."

"Oh? That's too bad," Vesswan murmured casually, as if she hadn't even known Lelldour.

"He was your teacher, wasn't he?" Juss asked, scowling.

"Years ago." Vesswan glanced from him to Shenza. "Since you mention it, I assume you know my training ended badly. Lelldour and I disagreed on too many things." Her tone held a hint of distaste, and Shenza noticed she didn't accord Lelldour the usual honor of calling him master.

"I did hear something like that," Shenza said. "I'm glad to hear the truth directly from you."

Vesswan frowned faintly. "May I ask who was passing my name around?"

"I can't disclose my sources," Shenza replied. She didn't especially like Groad, but his confidentiality was just as important as Chimi's. "If you don't mind my asking, how did you complete your training after Lelldour had dismissed you?"

"Necromancy doesn't require much training." Vesswan spoke carelessly again, but Shenza didn't miss the tension in her voice. "You either have the sensitivity, or you don't. Afterward, I expanded my training into other areas, partly so that I wouldn't compete against him."

"What kind of training?" Juss wanted to know.

Vesswan raised her eyebrows in a show of surprise. Even Shenza, who was used to his interruptions, shook her head quickly. Juss sighed and sat back.

"Didn't necromancy demand your full devotion?" Shenza asked, remembering Lelldour's scorn toward his former pupil.

"It isn't a highly paid specialty," Vesswan answered coolly, "and I didn't wish to pursue a menial trade in order to support my art. I'm a sorceress. I merely sought to broaden the scope of my abilities so that I could live on magic alone. Rather as you do, Magister."

Shenza ignored the barb. "Were you able to find other teachers here in Chalsett?" she asked, approaching Juss' question more subtly.

She assumed Vesswan would name Nurune Sengool of Sengool. It would make sense that Vesswan began her association with his coven while she was at loose ends. However, she evaded the question.

"One or two, but not here. I studied in Amethan, Sardony and Porphery, to name a few. May I ask why this matters to you?"

Her counter-question took Shenza by surprise. "I'm just curious," she said.

Shenza saw a flicker of emotion in Vesswan's eyes. Relief, or suspicion, or guilt—it was hard to tell.

She went on, "I don't know much about necromancy, and it could have a bearing on Lelldour's passing."

"Each school has its own ways, as you know." Vesswan spoke pleasantly enough, but the warning was clear. She wouldn't be open to any more questions about necromancy.

"Returning to my inquiry, then," Shenza said. "Lelldour's death hasn't been explained. I wonder if you remember him having any enemies who might wish to harm him?"

"No, it's been too long," Vesswan said.

"And do you happen to know where his family lives? I need to notify them."

"Sorry." Vesswan was already shaking her head. "We didn't keep in touch. Nobody pays attention to the necromancer unless they have a haunting spirit."

She gave a sardonic chuckle. It sounded as if Vesswan didn't even like being a necromancer. Before Shenza could ask any more questions, a chime's mellow voice resonated through the garden. Immediately, Vesswan sat straighter.

"Forgive me, but that's a client I was expecting. If you have nothing else?"

Though she phrased it as a question, Vesswan was already rising. It was frustrating to admit, but Shenza didn't have any more questions. Whatever suspicion she felt, Vesswan hadn't been implicated in Lelldour's death. To press her further would insult a Sengool ally, and Lady Izmay had already warned Shenza not to do that. She rose and bowed to her old adversary.

"I appreciate your time," she said.

"Of course, Magister."

Vesswan's maidservant reappeared at the base of the steps. Shenza and Juss followed her back to the gate. There they found a minor surprise: Tonkatt Akanti of Sengool, who Shenza remembered vividly from a very embarrassing incident during her investigation of Lord Anges' murder. Tonkatt was unchanged, a tall and charismatic young man with black hair swept straight back from his forehead. His handsome face hardened momentarily, but he gave a curt bow. Shenza merely nodded as she passed.

When they had gone a little way down the street, Juss glanced over his shoulder. "Isn't that the guy who was involved in your poisoning?"

"Yes," Shenza said, and dutifully reminded, "but it wasn't his fault."

"Huh." Juss grunted his skepticism. "And he's her client?"

"Apparently." Shenza said. "Since they're both part of Sengool's coven, it could be just business."

"Huh," Juss repeated. He added, "She's a cold one, isn't she?"

"Well, she is a necromancer," Shenza quipped. She remembered the chill she had felt last time she touched Chimi's shoulder.

"Ha, ha," Juss grumbled. "You know what I mean. She didn't even care that her own teacher was dead."

"I noticed."

Shenza fell into thoughtful silence as they walked along the street. Vesswan certainly returned Lelldour's contempt for her. The remark about menial labor probably referred to Lelldour's making rubber. It made Shenza realize how lucky she had been when Master Laraquies chose her as his student.

Thinking back to their interview, Shenza did feel that Vesswan had been a bit too quick with some of her answers. Her indifference seemed calculated. As if she had rehearsed her story? It reminded Shenza of Lord Aspace, always saying the opposite of what he felt. But then, everything reminded her of Aspace. She wondered if she would ever stop thinking about him.

The ground rolled under their feet with the latest of many tremors. Shenza glanced to her left, where the volcano continued its steady growth. After only a few days, the tip was already level with the third tier. It blew out a plume of dark vapors. A film of floating ash gave the surrounding waters a scabby look.

Shenza looked away. She had no more answers in the theft of the sand than she did in Lelldour's death. Nothing was becoming any clearer. She didn't know what to do. There was so little evidence, and nothing to make her suspect Vesswan except, Shenza admitted, that she was naturally suspicious of Vesswan. Was there something she had overlooked, some detail she had missed? There was no point in going back to Lelldour's without Chimi, but where else could she go?

"Shenza?" Juss' voice brought her out of her reverie.

She looked up to see a courier racing toward them. He was a young man, dressed in the bright blue of the first lord's staff from the plumes on his headcloth to the straps of his sandals. Shenza had an idea what his message might be. The afternoon suddenly felt terribly warm, but she made herself wait for him.

"Magister, I'm glad I found you." The messenger breathed deeply, and sweat beaded his shoulders, but his words came evenly. "My Lord would have you know that Lord Manseen Bosteel of Bosteel is here. There will be a feast at sunset. You are commanded to attend."

"As my Lord wishes, so I will do." Shenza forced the words out of a tight, dry throat.

The courier bowed again and jogged back the way he had come. Shenza closed her eyes for a moment. This news filled her with gloom. The brief moment when Lord Aspace had seemed to like her was no more than a fading dream.

"I guess I'd better report in," Juss said. "Are we done for today?"

"Yes, and thank you." Shenza started walking again, following the messenger toward the central stairs.

"I didn't do anything," Juss said as he came with her.

"Your help is always welcome," Shenza told him. "I should go prepare. Obviously, this is going to delay our inquiry. I'll let you know when we can start again."

"All right. Maybe I'll see you tonight."

Shenza merely nodded. They were at the top of the stairs. With a wave, Juss started down with a halting stride. Shenza took her time, as if she could delay the unpleasantness by walking more slowly. The volcano's looming presence across the harbor did nothing to put her at ease.

Inside, she felt foolish and helpless. She had said she must get ready for the feast, but she had no idea what to do. Chimi would know, of course. It annoyed Shenza to need her sister. They hadn't spoken since their argument. Was she supposed to forget what Chimi had said and pretend it had never happened? The way she had to pretend she didn't care about Lord Aspace's bridal negotiations, all during the feast? It seemed wrong for sisters to play at friendship and feel nothing.

Chimi should be working at this time of day. It would be easy to find her. But when she reached the third tier, Shenza turned aside. It was going to be a difficult night. Who knew how long the festivities would keep her at the palace? This might be her last chance to write out her notes. Just for a while, Shenza wanted to stay at home and go through her familiar routines. When she was ready to have everything turned upside-down, she would go find Chimi.

Chapter Sixteen

Midnight and Pearl

Chimi rushed home without waiting to see if Rellad would come. In fact, she hardly even waited for Grandmother to keep up. Chimi had spent the afternoon with a tantalizing view of the docks, watching tiny figures step off the magnificent boats and be met by palace guards. She hadn't been able to see any of the procession through the marketplace. It made her all the more eager for a glimpse of the mysterious Seelit.

Now Chimi and Shenza had washed, smoothed on fragrant oils, and donned their finest clothes. Not that Chimi had much choice, with only one really good robe to her name. Her only decision was what jewelry to wear.

"What do you think, this one or this?" Chimi held up two necklaces, showing them around the room.

On one hand she held a string of amber stones, smoothed by waves and sand. There were matching earrings with it. She was dying for an excuse to wear them. On the other hand dangled a long string of pearls, which always looked good against dark skin. Pearls were easy to get, and she had several bracelets to wear with it.

"The pearls," said Grandmother, who had been watching with her usual sharp attention.

"I think so, too," Mother added as she fastened Shenza's headcloth with an ivory pin.

"But the amber is more expensive," Chimi argued. She had just bought the necklace from Ginro's shop and hadn't had a chance to wear it yet.

"The pearls," Grandmother repeated. From her cranky look, she was about to remind Chimi that she was only being released temporarily. As if Chimi needed to be reminded.

"Amber is too close to the yellow in your robe," Mother said. "It won't show up like the pearls do."

As a last resort, Chimi called on her sister. "Shenza, what do you think?"

"Hmm?" Shenza looked up distractedly. She had been staring into her lap all afternoon. She looked beautiful in her turquoise silk robe, except that her expression was as gloomy as a rainy afternoon.

"Oh, never mind." Chimi held the necklaces up on front of herself again, comparing them. It was hard not to resent how much nicer Shenza's robe was. Shenza didn't seem to appreciate having it. On the other hand, she hadn't noticed that Chimi wasn't wearing her hoka any more.

"Wear the pearls," Grandmother commanded. "You'll be among folk who stand higher than you. Don't try to show off in front of them."

"The only thing I want is to have a good time." Chimi tried, but she couldn't keep the words from coming out sour.

"You have more pearls, anyway," Mother said. She gave Shenza's shoulder a gentle pat and then came to Chimi's side. "This will look better."

Giliatt took the strand of pearls from Chimi's hand and looped them over her neck. They spent a few more minutes putting earrings and bracelets on and taking them off, seeing how they went together, until Chimi found just the right combination. No matter what Grandmother said, she planned to look her best. Who knew if some young nobleman might see her tonight? Azma wasn't the only one who could make a match.

Although their hands were busy with baubles, Chimi didn't miss how Giliatt kept turning her head toward Shenza. Their mother was worried, though she tried not to show it. Even Chimi had to admit that Shenza was acting unusually depressed.

She had suspected that Shenza wouldn't be ready for the feast, so she had stopped by her house after the market closed. Grandmother had chosen Shenza's new robe. Then they'd had to drag her home with them. Honestly, leave it to Shenza to hide in her workshop while the most exciting event of the season went on!

On the other hand, Shenza hadn't mentioned their fight in front of Mother and Grandmother. She just stared through the table top and occasionally rubbed her hands against her knees. It was like she didn't know what to do without that travel case she always dragged around—which Chimi had forced her to leave at home tonight.

Inside herself, Chimi threw up her hands in disgust. If Shenza was so convinced that she wouldn't enjoy herself, she was sure not to. How was that Chimi's fault? Without meaning to, she sighed out loud. Giliatt turned to her with a fresh flicker of concern in her eyes. She didn't know which of them to worry about more, Chimi guessed.

She fiddled with her bracelets, trying to hide her feelings. Getting ready for a feast was supposed to be fun. Instead, she was being tortured by her family. Longing for escape, she cast an eye outside. Sunset was starting to paint the clouds with fiery hues. The feast was supposed to start at dusk, which meant it was still too soon for them to leave. Shenza was no help—she had gone back to her staring. It was almost painful to watch her. Really, she spent so much time studying, she didn't know anything beyond work.

Suddenly Chimi realized this might be exactly the problem. Shenza was probably still thinking about Lelldour—a topic Chimi was quite ready to have her forget. She needed someone to break the obsession and show her how to have fun again.

Now Chimi knew what to do. She held up her hands, letting her bracelets chime against each other.

"That's good enough," she declared.

"All right." Giliatt sounded relieved that Chimi had made up her mind. To Shenza, she asked, "Do you want a little more tea?"

"Hmm?" Shenza seemed surprised that everyone was looking at her.

"What we need," Chimi said, "is to get going. All we're doing is sitting here getting more nervous. Let's walk around for a while."

"Don't be in such a hurry," Mother chuckled fondly. "It's still too early."

"We might meet someone we know," Chimi said, ignoring her. "Then we can all go in together, without everybody staring at us."

Shenza seemed to like the idea, but the older women didn't.

"I don't know," Giliatt began.

And Grandmother demanded, "Who would you be meeting?"

Too late, Chimi realized her mistake. Meeting a boy, that was what they both assumed. Would Grandmother never give up on that idea?

"Winomi and her parents," Chimi answered, clinging to her patience. "Shenza hasn't met them, and they're part of the Kesquin family. She needs to start making contacts."

Chimi tried to cover her irritation, but she felt a cold, tight lump of anger lodge in her throat. It grew tighter as another doubtful glance passed between Mother and Grandmother. Before they could speak, Shenza gathered her robes and stood up.

"Chimi's right," she said softly. "I am nervous. It would feel good to walk around. I'm ready to go, so there's no reason to stay here."

As she spoke, Shenza put her arm around Chimi's shoulders and began to walk toward the main room. Chimi felt her rage ease as she followed her sister's lead. Mother and Grandmother came after them, but the younger women stayed ahead. Byben, who hadn't been allowed into Chimi's room while they were dressing, greeted them with a broad smile.

"Oh, two such beautiful ladies!" he exclaimed.

Chimi played along, twirling through the main room while Shenza led the way toward the street. Sachakeen was out working, earning extra money by sweeping the streets after the new volcano dropped ash on Chalsett-port. Chimi didn't miss her brother. He'd been just as bad as Grandmother lately.

"Are you sure it isn't too early?" Giliatt asked as she came in behind them.

"Even if I'm early, they won't make me wait." Shenza sounded weary as she made this prediction. "I don't know when the feast will be over, but don't worry. Chimi will be with me the whole time."

Giliatt looked at Shenza with that shadow in her eyes again. Impulsively, Chimi turned back and gave their mother a quick hug.

"Thanks for letting me go. I won't do anything to shame our family," she promised.

"I know," Mother began, but she broke off. "Your hands are so cold!"

Instantly, Chimi broke away. "Too much working in the fish market," she said with a shrill laugh. "Let's go, sister!"

Chimi hurried Shenza toward the street, hoping it looked like she was eager and excited instead of running away from her mother's questions.

Despite Chimi's claim, they didn't wander aimlessly through town. Chimi led Shenza directly up the main stair and along the eighth tier. Shenza lagged behind when it looked like they were going to the palace, but Chimi grabbed her hand and dragged her forward. The two sisters passed the palace, crossed a low saddle between two hills, and came out in a small plaza with a view of Chalsett-port. Shenza joined Chimi at the rail, trying to control her agitation.

The harbor faced southeast, so that the sun sank in a golden haze on their right side. Its rays drenched the town in fiery light. Even the smoldering hulk of the volcano had a strange beauty in the last daylight. As they watched, a flock of birds took off from the harbor and swirled like sparks before they lit in the trees near the shrine. A moment later, they surged skyward again.

Shenza felt just like that. Her thoughts spun in circles with nowhere to go. She had been trying to meditate while Chimi dressed, but the constant chatter had been too distracting. Walking only helped a little. Her knees felt wobbly, too weak to support her.

Lord Aspace had commanded her to attend this banquet, and she couldn't refuse. She would have to watch him woo Lady Seelit. How could he be so cruel?

It would have been better if I never knew him, Shenza thought bitterly.

Neither of the sisters spoke. It bothered Shenza a little that they didn't talk. She knew how Chimi felt about becoming a necromancer. Chimi knew how she felt about taking responsibility for her sorcery. After their last argument, what else was there to say?

Chimi stirred restlessly. She glanced over her shoulder, in the direction of the palace. Shenza summoned all her will to tease her.

"Are you that anxious for sunset?"

"Shouldn't I be?" Chimi spoke cheerily, but she didn't look at Shenza and there was a sharp edge to her voice.

Shenza was saved from answering by the sound of voices behind them. Chimi whirled, her face alight with excitement. Shenza turned, almost afraid to see who was coming.

A procession emerged from the walled estate on the crown of the hillside. At the head was an ornate carrying chair, draped for privacy and held by eight muscular men. From the brilliant magenta kilts on the bearers, this must be Lord Kesquin. A cluster of richly garbed men followed the palanquin. Then came two more chairs, where Lord Kesquin's wives must be riding. A larger group of women trailed after, older ones coming before younger. They were flanked by men armed with shields and spears. The weapons were large and showy, intended more for display than actual use, Shenza guessed.

She instinctively stepped back as the procession filled the courtyard. Then a voice called out to them.

"Chimi!" A plump girl waved vigorously near the back of the entourage.

"Winomi!" Chimi waved back, then dashed forward. The other girl stepped out to meet her. They embraced and stood giggling at the edge of the procession.

This must be Chimi's much-spoken-of friend, Winomi. Chimi must have had this encounter planned all along. And her plan had been precisely what she said it was. Maybe Shenza shouldn't have been so surprised that her sister told the truth. It was just hard not to absorb Grandmother's pessimism.

The lead chair stopped beside Shenza, blocking her view of Chimi. A man's hand, heavy with silver bracelets, pushed the heavy fabric aside.

"Good evening, Magister," said Lord Fastu Kesquin of Kesquin.

"And to you." Shenza pressed both hands to her chest and bowed, although she wondered how he recognized her without her usual robes and mask.

Fastu was a weighty and dignified man. His shoulder-length hair had been artificially straightened, but was still graying at the temples. Small black eyes surveyed her impassively from his fleshy face.

"We were enjoying the sunset," Shenza told him. Even to her, the explanation sounded awkward. However, Lord Fastu graciously agreed with her.

"I have always enjoyed the view from this plaza," he said. "It is quite striking."

He wasn't actually looking at the sunset, Shenza noted, but instead regarded her with veiled speculation. For a moment, she had the horrible sense that he knew exactly how she felt about tonight's festivities. Then Shenza saw that Chimi had edged around to stare at her with a pleading gaze. Shenza remembered the second part of Chimi's plan.

"May we join your family this evening, Lord Fastu?"

"That would be my honor," Fastu answered so promptly that Shenza suspected he had been waiting for her to ask. "Your charming sister is well known in our house."

"I appreciate the kindness," Shenza murmured, bowing again.

Lord Fastu motioned to his bearers and let the curtain fall. The retinue began to move again. Shenza stepped back and waited for Chimi and Winomi to come even with her. Chimi couldn't wait, however. She grabbed Shenza's hand and led her to the cluster of young women. From her wide smile, Shenza knew Chimi had heard Lord Kesquin's compliment.

Shenza was quickly drawn into the vortex of highly excited and beautifully dressed young women. She even looked like one of them, in her fine silk robe. This was Chimi's dream come to life, but it was Shenza's nightmare. Wearing such extravagant clothing made her feel like a stranger in her own body.

There were so many introductions that Shenza could hardly remember them all. Winomi's mother was named Anamatt. Her younger sisters were Taldeena and Losiri. Then there were many aunts and cousins. At least the group was friendly, except for a cousin named Azma whose greeting to Shenza was so haughty that it was barely polite. Shenza ignored her and let the crowd sweep her along.

In a way, she was glad to encounter this family early in the evening. The Kesquins were generally less hostile than the House of Sengool. Was this why Chimi had suggested coming to the feast with them—to imply some kind of alliance? Or maybe it was an opportunity to start one. Shenza wondered if that was a good idea. She was supposed to be independent. She wondered what Lord Aspace would think.

Meanwhile, Winomi whispered behind Shenza, "You look really nice, Chimi."

"Thanks," Chimi said. "I can hardly wait to see what Lady Seelit is wearing—and all the latest styles from Sardony!"

"They're really close to the capital," Winomi said.

Shenza bit her lip and wished they hadn't mentioned Seelit's name. She felt surrounded as it was, by the rustle of sandals over cobblestones and the murmur of voices talking about trivia.

"So tell me, Chimi," interrupted a girl with a sly voice, "have you had an offer yet?"

Shenza turned sharply at the tittering that followed. The girl just behind them was smirking, so she must have been the speaker. Shenza wasn't surprised to see who it was.

"Azma!" Winomi protested.

"What does that have to do with anything?" Losiri demanded.

"Stop your snipping," Taldeena snipped at Azma.

"I'm in no hurry to get married," Chimi said, but she couldn't hide her hurt scowl.

"No she has not!" Shenza answered at the same time. She spoke sharply, startled by the rude question. Who was this Azma to speculate on their family's private affairs?

"Your match hasn't been settled yet, either, daughter," one of the women scolded up ahead of them.

And Anamatt put in, "It isn't too late to send you back. Lady Panubi would understand."

"I'm sorry," Azma answered, but Shenza didn't think she looked very sorry. Winomi and her sisters drifted back a little, pushing Azma farther away from Chimi. The younger ones continued glaring at their cousin.

"Those girls," Anamatt sighed to Shenza a moment later. Shenza realized that she must have been afraid Azma's insolence had offended her.

"It doesn't mean anything," Shenza said, though the incident did rankle. It was one thing that she faced the scorn of the nobles. That came with her position. But there was no reason for anyone to punish her sister.

While the women went back to their chattering, Shenza glanced upward, trying to rise above it all. The sky had darkened from sunset blush to evening's soft lavender. Three of the moons, Inkesh, Prenuse and Quaiss, were suspended among the glittering stars like a string of mismatched baubles. There was no sign of Skall, and that annoyed her. It was a bit like having a spider in the room. She didn't want to see it, but she didn't like not knowing where it was.

Skall's brief appearance might be linked with the theft from the spirits and the new volcano. Shenza wondered if she would ever know for sure.

The buzz of conversation around her took on a different tone. Everyone started to walk faster.

"What's happening?" Shenza asked Losiri, who was closest to her and Chimi.

The younger woman shrugged, but one of the women ahead of them answered, "It's the Sengools."

"They're coming up ahead of us," Azma's mother added.

At once, the Kesquins began walking even faster. Sandals pattered over the cobblestones like a brisk afternoon rain.

"They used to be part of our house," Winomi explained, panting a little. "We can't let them get there before us."

"Of course not," came Chimi's loyal reply.

"They broke away without permission," one of the aunts sniffed.

Shenza merely nodded. She had already heard about this long-ago scandal. Azma made some other response that Shenza couldn't hear. Winomi's sisters glared at her even more fiercely than before. Shenza hid a bemused smile. Couldn't the noble families even get to the banquet before acting out their rivalry?

The first lord's gate was just ahead, blazing with lamps in the dusk. Beyond the swaying chairs of the Lord and Ladies Kesquin, Shenza glimpsed an opulent column approaching from the opposite direction. Those servants wore Sengool orange, and they seemed to be in as much a hurry as the Kesquins. Details of fine clothing and tense faces became clearer as the two retinues got closer. It was ridiculous to see the nobles race each other, while trying to pretend they weren't racing.

The competition ended when Lord Kesquin's chair reached the gate before his rival's. The rustling and murmuring around her took on a self-satisfied tone as the front of the Sengool train had to slow down abruptly.

The bars of the gate stood wide open in welcome. One of the Kesquin servants strode ahead, loudly crying his master's name, while the procession turned to enter the estate. Although they had been invited, Shenza noted many guards. Most wore the brilliant blue of the first lord's personal guard, but she also saw men in the dark gold of city peacekeepers. She looked half-heartedly, but didn't see Juss among them.

Shenza almost ran into the back of Winomi's mother before she realized that the carrying chairs were moving slowly again. Lord Kesquin was taunting his rivals with the leisurely pace. As Shenza passed the gate, she saw the noblemen at the head of the Sengool train chatting with elaborate unconcern. Drapes covered Lord Sengool's chair, so Shenza couldn't see his face, but she did glimpse his feet twitching impatiently through a gap in the fabric.

Once they were onto the grounds, the company had to stretch out because the paths were narrower. Serving girls paced beside them carrying lamps on poles, though the light didn't reach far. Shenza knew the estate well, but she found the twilit gardens eerie and strange. Familiar shapes of arbors and pavilions were vague in the dusk beneath the trees. She smelled damp stone and night-blooming flowers. Just behind her, Chimi and Winomi whispered about how pretty it was.

An amber glow outlined a tall hedge ahead of them. Moments later, the servants led them into an opening where lamps shone around a grand pavilion. Shenza blinked against the sudden, harsh light.

"Keep going!" Cold hands pushed on her shoulder as Chimi nearly walked into her.

"I am," Shenza said.

She knew where they were now. Not so long ago, Lord Anges' body had been laid in state here. Shenza remembered the peaked roof, its blue tiles merging into the darkening sky, and the scarlet columns rising to support it. Gems and silver inlay glittered everywhere. Low tables crowded the pavilion, instead of a funeral bier. Servants moved among them, setting out dishes, and cooking odors mingled with the perfumed lamp oil.

A platform had been set up in front of the pavilion. Lord Aspace sat waiting to receive his guests. Laraquies and Lady Izmay stood together on his right, Izmay a step higher as befitted her rank. Two men were positioned on Aspace's left. Shenza recognized Udama, so the man in splendid dark blue robes had to be Lord Manseen Bosteel of Bosteel.

"Look—there she is!" Winomi breathed loudly.

"Don't point," Anamatt scolded, but not as if she was really angry.

A young woman sat on the top step, a favored position, between Aspace and Manseen. Shenza had an impression of filmy, pale robes before the other girls crowded in front of her. Even the sour Azma stood on her toes, trying to see past the others. Shenza gladly stepped back to let them stare.

She supposed that she should be studying the Bosteels, but she couldn't look any farther than Lord Aspace. He was resplendent in a greenish-blue robe, full length, with peacock feathers trailing behind his headcloth. Copper chains draped his neck, while winking gems adorned his wrists and ankles. Useless as it was, Shenza couldn't help her feelings. No other man made her feel the way Aspace did.

Then, as she watched, he leaned forward and offered something to the girl sitting at his knees. Shenza's stomach turned over as Seelit took it with a shy smile. She tried to remind herself what Aspace had said, that he was more interested in Lord Manseen than his daughter, but it certainly didn't look that way.

The retinue slowed to a halt as Lord Kesquin's chair stopped and the bearers knelt. Fastu stepped out. The noblemen followed as he went to greet Lord Aspace. Closer at hand, the chairs of Lady Panubi and Lady Rahjeena also came to earth. The palanquins blocked Shenza's view, so she didn't actually see the Kesquin nobles greet their ruler.

A rumble of voices behind Shenza distracted her. Glancing over her shoulder, she saw that the Sengool procession was close behind. Though she was hidden among the women and none of them spared her a glance, Shenza felt a burst of fear. There were so many people here, and most of them didn't like her! She couldn't do this. No matter how pretty her clothes were, she was just a fisherman's daughter. She didn't belong with them.

The receiving line moved, dragging Shenza along. Her knees trembled with the need to flee as the pavilion loomed overhead. The evening air seemed stifling, too humid and thick to breathe.

Chimi turned toward her, all but dancing with anticipation. "We're almost there." Then she frowned. "Sister?"

Her voice was impatient, but her cool hand felt good on Shenza's shoulder.

"You don't look well," Winomi said from Chimi's other side.

"Oh..." Shenza summoned a shaky laugh. "I'm just not used to all this."

The line shuffled forward. Chimi rolled her eyes slightly, but apparently Winomi didn't see her reaction.

"It is a little scary the first time," she said with buoyant reassurance, "but you'll have fun. Lady Izmay is really nice." Then she paused. "I thought you would have met her by now."

"I have," Shenza admitted, "and she is."

Winomi angled her head, puzzled, but added brightly, "Well, the food will be outstanding, too. And there will be dancers."

"I love them," Chimi said.

Shenza, who had no appetite at all, controlled the impulse to rub her sweaty palms against her new robe.

The line crept forward. Winomi stood on her toes to see ahead of them. Once she had turned her back, Chimi shook her head at Shenza. The pearls dangling from her headcloth clicked together like Grandmother's scolding tongue.

"What *is* the matter?" Chimi hissed with equal parts irritation and despair. "This is a feast. We're here to have a good time. No wonder people won't talk to you, when you go around looking like—"

Chimi broke off and turned her head sharply, leaving Shenza to wonder what she had been about to say. Before she could respond, Chimi sighed lightly and tried again.

"I don't know why you carry on like this, sister," she said. "No one cares about *you*. Not tonight. They came to see *her*."

That was exactly the problem, Shenza thought rebelliously. Everyone wanted to see Seelit—especially Lord Aspace.

"Just stop thinking about yourself," Chimi went on. "As long as you don't get sick again, you'll be fine."

"That's not fair," Shenza protested, but Chimi turned to join the procession as it moved forward again. Shenza stared into the darkness, unable to believe her sister's callousness. It was true that she had been sick at the last public feast, but she had been poisoned! Why did Chimi have to remind her of that? And what gave her the right to lecture as if she was the older sister?

Shenza moved with the line, only because she didn't want to be left in the midst of the Sengool family. A shiver ran up Shenza's arms as she glimpsed Lord Aspace through the crowd. She rubbed them briskly, trying to put him out of her thoughts. She had known all along that she didn't have a chance with Aspace. Her mind knew it, but her heart never would.

And yet, as Chimi had reminded her, Shenza had already made a fool of herself once at the palace. She vowed to herself that she wouldn't do it again. She straightened her back and took deep breaths, drawing calm around herself.

Chimi greeted Master Laraquies with shrill enthusiasm. She also introduced Winomi, and both girls bowed excitedly as he presented them to Lady Izmay. They chattered like birds, Shenza thought, making a lot of noise but no sense. Lord Aspace was only a few feet from her. She felt his presence like the warmth of the night air, like a fragrance borne on the breeze.

She dared a glance in his direction. Her heart seemed to freeze when she saw his head turned, watching them. A faint smile lit his eyes, and Shenza trembled like one of the peacock feathers behind his head. In all the jeweled throng, she saw only the sheen of his silken robes, the glint of fine chains around his neck.

Someone touched her elbow. "Good evening, child," Master Laraquies said.

"Hello." Shenza jerked around. For a moment, she couldn't remember where she was, or why.

"I hope you'll enjoy yourself." On Laraquies' other side, Lady Izmay nodded with a twinkle in her eye.

"Thank you for the invitation." Shenza bowed with a jerk. A space had opened up as Chimi and Winomi moved forward to bow before Lord Aspace. Shenza steeled herself to face him.

The first lord lounged on his elevated chair, scanning the crowd with obvious boredom. He didn't look at Shenza now, and she felt a moment's panic. Had she done something wrong?

"My Lord," Shenza bowed, tongue-tied. In her mind, she could hear Chimi scolding her to stop worrying so much.

"I'm glad you came." Aspace lifted his hand in casual acknowledgement. Turning to Lord Manseen, he added, "My magister, Shenza Waik of Tresmeer."

It was a relief to turn toward Lord Manseen, who bowed politely. Shenza bowed in return. "Good evening."

Lord Manseen Bosteel of Bosteel was of medium years, neither as heavy set as Lord Fastu nor as tall as Lord Oriman. He wasn't very handsome, especially beside Lord Aspace. He was conservatively dressed in a deep blue robe embroidered with silvery shells. Pearls nested within the stitchery. At least he kept his hair in a natural curl, and didn't try to hide the streaks of silver.

Shenza recognized Udama, who stood slightly behind his lord. Udama bowed to her, his face alive with interest. She quickly nodded back. Beside her, Chimi greeted Lady Seelit effusively, asking about her journey. Lord Bosteel eyed them with wary amusement. Keeping an eye on his daughter, as any father would.

Shenza knew she couldn't put off the worst any longer. She looked at Lady Seelit and was startled to see that she was very young. Even younger than Chimi.

Seelit did look the part of a radiant princess. She wore a close-fitting sheath and headcloth of shell pink with an over-robe of undyed feather-flower silk. The stuff was so sheer and fine that it seemed to drift around her like mist. Her earrings and necklaces were of pink and white coral. A few curls framed her face, dark against the pale fabric.

With an ugly start, Shenza felt thorns of envy drive into her heart. How could this child be her rival? She heard a distant rumble, and the ground rolled beneath her feet. The disturbance suited her mood perfectly. Around her, the buzz of talk died away as everyone felt the earth's movement.

"Do you have many earthquakes?" Manseen asked. Seelit had leaned slightly toward him, and he patted her shoulder.

If it would make him take his daughter and leave, Shenza would gladly have told him the truth, but Aspace merely shrugged.

"The spirits have been restless lately," he said, as if the volcano growing across the harbor was of no consequence.

And Chimi smiled at Seelit reassuringly. "Oh, that's nothing." Shenza wanted to kick her.

The receiving line seemed to stand still forever, forcing Shenza to confront Seelit, whose beauty she could never hope to equal. At last the queue moved, and she murmured something else, she wasn't sure what. Chimi didn't want to go on, but now it was Shenza's turn to push. She shouldn't give herself time to say something inane. Or hateful. Or both.

Chimi and Winomi hurried through the line together, giggling every step of the way. Azma managed to push past them, despite Winomi's sisters trying to trip her.

"I don't care," Chimi whispered to them. She had been dreaming of this night for weeks now. Shenza's gloom wasn't going to ruin it for her, and neither would Azma's spite.

The girls settled down when it was time to greet the nobles, because it was important to give a good impression of Kesquin House. Shenza would have been proud of how polite Chimi was to Master Laraquies and

Lady Izmay, but she wasn't paying attention. Neither was Lord Manseen, in his robes of midnight and pearl. It didn't matter. Chimi only had eyes for Seelit.

Seelit was a vision. Everything about her was beautiful, from the touch of colored powder on her eyelids to her headcloth knotted just so, to the hint of fragrance that clung to her. The over-robe was so sheer, like a ray of moonlight. Chimi was deeply jealous, yet she felt no malice as she would toward a girl like Azma. Some day, she wanted to look exactly like that.

As Chimi got a better look at Lady Seelit, she saw that the girl was younger than any of them besides Taldeena. Winomi was telling Seelit how happy they were to meet her. The girl smiled in response. She had lovely dark eyes, soft as a baby calf's. Seelit was poised and confident, the way Chimi wished Shenza would be. If she would just smile, everyone would see how pretty she was.

Finally it was Chimi's turn. She bowed low and said, "I'm Chimi Waik of Tresmeer. Welcome to Chalsett-port." Then she realized that everyone must have been saying the same thing all night, so she added, "I noticed your jade bracelet. It's really pretty."

A warmer smile flickered across Seelit's face. "It was a gift from my mother." She raised her left hand momentarily, so that Chimi could see her bracelet, a close-fitted silver cuff with several jade stones. The largest one was carved in the shape of a flower.

"She has good taste," Chimi said, quick to cement a connection with the glamorous guest.

Everyone stopped what they were doing as the earth suddenly trembled. "What was that?" Seelit asked.

Her father laid a protective hand on her shoulder. "Do you have many earthquakes here?" he asked.

Lord Aspace said something reassuring, and Chimi quickly added, "Oh, that's nothing."

Then she was distracted by the short man who stood beside Lord Manseen. Oddly, he was smirking to himself. When he saw Chimi looking at him, he bobbed a quick bow.

The pause also gave Chimi time to realize that Lord Manseen had only brought Seelit with him. Her mother hadn't come along. Chimi wondered why not. Didn't Lady Bosteel care what kind of man her daughter married?

Unfortunately, Chimi didn't get a chance to say anything more to Seelit. Shenza was at her shoulder, anxious to keep up with the line. Chimi trailed after Winomi and her sisters. The Kesquin girls drew into a gossiping cluster near their mothers, and Chimi knew she should join them. Azma was there, though, and Chimi caught the faint buzz of her telling them oh-so-wisely that they didn't have to kiss Lady Seelit's fingers like some other girls around here.

"That's not nice," Winomi whispered, glancing in Chimi's direction. And one of her sisters retorted, "She wouldn't let you, anyway."

Chimi turned away. She didn't have to waste her time on Azma. She looked around for her sister, but Shenza seemed to have vanished. Confused, Chimi turned side to side and finally spotted her near a table where servants were laying out trays of fruit. She was by herself, of course. Only Shenza could be alone in this crowd, Chimi thought with disgust.

The expression on her face made Chimi look twice, though. Her cheeks were glowing, her eyes brilliant with emotion. Maybe it was shame, for Shenza looked down, picking at her robe with agitated fingers. Then she looked up again, as if she didn't want to but couldn't stop herself.

What in the world was that about? Chimi turned her head, trying to follow Shenza's line of sight. She could tell Shenza was looking at the receiving line, but there was such a throng as Lord Oriman made his bows that she couldn't tell who Shenza was so interested in.

"Chimi!"

The sound of her name made her turn back to her friends. Winomi was waving urgently, and Chimi could see that Azma's mother had called her over to the Kesquin women. Chimi glanced back at Shenza, but she knew Winomi's feelings would be hurt if she didn't come right away. She put Shenza's odd behavior aside and went to join her friends.

Chapter Seventeen

A Sister's Secret

Shenza retreated to lose herself in the growing crowd. The babble of voices washed over her as she sought a place where she could see what was happening without being obvious. She found it near one of the pillars that supported the pavilion roof.

This was the duty Chief Borleek had assigned her—watching Lord Aspace in case any spells were cast around the dais. It had seemed like a logical choice, but Shenza hadn't considered how much it would bother her to see that enchanting slip of a girl so close to Lord Aspace.

From her vantage, Shenza did notice one thing she hadn't before: Lord Manseen didn't have as much of an entourage as she'd expected. He could have brought along his wife, Seelit's mother, or a cadre of advisors. Even his son, Tenbei, since he already knew Aspace. Lady Seelit should have friends or attendants. Udama was there, surveying the scene much as Shenza was, but only one other man had come with them. Though he carried no weapons, he had the bearing of a fighting man. Unlike the Kesquin clan's ceremonial escort, he seemed very serious about his work.

Shenza thought about that. Security was Lord Aspace's responsibility as host, so why did Manseen have a bodyguard? Was he expecting trouble?

Intense whispering behind Shenza distracted her. She glanced back to see the Kesquin women in a tight knot around Fastu's chief wife, Lady Panubi. They were all staring resentfully. Shenza turned the other way to see what had them so annoyed.

Lord Orishem of Sengool was exchanging greetings with Lords Aspace and Manseen. Orishem's brother, Nurune, stood close at his side, his leathery face wreathed with smiles. For once, Nurune wasn't wearing his sorcerer's purple. All the Sengools wore layers of contrasting robes. This had been the style of Lord Anges' court, and Shenza was surprised they had chosen something so outmoded. What message were they trying to send?

Orishem moved on, swaggering a little. He looked quite pleased with himself. It all seemed very cordial, although Shenza did wish she had her mask. Then she could have heard what they were talking about.

She expected the Kesquins to step back and let the Sengool entourage mix into the throng. Instead, they held their places. Shenza watched Lord Orishem's smirk tighten into a petulant sneer.

"A pleasant evening to you." Lord Fastu greeted his rival with a mocking bow.

"It was," Orishem replied coldly.

He turned slightly aside and shouldered past the men of Kesquin's household, who seemed not to have noticed his approach because none of them budged. There was a period of jostling as the Sengools moved into the grassy area. The men bumped elbows and stepped on toes, until the women came near. No one wanted to be accused of molesting a noblewoman. The Kesquins gave them slightly more room.

Once again, the pettiness was both amazing and amusing. The contest was so juvenile, yet they all took it very seriously. Now Shenza understood why Lord Aspace's staff had put refreshments on both sides of the grass. She noted, too, that Lord Manseen's bodyguard and a pair of peacekeepers watched the process with steely focus. It made Shenza wonder if there was any danger of a real fight.

She turned her attention back to the receiving line. The elder Sengool women had already passed, and Oriman's oldest daughter, Innoshyra, was before the dais. Like her family, Innoshyra was draped in overlapping robes of azure, emerald and lemon yellow. Strands of matching beads were wound into her headcloth, which had been wrapped into a tall peak.

With the noise of the crowd, Shenza couldn't hear what Innoshyra said. Although she had once proclaimed the deepest devotion to the murdered Lord Anges, she now fluttered a fan coyly up at Lord Aspace. Lord Manseen said something, and Shenza couldn't miss Innoshyra's shrill laugh. Seelit smiled valiantly in response to something Innoshyra said to her. The fan concealed part of Innoshyra's face, but Shenza caught the poisonous gleam in her eyes as she confronted Seelit's beauty.

When the last of the Sengools had gone by, Aspace rose from his chair. He shifted his shoulders a little, perhaps easing the stiffness from sitting so long. Aspace spoke briefly with Laraquies and Lady Izmay, then turned toward Lord Manseen. A moment later, Aspace and Seelit strolled off toward the banquet table on the Sengool side of the grass.

Lady Izmay touched Laraquies' arm lightly, and they separated to mingle with the guests. Shenza stayed where she was. Aspace and Seelit moved easily through the crowd, acknowledging bows and stopping to chat. If she tried, she could ignore Seelit, who was short enough to disappear behind taller people.

Remembering that she was supposed to be monitoring everyone, not just Aspace, Shenza tore her eyes away from time to time. That was how she noticed Tonkatt Akanti of Sengool edging away from his family's contingent. Tonkatt wove through the press casually, yet he moved with a purpose and glanced around as if he didn't want anyone to notice him.

Tonkatt was one of Nurune's senior apprentices, or had been until he disgraced his coven. Shenza hadn't seen him again until he turned up at Vesswan's house. She narrowed her focus, trying to see if Tonkatt was wearing any magical talismans. She couldn't pick anything out among the jeweled strands around his neck.

Then she felt a sharp prickle across her shoulders. With a slight frown, Tonkatt turned in her direction. Shenza pretended to be interested in what Winomi's mother and aunt thought of Innoshyra's robes. She silently scolded herself for staring too long. As a trained magician, Tonkatt might be able to sense her interest.

She hazarded another look. Tonkatt bowed to Lord Manseen. They spoke briefly. The younger man backed away with more bows, while Manseen returned to his conversation with one of Lord Fastu's brothers. Manseen's bodyguard might have been looking at her, so Shenza lowered her eyes. When she looked up again, Tonkatt had rejoined his clan. He approached Nurune and a woman dressed in scarlet—Vesswan.

Shenza glanced away again. If Tonkatt sensed her spying, Vesswan and Nurune could, too. She frowned slightly as she gazed across the crowded square. Shenza hadn't thought Vesswan would be invited. She must have come in with the Sengools. Still, Shenza found her presence disturbing. She knew why she had come in with the Kesquins, but why was Vesswan sneaking around?

* * *

Chimi enjoyed nibbling on refreshments along with Winomi and her sisters, but she couldn't forget the expression on Shenza's face. Curiosity tingled within her. Who had Shenza been staring at?

After long minutes of wondering, Chimi touched Winomi's shoulder. "Let's find Shenza," she said. "My mother wants us to stay together."

"All right."

The two of them wound their way through the gathering until Winomi tugged on Chimi's elbow.

"Over there."

Shenza leaned against the same crimson pillar, watching the celebration. How could she stand apart on a night like this?

"Sister, there you are," Chimi said.

"Yes?" Shenza sounded surprised to see her.

"You don't look like you're having fun, Magister," Winomi said with gentle concern. "Can we bring you something?"

"Yes, she is," Chimi interrupted playfully. "She's been watching someone. I can tell."

Shenza blurted, "I am not!"

"It must be a man," Chimi crowed, delighted by Shenza's reaction. "Look at her blush!"

"Sister!" Shenza's stern voice couldn't hide the color in her cheeks. Winomi giggled. She saw it, too.

"There's nothing wrong with looking. Even my mother says so." Winomi leaned closer and confessed, "I like that Sulimor. See him, over there? I know he's a Sengool, but..."

Chimi turned to follow her friend's gaze. She nodded approvingly. "He has nice legs."

"Girls!" Shenza sounded desperate. "It's nothing like that. My duty..."

"Well, maybe it should be," Chimi retorted. "We're both old enough to marry, and you're the magister. You're *eligible*, sister. Think about the possibilities."

For a moment, Chimi thought Shenza would march her back home. Then her sister blushed even hotter than before. Chimi and Winomi glanced at each other and fell into fresh giggles.

Then Shenza straightened, and Chimi turned to see who was behind them. A middle-aged woman approached, garbed in the bright blue robes of the first lord's household.

"What is it, Tio?" Shenza asked.

"Magister." The serving woman bowed. "The guests will be seated soon, and my Lady Izmay would like you and your sister to attend her. You also, Lady Winomi."

The first lady? Chimi's heart leapt within her, but all Shenza said was, "As my Lady commands."

"Me?" Winomi squealed with excitement. "I mean, of course, if my Lady wishes it."

"Allow me to guide you." Tio bowed again.

Chimi's heart skipped within her. She could hardly believe it—they got to eat with First Lady Izmay! After this, she could forgive Shenza for just about anything. Meanwhile, Winomi frantically beckoned to Losiri and whispered news of the invitation.

"Tell Mother where we'll be," she said urgently.

The younger girl pouted, but nodded. "You have to tell me everything!"

"I will, tomorrow," Winomi breathed the promise.

Tio led them toward the pavilion. Feeling bold and important, Chimi walked at Shenza's shoulder.

"I'm so excited! I didn't think Lady Izmay even remembered me," Winomi said to Chimi.

Suddenly she regarded Chimi with a new kind of respect. Because, Chimi thought, they had been friends for a long time, but it was always Winomi who did favors for Chimi. Now this opportunity came to Winomi because of her.

"I know," Chimi said, happy that she could help her friend for once. "I..." She broke off at the sight of a familiar face nearby. "Nomi, look!"

It was Azma, and she was practically on the Sengool side of the grass. Chimi couldn't see the face of the person she was talking to, but there was no mistaking those garish robes. It had to be Innoshyra. Azma smiled up at the older girl with obvious flattery. It wasn't like Azma to be so submissive. And with a Sengool, at that.

"She's never that nice to me," Chimi muttered.

"Never mind that," Winomi answered, her voice a thread of delighted scandal. "What does she think she's doing?"

Just then, Azma caught sight of them following Tio. She flinched for a moment, but straightened her back defiantly. Eyes narrowed, she said something. Innoshyra whirled, frowning. She must have realized that they were being invited where she wasn't, because the fan in her hand closed with a convulsive snap.

"Didn't Jeruki say Azma had an offer from a Sengool boy?" Chimi asked, reveling in the moment. "Maybe she's trying to get Innoshyra to introduce them."

"Before Lord Fastu even agrees?" Winomi gasped. "Just wait until I tell Mother!"

The three young women followed their guide into the pavilion. Others were doing the same, gliding up the steps like butterflies on a breeze. Chimi, who had never been to a formal banquet, watched everything with delight.

The tables had been arranged in two curving lines, a wide gap between them. They were large enough for six to sit on the cushions around them. People sorted themselves out and chose seats. The men sat apart from the women, closer to the two head tables, and the Sengools stayed well away from the Kesquins.

Two tables were placed on another dais at the far end of the pavilion. Near one of them, Lord Aspace and Master Laraquies greeted Lord Fastu. Lord Manseen strolled toward them. At the other table, Lady Izmay chatted with Lady Seelit, who smiled shyly. A guard in a short gray robe loomed behind her. Chimi felt a fresh surge of elation. She and Winomi wouldn't just meet Seelit once, they would really get to talk to her!

Tio bowed at the base of the steps and Shenza led them onward. They all bowed to Lady Izmay with hands crossed on their chests.

"Welcome," Izmay said. "So good of you to join us."

As if they would have turned down her invitation, Chimi thought.

"It's our honor." Shenza mumbled as if her mouth was full of ashes.

"Thank you for asking us," Chimi said, making up for her sister's lack of enthusiasm. Izmay and Seelit both smiled.

"Not at all," the first lady replied. "I'd like to get to know some of you young ladies better."

Lady Izmay wore a stunning robe of creamy silk with fishes the exact color of ripe apricots. Their bubble eyes and swirling fins had been painted with amazing skill. It was just as nice as Lady Seelit's diaphanous robe, and Chimi couldn't decide which she liked better.

"Hello again," Winomi added, looking directly at Seelit.

"Good evening," Seelit said. Her dark eyes sparkled. "I'm getting hungry. Are you?"

"Come, then." Izmay guided the four of them down the length of the pavilion to her table. She seated Seelit first, and then Shenza, taking the place between them for herself. Lady Izmay was giving Shenza a big honor, Chimi thought, and she didn't seem to know it. Chimi quickly settled at Shenza's right, across from Seelit, and Winomi knelt beside her.

Each of the places was marked with a small gift. Chimi got a jade bracelet carved with vines. She slipped it on even though it didn't go with her robe. Winomi had a silver gull brooch inlaid with white shell. Shenza's was a string of gleaming emeralds. Once again, the first lady showed her special favor, but she didn't appreciate it.

"How nice," Chimi said as she fastened the bracelet around her sister's wrist.

One place was still open at the table. Just as Chimi wondered who it was for, Lady Izmay smiled in welcome.

"Lady Nepanta, please join us."

"My Lady honors me," a new voice replied.

Shenza look up suddenly, and Chimi felt Winomi tense slightly as a stranger sank onto the pillow between her and Seelit.

"Have you met Winomi Igola of Kesquin? This is Nepanta Shuzoli of Sengool, and of course, our honored guest, Seelit Bosteel of Bosteel."

"Good evening," Nepanta said, wary but polite.

Winomi nodded a bit stiffly. Chimi reached out to squeeze her friend's hand under the table. It could be awkward, having to sit beside her family's rival. If Chimi had known, she would have switched places, but it was too late now.

At least they wouldn't have to put up with the abrasive Lady Innoshyra. Nepanta was close to the ages of the other girls. Her silken robe was pale green shaded into blue. From the relatively modest garments, she must be a secondary relation of the Sengools, equal in rank with Winomi.

"It's nice to meet you," Winomi said, making an effort at friendliness. Nepanta seemed to relax.

Both of them turned to Seelit, who smiled in return. "I'm glad to hear everyone's names again. I've met so many people today."

Then Nepanta turned to Chimi. "And your name?"

Chimi looked to Shenza, who was the older sibling and should make introductions.

"Excuse me." Shenza straightened slightly, as if coming out of deep thought. "I am Shenza Waik of Tresmeer. This is my younger sister, Chimi."

"The magister?" Nepanta asked. "A pleasure to meet you."

She might have said more, but Tio reappeared. She knelt, reaching between Winomi and Nepanta to set a tray on the table. A teapot steamed there, with little cups clustered around it. A small bowl was heaped with gleaming pearls molded from sugar crystals.

Lady Izmay took up the pot and one of the cups. "Who would like tea?"

Everyone said yes, even Shenza. The first lady poured tea with her own hands, rather than waiting for Tio to do it. The drink was pale as amber, yet wonderfully fragrant. It smelled like orange blossoms and tasted of cassia. Chimi used a pair of tiny tongs to drop two sugar pearls into her drink.

Nepanta asked, "Are you also a sorceress, Chimi?"

Trust a Sengool to remind everyone of her lower rank, Chimi thought. Both Shenza and Winomi tensed beside her. However, Nepanta's expression was courteous, not malicious, so maybe it was an innocent question.

"I work in the fish market," she answered. "I sell fresh fish and mussels, mostly. Sometimes other things, like sea-whip."

Nepanta's eyebrows rose, and Seelit glanced at her, surprised. Chimi felt her cheeks tingle with color. Young ladies of noble rank never even had to do chores around the house. They must wonder why she was sitting with them at all.

"Is that hard work?" Seelit sounded genuinely curious. Well, Chimi's job was nothing to be ashamed of.

"It's mostly talking," she said. "Finding out what people want, or convincing them they want what I have. Bargaining is fun, too."

Seelit smiled at that.

"Shopping is her favorite hobby," Winomi put in.

"Chimi helps support our family," Shenza said. She sounded a bit defensive, to Chimi's ears. "We also grow feather-flowers for the silk."

"We might be wearing some of it now," Winomi said.

Chimi, whose robe was only hemp, shrugged. "Maybe you are."

"It's an honorable trade," Lady Izmay said. Turning to Seelit, she asked, "Do you or your father have any favorite hobbies? We want our guests to have a good time."

"I grow flowers, too." Seelit shared a smile with Chimi. "I love orchids. Sometimes I walk in the rain forest and look for wild orchids. Since I've never been to Chalsett before, I'm sure I would find some new ones."

"My uncle also collects flowers," Winomi said. "You'll have to come see his pond lilies and lotuses."

Not to be left out, Nepanta quickly added, "I'm sure my uncle would loan you a boat and a guide if you'd like to explore the coral isles. There are plenty of wild orchids there."

"I'd like to," Seelit said, although Chimi noticed she didn't say which offer she favored.

"But don't go near the volcano," Shenza cautioned. A silly warning, Chimi thought with disgust.

"Why would we?" Nepanta asked. "Nothing is growing there."

While Izmay refereed the discussion, Tio came back to switch the teapot for a small dish of pickled vegetables. Chimi helped herself to the spicy-sweet treats and settled back to enjoy the meal.

* * *

Izmay and the younger girls were intent on negotiating their social schedule. Shenza glanced around, trying not to let her disinterest show. If she got the chance, she wanted to ask Seelit if the Bosteel ships had encountered pirates on their journey. That might explain why they had their own guard; the fellow still lurked near the pavilion steps, in a position to watch both Seelit and Manseen. He looked just as unfriendly when she saw him up close.

Until she got her chance to speak to Seelit, Shenza kept an eye on the neighboring table. Like Izmay's table, it was carefully balanced to include both Sengools and Kesquins without giving an advantage to either. In addition to Lords Aspace, Manseen, Oriman and Fastu, she saw Laraquies, as Vizier, and Chief Peacekeeper Borleek. Shenza wondered a little at that, since she knew neither Aspace nor Laraquies liked Borleek. However, she did see the advantage of placing Borleek's burly mass in between Oriman and Fastu. Or maybe Lord Aspace was trying to make a point to Lord Manseen and his dour bodyguard.

The conversation seemed jovial enough. Even Borleek wasn't scowling as much as usual. Both Fastu and Oriman were focused on Manseen. They seemed to be offering him business deals. Shenza found her eyes lingering on Lord Aspace, who leaned over to hear something Laraquies said. The hum of voices fell away, leaving silence and the brilliance of his smile. Shenza forced herself to drink her tea and break the spell.

Somewhere nearby, a flute began to whisper. Dancers flitted into the space between the rows of tables. Translucent, silvery veils floated around them as they bowed toward the head tables. Shenza knew the lead dancer, Aoress Lirelik of Catensa, who was considered the best dancer in Chalsett-port.

The rumble of a drum and wail of a single violin joined the reed flute as the performance began. Rich colors shimmered over the dancers' veils, transforming the cast into a young couple clinging to their foundering boat. Shenza recognized a popular folk tale about faithful lovers separated by shipwreck and storm. She tried not to sigh. No one had to remind her how difficult love could be.

Tio returned to their table with the next course: fried noodles topped with greens and several bowls of sauce to pour over it. Shenza took only a small portion. It would insult Lady Izmay and her cooks if she didn't eat, but she really wasn't hungry.

To her surprise, Lady Izmay leaned closer. "Try to eat something," she murmured. "You'll feel better."

The first lady's voice was soothing. Shenza was startled by the concern in her eyes.

"I'm sorry," Shenza whispered, hoping not to disturb the other girls as they watched the dancers. "It looks delicious, but I've been worried about..." Shenza hesitated. She had no right to complain about Aspace's courtship, especially when Seelit sat so close by.

"This is all nothing," Izmay murmured back, taking in the banquet with a wave of her hand. "My son is up to something. He thinks I can't tell." For a moment she looked exactly like Aspace, intense and inscrutable. Then she chuckled. "I'm too old for such games. However, I suspect that he already knows who he wants to marry."

Izmay raised her cup for a sip of tea, but she angled a coy glance at Shenza. Shenza stared at the dancers without seeing them. What was Izmay trying to tell her? That Lord Aspace had feelings for her? She longed to believe that, but it couldn't be true.

And yet, when Izmay spoke to Seelit, Shenza could almost imagine a trace of pity in her voice.

For the first time, Shenza looked at her rival not as a symbol of inevitable disappointment, but as a person. Seelit was very pretty, and she was trying hard to be friendly, but her bodyguard loomed behind her like a dark cloud. Could it be that his job wasn't to protect Seelit, but to make sure she did what she was told?

That was ridiculous. What woman could not want Lord Aspace once she had met him? Shenza's eyes found their way to the next table, where Aspace served food for his guests. Only days ago, she had been sitting with him, alone except for the falling rain. Shenza felt her cheeks burn at the memory. The way he had looked at her then, maybe Izmay was right. Maybe she did have a chance.

Her stomach growled, bringing her back to herself. Shenza was surprised to feel real hunger. The noodles suddenly looked delicious, and Tio was just laying down a platter of fish and crabs. Shenza picked up her utensils to eat.

* * *

Chimi and Winomi sighed together as the story ended with the lovers joyfully reunited. Chimi caught a furtive movement in the corner of her eye and looked around to see if Nepanta was really wiping her eyes. Then she joined the audience in clapping and cheering. The dancers bowed gracefully and ran from the stage with their sheer veils drifting behind them.

"That was so beautiful," Chimi said.

"I love that legend," Winomi answered.

On Chimi's other side, Shenza merely mumbled. Chimi turned to scold her sister for ignoring such an amazing performance. When she saw Shenza's fixed gaze and the glow of color in her cheeks, she swallowed the words. Chimi had forgotten that Shenza was acting like this earlier. Now she had another chance to discover who her sister had a crush on.

She turned her head, trying to follow her sister's line of sight. The only table in that direction was Lord Aspace's. Just a few feet away, Master Laraquies was pouring wine for Lord Manseen, and Lord Oriman was saying something to Chief Borleek. Powerful as those men were, there was only one person at the table worth looking at the way Shenza was looking.

Chimi bit her lip to keep from shrieking out loud. She had been right—Shenza was staring at a man. It couldn't be, but it was true. Shenza was in love with Lord Aspace!

Chapter Eighteen

Gifts of Friendship

Chimi yawned as she propped her elbows on the counter of her booth. Waves on the harbor sparkled with morning light. She tried to watch the boats moving to and fro, but her eyes kept losing focus and her head felt heavy as a jug of water from the neighborhood well. Chimi raised her hands to cover another yawn.

"Now stop that," Byben scolded beside her. "You'll make me fall asleep."

"Sorry." Chimi smiled, rubbing yawn-tears from her eyes.

Thank goodness Byben had come to work with her this morning. So far, he'd spent most of his time catching up on family news with Nakuri, who was his cousin. Or maybe his niece. Chimi could never remember. That left the sales work to Chimi, but it was still better than Grandmother's grim presence.

Chimi was exhausted, but in the best possible way. She and Shenza had come home very late, of course. The feast had been delicious, and there had been more dancing. Even Shenza had finally relaxed enough to enjoy herself. Conversation had been lively as the wine began to flow. When they got home, Mother and Sachakeen had met them with all kinds of questions. Who had they talked to, what had gone on? Most of the moons had gone down before the sisters went to bed, Chimi in her hammock and Shenza on a pallet beside it. Even then, Chimi had been too excited to sleep. From the way Shenza kept turning over in the dark, she hadn't been sleepy, either.

Not that Chimi blamed her. She had been delighted to figure out Shenza's secret, but horrified, too. Shenza, in love with Lord Aspace? Today, in the bright light, it seemed unbelievable. Chimi laughed inside as she remembered telling her sister to look at the men around her. Shenza was already looking, but she set her sights high. Maybe impossibly high.

Lord Aspace would sure be a prize catch. The way Lady Izmay had been favoring Shenza, maybe she even had a chance. And wouldn't that be something! Mother wouldn't even have to try to find a husband for Chimi. As a first lady's sister, she would be highly desirable. Young men of noble houses would line up to offer for her.

She knew she couldn't count on anything like that, but there was no reason not to dream. Chimi smiled to herself, then yawned a yawn as vast as the sea.

"You did have fun last night," Nakuri chuckled.

Chimi grinned. "Just a little."

Nakuri and Byben went back to their conversation, and Chimi pretended to dust the counter. The hardest thing was to keep quiet about what she knew. Nakuri had been as full of questions as Mother, when their stalls opened, but Chimi hadn't said a word. Oh, how she longed to tease Shenza. Such an obvious infatuation made a tempting target.

She couldn't do it because of Mother and Sachakeen. Chimi was sure they already knew. Certain details, like the way they had been acting at dinner on the day she met Yail, only made sense if they knew. Chimi was highly annoyed that they hadn't told her. Until they mentioned it, the blame would be on her if she said anything. It was a kind of torture.

She yawned yet again, then lifted an edge of her robe to blot the tears that gathered in her eyes. "Sorry," she murmured to Byben.

The old man patted her shoulder. "Maybe you should sit in the napping chair today."

"No, really, I'm fine."

The family's silence meant that Chimi couldn't even share Shenza's secret with Winomi, and she always told Winomi everything. She had never held back good gossip before. It felt wrong, like she was betraying their friendship.

It would be worse to tell on her sister, though. Shenza took everything *so* seriously. Half the girls in town had a crush on Lord Aspace, but she acted like she was the only one. Maybe she just thought she was the only one who mattered, Chimi thought irritably.

A distant movement caught her attention, and she blinked her eyes into focus. A passenger canoe glided into the harbor, past the foaming surf at the breakwater. She watched idly. It was a large craft, its pointed prow carved and painted to look like a swordfish. There were eight oarsmen with bronzed muscles gleaming as they worked, and nearly a dozen women in brightly colored robes. The only male passenger was a big man in a short gray robe and kilt. When Chimi noticed him riding directly behind a shorter figure, she perked up. That was Seelit's bodyguard from last night. Seelit and the Sengools must be coming back from their orchid expedition.

"Welcome!" Byben suddenly called.

Chimi turned with a start and saw an elderly woman at the counter. Reminded of her job, Chimi smiled.

"Good morning! We have eels, redfish and clams today. What would you like."

"Is the redfish cut in fillets or steaks?" the old woman asked.

Hearing her tremulous voice, Chimi groaned internally. She recognized this customer. It was the same woman who had taken so long to make up her mind the last time she was here. Dutifully, Chimi peered into the basket beneath the counter. She was so tired this morning, she hardly remembered what kind of fish it was, let alone how it was cut.

"Fillets," she reported.

"Let me see some," the customer said.

Chimi lifted out a section of soft, pinkish flesh and laid it on a banana leaf on the counter. All the while, she tried to keep an eye on the pier where the canoe was putting in.

"Is this all you have?" the old woman asked. "Are they all this size?"

Chimi was forced to look back at her customer. "What do you mean?" The fillet was big enough to feed a family.

"Do you have any smaller ones? I can't eat that much."

"Of course, matron." Chimi knelt down to put the redfish away. She searched through the bin for a smaller portion. "How's this?"

The old woman poked at the fish, feeling for bones, and bent down to sniff how fresh it was. When she did that, Chimi looked over her back. The Sengool women were gathering in a circle, waiting for Seelit's bodyguard to help her off the canoe.

"I don't know," the customer murmured. "Maybe I should have an eel, instead."

"Whatever you want." Chimi forced a smile, then knelt behind the counter to hide her scowl. Why did there have to be a customer, just when there was something interesting to see? And why did it have to be this customer?

She placed another banana leaf on the counter and set three eels on it, giving the old woman a choice so she wouldn't ask to see a different one right away. The eels were so fresh that their eyes still glittered.

"Don't they look delicious," she said. "One of these would make a fine meal with some onions and ginger and rice."

"Would you gut it for me?"

"Of course, matron. There's no charge, once you've paid for it. Have you decided?"

"Not yet..."

While the old woman studied the eels, Chimi hazarded another glance at the dock. To her dismay, no one was there but the oarsmen. Seelit was gone!

Discouraged, Chimi turned back to her customer. She was surprised to catch the tail end of a shrewd glance coming back at her. The old woman wasn't confused at all. She was playing at it, taking advantage of Chimi's distraction. Maybe she thought she could make her desperate for the sale and get a better price.

A cold surge of anger rolled up Chimi's spine, but she swallowed her harsh words. Successful shopkeepers couldn't tell their customers what they thought, even when they did something this sneaky.

"Take as long as you like," Chimi said. She tried to sound like she didn't care what the old woman did. Looking at the eels' needle-like teeth, she wished one of them would bite her.

The customer stepped back, still pretending to be undecided.

"I'll have to think about it," she quavered, and shuffled off down the aisle. Just like she had last time, Chimi recalled.

"Come again soon," Chimi said. Even she could hear how grudging the courtesy was.

She quickly wrapped the redfish in its banana leaf and put it back in the bin. If the woman did come back, she could find it more easily.

"Don't be upset," Byben consoled her, passing the eels down from the counter. "You tried hard. I could tell."

"Oh, it doesn't matter," Chimi said. Now that the difficult customer was gone, she let her disgust show. "It's just a game she plays. She'll be back later."

"You know our clients best."

Chimi yawned as she put the eels away. After a moment, she drooped against the counter. For the first time, she thought how stupid it was to work in a fish market. If she could marry the right man, she'd never have to work again. She just had to get Shenza to take her to more banquets. Then she could find her future husband. If he was rich, even Grandmother couldn't criticize her for making her own match.

A flash of moving color on the nearby stairway caught her eye. The Sengools! Chimi straightened eagerly, hand raised to wave. Then, in sudden panic, she ducked back under the counter. Innoshyra of Sengool was leading the group. Nepanta might not have sneered at Chimi, but Innoshyra wasn't nearly as nice.

Cautiously, she peered over her counter. The women halted at the top of the steps up from the pier. Innoshyra was arguing with Seelit in a fakey-nice way that did nothing to disguise her jealousy. Seelit of Manseen seemed to be apologizing for something. She bowed gracefully.

"But you can't wander around alone." Innoshyra's strident voice carried easily over the distance. A chorus of the other Sengool women supported her.

"A young lady..."

"It's not right!"

If Innoshyra thought she could appeal to the bodyguard who loomed behind Seelit, she was wrong.

"She won't be alone," he said. His flat, almost toneless voice was somehow very threatening.

So Seelit was trying to get away from the Sengools? Chimi didn't blame her.

"I've enjoyed visiting with you," Seelit said in a pleasant but firm tone. "I just want some free time now."

Chimi glanced down the aisle, making sure no patrons were about to interrupt her. Byben and Nakuri were chatting again, oblivious to the drama unfolding nearby. Chimi watched avidly. This was something she could tell Winomi about later.

The discussion went on a little while longer. Innoshyra's cheeks, already rouged, burned crimson with anger but in the end Seelit got her way. The Sengools huffed off after Innoshyra, leaving Seelit with her bodyguard. Chimi was proud of her for standing up to them.

Unexpectedly, the guard glanced toward Chimi. As she met his gaze, cold tingles ran up her arms. He leaned closer to Seelit, saying something Chimi couldn't hear.

Embarrassed to be caught staring, Chimi jerked her eyes away and pretended to wipe her counter yet again. The ruse didn't work, though. She heard the rustle of robes coming closer.

"Chimi?" Seelit asked.

"How are you today?" Chimi asked. She quickly confessed, "I saw that you were talking. I didn't want to interrupt."

"That's all right," Seelit said. She was wearing an ordinary headcloth and robe this morning, soft green silk with white flowers. White beads draped her neck, and a set of thin silver bangles chimed together as she raised her hand to tuck a dark curl behind her ear. On her other wrist, she still wore the jade bracelet Chimi had noticed the night before.

"I didn't think you would be able to find me here," Chimi said, "but I'm glad you did."

"We passed by earlier, but you were busy," Seelit said.

"I'm sorry to miss you."

Seelit's dark eyes roved with friendly curiosity. "Is this where you work?"

"This is it!" Chimi spread her arms wide. "We have the best eels today."

Inside, she felt puzzled. Seelit couldn't need to buy food. Lady Izmay and her staff would take care of all that.

"And this must be your grandfather," Seelit said, for Byben was watching them with interest.

"No," Chimi said. Seeing a trace of disappointment on the old man's face, she added, "Well, he's an honorary grandfather. This is Byben Calloob of Cessill, a good friend of my family. And he's my boss."

"But not too bossy," Byben put in. He chortled at his own joke, while

Nakuri groaned in the next stall. Seelit laughed.

All this time, the guard studied Chimi coldly, as if she was an eel herself. She wished he would stop doing that. It made her think a girl who worked in a fish market wasn't worthy to talk to someone like Seelit.

"It's a beautiful day," Chimi said before the silence got awkward. "Did you see any orchids when you went boating?"

"Oh, yes. Many," Seelit said with real enthusiasm. "There was one with a long tail at the back, curling like a monkey's, but it had stripes on its face like a marsh tiger. And there was one that looked exactly like a white moth. If I can, I want to bring one of those home with me."

"I hope you can," said Chimi, who had never paid much attention to flowers. Again she wondered why Seelit had come to see her. With the guard's frigid gaze on her, she didn't dare ask. Chimi cast about for something else to say.

"Would you..."

"Do you..."

Both girls started talking at the same time, then stopped together. Chimi couldn't help laughing. "You first."

Seelit relaxed, enjoying the moment's humor. "Can you come to the market with me? That girl, Winomi, she said you know all the best places."

"I'd love to, but..." Chimi hesitated as feelings warred within her. It was exciting that Seelit wanted to be friends, but this was Shenza's rival. How could she favor Seelit over her own kin? And anyway, she had left her money at home.

"What are you waiting for?" Byben's voice at her shoulder startled her.

"But it won't rain for hours." Chimi gestured skyward, where the first clouds were blooming in the sky.

"Do you think I can't watch the shop?" Byben scolded, but his eyes sparkled with good humor. "I did it by myself for years before you came along."

"I know." And Chimi remembered the stories Nakuri had told her about how badly Byben used to do the job. "Grandmother said..."

"She doesn't need to know," Byben said in a conspiratorial tone. "Nakuri won't tell, will you?"

He turned to his cousin, who grinned. "She won't hear it from me."

"There, you see?" Byben lifted the section of counter and pushed Chimi toward the gap. "Go on. I'm your boss. I say you've earned some free time."

"If you say so—boss," Chimi teased as he shut the counter behind her. "But if Grandmother gets mad, I'll tell her it was your idea."

"Your grandmother might get mad?" Seelit sounded concerned.

Chimi wasn't about to start on that sore subject. "She thinks I need a chaperone, but I don't think anyone is going to bother us." She flashed a pert smile up at the bodyguard.

"Oh," Seelit said. "This is Hydara Tocarei of Bosteel. He's one of Father's servants."

The man looked more like a warrior than a servant, but Chimi wasn't about to argue. "Nice to meet you," she said.

Hydara didn't respond. He seemed intent on scanning the busy crowd.

Feeling slightly foolish, Chimi started to follow Seelit along the row of fish stalls. After a moment, she turned back.

"Byben!" she called. "If that lady comes back, don't let her talk you down. Our redfish is the best. Make her pay a fair price!"

Byben waved his hands in a shooing gesture. Chimi's exhaustion dropped away as she caught up with Seelit. This was so lucky, that Seelit wanted to be her friend. She had just been thinking how she needed to meet the right man. Seelit could help her even more than Shenza.

"Thanks for inviting me," Chimi said. "This will be fun. What do you want to look for?"

Seelit hesitated at that. "I'm not sure," she said. "I hadn't planned that far, actually."

She laughed with a note of embarrassment, but she also glanced uncertainly at Hydara. Chimi wondered what he had to do with it. Surely he didn't tell her where she could go shopping. Still, if Seelit didn't have any ideas, there was no reason Chimi couldn't offer one.

"I know some of the jewelers," she said. She hoped Seelit wouldn't want clothes. The shopping trip with Shenza had been such a fiasco, and Chimi had no reason to be friendly with the House of Melleen anymore. "Or we could get something to eat first."

Seelit brightened, saying, "I'd really like a cup of tea. After last night, I feel like I won't be hungry again for a hand of days."

"Come on," Chimi said. Smiling, she led the way to the aisle where the food sellers were. Inside, she wondered why Seelit was so unsure of herself. She hadn't acted that way last night. Maybe she had changed her mind about shopping together, now that she had seen where Chimi worked. Chimi didn't want to think about that.

Determined to have a good time, she led Seelit to a stall where the vendor offered pieces of sugar cane. She ordered a pot of tea and two pieces of cane. As an afterthought, she glanced at Hydara. "Do you want some?"

"No."

"He's on duty," Seelit apologized.

"That's fine," Chimi said, but Hydara's attitude was starting to annoy her. The vendor brought their food in a cheap wicker basket. Chimi considered telling Hydara to carry it, but she wasn't quite brave enough to try.

Instead, she carried the hot teapot herself, toward the giant fig tree. There was a small chance Winomi might be there. The Sengools had already monopolized Seelit, and Chimi knew her friend would want an equal chance. It would surely be fun to see Jeruki or Azma's face when they found her sitting with Seelit! No one from the family came by, though. Chimi told herself not to be disappointed.

Seelit and Chimi sat in the shade and sucked on their sweets. Chimi asked about the fashions on the inner islands. Soft colors were popular, Seelit said, and plainer fabrics rather than complicated designs. Chimi nodded, remembering Lord Manseen's garment from the night before.

"Your robe last night was beautiful," Chimi said. "The way it was practically invisible."

Seelit's cheeks glowed as she admitted, "I thought of that myself."

"It was so perfect! Everyone is going to be wearing their robes like that, just you wait," Chimi assured her.

When they were done, Chimi put the empty cups and teapot back in their basket while Seelit rinsed her hands in a small fountain nearby. Chimi moved through the market purposefully, stopping only to return the crockery to the food seller or if Seelit wanted a closer look at something. It was crowded, but there was never any danger of them getting separated. People tended to give way when Hydara scowled at them.

Knowing that Seelit wouldn't have to worry about money, Chimi passed by the stalls selling strands of wood or common shells. With a twinge of guilt, she even skipped Ginro's stall. She led her friend to a tiny square, screened by thick vines. It was almost like a private room among the noise and hurry of the marketplace.

"This is lovely." Seelit touched a vine flower with gentle fingers.

"This place is always nice." Chimi looked around slowly, savoring the temptations all about her.

The finest jewelers offered their wares in this cool bower, away from the day's rising heat. Isolated rays of sunlight pierced the leaf cover, making gems blaze. Some were cut in glittering facets, while others glowed with a softer polish. So many colors, ruby and sapphire, emerald and opal. Chimi sighed with delight.

"What kind do you like?" Seelit asked.

"All of them," Chimi answered wistfully. "I come here just to look," she admitted. "It's too expensive for me. But you can get whatever you want, right?"

At a glance from Hydara, Seelit quickly demurred, "If my father says it's all right."

"Of course," Chimi said. Her eye stopped on a stall where ropes of gems gleamed like strings of sunshine made solid. Chimi beckoned to Seelit.

"How about some amber? It comes all the way from Amethan, on the far side of the Jewel Sea. And see this one, with the tiny fly inside it? I think it's fascinating how that can happen."

"You like amber?" Seelit asked.

There was an odd catch in her voice, and Chimi looked at her curiously. She also realized that the shopkeeper was lingering nearby, hoping to make a sale.

In a spirit of solidarity, she said, "I love the way it glows in the light. I feel warm just looking at it." Chimi stroked a nearby brooch with a longing hand. The merchant's eyes narrowed suspiciously, and her sympathy for him dimmed. She went on, "I got some recently. I couldn't really afford it, but I had to. Mine is smaller than these ones. Anyway, this color is better with your eyes, I think."

Chimi turned, assessing the match, and found Seelit gazing at her with something like dismay.

"It's okay if you don't like it," Chimi quickly said.

"It's just funny," Seelit said with another nervous smile. "Actually, I wanted to give you something. I didn't know if you would like it."

"Something for me?" Instantly, Chimi turned her back on the display. She didn't want Seelit to think she was only begging for a present. "You don't have to. Really."

"It's a gift, to thank you for your hospitality," Seelit said. "That's our custom on Sardony."

Seelit held out her hand. Well, Chimi wasn't about to refuse a gift. Something warm and light settled into her palm. She looked down in anticipation, then gasped. The bracelet was of twisted copper wire, gleaming around a large amber stone. It was rounded and polished, with something dark at the center. Chimi held it up to see more clearly.

A tiny scorpion, no longer than her thumbnail, hung suspended in the center. Every detail was visible, from the crumpled legs on one side to the infinitesimal orbs of its eyes. It seemed so alive that it might jump out and sting her at any moment.

"This is beautiful," she breathed. "I can't..."

"Please take it," Seelit answered. "Father let me have a few things to give away, so don't worry about..."

"Thank you so much!" Chimi hugged Seelit, while both Hydara and the jewel seller glared at her. Then she fumbled with the wires, trying to make the bracelet fit properly. "This will go perfectly with my necklace."

"I'm glad you like it." Seelit sounded resigned now. "Let me help you with that."

Chimi held out her right hand and let her friend twist the cool wires to tighten the bracelet. Hydara continued watching with sharp eyes, but Chimi ignored him. What did some stupid soldier know about jewelry? More important was the way Seelit's hand suddenly trembled.

"You look really tired," Chimi said, concerned. Seelit's dark eyes flickered to her face, searching for something. Chimi couldn't tell what. "I know I am. We were up pretty late last night." She made a show of yawning, so she could revel in the new weight of the amber on her wrist.

"Maybe I am," Seelit said. "It's been a busy morning."

"That Innoshyra would wear anyone out," Chimi put in tartly. She had heard enough from Shenza to know how hard Seelit's morning must have been. "Maybe you should go back to the palace and rest. We can meet again in a day or two and do some more shopping."

"Thanks for understanding." Seelit's expression was pensive. Chimi couldn't bear to see her look so sad.

"You'll feel better when you've rested," Chimi assured her. "Anyway, Byben didn't say I have to go back to the shop. Maybe I'll find someplace to take a nap myself."

"I'll see you later." Seelit raised her hand in farewell. Hydara was close behind her now, almost forcing her away. He was pretty pushy for a servant. Chimi watched them go, wondering if there was any way to make sure he got left behind next time.

* * *

Chimi's happiness quickly faded, giving way to exhaustion that rode in her belly like a stone. Still, she had no intention of resting. There was so much to tell Winomi that she couldn't wait. Chimi headed for a side stair that would take her up to the Kesquin estate without the risk that Seelit's bodyguard might see her.

The upward climb was always long, but today it felt endless. She had to rest on every other landing, it seemed. By the time she dragged herself to the Kesquins' gate, she was drenched in sweat, yet she didn't feel hot. In fact, she was numb and cold to her core. Chimi was relieved that the gate guard recognized her and let her in. She didn't have the energy to argue with him.

A maidservant led her through the garden, where the surfaces of the ponds were covered with lilies in creamy yellow and palest pink. Seelit would like those, Chimi thought. She had to get her to come here somehow.

The women of the household had retreated to a shady arbor. Before her escort even announced her, one silhouetted form jumped up from the cluster of shadowy figures.

"Chimi!" Winomi cried.

Chimi smiled at her friend, but made sure to bow to the two Kesquin ladies before she went to join the younger girls. The women paid little attention, although she did catch a quick smile from Winomi's mother.

"I wondered if you would be up yet," Winomi said.

"I had to work," Chimi replied as she sank down between Winomi and Taldeena. "But you won't believe who I saw this morning—Seelit!"

"She went out with the Sengools. I remember," Winomi sighed. "Would you like something to eat?"

She gestured toward a table where trays of sliced fruit offered refreshment. Normally the pineapples and mangos would have been tempting, but Chimi had no desire for them today.

"I'm not hungry, thanks," she said. "Listen, Seelit might have gone out with them, but she didn't stay there."

Chimi eagerly described what she had seen on the docks. The girls listened raptly. Even the adult women took an interest. Chimi preened as she enjoyed the attention.

She had to pause for a yawn before concluding, "And then she gave me this. Look!"

She held out her hand to show off her new bracelet. The three girls leaned forward to admire it. Chimi felt the warm tickle of their breath on her arm.

"Oh, look at the scorpion," Losiri murmured.

"That's a nice one," Winomi approved. "She must really like you."

"I like her, too," Chimi said. "Remember how everyone was just on top of her last night? I felt sorry for her."

"She looked like she was used to it, though," Winomi said. "She's a first lord's daughter, where she comes from."

"But she had that mean-looking man, Hydara, following her everywhere. I didn't like him at all." Chimi rubbed at her wrist. The sweat from her long climb felt sticky and chilly on her shoulders. The wires of the copper bracelet, which had been so warm when Seelit gave it to her, felt tight. They dug into her skin. Instead of taking on her body temperature, the bauble seemed to suck out her warmth. Chimi thought about taking it off, but she didn't. It was a triumph to receive such a gift. She had to show it off as much as she could.

"Did you say there's other news?" Chimi asked after another yawn.

"Oh!" Winomi grinned. She and her sisters crowded closer. "Remember last night, when you saw Azma talking to Innoshyra?"

"Of course. Where is she, anyway?" Chimi glanced around. From Winomi's low, confidential tone, Azma's forwardness was being punished. Chimi looked forward to watching her suffer.

"Well," Winomi began with glee.

"Daughter," Anamatt interrupted. All four girls looked around. Their mother smiled, but scolded, too. "As much as we like Chimi, this is family business. Since we're all tired from last night, maybe we should take the opportunity to rest together. No more talking."

"Yes, Mother," Winomi answered, while her sisters pouted.

Chimi lifted her shoulders in a shrug as Winomi gave her an apologetic glance. She was sure she would hear everything soon. If only she could tell Winomi everything, too, Chimi thought with a twinge of guilt.

As instructed, Winomi and her sisters started arranging the cushions so everyone could lie down. The maidservant began to pluck the strings of a zither. Its gentle tones drifted like a cool breeze beneath the arbor. A patch of sunlight slanted between the vines near Chimi, and she moved a pillow over there. It felt amazingly good to lie down.

As she started to doze, Chimi felt the ground shake beneath her. The zither stopped abruptly, and the girls sat up with startled exclamations. Chimi wanted to sit up, too, but she couldn't seem to move. No sound emerged from her lips when she tried to speak. A moment later, the girls settled down and the music resumed.

Chimi felt the first flutter of panic in her chest. Fighting hard, she forced her eyes open. Vague shapes formed before her. She couldn't bring them into focus. She tried again to sit up, but she couldn't move. Her whole body felt inert, disconnected from her will. She wasn't even sure she was breathing.

Something was wrong. If she hadn't been so tired, Chimi might have been able to figure out what it was. She couldn't move, couldn't speak, and even though she lay in the sun she felt very cold. Not just a little chilly from shade and sweat—she was cold to her core.

No—cold as a ghost, she thought with a new surge of terror. That was impossible, her cloudy mind insisted. The ghosts wouldn't bother her any more. Vesswan had promised.

If Chimi could have moved, she would have run screaming to a necromancer. Even to Lelldour. Someone had to know what was wrong with her. But Chimi couldn't run. She could only lie there, as still as a stone statue or the trunk of a fallen tree.

Chapter Nineteen

Invisible Witness

Chimi didn't know how long she lay there, paralyzed. The chill within her sent waves of stabbing pain through her body. No matter how hard she tried to cry for help, she couldn't get her lips to move. The agony faded abruptly, and she found herself floating, looking down on her own limp body and slack face.

Her spirit was out of her body! Chimi tried to dive back down and reclaim her physical shell, but nothing happened.

All around her, the girls and women of Kesquin House chatted lazily, as if nothing was wrong. Chimi heard them clearly, but nobody noticed when she waved her arms and screamed Winomi's name. She was invisible to them, just as the ghosts had been to Shenza.

With sinking dread, Chimi realized she was almost a ghost herself. The only person who could help her would be a necromancer. With Lelldour already dead, it would have to be Vesswan. At least Chimi had some confidence in her.

She turned, orienting herself. Since she didn't have feet to run with, she willed herself to fly toward the eastern side of the island, where Vesswan lived. She was halfway across the nearest lotus pool when she stopped moving. It didn't exactly hurt, although there was a sort of pressure in her chest. Chimi focused her will as if she was casting a magic spell, but she couldn't get any farther from her body.

Dejected, she floated back to hover over her motionless self. It was maddening to watch Taldeena lean over, waving a fan to blow a draft in her body's face. If Chimi had been in her body, it would have tickled. The body didn't react.

"She's really sound asleep," Taldeena giggled.

"I guess she wasn't used to staying up so late," Losiri said. With a mischievous grin, she leaned over to fan along with Taldeena.

"Leave her alone," Winomi scolded, aiming a slap at Losiri with her own fan. "She's my friend."

They were laughing at her, Chimi thought bitterly. They all thought she was asleep after the feast the night before. Even Winomi didn't understand. Trapped in spirit form, Chimi couldn't cry, but the memory of tears crossed her face like a breath of dry air. When would someone realize she was in terrible trouble?

"You're such a fool," sneered a new voice. Winomi tensed as Azma strolled under the arbor. Anamatt frowned, but Lady Rahjeena spoke first.

"Were you invited to join us?" the younger Lady Kesquin asked. Even the servant who was playing the zither paused at the cool challenge in her tone.

But Lady Panubi, who had always resented the second wife, quickly replied, "I think it's all right."

Lady Rahjeena nodded, though she irritably flicked at an imaginary bit of dirt on her knee. Azma bowed her gratitude to Lady Panubi and went to join Winomi and her sisters. She hadn't changed a bit, Chimi thought angrily. Still the straight hair cut in a hard, false line across her forehead. Still the gleam of malice in her dark eyes. Azma sat close beside Winomi, forcing her to move over.

"She isn't your friend, you know," Azma went on, making no effort to keep the conversation private. "She was never our friend. Chimi just wants to build herself up and get closer to royalty. She was using us to do it."

So that was what Azma thought? Chimi wanted to shriek at the unfair criticism. Or dump the nearest platter of fruit over Azma's lying head. Her wishing did no good.

The older women listened, glancing between Azma and Winomi, assessing the accusation. Lady Panubi appeared slightly interested. Lady Rahjeena looked like she had something to say but didn't want to argue with Panubi.

"Chimi wouldn't... She..." Winomi sputtered, almost too angry to speak. Finally she burst out, "She would never do that! Chimi doesn't have a mean bone in her body—unlike you, Azma!"

Chimi wanted to hug her.

Azma raised her eyebrows at the hot words. Her smug expression said that she felt she had scored a point by making her cousin so angry.

"Oh, think about it," she retorted. "Her family is so poor, not like ours. All she talks about is getting a rich husband. Who did you think she had in mind—maybe my brother, or one of yours?"

No one heard Chimi's angry gasp. Of course she had been thinking about marriage and her future. All girls did. Azma had been her friend. Maybe not as close a friend as Winomi, but Chimi had never thought she should hide her dreams. Now Azma used her confidences against her. She had no heart at all!

"It's not like that," Winomi said, but she sounded shaky.

"How can you criticize, Azma?" Anamatt put in. "You who are so ready to make your own match. What of your ambitions?"

Azma opened her mouth to retort, but a thinking laugh from Panubi cut her off.

"What if Chimi did use you?" She smiled as if Winomi was a child. "All friends use each other. It's the way of the world. And if she uses us, we also use her. Her sister is doing well as magister. The family's power is increasing. Soon they may be our equals."

Azma scowled, but didn't dare interrupt Lord Kesquin's senior wife.

"My husband doesn't wish to alienate a potential ally," Panubi continued. "That's why he approves of Chimi's visits to our house. You've done well to encourage her." Panubi nodded to Winomi, who accepted the praise with a nervous flutter. Then Panubi turned to Azma with sudden severity. "Consider this before you antagonize the House of Tresmeer any further."

Chimi spun away from them, phantom hands pressed to insubstantial ears. She couldn't bear listening to them talk about her when she was lying right there. Chimi darted over the lily pond, where bright yellow blossoms mirrored the sun.

Part of her—the largest part—was furious at Azma for assuming she knew what Chimi wanted. It was jealousy, that was all. She could tell from the way Azma had frowned when Panubi mentioned Shenza. Azma hadn't minded being friends as long as it was clear that she, Azma, was superior. Now that was changing and she showed her viper's fangs. Chimi kicked at the blossoms beneath her, wishing she could strike at Azma instead. Marry her brother, indeed!

Then a tiny voice in her heart asked if it wasn't possible that Chimi had been bragging about Shenza a bit too much. Had she insisted on dropping names, like Laraquies', even though she knew it bothered Azma? Maybe Azma wasn't totally to blame. Maybe Chimi hadn't been the best friend she could be.

That was no excuse, she snapped to herself. Even Lady Panubi said that Azma should have been more friendly once Shenza got her promotion. She had spoken of the House of Tresmeer, dignifying Chimi's family name in a way she could never have imagined.

Deep inside, Chimi knew that was no excuse, either.

Somewhere behind her came the faint rustle of robes. Winomi said, "I think I'll go inside. Chimi, do you want to come?"

Without moving, Chimi found herself back under the arbor, hovering over her motionless body.

"She's been asleep a long time," Losiri observed.

"We should pour honey in her ears," Taldeena suggested with a wicked smile. Azma laughed sarcastically.

"Chimi?" Winomi repeated, tugging at her shoulder. Chimi longed to feel the warmth of her friend's hand. She could only watch as Winomi pulled back with a startled jerk.

"She's so cold!" Winomi cried.

At last, somebody had noticed that she needed help!

Now it was Azma who had to move out of the way while Anamatt and the other women converged on Chimi's limp form. Chimi watched them shake her, roll her over, pinch her arms and slap her cheeks while the frantically called her name. None of it did any good.

"This isn't normal," Anamatt finally said. "What could be wrong with her?"

"It's almost like she's dead," Azma's mother murmured.

"Don't say that," Winomi shrilled at them. "Her heart is still beating. She can't be dead!"

Winomi slumped over Chimi and sobbed, while her mother and sisters clustered near to comfort her.

"Don't worry," Anamatt soothed. "It will be fine."

"This won't do," declared Panubi, who had been watching the process from a safe distance. "Send for a healer at once."

She probably just didn't want to kill a potential ally, Chimi reflected bitterly.

"As she keeps saying," Azma said, annoyance coloring her tone, "her sister is the magister. Maybe she'd know what to do."

"You may be right." Panubi motioned to the maidservant who had been playing the zither. "Send word to the magister."

"As my Lady commands." The young woman bowed and hurried off.

"Let's make her comfortable," Lady Rahjeena suggested anxiously.

As Chimi looked on, they put a pillow under her head and covered her with an assortment of fine silken robes. They meant to keep her warm, but Chimi doubted it would help. Winomi held vigil over her body, sniffling occasionally. At least her friendship was genuine.

Chimi hovered nearby. She wished she could comfort Winomi, and wished too that Shenza would hurry. Since she couldn't tell anyone to call Vesswan, Shenza would have to do. Chimi circled the lily pond impatiently. The wait seemed endless.

* * *

Out in the street, the gong rang. Its mellow voice usually warmed the afternoon air with welcome and promised help to those in need. Today, the sound was unbearably loud and shrill. Muffling a groan, Shenza dragged herself up from the table and shuffled toward the front of the house.

It seemed she took too long to reach the door. Juss' voice rang in the street outside. "Good morning!"

Shenza was glad it was him. If a client had come to see her, she would have had to pretend she was awake. After last night's revelry, there wasn't enough tea in the world to wake her up. She had only just crept home from her mother's house, bathed and changed into her normal robes, and it was almost noon.

Brilliant daylight made Shenza wince as she pushed aside the curtain of tiny shells that screened the doorway. Juss had already come up the steps and was waiting just outside. She rubbed her tired eyes and opened the grille for him.

"Did you have fun at the feast?" Juss grinned with sadistic good humor.

Shenza nodded, trying not to yawn in his face. "I didn't see you there."

Juss followed as she started back to the table, where she had been trying to wake herself with a fresh pot of tea.

"They made me stay at the ward," he complained. "Shamatt said he needed someone reliable down there while he and the chief were up the hill."

"That's too bad," Shenza sympathized.

She had thought she would be miserable all night, watching Lord Aspace flirt with Lady Seelit, but Lady Izmay had definitely been dropping hints. Despite all Chimi's friendly overtures, it had been Seelit who sat on the outside. Shenza gazed across the garden, not seeing the brook's sparkling water. A smile of startled joy tugged at her lips. The royal banquet hadn't been what she expected at all.

"I heard the food was amazing," Juss said as he joined her at the table.

"Are you hungry?" Remembering basic hospitality, Shenza gestured to take in the bowl of steamed breadfruit on the table. This simple food was all she could face after the rich fare at Lord Aspace's table.

"No, I ate on the way here. You go ahead."

She nodded and took a piece of breadfruit. As soon as the chewy morsel reached her stomach, her head began to clear.

"Was there really an armed man with him?" Juss asked after a moment.

"With who? Oh." Shenza paused, redirecting her thoughts. She had almost managed to forget Lord Aspace's forebodings about Lord Manseen's visit. "Well, there was a guard. I didn't see any weapons." She shrugged, knowing it would have been easy enough for the man to hide one. "What did Chief Borleek say?"

"Nothing. I heard from Rakshel, and he was there. I just..."

Again the chime rang from the street, cutting Juss off in mid-phrase. Shenza quickly took a bite of breadfruit as she rose to go to the door.

"Are you expecting anyone?" Juss asked.

Shenza shook her head as she walked. Laraquies hadn't been here when she got home. Either he had rested and gone on his way again, or he hadn't come home last night. Sometimes Shenza wondered how an old man had such stamina. She yawned again, wishing she had that much energy.

Tiny shells clattered around Shenza as she pushed through them. "Good day," she called.

A young boy looked up from the base of the steps. He was dressed in a short kilt of bright magenta and matching headcloth. A servant from Kesquin House? The lad bobbed in a bow.

"Magister Shenza?" he piped. "Lady Panubi has sent a message for you." Shenza nodded, and he continued.

"Your sister came to visit us this morning," the boy said with serious concentration. Shenza listened, surprised. She had thought Chimi would be working. "Now she is ill. Will you please come and advise us?"

"Of course," Shenza said. "Wait just a moment." Torn between irritation and amusement, she turned back into the house. "Chimi's not feeling well," she called to Juss.

He replied with a snort of laughter. "Stayed out a little too late, did she?"

Shenza chuckled, too. To be honest, she didn't feel very well herself, and she hadn't sampled the wine, as Chimi had. Bending over the table, she snatched a few more bits of breadfruit and mumbled, "I have to go get her. Can you do me a favor?"

"Carry her home? Sure." Juss stood up. "She won't weigh a thing."

"Actually, I need you to tell my mother what's happened." Shenza hurried through the work room and snatched up her travel case. She didn't expect to need her mask and tools, but she always felt she wasn't completely dressed if she didn't have them with her. "You remember where our house is, don't you?"

"I think so," Juss answered. He came to join Shenza as she paused in the doorway, pulling on her sandals.

"Tell Mother she's up at the Kesquin estate. I'll go straight there and she can join us."

"Right."

Juss tapped his chest in a quick salute and jogged down the steps, past the messenger boy. Shenza ordered the gate to lock itself behind her.

* * *

Time blurred into a fog of anxiety and boredom for Chimi. Her sister finally arrived behind a breathless page. Winomi, Losiri and Taldeena swarmed to meet her, all of them talking at once.

"Thank goodness you're here!"

"We didn't do anything, not even Losiri."

"She fell asleep and we couldn't rouse her."

"She's never done this before."

"Girls," Anamatt scolded. "One at a time!"

Shenza chuckled in the resulting silence. "It seems she didn't get enough sleep last night. I'm very sorry to bother everyone." She directed this last to Lady Panubi.

Chimi fumed invisibly. Even Shenza had no respect for her!

Panubi shook her head graciously. "Please believe that I wouldn't call on you for a minor thing."

"It's more than that," Anamatt said. "Please come look at her."

Chimi watched her older sister's expression change from mild amusement to confusion as she saw Winomi's blotchy face. Anamatt tugged at her arm, drawing her toward the heavily swaddled bundle of Chimi's body. Shenza knelt beside it, sitting her travel case at her knee.

"Sister?" she called gently as she ran her hand over the body's forehead.

Chimi felt something like a crackle of lightning in the air. Her sister tensed. However, unlike the other women, Shenza didn't look surprised. She sat very still for a long moment. Only her eyes moved, roving side to side as if she could focus on something that wasn't there.

"You see? This isn't normal." A shaken Anamatt broke the silence. "I've tended my share of sick children, but never anything like this. She's so cold."

"Yes," Shenza murmured.

She reached for her travel case, which opened itself before she even touched it. The gleaming face of her mask gazed up at the silent watchers. Shenza picked it up and raised it to her face.

Suddenly she seemed like a stranger in her purple robes and golden mask. Its serene smile was marred by a spider-web of cracks on one side. That had never bothered Chimi before, but now she wondered why Shenza hadn't repaired it. Did she want people think she, too, was broken and imperfect?

That was much less important than Chimi's plight, however. Chimi watched impatiently as Shenza surveyed her body. Why didn't she do something? After a moment, Shenza leaned over to lift Chimi's right hand from under the coverings. A ray of sunlight struck false fire from the bracelet with the scorpion entombed in amber. Shenza spoke at last.

"This is new, isn't it?" Her voice was too calm, thoughts unknowable behind her mask.

"That's right," Winomi said in a trembling tone. "She just got it today."

"Did she tell you where she got it?"

Something in Shenza's voice made Chimi drift closer, to hear better.

"From Seelit," Winomi replied, blank and confused. "Chimi said it was a friendship gift."

"She wouldn't stop talking about it," Azma added sullenly, from the back of the gathering. Chimi kicked the air in her direction.

"That's not fair," Losiri protested.

"It's the truth," Azma retorted.

"If you got something from Seelit, you'd brag, too," Taldeena swiped back.

"Girls!" Rahjeena scolded. "Let the magister work."

Ignoring them, Shenza carefully picked at the wires that held the bracelet in place. Chimi knew her sister's mask was enchanted to show her things others couldn't see, but what was she seeing now? Why didn't she tell anyone?

Shenza loosened the thin wires and worked the bracelet off the body's hand. There were grooves where the wires had pressed into her skin. Chimi remembered how it had pinched. She closed her eyes and concentrated, willing her spirit to re-enter her body. How she longed to lie in her cold, flaccid skin and make it warm again—so she could sit up and tell them she had heard every word they said about her!

It was no use. Chimi remained a floating spirit, helpless to influence the real world. Shenza sat back, as if she too was waiting for Chimi to revive. When nothing happened, she closed her fist for a moment, knuckles whitening around the amber stone. Then she slipped the bracelet into a small pouch from her case. Leather cords twirled, tying a knot, and Shenza returned it to her case. Silently, with surprising tenderness, she stroked the body's face once more.

"Can't you help her?" Winomi sniffled.

When Shenza didn't answer right away, Chimi felt the cold weight of dread on her intangible shoulders.

"I don't think so," Shenza finally admitted. "This is beyond my experience."

At these words, true fear tightened around Chimi's throat like a strangling vine. "It can't be," she squeaked. Shenza couldn't be helpless. Chimi depended on her. She had always been able to count on Shenza, even more than on their mother. How could her sister fail her?

"But what's wrong?" Winomi cried. Anamatt patted her shoulders, murmuring words to calm her, but Winomi stared at Shenza with frantic eyes.

"I'll have to take her to a healer," Shenza answered in such a calm voice that Chimi guessed she was also fighting panic. The older women glanced at each other, maybe because Shenza hadn't answered Winomi's question. Shenza bowed once again to Lady Panubi. "I'm sorry to impose, but may I..?"

"Please don't apologize." Panubi waved her words away. "We're all very fond of Chimi. We'd do anything to help her."

Chimi growled to herself at Panubi's self-serving lies. The tiny voice in her heart asked why she had ever believed them. Maybe, Chimi admitted, because she had wanted to believe so badly.

Panubi clapped her hands, and a group of menservants hurried under the arbor. They were bare-chested, wearing short kilts in the magenta of Kesquin House. Some of them carried a litter. They must have been getting it ready while Chimi's spirit roamed around the lily pond.

"I appreciate it." Shenza stood out of the way while the men set the litter beside Chimi's body. "Just a moment. I don't think we need those."

She leaned forward, swishing the extra robes away. Chimi watched with horrified fascination as her body was lifted onto the litter. Her arms flopped at her sides, and her head rolled loosely. Then the men took up the poles and rose together in an easy motion.

"Wait!" Winomi jumped to her feet. "I want to come, too."

"This is a family matter," Anamatt began in a calming tone.

"She's like my family, you know that, Mother!" It was the first time Chimi had ever heard Winomi argue with an adult. "Please, Magister, I won't intrude. I just want to be with her."

Chimi willed Shenza to agree. Of all her supposed friends, Winomi was the only one she trusted anymore.

"I think Chimi would like that," Shenza answered at last.

As one, Winomi and Chimi heaved sighs of relief. "Thank you!" they both cried, though only one of them was audible. Then Chimi saw Rahjeena and Panubi's approving smirks, and Azma rolling her eyes. Maybe it was a good thing no one could hear her. If Chimi had been able to speak her mind, she would never have been welcome in Kesquin House again.

The carriers set off after Shenza. Winomi snatched up one of the extra robes and wrapped it around her shoulders as she followed. Chimi fell back to drift beside her. For some reason, she didn't feel as helpless with her friend nearby.

They had to move slowly on the central stair. There was a lot of traffic, most of it going the other way. Whole families walked together, adults with bundles on their backs and older children leading younger ones. Chimi remembered how Mother and Sachakeen had talked about getting away from the volcano. It looked like a lot of people had decided to do it.

Despite the crowd, the bearers carried Chimi's body so smoothly that its head didn't even jiggle. Chimi thought she recognized them from the night before. These were Lady Panubi's own servants, who carried her chair when she wanted to go somewhere. The lady's generosity no longer impressed Chimi.

They had just passed the fifth level when she heart Juss' voice from ahead of them. "Excuse me," he said, and "Let us pass, please," getting closer all the time. Chimi saw the peace officer coming up the steps. Giliatt followed close behind him, and then Sachakeen with Grandmother leaning heavily on his arm.

"Oh, there you are," Juss said as he came even with Shenza.

Giliatt rushed up the last few steps, forcing the bearers to stop.

"Have you found her?" Giliatt asked. Her voice trailed off when she saw the body lying on the litter. Stricken, she asked, "What's wrong with her?"

"What does it look like?" Sachakeen laughed sarcastically, and Chimi felt a fresh burst of indignation. Why did everyone think she had only fallen asleep?

Sachakeen fell silent as Giliatt glared at him, and Grandmother yanked imperiously on his arm.

"They wouldn't have called us for nothing."

"I'm taking her to a healer," Shenza said, possibly trying to head off an argument. "Come with me, Mother, and I'll tell you what I know."

Giliatt stared at Shenza as if trying to see what the golden mask concealed. Then she nodded, and they turned back down the stairs. Giliatt's hand rested in the crook of Shenza's elbow. As they followed the litter, Giliatt tottered like an old woman. Her face was even more pale and pinched than usual.

Because she was worried, answered the tiny voice from Chimi's heart. Giliatt didn't know that Chimi was only trapped outside her physical shell. She only saw the body of her youngest child, which certainly looked close to death.

And Chimi was trapped in another way, too. Shenza was going to tell them about everything: the ghosts, the necromancer. Winomi would probably hear it, too. Chimi could just imagine what Grandmother would saw when she learned that Chimi, who had already been marked as a trouble-maker, had also been touched by dark magic. She would be forced to listen again, powerless to deny anything they said about her.

She had no choice in that, either. The bearers moved slowly downward. She was drawn along with her body, willing or not. It was terribly unfair.

Chapter Twenty

The Truth Trap

The family raced to Kafseet's clinic as fast as the Kesquin servants could get them there. The bearers took Chimi into an alcove facing the lily pond and set her on a narrow table. When they were gone, Shenza took off her mask. The day's heat closed around her like a stifling, heavy robe.

She found a place between Mother, Grandmother, and Sachakeen. Winomi was with Juss, near the walkway. They all watched in silence as Kafseet moved her hands through the air above the unconscious girl, never quite touching her. Giliatt hugged herself, and Sachakeen laid a comforting arm over her shoulders. Seeing their mother's desolate expression was almost worse than feeling the chill that radiated from Chimi's body. No woman should have to see her child lie so cold and limp. Especially someone like Chimi, who had always been so full of ego and vitality.

"What's wrong with her?" Sachakeen's voice came suddenly harsh in the quiet of the clinic.

Kafseet turned, surprised. "You'll need to give me a little more time, boy," was her tart reply.

Sachakeen glared at Shenza as if she was to blame for Chimi's condition. Giliatt, too, looked a question at her. Shenza sighed, wondering how she could ever explain.

"I'll tell you what's wrong," Grandmother Myri snorted before Shenza could speak. "This young lady has taken it into her head that she can do everything her own way. She doesn't need to follow tradition or heed her elders!" The old woman's black eyes glittered, and her jowls trembled with wrath. She, too, glared at Shenza. "Why should she, when her older sister does whatever she wants!"

"Grandmother," Giliatt protested.

"Chimi needs help," Shenza said. Despite herself, she felt her fury rise. How could the old woman bring up a family quarrel at a time like this?

And Kafseet retorted, "I hardly consider Shenza a prodigal."

"Chimi isn't like that!" Sachakeen interrupted. His angry voice overrode both Shenza and Kafseet. "Chimi never ran around with boys."

Shenza watched him, surprised. Sachakeen didn't usually shout.

"That's right," Winomi added indignantly. Then she looked embarrassed at intruding into family matters.

"You can't blame this on Shenza," Sachakeen went on with frustrated ferocity. "Chimi won't force anyone to marry her and hide her shame. That was your life, Grandmother."

Myri glared at him, while Kafseet raised her brows in wry amusement.

"What?" Shenza asked faintly.

It sounded like Grandmother Myri been forced to marry Grandfather Onuro rather than face the shame of unwed motherhood. The old barracuda who despised her grandchildren as rebels and deviants? How could Myri pass judgement on them? And how did Sachakeen know about this when Shenza had never heard a whisper?

"Who told you a story like that?" Grandmother hissed.

"Some of the oldtimers still remember," Sachakeen said. "Like Thell's grandpa. He told me you got married in a hurry, and our father was born too soon afterward."

"That thieving gull." Myri waved her hand to dismiss the rumor, but Shenza noticed she didn't deny Sachakeen's story.

"He told me our father might not even have been Onuro's son." Sachakeen took a step closer, daring Myri to contradict him. "He said they didn't look anything like each other."

Shenza felt her heart drop. She waited for Myri to say it wasn't true. Behind her, Winomi backed toward the door.

"I-I'll just take a little walk," the girl stammered. "A-around the garden."

"I'll come with you," Juss immediately volunteered.

"Stop!" Giliatt commanded. Her voice was like the lightning that sometimes came with summer storms. Juss and Winomi halted in their tracks. A resounding silence fell.

"We can't have this discussion right now," Giliatt told Grandmother. Though she used a gentle tone, it was one that allowed no argument. "Chimi is sick. We have to think about her first."

"I am thinking about her," Grandmother said. Her eyes glittered with some emotion Shenza couldn't name. Rage or shame, perhaps. "I want to make sure she never gets judged the way I was."

"Enough." For once, the longsuffering Giliatt didn't compromise. Turning to Sachakeen, she went on, "That all happened a long time ago, and it never changed how I felt about your father. Please don't say any more about it."

Sachakeen shrugged, which Shenza guessed was as close to agreement as he was likely to come.

Finally, Giliatt appealed to Shenza and Kafseet. "Don't you have any idea what's wrong with her?"

"I wish I did," Kafseet answered with sincere regret. "She's full of some kind of energy that I don't recognize."

"Shenza?" Giliatt pleaded.

Suddenly the task Shenza had been dreading was very simple. At least, it was better than watching her family attack each other like hungry sharks.

"It's negative energy." Shenza found it easiest to face Kafseet, so she spoke to her. The curomancer seemed puzzled, so Shenza added, "Death energy."

"Death?" Giliatt asked in a strangled voice. Winomi gasped.

"She's not going to die," Shenza explained quickly, "not necessarily. Chimi has been chosen as a necromancer, but she didn't want to do it. She refused the training. I think the negative energy has been building up inside her, until she finally collapsed."

Kafseet's keen glance rifled through the family's startled expressions before she said, "And you didn't mention this earlier?"

"She didn't want anyone to know." Ducking her head, Shenza mumbled to Giliatt, "She made me promise not to tell you."

"Is that all?" Giliatt gave a shaky laugh. "My uncle Panjeun was a necromancer. Didn't you know?"

Shenza shook her head. "I guess there's a lot I didn't know about our family." She glanced warily at Grandmother. "Chimi thought you would be angry. I told her she was letting you think the worst, but she insisted."

"So the man she said was following her that time," Sachakeen said. "That was a ghost?"

"It must have been," Shenza answered, "but only Chimi could see him."

"Wait a minute. She's a necromancer?" Juss demanded.

"It's an honorable profession," Winomi said, though the words came out almost a question.

Grandmother humphed in her throat.

"No, I mean, we spent half a day digging up a skeleton from the necromancer's yard," Juss said. He jerked his thumb toward the adjoining alcove, where Lelldour's bones lay. "They're his bones, right? Those are the necromancer's bones."

Shenza nodded, but when she saw her mother's face, she added, "That's not important to Chimi's situation." To Kafseet, she went on, "This isn't my specialty, so I don't understand it very well, but—"

"It's not mine, either," Kafseet said.

"The one time I talked to Lelldour, when Chimi was there, he said that necromancers absorb the negative energy of ghosts they help, so it doesn't stay among the living," Shenza said. "If we can drain it off, maybe she'll wake up. Do you know any way to do that?"

Kafseet shook her head. "I'll have to do some research on this. Curomancy only deals with life energy. I don't know if I can manipulate death energy the same way, and I don't want to make her any worse. You do bring me the most interesting challenges, Shenza."

"What about the other necromancer," Giliatt began, then broke off. "No, if he's dead..."

"There is another necromancer," Shenza admitted. "I can ask her for advice, but I have to tell you, Mother..." She hesitated, searching for words once again.

"I've met her," Juss put in. "You can't trust her."

"And it will be expensive," Shenza said, finding no way to soften the truth.

"It would be," Giliatt murmured. Money had always been their family's weakness, a power not even magic could overcome. She came to Chimi's side and took her slack hand.

"I think I've heard of that other necromancer," Kafseet said. "Let me try first."

"As magister, can't you have it paid for?" Sachakeen said.

Shenza shook her head. "This isn't official business. It's family. I can't abuse my position."

"Not even because it's family?" her brother growled.

Once again Shenza groped for words to explain. A magister had to serve the public good, not use the public purse for personal gain. Yet part of her knew Master Laraquies would approve the expense if she asked. How could she refuse to help her sister?

Still, she forced out a harsh whisper: "It would be wrong."

"Then let me help," Winomi offered. "I can ask my uncle—" For some reason she broke off, then pushed her chin out determinedly. "Chimi's my friend."

"That's very generous," Giliatt began, and Shenza could tell how hard it was to refuse assistance from a wealthy family.

"Lord Fastu would want to do it," Winomi insisted.

Everyone stopped talking as a loud rumble touched their ears. It came from the direction of the harbor. The tremors started before Shenza could even turn toward the noise. First was a bang and a shock, then rolling vibrations that nearly threw her off her feet. She and Kafseet grabbed the table where Chimi lay, while Sachakeen helped Grandmother keep her feet. Juss moved to steady Winomi. Fearful shrieks rang from the distance.

The shaking seemed stronger than ever before, and the low rumbling went on even after the treetops had stopped swaying. Shenza fought the urge to run and see what the volcano was doing. Her family needed her here.

"Those are getting worse," Grandmother said at last.

"I know," Sachakeen answered. He sounded a little defensive, as if the old woman might blame him for the earth's whims.

"Chimi is my patient," Kafseet interrupted, getting back to the subject. "If Shenza is right, she won't get any worse right away. Let me see what I can do before you go into debt."

"All right," Giliatt said. She gazed at Chimi again, helpless and forlorn as a child despite her mature years.

"There's one other thing I can show you," Shenza said to Kafseet. She opened her travel case on a side table and retrieved the amber bracelet from inside. "Chimi was wearing this when she collapsed."

Kafseet held the bracelet in a ray of sunlight. It winked as she turned it.

Winomi blurted, "But Chimi just got that today."

She broke off when Shenza raised her hand. "I know where she got it," Shenza replied grimly, "but I can't make any accusations. Nobody can. Do you understand?"

Winomi nodded. Both hands covered her mouth. "But why?" she whispered through her fingers.

"I don't know," Shenza said. She turned back to Kafseet. "That's evidence, and I'll need it back. Take good care of it."

The curomancer eyed her. "Of course."

Shenza closed her case and felt magic seal it. Beneath the confusion of Chimi's illness and her family's old quarrels, questions had been circling like sharks in her mind. Now they surfaced again. Had Seelit known the bracelet was enchanted? Had she guessed how it would affect Chimi? Even if she had, why attack Chimi?

Or maybe this wasn't Seelit's plan at all. She was probably just following her father's orders. Still, again, why would Lord Bosteel target Chimi? She was nothing to him.

Shenza was aware of her family's tense stares as they waited for more information. She had nothing to tell them, not yet. Shenza expected Sachakeen to start yelling again, but he only asked, "What about us? What should we do?"

With the volcano growling across the harbor, her first impulse was to tell them all to leave Chalsett while they could. Yet she knew they wouldn't go anywhere until Chimi got better.

"I still have to talk to Vesswan," Shenza said. When Kafseet frowned, she added, "She might be able to advise us."

"You're not going without me," Juss said.

Shenza had suspected he would say that. She allowed herself a tired smile.

"I'd also like to let Master Laraquies know what's happened," Shenza went on. "I think he would want to know."

"We have messengers," Kafseet assured her. "If he comes down, he can look at this bracelet with me."

Shenza nodded. "Fine."

"Then I'm going to stay here," Giliatt said. "Son, we were in the middle of husking those feather-flower pods. If you can bring them, I'll work on them here. Then someone needs to help Byben take down the market stall when the rain comes."

"I'll do it," Sachakeen said.

"And someone will have to cook tonight." Giliatt glanced at Grandmother. The old woman had been staring at Chimi, absorbed in her own thoughts. She nodded grudgingly.

Another distant rumble filtered into the alcove. Everyone tensed, but there was only a little shaking this time.

"I'll be back as soon as I can," Shenza told them. To Juss, she said, "Let's go."

* * *

The family scattered like leaves in the wind. Chimi watched them go with helpless frustration. She wanted to follow Shenza, because Vesswan was probably her only hope, but she still couldn't get far from her comatose body. She floated there while Giliatt bowed her head in despair. Winomi hesitated in the doorway, then came to Giliatt's side.

"I'm scared, too," Winomi whimpered.

The two women quietly wept together. Unable to bear it, Chimi fled across the garden. Once again she glided over a pond of lilies. It was hard to believe the things her family had been saying to each other. She was especially amazed that Sachakeen had spoken up for her. He was usually such an annoying big brother. And then there was Grandmother with her sordid past. No wonder she was so obsessed with Chimi's chastity! Strangely, Chimi wasn't even angry with Grandmother. The whole issue was so irrelevant compared to Chimi's actual problem.

She would have liked to shake Shenza. Her life was at stake, and she was too proud to ask for help? It would be wrong, she said. Sun and sand, what a prude!

"Well, well," said a voice nearby.

Chimi spun on air to find Lelldour floating beside her. The red-robed necromancer eyed her with no curiosity.

"What are you doing here?" Chimi blurted.

Lelldour gestured behind them, where one of the alcoves held a long, low bundle. It looked the right size for a human body, but lay strangely flat under a layer of red fabric.

"I can't leave," Lelldour replied with resigned impatience. "My bones are over there. The curomancer is collecting us like fireflies in a lamp. I don't think she even knows it."

Now that he mentioned it, Chimi remembered Juss saying something about a necromancer's bones being here. She hadn't thought he meant this!

"Well, I'm not dead," she said rebelliously. "Isn't there some way I can get back into my body?"

"Perhaps."

Lelldour regarded her as he always did, with determination and distaste. Chimi felt a faint prickle as the memory of hairs rose along the back of her neck.

"Not this again," she moaned.

"Why not?" Lelldour asked. "I couldn't help hearing what they said. You already have a necromancer in your family. Why not do it?"

Trust him to throw that into her face, Chimi thought bitterly. She hadn't even known her mother had a necromancer for an uncle.

"I just want a normal life," Chimi answered. "That isn't who I want to be." She drifted away above the garden path, though there was only so far she could go.

"And this is?" Lelldour suddenly reached out. Chimi jumped as his hand passed through her chest, leaving a cold shiver in its wake. "Being a helpless pawn in someone's scheme, is that what you want?"

Chimi answered her mouth to say no, that she wanted to be the one who schemed. Something made her swallow the words. It bothered her that she had to ask, "What do you mean?"

"I have my theories," Lelldour told her, "about what happened to you, and to me, and what could happen to this whole island."

"Theories?" Chimi snapped. "You sound just like Shenza. If you mean the earthquakes, this doesn't have anything to do with them."

"I even have an idea how to restore you to your body," he went on, ignoring her argument. Lelldour sounded so casual, he might have been talking about the day's weather, or the tides.

Now it was the necromancer who moved away along the path. Chimi was forced to trail after him.

"You want something in return," she accused.

Chimi remembered how Shenza had told their mother Vesswan could help, but the price would be high. It was true that Vesswan had charged Chimi before. Yet Lelldour's price was even higher.

"I know what you want. You're no better than Vesswan." Chimi felt her intangible chin quiver with anger and self-pity.

"I'm nothing like Vesswan," Lelldour answered with cold, outraged calm. "And frankly, I'm not sure someone as selfish as you can ever be a true necromancer."

He kept moving along the path, but Chimi had reached her limit. She stopped in mid-air, pulling against the unseen tether that bound her to her body.

"Selfish?" she shrieked after him. "Selfish? Who are you to call me selfish? You who can't see beyond your own demands!"

Lelldour didn't answer her right away. The sky darkened as a plume of volcanic mist passed over them, and another tremor ran across the garden. It rifled the pond's surface but left the two ghosts untouched. Then his voice came to her across the eerie quiet that followed the shock.

"Now you know how we feel," he said. "We ghosts who can see but not be heard, who can feel but not touch, who know what to do but can never help those we care for the most. I hope you like how it feels. Unless you change, this is the way it's going to be."

It wasn't a threat, but Chimi cringed all the same. The quiet voice in her heart spoke up. How could Chimi complain about Lelldour's demands? Wasn't she the one who expected help without giving anything in return?

She had always been the baby of her family. Not a complete brat, but still, she had been sheltered by her mother and older siblings. Chimi had spent so much time lately wondering why they treated her like a child. Maybe it was because she kept acting like one.

Now Lelldour needed someone to take up the burden of sacrifice that was a necromancer's lot. It wasn't a selfish whim, but a necessity. A ghost himself, Lelldour couldn't fill that role any more. Someone else had to do it.

That meant Chimi. And she knew she couldn't bear to go on like this, both dead and alive at once. She had already seen more than she wanted of Lady Panubi's ambitions and Grandmother's shameful secrets, even of her mother's tears.

Her inner voice, so hateful and so truthful, replied that Chimi had the power to save herself from this un-life. She had always had the power. She just had to forget her pride and use it.

* * *

"It's too bad about Chimi," Juss said as he and Shenza mounted the grand stair.

Shenza merely nodded, saving her breath for the long climb to the top of the city. After leaving the clinic, she had wasted several minutes staring at the volcano. The sullen mountain glared back at her, growling constantly and belching out vapors that drifted across the water to envelop Chalsett-port in a foul haze. Under their feet, the ground twitched steadily. Shenza felt a stab of guilt as she remembered the spirits' anger and that she hadn't done anything to appease them. But what could she do now, with Chimi so ill?

Sweat broke out on her back as she climbed the many steps. The wind, heavy with volcanic fumes, turned her sweat cold. Even the air seemed to hold a chill, like a lingering memory of Chimi's body temperature. Shenza missed wearing her mask, which would have moderated the extremes. Reaching the top at last, they turned toward Vesswan's house. It was a relief to walk on level ground.

"Do you think Vesswan will help you?" Juss asked, breathing hard from the pace of their climb.

Shenza held back a burst of irrational anger. Why did everyone expect her to have all the answers? Even the spirits. It wasn't fair.

"Who else can we ask?" she retorted. "Master Laraquies doesn't know any more than I do, and I can't talk to Master Lelldour without Chimi."

"Just asking," Juss muttered.

Vesswan's arched gate loomed out of the mist. The lantern set in the arch was lit, a flicker within reddish glass that cast no light onto the street below. She tried to remember if it had been lit when they visited before, but she didn't know.

They stopped at the gate. Juss took up the mallet and struck the gong beside the arch with more force than seemed necessary. Shenza was trying to decide if she should apologize for snapping at him when Vesswan's maidservant appeared around a hedge. She gazed at them for a moment, silent and serious. Her free hand pleated a sharp line in the orange fabric of her robe.

"Good afternoon." Shenza spoke up when the servant didn't. "Is Necromancer Vesswan free?"

"I'll ask," the servant replied. She vanished behind the hedge.

"Always so friendly here," Juss quipped.

Shenza nodded, wondering if she had imagined the gleam of speculation in the servant's eyes. She wanted to retrieve her mask from inside her travel case. She would have felt less vulnerable with it on. Yet she left it where it was. The mask was only for official business, and she was here for her family.

Raindrops began to fall in pale flickers against the dark hedge. The volcanic tang on the air got thicker. More drops fell, faster and faster. A gentle rumble sounded in the gloomy sky above them. Shenza felt Juss shift behind her as they waited in the rain. Eventually the servant reappeared holding a parasol, which she offered to Shenza.

"Thank you," Shenza said as she accepted it.

"This way."

Raindrops tapped on the tightly stretched fabric as they followed the serving woman through the gate. Across the garden, Shenza glimpsed the small pavilion where they had met with Vesswan before. It stood empty and dark. This time they went to the house itself, a round stone structure with a tiled roof. The central chamber was flanked by several smaller ones, making the whole seem like a clump of mushrooms growing in the rain.

As they climbed the stairs, Shenza saw Vesswan bent over a table in the center of the room, sweeping up pens, ink bottles and a scroll of cloth. She rolled the fabric into a neat bundle and tucked it into a scroll rack on the far side of the chamber. Slender in her scarlet robe, she glided to meet Shenza and Juss.

"Forgive the delay," Vesswan said with a smile and a bow. The bone strands around her neck clicked together. "I was in the midst of some research."

Shenza handed the parasol back to the servant, who took it and held out her other hand. After a moment, Shenza realized she wanted to take the travel case, too.

"No, I'll keep it." Shenza quickly stepped back, and the woman left. Disconcerted by her manner, Shenza did her best not to stammer as she returned Vesswan's greeting with her own bow. "I'm sorry to interrupt you."

"Don't give it another thought." Still smiling, Vesswan motioned toward the table, where a different servant was setting down a tray. "Won't you join me?"

"Thank you," Shenza said. Juss sat close at her shoulder as she sank onto a cushion beside the table. A broad carpet covered the floor beneath the furnishings. It was deep red, very thick and soft. Shenza noted a circle of runes woven into the pattern. She didn't recognize the spell, but assumed it was meant to shield the table from magical spying. It didn't surprise her that Vesswan needed that kind of protection.

"I saw you at the feast last night, but I didn't get the chance to say hello," Vesswan remarked. "Tea?" She gestured to the tray, which held a bowl of dried dates, a steaming teapot, and three cups.

"No, thank you," Shenza replied. She still wasn't hungry. With an effort, she remembered to make small talk. "Did you have a good time at the banquet?"

"Oh, very much." There was a glint of humor in Vesswan's eyes. She looked to Juss. "Tea, officer?"

"Thanks," Juss said.

Vesswan bent her head momentarily, pouring tea for herself and Juss. The strands of her many braids made a pattern much like the bone necklaces around her neck. As Vesswan set down the teapot, her dark eyes were on Shenza.

"Do you have more questions for me?"

"No," Shenza replied. Even now, it galled her to admit that she needed the woman's help. "I have a family emergency."

"You?" Vesswan asked, surprised. "Please, tell me how I can help."

Shenza spoke haltingly at first, interrupted only by the occasional slurp as Juss drank his tea. She felt that she was confiding her family's deepest pain to the least reliable person in Chalsett-port. Vesswan listened, slipping a date into her mouth from time to time.

"That's terrible!" she exclaimed when Shenza finished her tale. "You must be frightened for her."

"Yes." Shenza remembered her mother's anguished eyes and thought frightened wasn't a strong enough word. "As a necromancer, is there anything you can do?"

"Let me think."

Vesswan rose and strolled toward the shelf of scrolls Shenza had seen earlier. Shenza felt a prickle of disappointment. She didn't like Vesswan, but she had expected her to have some kind of answers.

Beside Shenza, Juss yawned. Puzzled, she glanced at him. If he had been drinking tea, it should be waking him up. He covered his mouth and mumbled an apology. Even as Shenza wondered, she heard the rustle of fabric and felt a flare of heat. She turned, a moment too late. Vesswan slapped one hand onto the circle of runes woven into the carpet they were sitting on.

"Seal the circle!" she cried, and quickly stepped back.

"What is this?" Shenza demanded, but she already knew. Vesswan had put up a warding circle, trapping them inside it.

"Let us out, you!" Juss cried. Despite his yawning, he was fast enough on his feet. His knees wobbled a bit, but he lunged at Vesswan.

"Wait!" Shenza said.

Once again she was too late. Juss struck the warding circle with a flash and a loud crackle. Shenza scrambled out of the way as he was flung backward. Barely missing the table, he landed heavily on the carpet. Vesswan laughed softly.

"Lie still," Shenza said as she knelt beside him. Juss didn't respond, though his eyelids flickered when she rolled him over. He was stunned, or maybe Vesswan had drugged his tea.

"What are you doing?" Shenza straightened to confront Vesswan through the glowing wall.

"Springing a trap," Vesswan answered smugly. "You really did make it easy for me."

The necromancer glided around the ward, rolling a date idly between her fingers. Shenza watched, trying not to let her dismay show. Without understanding why Vesswan was doing this, it was hard to gauge the danger.

"Your poor little sister," Vesswan crooned with mock sympathy. "She told me all her woes. It never occurred to her that I don't want another necromancer in town. Especially not now. It was hard enough getting Lelldour out of the way."

"I thought he was bitten by a spider," Shenza probed.

"It wasn't just a spider, not after I got done with it." Vesswan popped the date into her mouth and chewed with slow relish. "All those enchantments Lelldour didn't want me to try... I used every one of them."

At least this answered Kafseet's questions about how a little spider had killed grown man. Shenza waited and watched, hoping Vesswan wouldn't realize how much she was revealing and stop talking.

"He's such a fool," Vesswan hissed with sudden venom. Then she laughed. "So is your sweet sister. She gave me everything I needed to destroy her. But she did make good bait."

"Bait?" Shenza glared at Vesswan. It wasn't so surprising that she had been responsible for Lelldour's death, but to think that Chimi had come to see her, despite Shenza's warnings!

Vesswan must have seen how hard Chimi was trying to make friends with Seelit at the banquet. She must have given Seelit the bracelet, with instructions to make sure Chimi got it. With Lelldour dead, Shenza had no one else to turn to when her sister collapsed. Chimi had led them both into Vesswan's trap.

"Bait," Vesswan affirmed, smiling with cool and vicious amusement. "Seelit, too. A pretty girl is a perfect distraction. Any more questions?"

Shenza felt she would rather choke than play Vesswan's twisted game, but as long as she was trapped inside the warding circle, she had no choice. Any information might be useful, assuming she could somehow escape to use it. Besides, there had to be more to this than just eliminating competition. Otherwise, Seelit wouldn't be involved.

"Why are you doing this?" Shenza's voice sounded sullen in her own ears.

"Because you also make good bait," Vesswan said. She waited a moment and then asked, "Don't you want to know who you're the bait for?"

Chapter Twenty-One

Riddle of the Runes

"What are you waiting for?" Lelldour asked.

"I'm not!" Chimi protested. If she'd had solid teeth, she would have ground them in frustration. She and her unwanted teacher hovered over the table where her body lay. Giliatt and Winomi sat in the alcove, totally unaware of them. The only sound was dry crackling as Giliatt split feather-flower pods.

"All you have to do is meditate," Lelldour said with flat contempt. "Don't you know how?"

"Of course I do," Chimi retorted. "We studied it in school."

Of course, she hadn't paid as much attention as some of the other students. She hadn't thought meditation would ever be important to her.

"Then you're not trying," the necromancer scolded.

"Yes, I am!" Chimi snapped. "The teachers told us you can't meditate if you're too tense or upset."

"Then calm down," Lelldour replied with infuriating stoicism.

"I can't!" Chimi wailed with sudden despair. "They said you should relax your shoulders and your neck and your back. They taught us to breathe deeply. But I don't have a neck or back. I'm not even breathing! How am I supposed to do this?"

She circled the chamber at the limit of her flight, passing through walls and furniture without feeling them. Lelldour merely watched until she slowed down.

"I don't understand it, either," he finally said. "You should slip back into your body. But panicking won't help. We must try to think."

"Think?" Chimi shrieked.

"As you just pointed out, we've lost the physical resources we once took for granted. We have no hands or voices. All that remains is intellect."

With an upward quirk of one eyebrow, he reminded Chimi how deficient she was in this respect. Irritated, she drifted back toward her empty body.

Chimi hadn't realized how lucky Shenza was to have Laraquies as her teacher. Laraquies was wise and kind, always laughing about something.

Chimi couldn't imagine Lelldour ever smiling. She would never call him master, in the tone of trust and respect Shenza had for Master Laraquies. Lelldour was so... so dead. And Chimi was alive. How could she learn anything from him?

A flurry of movement drew her attention back to the curomancer's clinic. Winomi and Giliatt jumped to their feet as Laraquies hurried in. Winomi made a quick bow, while Giliatt went to meet him.

"Master Laraquies, thank you for coming!"

"I came as soon as I heard." Laraquies embraced Giliatt. "I only hope I can help. Please tell me what happened."

"Shenza says its necromancy," Giliatt began.

And Winomi said, "She fell asleep at our house."

They both stopped as Kafseet swept into the alcove.

"Vizier?" she called. "Oh, excellent timing. I've just been looking at these runes. Can you confirm what they do?"

She held out her hand, and Chimi saw the golden gleam of amber.

"Is this something of Chimi's?" Laraquies asked as he took the bracelet.

"Apparently she was wearing it when she collapsed," Giliatt answered. Winomi nodded.

"The symbols are on the reverse," Kafseet added.

Laraquies turned the bracelet over so that the amber faced downward. Chimi drifted closer, but she could only make out faint scratches on the stone.

To her surprise, the old man turned suddenly. He looked straight at Chimi, and she felt a flutter of hope in her chest. Then his gaze passed through her without focusing.

"There's quite a chill in the air." Laraquies rubbed the back of his neck.

"It's been getting colder all day," Kafseet agreed. "Not right for this season." Then she nodded toward the bracelet. "Those runes?"

The old magister glanced around the alcove once more before he went back to studying the bauble.

"He's aware of us," Lelldour said, surprised.

"Master Laraquies is very wise," Chimi said. "If I keep standing close to him, do you think he'll see us?"

"Since he's not a necromancer, I doubt it," Lelldour told her. "But, by all means, try."

Chimi wafted to Laraquies' elbow. She could see every fold of his purple robe and every silver strand in his curly ponytail, but she couldn't bear to actually touch his body. Her phantom skin prickled, just as if she were standing too close to a stranger. Unfortunately, Laraquies paid no more attention.

"As I read it," he announced a moment later, "this spell is just to keep the bracelet from falling off."

He angled a glance at Kafseet, who gave a sharp little nod.

"Shenza said Chimi just got it today. She seemed to think it has to do with her condition, but I don't see how."

"Why use a spell?" Laraquies turned the bracelet, fingertips probing the amber stone. "See how the wires twist together? That should keep the bracelet on."

"Because it's magic?" Winomi suggested. When Kafseet and Laraquies both looked at her, she hurried on. "I mean, anyone could twist the wires to keep their jewelry on, but I've never seen such a big amber before. Someone who's rich enough to buy something like that would want to be sure they didn't lose it."

"Maybe," Laraquies said, but Chimi thought he didn't sound convinced.

Neither was Kafseet. "If that's true, they did a poor job of it. Those runes are just sloppy."

"They are," Laraquies said. "One could almost think the markings are a ruse to throw off investigators." He and Kafseet exchanged dark glances. "If I had my mask with me, I could look for other enchantments hidden on it. Before I go get it, Giliatt, you said something about necromancy?"

"Yes, Shenza said..." Giliatt began the long explanation, but Chimi stopped listening.

Why had Shenza made such a big deal about Seelit giving her the bracelet? All her talk of not making accusations, and the jewelry had nothing to do with Chimi's situation!

Then Chimi paused. How did she know the bracelet was harmless? Shenza had been wearing her mask part of the time. Maybe she had seen something that Kafseet and Laraquies couldn't.

Just this morning, Chimi had been certain Seelit was her friend. Now she wasn't so sure. Seelit had been awfully quiet. Chimi had thought she was just tired. What if, instead, Seelit had been feeling guilty? Chimi also remembered Hydara, the grim-faced guard who had shadowed their every movement. Maybe Seelit had been afraid of him.

"Did you say where Chimi got this?" Laraquies asked, showing the bracelet to Winomi.

"From Lady Seelit. She said it was a friendship gift," Winomi told him. "I don't understand why anyone would give Chimi a cursed bracelet. You'd think they would go after someone important."

"Necromancers are important," Giliatt said. "My uncle said they help maintain the natural balance. If the old necromancer is dead, Chimi might be more important than anyone thinks."

Chimi wished she felt better about that idea.

"There is another necromancer," Kafseet was saying. "Ves... something.

Shenza went to see her."

"Vesswan?" Laraquies raised his brows.

"Yes, that's it."

"Maybe this wasn't intended for Chimi at all," Winomi said. "What if they gave it to Seelit, and they meant it for her, but she didn't like it, so she gave it away."

Chimi sighed to herself. She would have loved to believe Seelit had made an innocent mistake, but she couldn't forget how Panubi had schemed to use her for the Kesquin clan's benefit. Seelit didn't seem to be any different. It made Chimi sad to realize she no longer believed people did things just to be nice.

Except for Winomi. Chimi hadn't realized how hard her friend tried to think the best of everyone. But then, Chimi was just as much a fool for not thinking it was odd that Seelit came to see her. That must be why she and Winomi were such good friends.

"You could be right," Laraquies told Winomi in a soothing tone. "Believe me, I'll investigate every possibility. Now, since Shenza's gone to visit Vesswan of Zeell, I'll take the bracelet home and see what I see. When Shenza gets back, let her know where I'll be."

"All right," Giliatt said.

"She said that's evidence, and I wasn't to lose it," Kafseet cautioned.

"Since it's you, I don't think she would mind."

Laraquies tucked the bracelet into his robe. Chimi watched him leave with another deep sigh. For a moment, he had seemed to sense her presence. Now he left without acknowledging her. Chimi tried not to feel that Laraquies, too, had failed her.

"Well, that didn't help," she complained to Lelldour. "We still can't leave our bodies, and I can't get back into mine. Does your vast intellect have any suggestions?"

Lelldour didn't answer right away. Fearing that he would go away and leave her completely alone, Chimi turned to look at him. The old man eyed her thoughtfully.

"Perhaps we cannot leave our bodies," he said, "but we have friends who can."

"Friends?" Chimi scoffed. "My best friend is sitting right there, and she can't even see me."

"Not her, you foolish child," Lelldour replied. "I mean the ghosts."

* * *

Slowly and carefully, Shenza sat down. Juss had fallen on the cushion where she had been sitting, so she had to move into Vesswan's place. That bothered her almost more than being trapped within the warding circle.

"Oh, come now," Vesswan exclaimed with another little laugh. "Aren't you even a bit curious?"

Shenza didn't answer. Vesswan of Zeell went on circling the chamber, savoring her helplessness. More than ever, the red-robed necromancer reminded her of a snake—graceful, controlled, and deadly. Shenza couldn't stand to meet her mocking gaze, so she studied the table top, where Juss' tea was rapidly cooling.

Dark possibilities crowded her mind, so many that she could barely think. Her worst fear, which she couldn't seem to shut out, was that something would happen to Lord Aspace because of her. Shenza knew that was stupid. Aspace didn't care enough to put himself in danger for her sake. Master Laraquies would, though. If he also fell into Vesswan's trap, Lord Aspace would only have the lesser magicians to protect him. And his guards, of course, but they were no more a match for sorcery than Juss.

"Such pride." Vesswan seemed annoyed by Shenza's silence. "Very well, I won't tell you. You can try to guess on your own."

The necromancer strolled across the chamber to the scroll rack, where a small brass chime stood on a wooden frame. She lifted the hammer and struck it twice. As the ting-ting pierced the steady drumming of rain outside, Shenza straightened one leg under the table. Her toes found the side of her travel case. She managed to hook a strap with her foot and drag the case out of sight under the table. Her tools were inside it. She couldn't use them yet, but she hoped Vesswan would forget that she had them.

Footsteps sounded, coming closer. Shenza sat up straight as two men strode into Vesswan's work room. She tensed as she recognized Nurune Sengool of Sengool and Tonkatt Akanti of Sengool. They must have been hiding in the back of the house while the necromancer sprang her trap. Seeing those two, she understood a little more of what was happening.

Nurune, Lord Orishem's brother, wore a purple silk robe that gleamed with silver stitchery. Deep lines of age and experience made his face into a mask, one he could manipulate as he wished. Tonkatt, his nephew, was part of Nurune's coven. He was very handsome, a little older than Shenza, and walked with an arrogant swagger. He, too, wore a purple silk robe and glittering jewels.

At one time, Shenza had found him all too attractive. Now, something about him repulsed her. Tonkatt had changed in the weeks since their disastrous flirtation. His face looked thinner, and lines were forming around his mouth and eyes. Despite the age difference, Tonkatt was starting to look exactly like Nurune. They might be wealthy and well fed, but something inside them was shriveled like rotten fruit.

"You see?" Vesswan gestured toward Shenza, as if displaying a prize.

"Here is the magister, just as I promised."

Nurune gazed at Shenza with cold hauteur. She wondered if he expected her to say something. To rage at him, or demand an explanation, or even plead for freedom. After a moment, he turned away.

"Well done," Nurune said. "My Lords will be pleased."

Shenza wasn't surprised to learn that Lord Orishem was involved with this, any more than she was to hear that Vesswan had murdered Lelldour. Sengool's ambition had never been far below the surface. From the moment of Lord Anges' death, Orishem's daughter, Innoshyra, had been trying to win Lord Aspace's affection. Orishem must have grown impatient with her lack of progress.

Yet Nurune spoke in plural—lords, not lord. That meant the Sengools were part of a larger conspiracy. Who was the second lord?

Although Nurune had turned his back, Tonkatt was still watching Shenza. His dark eyes brimmed with malice. He seemed to enjoy seeing her trapped.

"It's too bad this had to happen," Tonkatt smirked with false sympathy. "If I'd had my way, we'd be very close friends by now, but that idiot, Makko, had to interfere."

Shenza's face grew hot with remembered humiliation. Tonkatt had tried to snare her with a love charm, but Makko's poison had made her desperately sick. Caught with the charm, Tonkatt had claimed innocence. Now she knew the truth. In a bizarre way, Makko had saved her.

"We could never have been friends," she answered defiantly.

"Quiet!" Nurune snapped.

Shenza glared at both of them. If Tonkatt had tried to deceive her, it had probably been Nurune's idea. What kind of cheap woman did they think she was?

Tonkatt suddenly asked, "Are you sure she can't get loose?"

Shenza quickly lowered her eyes. Her enemies were all trained sorcerers, sensitive to mood and intuition. They might be able to detect her thoughts, especially if she kept staring at them. She shouldn't have forgotten that.

"What can she do?" Vesswan asked casually. "She's bare-handed, and that lout who came in with her..."

"Dead?" Nurune asked.

"Drugged," Vesswan replied. "I didn't want to kill him yet. He does look strong, and I have an amulet that might change his way of thinking." Her chuckle made the hairs rise on Shenza's arms.

She was glad Juss wasn't dead, and Vesswan seemed to have forgotten she had her travel case with her. Trying to hide her emotions, she kept her eyes focused on the basket of dates.

"What about her?" Tonkatt asked.

Shenza clenched her fists in her lap, feeling the hot weight of his eyes on her. She wouldn't give him a second chance to seduce her.

"That's for Orishem to decide when he becomes First Lord." Nurune spoke his brother's hoped-for title with relish. "For now, the magister is secure, but we don't know how long we have before someone comes looking for her. Vesswan, are you ready for the next phase?"

"Completely," the necromancer said. "Lelldour is dead, and dear Chimi can't interfere."

Shenza tried not to bristle at Vesswan's boasting. She hazarded a bitter glance at the necromancer. She was just in time to see Vesswan pick up another small object from the top of the scroll case.

It was a doll made of bent twigs, the kind of toy little Sujah might have. This one was bound with scarlet cords and had some kind of medallion dangling where its face should have been. Shenza's throat got tighter. That must be how Vesswan had brought Chimi down.

Luckily, Vesswan seemed more interested in preening before Nurune than in Shenza's reaction. She went on, "The earth and air are saturated with dark energy. Since the nature spirits are pure light, they can't intervene, either. I doubt they can even get on the island."

"What about the volcano?" Nurune asked.

Shenza thought this was a very good question, but Vesswan brushed it aside.

"It's too far away to trouble us. I've also captured several wandering ghosts. Those will give our constructs life."

"Very well," Nurune said. "You've both studied the manuscript Makko provided?"

"It should be simple enough," Tonkatt said.

"Then," Vesswan said with a smile, "Master Nurune, if your servants will fetch the sand, we can begin."

* * *

Chimi was so tired of being trapped in spirit form that she did exactly what Lelldour told her. She floated above her body and thought about Yail and Hawadi. It seemed like months ago that she had aided the two ghosts. Since Yail was only a child, Chimi settled on Hawadi as a better helper. She closed her eyes and pictured the old woman in her gem-studded robe and headcloth.

"Grandmother Hawadi," Chimi called in her mind. "Come to me. I need you." She repeated it several times. The force of her concentration made a faint pressure against her phantom skull.

"I can feel that," Lelldour remarked. "Perhaps you're not completely without ability."

Chimi ignored his patronizing tone. Aloud, she asked, "Why do I need to summon her?"

"There must be some reason you can't return to your body," Lelldour said. "Since Vesswan is the only one who could benefit from both of us being laid low, we'll probably find the reason in her house."

Chimi started to protest that Vesswan was nice. She wouldn't try to hurt them. Then, remembering all she had learned in this very long afternoon, she focused on Hawadi instead.

"Since you helped Hawadi, you have the power to command her," Lelldour continued. "She isn't trapped, as we are, so she can go to Vesswan's house for us."

"Oh," Chimi said. "Will she be here soon?"

"Sometimes it takes longer than others," Lelldour said. If he meant to be encouraging, he spoiled it by adding, "If you had kept the bone she gave you, this would be easier."

"I didn't think I needed it," Chimi said. She was getting irritated again, and her concentration wavered. She renewed her focus on Hawadi's silent dignity as she comforted her grieving husband. Silently, she pleaded, "Hawadi, I need you."

"Stop for a moment." Chimi felt the chill of Lelldour's hand on her insubstantial shoulder.

She opened her eyes. Master Laraquies came into the alcove, holding a parasol as protection against the steady rain. He had his mask on. Chimi hadn't seen him wear it very often. The gleaming golden face, with its fixed smile, made him seem like a stranger.

"No word from Shenza?" Laraquies asked. Giliatt shook her head. "In that case, Lady Winomi, I must ask you to come with me."

"Of course, Vizier." Winomi stood up, but she sounded uncertain. "Where are we going? Should I send a message to my parents, so they'll know where I am?"

"We'll be speaking with Lord Aspace," Laraquies said as he beckoned Winomi to join him on the path. "If my suspicion is correct, I'll be sending a message to Lord Kesquin very soon."

"From Lord Aspace?" Winomi giggled. Chimi knew she always had thought Lord Aspace was terribly cute. "How will this help Chimi?"

"We need to find the source of the cursed bracelet," Laraquies explained. His voice got fainter as they left the alcove. "Lady Seelit is my Lord's guest. If there's any chance someone meant her harm..."

Chimi hovered for a moment after their voices dissolved into the chatter of the rain. Something wasn't right. She didn't know how she could tell, but she was sure Master Laraquies had been hiding something.

Why would he do that?

She shook her head. Aside from Shenza, Winomi and Giliatt, Laraquies was the only person Chimi trusted. He couldn't be involved in anything evil. She turned to ask what Lelldour thought, and was surprised to find herself looking up at Hawadi. The old woman was just as Chimi had remembered, from her embroidered robe to the kind eyes in her weathered face.

"Grandmother Hawadi," she choked out with surprise and relief. Finally, she had done something right. "I did it!"

"Yes, I see her," Lelldour replied with grudging respect.

Hawadi didn't even glance at him. She and Lelldour both focused only on Chimi. It was a bit weird.

"What is it you need?" Hawadi asked.

Chimi said, "I need you to spy on someone."

* * *

Servants carried the furniture out of Vesswan's work room. As they rolled up the carpet, Shenza had a brief hope that one of them would break the warding circle, but they stopped short of the runes. Sengool servants joined Vesswan's, so the room was cleared quickly.

Shenza didn't bother to pretend she wasn't watching. What else would they expect her to do? She saw grunting servants remove the scroll rack and come back with heavy baskets. There was also a set of boards, a brazier, sticks of incense, and a wicker cage holding four gray doves. None of this made sense for any ritual Shenza recognized, but she was getting used to that. She was also aware of the floor constantly shifting under her knees as tremors shook the island. They, too, seemed almost normal.

Ignoring the dense mist that blanketed her garden, Vesswan went out to the small pavilion. She returned with four glass bottles. They glinted red in the faint daylight.

Tonkatt had been standing to one side, studying a scroll Vesswan gave him. Glancing at Shenza, he asked, "Should we let her see this?"

"There isn't time to clear another room," Vesswan said, "and I want all my tools here in case something goes wrong."

"Something could go wrong?" Nurune interrupted.

"Something can always go wrong, Master Nurune," Vesswan replied smoothly. "Will it? Not likely. Besides, our dear magister probably won't be telling anyone what she sees."

Vesswan smiled mockingly, and Shenza suppressed a chill. Lowering her eyes, she pressed her foot against the reassuring bulk of her travel case hidden under the table. Anyone could make threats. Carrying them out was something else. Still, the scent from the bowl of dates on the table nauseated her. With a quick hand, she pushed it farther from her.

A faint noise made Shenza glance aside. Juss lay as he had fallen, but his hands were twitching. His breath caught, then eased back into a regular rhythm. Vesswan's drug must be losing its hold. That was good, but Shenza hoped Juss wouldn't wake up too suddenly—or too loudly. She wanted to see what the Sengools were up to. The information might make her captivity worthwhile.

The servants laid out a square of boards on the bare floor. With Vesswan supervising, they tipped one of their heavy baskets over. Out flowed a cascade of sand mixed with small shells and bits of seaweed. It smelled like it had come straight off the beach. Tonkatt backed away, coughing at the dust.

Vesswan ignored him. She knelt beside a smaller basket and scooped more sand into a bowl. This sand was different, so white that it almost glowed in the dim light. Now Shenza knew who had stolen from the spirits. Vesswan carefully spread the clean sand over the rest, and then indicated with a gesture that one of the Sengool servants should mix the two together in the form.

She straightened, brushing sand off her hands, and turned to her own household. The dour serving woman had been busy cutting lengths of heavy red cord and tying them around the necks of the four bottles to make crude necklaces. She held one of them up for Vesswan's inspection.

"Excellent," the necromancer approved. "Tonkatt?"

"Ready," the sorcerer said, though his voice was still raspy from the dust.

"Prepare yourselves," Vesswan said. She took one of the necklaces from her servant, and a knife from the woman who had brought the drugged tea.

She raised her hands, and Shenza felt power swirling like a cold draft in the room. The air felt so clammy, she could well believe the atmosphere was saturated with death energy.

"Light, out," Vesswan commanded. As the lamps extinguished themselves, the workroom plunged into darkness. Even daylight from outside hardly seemed to penetrate the gloom. The glow of the warding circle became clearly visible. Shenza frowned as she tried to peer through it.

Tonkatt began to chant. Vesswan answered. They were nothing but vague, gray shapes in the darkness. Shenza couldn't see Nurune at all. Maybe this was what Vesswan had meant about her not describing the ritual; she couldn't see a thing. The chanting went on. Two voices, balanced and controlled, wove power in the darkness the same way hemp stalks could be twisted into strong twine.

One of the gray shapes moved. There was a creak, followed by startled cooing from one of the doves. Shenza heard it flap wildly, but its shriek of protest was suddenly cut off. She winced at the sound of blood dripping onto the sand in the framework. Had she once told Chimi that necromancy didn't have to be gruesome? She had been wrong.

Juss groaned more loudly than before. Shenza groped for his shoulder in the darkness.

"Don't move," she whispered, hoping the chanting would cover her words.

"What happened?" Juss mumbled. "My head..."

"You were drugged," Shenza breathed back to him.

"Drug?" His voice was a feeble echo of its normal, forceful tone.

"The tea. Lie still and rest until your head clears."

Juss stopped arguing. Shenza turned back to the ritual. One of the grayish shapes lifted its arms again. That had to be Vesswan, because there was a faint whoosh as dark power was sucked into the center of the chamber.

By the light of the warding circle, Shenza saw the pile of sand rise in response to Vesswan's magic. Tonkatt moved next, throwing something over the pillar of sand. He quickly stepped back. Shenza felt a shudder in the air. The ground beneath them rolled, too. A dull scarlet glow sprang up. It came from one of Vesswan's red bottles, which hung around the top of the pillar.

The sand took on a manlike shape, with rough lines of arms and legs. But its head was too low, sloping to merge with massive shoulders. There was no face, just a glowing circle in the middle of its head that was exactly the same color as the bottle. Even so, Shenza felt a malevolent awareness within the sand-creature.

"What is it?" Juss asked at her elbow.

"Shh!" Shenza tried not to jump. At least he was sounding more alert. "I think it's a golem, but please stay down. I want them to think you're still drugged."

"I guess," he grumbled.

Tonkatt and Vesswan finally stopped chanting. The necromancer's triumphant voice rang from the darkness.

"Master Nurune, I was requested to provide the perfect soldier. One who doesn't eat or sleep and won't disobey orders. This warrior can slay hundreds, yet cannot be killed, and—" she paused dramatically, "—will never complain about his wages."

"That's impossible," Juss muttered under the table.

Shenza squeezed his shoulder in warning. Vesswan might find humor in this grotesquerie, but she didn't feel like laughing.

"It will take a short time to construct the rest of the golems," Vesswan went on, "but you may tell Lord Manseen that his army is ready."

Chapter Twenty-Two

The Way Out

Hawadi glided swiftly up the grand stair. Concentrating, Chimi watched the ghost's progress even though she and Lelldour were still at the clinic with their bodies. She had heard about ghosts possessing people, forcing them to do what was necessary for the ghost to rest in peace, but Chimi was possessing a ghost! Without Lelldour, she would never have thought to try it.

At the top of the stairway, Hawadi paused. Chimi sensed that she was waiting for directions. She tried to project her will. *"Go right from there."*

She must have succeeded, because Hawadi did turn right. Chimi relaxed a little. She hadn't been sure it would work, even though Lelldour said it would.

Guided by her will, Hawadi soon came to Vesswan's gate. Chimi felt a strong pull ahead of them. It centered on the lamp in the top of the gate. Its sullen glare seemed unnaturally bright against the rainy sky. Hawadi stopped beneath it. Chimi felt her gazing upward, focused on the lamp. Hadn't Lelldour said something about his lamp? A special oil that would attract ghosts? She couldn't let her only ally be trapped.

"Don't stop," Chimi urged. *"This isn't what we need to know."*

It was a struggle, but she forced Hawadi onward. The necromancer's house was dark, yet voices echoed inside it. A man and a woman chanted together. It sounded like Vesswan was one of them. Good. If she was busy casting a spell, she might not notice Hawadi snooping around.

Hawadi seemed to sense that Chimi wanted her to stay hidden. Instead of taking the stairs, she passed through the shrubbery and drifted up through the side of the house.

The interior was even blacker than Chimi had expected. Glints and flickers of movement hinted at furnishings and people inside. Dark energy dragged at them like a flowing river. Hawadi resisted its pull. Directly before her, a glowing circle extended up to the rafters. Inside, to Chimi's shock, she saw Shenza and Juss. Vesswan had them trapped! With a sinking heart, she realized Lelldour had been right all along.

Chimi strained to see her sister in the gloom. Shenza sat at the table, facing away from Hawadi, while Juss slumped on the floor. Chimi hoped he wasn't hurt. Then she saw his head turn slightly and heard a rumble of speech. He was alive!

Still the chanting went on, voices blending until they no longer sounded human. Shenza's rigid back expressed her revulsion at whatever spell they were weaving. Chimi directed Hawadi to move around the warding circle so they could see what Shenza saw.

Something loomed in the darkness, given shape by the scarlet rays of a glowing bottle. Just looking at it made Chimi feel like she had stepped barefoot onto a beach covered with slimy algae. She could almost taste the stink in the air around it.

Chimi had no idea what it was. Maybe Lelldour would know. It did have an awareness, though. Chimi sensed it, just as she felt Hawadi's personality across the distance. Malice beat outward like the tremors from the volcano. Somehow Vesswan had imprisoned a human spirit within that monstrous being. Was it looking at Hawadi? Did it sense her ghostly presence?

To be safe, Chimi told Hawadi to move behind the warding circle. The creature's vicious stare didn't change.

Vesswan and her assistant finished chanting. Vesswan was talking to someone Chimi couldn't see, bragging about the horror she had created. A man strode off through the rain, while others started moving things around in the darkened chamber. The chanting started again, and some kind of animal screech came from the shadows.

"It's time to go," Chimi told Hawadi.

Much as she wanted to help Shenza, there was nothing she could do. Nor did she want to learn any more about Vesswan's kind of necromancy. She had to tell Lelldour what they had found out.

Besides, with Hawadi helping, they could always come back. She hoped Vesswan would be done with her foul enchantments by then.

* * *

Shenza thought Tonkatt and Vesswan would never finish their perverted ritual, but eventually they stood surveying a row of four hulking sand golems.

"That's that," Vesswan declared. She turned to smile at Tonkatt. "I'm impressed with your skill."

"I could never have done it alone." Tonkatt tried to sound as suave as Nurune, but his voice was rough from chanting.

"We need to get you a cup of tea," Vesswan said. "With elitherium, to keep your strength up." She smiled with more than a hint of flirtation.

"I'd like that." Tonkatt smirked back at her.

It was disturbing to watch them flirt in front of the golems. Shenza closed her eyes to shut out the sight.

While the two of them had been creating their monsters, Shenza used her enforced leisure to piece together their plan. Obviously, Lord Aspace had been right. Lord Manseen's visit was just a cover for helping the Sengools with their rebellion, although she wasn't sure how the House of Bosteel would benefit from it. There had to be a good reason for Manseen to violate Lord Aspace's hospitality like this. He even used his own child as part of the scheme.

For now, Shenza gave up on reasons. She concentrated on which tools she had in her travel case and how she could use them. She thought she had a plan of her own, if they gave her time to use it.

"Magister," Vesswan called in a sing-song. Shenza opened her eyes to find her two enemies gazing at her with malicious pleasure. "We must take our leave. Do forgive us."

Vesswan's voice dripped with sarcastic courtesy. Shenza didn't answer, since she knew they didn't really expect forgiveness. Or were they giving her one more chance to beg for freedom? Finally, she shrugged at them.

"Good-bye."

At least she had some satisfaction of seeing them scowl at her lack of fear.

"Let's go." Tonkatt turned toward the doorway, gesturing sharply at the servants, who scurried out of the work room.

"Don't let her bother you," Vesswan said soothingly. "Everything went perfectly. All we have to do now is wait."

The four golems followed her out of the work room with a harsh rustle of sand scouring the floor. It was so much the opposite of human footsteps that Shenza suppressed another shudder. The procession of servants, sorcerers and golems crossed the garden. They passed the pond and gazebo. From her previous visit, Shenza remembered a narrow path up the hill, half hidden in the underbrush. Nurune had already gone that way and not come back, so she guessed there was a gate at the top. It probably led directly into the Sengool estate.

No doubt Lord Oriman had already gathered his household's troops. She didn't think Manseen had more than one bodyguard, but that was little consolation. When Master Laraquies came to rescue Shenza, Vesswan would spring her third trap of the day.

Silence fell except for the steady beating of rain. A series of small tremors left her uneasy. The gloomy conditions were perfect for the nature spirits to appear and punish her for failing to get their sand back. Now that Vesswan had corrupted it with her evil spells, they probably wouldn't take it back.

"Can I move now?" Juss whispered.

"Not yet," Shenza murmured back. "The ward holds us, but it doesn't hide us. They want Master Laraquies to know where I am, so he'll come to save me. Then they'll get him, too. I don't want them to guess what I'm planning."

"You have a plan? That's nice to know."

"I'm sorry. I feel so stupid for letting her trap us." It was all Shenza could do to keep from wailing her frustration aloud. Juss didn't correct her, she noticed. "Yes, I have a plan."

Slowly, she reached under the table and pulled her travel case into her lap. She willed the case to open, then groped inside it. It was confusing at first, feeling the lumps and pouches and trying to remember what was inside them.

"Do you have a dagger with you?" Shenza asked while she searched inside her travel case.

"Yes."

"How sharp is it?"

Juss looked up at her, alert and tense. "How sharp does it need to be?"

"Sharp enough to cut through the carpet." Shenza felt the familiar, slick surface of her mask and the rough lines where it was cracked. Much as she longed for its protection, it wasn't what she needed yet.

"To cut the runes and break the circle?" he asked.

Shenza shook her head. "They'd sense it if the ward was disturbed, and come swarming back. We'd be caught before we could do anything. We'll have to get out through the floor."

"It's a dagger, not a saw," Juss responded. "Won't they see what we're doing and come after us anyway?"

"Not if I can find... Ah." Shenza's fingers closed over a small bottle. She hoped it was the right one. "If Master Laraquies was here, he'd tell us to do something the Sengools can't anticipate. I doubt Vesswan and Nurune have considered the crawl space under the house. They have servants to worry about things like that."

"I hope you're right," Juss said.

"There's no way to tell if they're spying on us," Shenza admitted, "but it's more likely they're watching the street to see if Master Laraquies is coming."

As she spoke, Shenza drew the bottle out of her travel case. Peeking into her lap, she was rewarded by a silvery glow. This was the one she needed.

"Shut your eyes," she warned, "but get ready."

Juss did as he was told. Once Shenza was sure he wouldn't get grit in his eyes, she stood up, cupping the bottle against her side to shield its glow. She tried to act as if she was only getting up to stretch stiff legs. Shenza paced around the warding circle, listening for signs that someone had stayed behind. She didn't hear anything.

She raised her hands, jerked the cork out of the bottle, and poured a generous pile of pearl dust into her hand. Concentrating, she cried, "Seek," and threw the dust upward.

Pearl dust swirled around her in a glittering cloud. With a soft crackle, it snapped into contact with the nearest magically charged object—the warding circle. Shenza moved quickly, spreading pearl dust. When the bottle was empty, the wall around them was coated with shimmering white. No one could see into it.

"I couldn't have stayed there much longer," Juss groaned as he rolled to his feet. "My neck hurts!"

"You did well," Shenza assured him.

She bent to retrieve her travel case, while Juss shoved the table as far to one side of the circle as he could. Shenza dropped the empty bottle into her case and drew out her mask. Heart pounding, she slipped it on and listened again for the Sengools' return.

Meanwhile, Juss limped around the warding circle, stopping to bounce lightly on his toes. The floor dipped slightly and Shenza heard a muffled squeal.

"Loose board." Juss knelt and drew his knife. He pushed the blade through the carpet with surprising ease, then cut a long gash away from himself. Heavy ripping filled Shenza's amplified hearing. He added a side slit and beckoned to Shenza. "Give me a hand."

Shenza grabbed the corner and leaned backward, pulling, while Juss slashed at the carpet. Fear that four golems would return gave her extra strength. Juss went to work on the opposite corner. Fine dust puffed upward as they peeled the carpet back to reveal a large square of floor. It was made of slats cut from thick rattan logs, sanded and coated with a heavy lacquer to smooth out the irregularities. Narrow gaps between the boards allowed for air circulation. Juss pushed his knife blade into one of these and pried at the boards.

"Get back," he warned.

Shenza edged away, clutching her travel case. Juss worked his blade along the crack until they both heard a creak.

"There it is," Juss said.

Fine dust filled the crack, coloring it gray against the pale wood. Juss pried at the floor. The rattan was thin, but tough. It resisted until Juss set his dagger's point in the break and leaned forward with all his weight. The wood cracked.

"Good," Shenza encouraged him.

Juss leaned sideways, twisting the blade so that the ragged edge rose slightly. Shenza winced as he pushed his fingers under it. Shoulders bunched with effort, Juss set his knee farther down the board and pulled upward. The wood groaned and bent. It finally broke with what seemed like a deafening snap.

"That's the easy part." Juss tossed the wood aside and started working on the neighboring slats.

"I wish I could help," Shenza said as he wrestled with another board.

"Do you know a spell to rot this wood?" Juss asked with grim humor.

"Only to keep it from rotting," she said.

It made sense to rely on brute force for now. Vesswan and Nurune's plan was based on magic. As long as she and Juss used the same methods, they would be at a disadvantage. Still, she felt guilty watching Juss' face darken with effort as he jerked his knife up and down through the stiff wood.

"I know a spell to sharpen your knife," she offered.

Juss gave a bark of laughter, but he sheathed his weapon. "This is taking too long." He stood up and aimed a kick at the partly-sawed board. It gave way on the second try. "Better."

Kicking was faster, but it seemed to take hours before they had a third and fourth board out. Shenza knew this had to be hurting Juss' scarred legs. Her stomach felt tighter and tighter. Surely someone was watching them. She had to get away!

"That's good enough," she said when Juss had the fourth board out. "I can fit through there. Can you?"

"Maybe." Juss eyed the dark opening doubtfully. "You don't want me to go first?"

"They'll have more wards on the exits from the crawl space," Shenza said. "Mostly to keep out pests, but some might affect people. I'll have to dispel them first."

To her surprise, Juss didn't argue. "Somebody has to warn the first lord about those creatures. If you can get through, you should go."

Shenza sat down with her feet in the hole. A cold draft blew around her ankles, and the gurgle of running water wafted up from the darkness.

"It will take me a moment to clear the wards," she said. "I'll wait for you outside."

"Don't," Juss said. "I'll catch up."

Shenza nodded. Groping inside her travel case, she brought out her spell-breaker. The talisman was a bamboo rod, as long as her forearm and tapered to a blunt point. Runes were carved in a spiral pattern along its sides. They blazed with purple light in the vision of her mask.

She checked that the case had sealed itself and said, "Here I go."

Bracing both hands against the edges, she shifted her legs and hips to slip into the hole. Her toes splatted into shallow water. She crouched, lowering herself, and twisted her shoulders to make it all the way through. Her headcloth caught on a jagged splinter, but she managed to pull free without it coming off.

Reaching back up, she grabbed her travel case. After a final glance up at Juss, she crawled into the darkness.

* * *

When Chimi told Lelldour what she had seen, he didn't speak for a long time. He just hovered over the rainswept pond while Chimi and Hawadi waited for his response.

"Say something!" Chimi finally burst out.

"This is worse than I thought," Lelldour answered gravely.

"What were those things?" Chimi shuddered as she remembered the sand creatures with their one-eyed stares of hate.

"Golems," Lelldour said. "Magical constructs. They move, but do not live. I had heard theories that such things could be made, but never a credible story that anyone had done it. Trust Vesswan to bring such an abomination into this world."

"She said it was going to be part of an army," Chimi told him anxiously. "But if it's magic, can't it be dispelled?"

"It isn't that simple," Lelldour said. "They contain life, of a sort, through the ghosts trapped within them."

"What can we do?" Chimi asked.

"We can't do anything," he replied with inexorable logic.

"But..."

"As interesting as this is, it isn't what I sent you to find out," he went on.

"This is more important." Chimi was getting angry again. "Shenza is trapped, and it's all my fault. She told me not to go to Vesswan."

"So did I."

"Rrr!" Chimi tried to beat her hands against her forehead in frustration. Since she was still a spirit, it didn't work. "I have to save her."

"It's true that you didn't help by ignoring our advice," Lelldour said, "but the blame isn't all yours. Vesswan was once my pupil. I know how she thinks. This isn't the sort of scheme she would develop on her own. Someone put her up to it."

"You think so?" Chimi was glad to give up some of the blame.

"There's no profit in it," Lelldour said. "Not unless someone is paying her well."

"Maybe you're right, but that doesn't fix anything," Chimi sighed.

Lelldour shrugged. "Your sister went there to find a way to help you. You must trust that she will."

"But she's a prisoner!" Chimi wailed.

"She's still the magister."

"I guess so," Chimi sighed. But Laraquies had been the magister for years and years, and he hadn't been able to help them at all. Trusting had never been so hard.

* * *

Shenza splashed her way through a stream of rain water just deep enough to cover her fingertips. She followed its chilly flow, though her robe was soaked and her back scraped the underside of the floor. The boards above her shifted slightly as Juss moved. Luckily, the crawl space wasn't totally dark. Dim grayish light penetrated the gloom through ventilation holes along the foundation.

As she had expected, a pale purple glow surrounded the access points. The nearest opening was blocked by a screen of woven bamboo strips. Apparently, even necromancers didn't want animals nesting under their houses. Since the runes were on the other side, she couldn't tell what the ward did, but it didn't really matter. She extended her spell-breaker and concentrated.

"Ward, off."

Shenza tapped the screen lightly. There was a flare of light and unexpected warmth in the clammy crawl space. It faded along with the ward's glow. She pushed at the screen. It didn't move. Behind her, she heard creaks and muffled cursing as Juss tried to follow her through the hole.

"I'm almost through," Shenza called.

"Don't worry about me," Juss answered. The frantic scrape of his dagger started again.

Shenza clutched the spell-breaker in her teeth and pushed at the stubborn screen with both hands. It shifted, but then stuck. She took a deep breath and hit it again, harder. At last the screen flew outward. It struck one of the bushes and fell with a slap in the mud.

She scrambled after it. Her knees and back felt stiff from bending over, but she kept to a crouch between the shrubs and the house.

"I'm out," she called.

"Good for you." Juss grunted with effort as he kicked at the edge of the hole.

Shenza scanned the yard for signs of pursuit. It was still raining hard. Despite that, mist hung in the air. It had a bitter volcanic tang. Under her feet, the ground twitched like an animal stung by a fly. Trapped inside the ward, she hadn't realized how bad things were getting outside.

She knew she couldn't stay where she was. Juss would expect her to run. Yet there was one more thing she had to do first. She broke from cover and dashed up the stairs.

When the servants had taken the furniture out, Shenza had made sure to watch where they put the scroll rack. She ran to it, though her wet robe tangled her legs and nearly tripped her.

"Where is it?" she muttered desperately. "That stupid little doll."

Juss called irritably, "Weren't you going the other way?"

"I can't leave Chimi the way she is." Shenza felt across the top of the case and shuffled through the compartments. The cold water had left her fingers thick and clumsy.

The twig doll wasn't on the scroll rack. She knelt to peer behind it and was rewarded by a flash of crimson. Inside the work room, Juss was kicking the slats again. Shenza felt the impact, just one more vibration in the floor. She heard a loud crack. He would be free soon.

Ignoring the tight fit, she shoved her hand into the narrow gap between the rack and the wall. Her fingertips touched something, but it pushed away from her. With a cry of frustration, she lunged forward. Her fingers caught and twisted in the red cord. With a cry of triumph, she dragged the cursed doll out of its hiding place.

In its own way, the doll was as grotesque as the golems. Its stunted limbs and loop of head were human only by suggestion. A frizz of curly black hairs—Chimi's, no doubt—were twisted into the scarlet cords. The shell medallion hung where a face should have been. If she had had time, Shenza would have studied the runes before tampering with the doll. Now she just threw it down and raised her spell-breaker.

"Dispel!"

A purple flash, a crack and a puff. The dry twigs burst into flames. Even though her clothing was soaked, Shenza jumped back. She watched the charmed doll burn. Deep inside, she was shocked at herself for destroying evidence that she could have taken before Lord Aspace, but there was no choice. She had to set Chimi free.

"What are you doing?" Muddy and dripping, Juss burst out of the bushes at the bottom of the steps. Suddenly he lunged up the stairs. "Shenza, look out!"

* * *

Sachakeen and Byben came back to the clinic after they had closed the market stall. Chimi listened half-heartedly as her mother explained the situation.

"She'll get better soon," Byben said, trying to console Giliatt.

"Isn't Shenza back?" Sachakeen asked.

Giliatt shook her head. "I don't know what could be keeping her."

Suddenly Chimi felt a kind of jerk at the core of her spirit self. She barely had time to realize what was happening before she was yanked back into her body.

Chimi opened her eyes, blinking away a film from her eyelashes. She took a deep breath. It was hard to believe she actually had air in her lungs. She sat up. She had solid weight again, felt the pressure of gravity against her hands as she lifted them to her face. It was true—she was back in her own body!

Mother looked at her and screamed.

Chapter Twenty-Three

Awakening

When Juss cried his warning, Shenza ducked and jumped to the right. Something snapped past her shoulder and clattered on the porch. She whirled to look behind her.

"You didn't think you could escape, did you?" Tonkatt sneered from the shadows of the doorway. He was damp and rumpled, holding a whip of many leather cords with sharp metal tips. Behind him, Shenza saw the glimmering cylinder of the warding circle, still coated with pearl dust. Pale gray, crumpled shapes lay scattered on the floor—the doves Vesswan had sacrificed for her vile ceremony.

"We already did," Juss said. With no sign of his usual limp, he lunged forward, trying to stomp on the whip's trailing ends. Tonkatt twitched them away.

"We got out of your trap," Shenza flared, "and we'll get away from here."

Still, she backed toward the rail at the edge of the porch. Tonkatt's whip didn't glow with magic, but it could still tangle her feet or bind her hands to her sides.

"Master Nurune saw what you were doing." A malicious grin distorted his handsome face. "Very clever, Magister. Cutting a hole in the floor. That took real magical talent."

"It worked," Juss retorted.

Tonkatt ignored him to focus on Shenza. He swished his whip and the lashes rattled over the floor. "Master Nurune sent me to keep you here. He didn't say I couldn't hurt you."

He grinned again, with a sickening twist that made Shenza's flesh crawl. Knife at the ready, Juss waved Shenza to move behind him.

"Get going," he ordered. "Leave this to me."

"You're a fool to think you can protect her," Tonkatt jeered. "You have no magic compared to mine. You even drank a necromancer's tea without wondering what was in it."

"It doesn't take sorcery to deal with someone like you," Juss answered tightly.

Shenza sidled toward the steps. Now that she had burned the cursed doll, there was no reason for her to stay here. Nothing moved in the sodden garden. It sounded like Nurune had only sent Tonkatt. However, that could change in a matter of moments.

Juss turned slightly to scowl at her. "Would you just go?"

While his attention was divided, Tonkatt swung his whip with a cry of fury. Shenza stumbled down the steps, out of reach. At the same moment, Juss sprang forward. He ducked under the arc of the flying lashes and slammed into Tonkatt. The magician staggered backward, tripped on his fine robe, and lost his grip on the whip.

Even as its handle clattered down, the two men crashed onto the porch. Struggling, they tumbled into the house. Shenza lost sight of them in the darkness. The thud of blows was strangely magnified in the empty chamber. Then came a strangled cry, and silence.

"Juss?" Shenza called. Her friend appeared from the dark house. His knife dripped red as he came down the steps. An image came to her mind, Tonkatt's body lying discarded on the floor like one of the doves. She didn't need to ask what had happened.

"That's one traitor taken care of," Juss said. His face, though pale, was calm and set. "Let's hope the rest of them were watching."

"Are you hurt?" The words came haltingly. She couldn't bring herself to ask any more. This might have been the first time Juss had fought to the death.

"We still have to get out of here," he said.

✶ ✶ ✶

Mother screamed. Sachakeen stared as if Chimi was some kind of ghost. Only Byben didn't seem surprised by her recovery.

"See now? I told you she would get better," the old man piped. "Welcome back."

"I—" Chimi started to answer. She broke off as Giliatt flung herself across the room and swept her into a hard embrace. Sachakeen was only a step behind.

"You're all right," Giliatt sobbed. "Thank the heavens!"

"What happened?" Sachakeen demanded, but not as he usually did, with the irritated snap of an older brother. For once it sounded like he really cared about her.

Chimi's throat closed up. Her vision wavered as all the tears she had been longing to shed gathered in her eyes.

"I wasn't dead," she choked around a knot in her throat.

"What's wrong?" Kafseet dashed into the alcove, followed by an apprentice curomancer in a green and white striped robe. She stopped when she saw Chimi sitting up. "Oh. Shenza must have made arrangements with Vesswan."

She couldn't know how wrong she was. Chimi closed her eyes for a moment, wishing she could burrow into her mother's embrace like the child she was. Or, she corrected herself, the child she had been acting like. She couldn't afford to be that child anymore.

"No, she didn't." Chimi heard her own voice come out brittle and flat, like a stranger's. "Vesswan is holding Shenza prisoner. And she's made some kind of creature. I saw it."

Giliatt, Kafseet and Sachakeen started talking at once, questions and demands that made Chimi's head throb.

"Just let me talk!" she cried. When they all paused, she rushed on, "I've been trapped outside my body. I was here, but only as a spirit. I could see everything that happened, and hear everything, too, but I couldn't get back into my body."

"Everything?" Sachakeen repeated. From his and Giliatt's expressions, they obviously remembered the family's argument earlier in the day.

"Yes, everything." Chimi smiled bitterly. "It isn't important. Some ghosts were helping me, because Shenza was right, I'm a necromancer." Despite her reluctant acceptance, Chimi's throat ached as she spoke those words.

"You're so cold." Giliatt touched Chimi's hands, then her forehead. "Just like Uncle Panjeun."

"I've gotten used to it, I guess," Chimi said. "But Mother, I saw Shenza and Juss at Vesswan's house. They're trapped inside a warding circle. And Vesswan made a golem. I think it's part of an army. We have to tell someone."

"An army?" Giliatt frowned at her, doubting.

Kafseet interrupted, "Tell me about this golem."

"It was all sand, shaped like a man, but rough," Chimi told her, "like something you would pile up on the beach, not a real person. It had one red eye and a glowing amulet on its chest." She shuddered. "It was evil. I could feel it."

"Can this be true?" Giliatt looked to Kafseet, perhaps hoping for reassurance.

"I've heard stories," Kafseet answered slowly, "but I didn't think any of our local magicians had the power."

"What's a golem?" Sachakeen asked. He sounded like himself again, expecting Kafseet to prove Chimi wrong. The annoyance was almost comforting.

"It's a kind of artificial life," Kafseet said. "Can't be killed, doesn't have to sleep, that sort of thing. If Chimi is right, and this is part of an army..."

"Lord Aspace wouldn't use that kind of magic," Sachakeen argued.

"Shush, son," Giliatt scolded.

"I don't think it's for Lord Aspace," Chimi broke in, irritated. "Vesswan's house is right by the Sengools. It must be for them. They're going to attack Lord Aspace."

"Are you sure?" Kafseet demanded.

"That's what Master Lelldour thinks," Chimi said.

"We have to warn someone," Giliatt said. Her hands shook as she hugged Chimi again, but her voice was firm. "Master Laraquies will know what to do."

Chimi nodded. "I wanted to tell him anyway, so he can help Shenza."

"If you're right, we're going to need anyone who can heal." Kafseet turned to her apprentice. "Satta, gather everyone who's here, and send word to whoever went home when the rain started."

"Yes, Mistress Kafseet." The young man bowed and scurried away.

Meanwhile, Chimi swung her legs over the edge of the litter she had been lying on. She nearly fell as it wobbled beneath her.

"Careful." Sachakeen reached out to steady her.

"I'm fine," Chimi said, though every muscle in her body felt tight after hours of inactivity. Then a cool draft reminded her of something else.

Hawadi seemed to have vanished when Chimi stopped concentrating on her, but Lelldour hovered nearby. His face showed no envy that she had been able to come back to life, but Chimi still felt guilty.

"I'm sorry!" she blurted.

"Who is your friend?" Byben asked.

Giliatt gasped, and Sachakeen's arm tightened protectively on Chimi's elbow. Kafseet pivoted in the doorway.

"You can see him?" Chimi asked. At first she didn't understand why everyone could see Lelldour, when they had both spent hours here as spirits and nobody had noticed them. Then she remembered what Shenza had said several days ago, that Chimi's power as a necromancer made him visible. She explained, "This is Master Lelldour. He was the necromancer before."

To her surprise, Lelldour bowed in greeting. Kafseet had enough presence of mind to return the polite gesture while her family stood stunned. Chimi wondered why they were all so surprised. Hadn't they believed her when she said she was a necromancer?

"So is that your body?" The curomancer gestured toward the next alcove, where Lelldour's skeleton lay.

"It is," Lelldour said. "Thank you for trying to discover the truth. However, I already know who murdered me."

"I see." Kafseet stared at him with interest.

Chimi wished she knew what they were talking about, but too much time had already been wasted to start catching up on news. "I'm sorry,

Master Lelldour," she said, "but I have to leave. You'll be stuck here."

As hard as she had been trying to get away from Lelldour, she could hardly believe she was saying that.

He sighed at her with his usual scorn. "Not if you take one of my bones."

"Oh!" Chimi ran out the door, though her knees still felt a bit rubbery, then turned back to Kafseet. "Where did you say his body is?"

"Over here." Lelldour walked through the screen.

"Sun and sand," Sachakeen muttered under his breath.

Now that Chimi was solid again, she had to follow Kafseet around the barrier between the two alcoves. There was the pallet she remembered seeing before, a cloth-covered bundle supported between two tables.

Even after what she had experienced today, it felt strange to lift the edge of the cloth and have a skull staring back at her. The rest of the bones were neatly arranged much as they would have been in life, except that they were bare and flat. Like a drawing, she thought, compared to a real person.

Lelldour was on the other side of the skeleton. His face showed no emotion at the sight of his own remains. Chimi was aware of her family gathered in the doorway, watching in horrified fascination.

"Which one?" Chimi asked.

"A finger," he said. "They're small and easy to carry."

Chimi gingerly took one of the bones from the side nearest to her. It had been his left hand. The bone was dry and cool, strangely light.

"What if she drops it?" Giliatt worried aloud. "She could lose it."

"That's why we usually put them on necklaces," Lelldour spoke to Chimi, ignoring Giliatt. "I don't have time to teach you the traditional ceremony. You'll just have to be careful."

"I won't drop it," Chimi protested. She wished they wouldn't say things like that. "Now let's go."

She turned away from Lelldour's skeleton and was surprised when everyone obediently followed her toward the street. Leadership didn't come naturally to the baby of the family. She wasn't sure she liked it.

"If you're going up to the palace, let Lord Aspace know we're getting ready," Kafseet called behind them.

"I will," Chimi said.

The rain hadn't slackened at all. Sachakeen paused to open a parasol for Giliatt, who promptly held it over Byben. They set off together, Sachakeen and Chimi flanking their elders. Lelldour drifted behind them, although only Chimi seemed aware of him.

The town square was very quiet as they passed through on the way to the central stairs. Beyond the patter of rain and splash of footsteps, Chimi heard the volcano growling in the distance. The ground shivered under their feet. A gusty wind was driving plumes of foul gasses through the town. Even the steady rain couldn't beat it from the air. It made Chimi's nose burn, and she saw Giliatt lift one end of her robe to cover her mouth.

"Mother, do you want to go home with Byben and Sachakeen?" Chimi asked, to break the silence. "I can go to the palace by myself."

"No, I want to be with you," Giliatt said. "And I want to know what happened to Shenza."

"If there's a battle, it'll be at the palace," Sachakeen pointed out nervously. "We might be safer at home."

"Myri and I can wait by ourselves," Byben countered. "We're old. Nobody will bother us."

As if in argument, the ground suddenly lurched under their feet. Stone creaked ominously, and vegetation thrashed around them. Sachakeen supported Byben as he stumbled. Chimi grabbed the rail for balance.

"We might not be safe anywhere," she said when they were all steady on their feet. A glance at Lelldour's silent visage reminded her how he had predicted natural disasters if she didn't restore the balance of nature. "The volcano's getting worse. I think you and Sachakeen should go, Mother. Take Grandmother and Byben to the dawn side of the island for a few days."

"I can't leave you behind," Giliatt gasped.

And Sachakeen scowled. "I can take care of them."

"That volcano's really close to town," Chimi snapped. "If it blows up, you won't have time to run! I think you should go while you can."

She pointed up the stairs, where another family was emerging from the fog. A man and a half-grown boy had large bundles on their backs. A woman with a baby strapped to her back followed them, leading a heavily laden water buffalo. Everyone watched in silence as they faded into the mist.

"Chimi could be right," Byben said at last.

"But what about Shenza?" Giliatt asked.

"She would want the rest of you to be safe," Chimi said. "You know I'm right."

The argument raged as they went on up the stairs. Chimi glanced over her shoulder to be sure Lelldour was still there. She couldn't make anyone do what she wanted. She was too young. She hoped they would listen, though.

As for herself, Chimi knew she couldn't run away. Somehow Shenza had freed her from Vesswan's spell. Now it was her turn to save her sister. Without Lelldour, she wouldn't have the first idea how to do it.

* * *

Ironically, Juss and Shenza only ran as far as Vesswan's gate before they stopped. The peace officer stood surveying the street warily, while Shenza peered past his bulky shoulders. The cobbled lane was empty. It seemed that the people of the town were keeping to their homes in the unseasonal monsoon. A strong tremor reminded her they might also have fled from the volcano.

"Go left," Shenza whispered.

Frowning, Juss glanced at her. "Isn't the palace that way?" He jerked his bloody knife to the right.

"Yes, but we'd have to go past the Sengool estate to get there." Shenza didn't know how many fighters the Sengools and Lord Manseen had, but she didn't want to run straight into the ambush they must have laid for Master Laraquies.

"You're right," Juss decided. "I've done enough patrols to get us through. Come on."

He set off at a fast limp, sticking close to the wall on the near side of the street. Juss seemed to feel better in the leader's role, so Shenza let him have it. She followed as he cut across the lane. A side stair led down, level after level, until it disappeared in the fog.

"Let's not go too far astray," Shenza cautioned.

"I know." Juss paused at the second landing down and peered around a hedge.

Truthfully, Shenza wished they could keep going all the way to the curomancers' clinic. She was desperate to know if she had succeeded in releasing Chimi. There was no time for that. The palace was where she belonged now.

* * *

It should have stopped raining by now. On a normal day the clouds would be thinning, with afternoon light breaking through. Instead, the rain got harder and colder. Fog clung to the ground in leprous patches, and Chimi's eyes stung after she went through it. She blinked furiously and pressed on.

It looked like Lord Aspace's staff knew something was going on. The gate to his estate was heavily guarded. Palace guards in blue kilts had been joined by peace officers in dark gold. All of them carried shields and spears or knives. Behind the stone wall and metal bars of the gate, soldiers were hastily laying down a line of what looked like pineapple stems. A sorceress who Chimi didn't recognize followed them, chanting quietly and waving a long staff over the pieces. They sprouted and grew with unnatural speed, forming a barricade of plants that bristled with thorny stems.

Chimi had finally convinced Giliatt and Sachakeen to take the elders to safety, but she had to stand in the rain and explain, three times, how badly she needed to see Master Laraquies. First she told the guards at the gate, and then their stiff-necked commander. Finally, a senior peace officer went by.

"Sub-Chief! Can you help me?" Chimi called. She remembered Shamatt from the investigation when Shenza had been poisoned.

Once he heard Chimi's story, Shamatt said, "I'll take you to the vizier," and politely offered her a parasol.

"Thank you." Chimi took it gratefully.

As she followed him, Chimi glimpsed a column of warriors coming from the south. They wore Kesquin's magenta, and Chimi was sure she saw Lord Fastu's son Miroth at the head of the line. They must be coming to help Lord Aspace. Maybe it was only because the Sengool family were the rebels, but she was still relieved to see them.

"Chimi?" Shamatt called.

"Sorry!" She trotted to catch up with him. "I just saw the Kesquins coming."

"Lord Aspace sent for them," Shamatt said as he led her past the wall of pineapples. "He'll be glad to know they're here, and Vizier Laraquies will be happy to see you. He's been worried."

"I'm sorry to bother everyone," Chimi murmured. She suddenly realized how she had compromised Chalsett's defense against the Sengool rebellion.

"Did you say you know where Shenza is?" Shamatt asked. "We hoped she would be here by now."

"It's complicated," Chimi said.

Shamatt eyed her for a moment, then shrugged. "You can explain it to Lord Aspace."

He made a sweeping gesture, and Chimi saw that they had come back to the same pavilion where the banquet had been held. Only the trampled grass hinted at last night's revelry. More guards and peace officers were laying down another living barricade.

"Useless," Lelldour murmured at her shoulder. Chimi turned to glare at him, hoping Shamatt hadn't heard. Lelldour shrugged. "I suppose we must allow them to try," he said.

"Don't be so pessimistic," she hissed. She followed Shamatt across the grass, trying to shake off her fear at Lelldour's dismal prediction. The pavilion swarmed with so many peace officers that it looked like a beehive. Sorcerers in purple robes clustered to one side, talking urgently. Lord Aspace's chair had been set up near the top of the steps, but he wasn't in it.

The first lord paced restlessly between the sorcerers and his throne. He had exchanged his flamboyant festival robes for a short kilt and mantle, bright blue with white waves painted on. His headcloth was tightly wrapped, to keep his hair back from his face, and he wore only a few close-fitted bracelets. She guessed he had taken off anything that might get tangled up if he had to fight. He also carried a short spear and shield.

The burly Chief Peacekeeper, Borleek, stepped forward to say something to Lord Aspace. Glancing over the head of the much shorter first lord, he saw Shamatt and scowled.

"Where were you?" Borleek demanded.

Chimi jumped, but Shamatt wasn't put off by his abrupt manner.

"Chimi Waik of Tresmeer has news for my Lord," he answered mildly.

Aspace whirled, and Chimi quickly bowed. She had the impression of his brilliant, sharp eyes before Master Laraquies burst out of the circle of wizards.

"Chimi?" The old man hurried down the steps to embrace her, wet as she was. "You've recovered! My child, we were so worried."

To Chimi's surprise, Lord Aspace swept down the steps after Laraquies. "Weren't you unconscious?" he accused.

"I was trapped outside my body," she said, too surprised to use the formal speech a first lord was due. "I have to tell you about Shenza and the golems!"

"Tell me, then." Aspace beckoned her to follow him up the steps, where he sat in his chair, spear across his lap. Chimi hurried after him, glad to get out of the rain.

"Did you mention golems?" Laraquies asked, following them.

"That's right." Chimi began her story. Laraquies, Borleek and Shamatt all interrupted with questions, but Aspace didn't say anything. He sat very still, though his knuckles got white around his spear shaft. His expression was remote and unreadable, but his eyes were terrible.

"And that's where Shenza is now?" Shamatt asked when Chimi had finished.

She nodded. "Vesswan has her."

Borleek made a kind of huffing noise, giving his opinion of Shenza's importance, but Aspace sent a sharp glance in Laraquies' direction. "Find her."

"As my Lord commands." Laraquies bowed and backed away, then turned toward the group of magicians, who had also been listening intently to Chimi's story.

"Should we send someone after her?" Shamatt asked.

"We can't do that," Borleek snapped. "We need every man here."

"Lord Miroth of Kesquin is just arriving with his troops," Shamatt said. "I would be willing to go, if I had three peace officers and a sorcerer."

"I need you most of all," Borleek scowled. "Juss is with her. She'll be fine."

Chimi listened tensely as Borleek dismissed her sister's predicament. However, Aspace looked up at Borleek with something like hatred.

"We won't abandon her."

His finality silenced the group, until Chimi asked timidly, "Can I ask something?"

Borleek snorted, but Shamatt nodded. "What is it?"

"How did you know?" Chimi voiced a question that had been nagging at her. "I mean, that the Sengools are going to attack?"

"The bracelet you were wearing when you collapsed," Shamatt explained. "It had a second spell on it. Vizier Laraquies recognized the craftsmanship of the Sengool coven, thus linking them to your mysterious illness. Also, Lord Manseen and Lady Seelit went to call on the Sengools earlier today, and they haven't come back. Obviously, we didn't know everything you found out, but we knew they must be taking shelter with their allies."

"I guess so," Chimi said. She wished she didn't have to believe that Seelit would betray Lord Aspace's hospitality, but there didn't seem to be any other explanation.

"What are we supposed to do about those golems, is what I'd like to know," Borleek growled, speaking mostly to himself.

"My Lord." Laraquies returned holding a large shell that gleamed white in the premature dusk. "I've scried the warding circle Chimi described, but no one is in it. There's just a hole in the floor." He smiled briefly, but then turned serious again. "Shenza isn't there, but I did see a body and quite a lot of blood."

"Blood?" Chimi squeaked.

Chapter Twenty-Four

Walls of Doubt

Shenza and Juss hurried off along the sixth terrace in silence except for their ragged breathing. Her mask kept the raindrops out of her eyes, but she could feel the stealthy trickle of water seeping through her headcloth. The wet fabric of her robe stuck to her ankles. She nearly tripped before she could jerk it loose. Juss stopped to glare at her. Then he stalked on. Shenza darted a wary glance at him. Juss hadn't spoken since their escape from Vesswan's house.

The endless drumming of rain seemed to absorb all other sound. Even their footsteps splashing through the puddles was barely audible. The quiet unnerved her.

"You aren't embarrassed, are you?" she finally asked. "Tonkatt would have said anything to bother you. You know that."

"But he was right." Juss scowled, looking ahead and behind, anywhere except at Shenza. "I shouldn't have trusted that woman."

"Are there so many poisoners in Chalsett that you should expect a tainted cup?" Shenza countered, hurrying to match his halting strides. "You beat Tonkatt. I'm the one who should apologize. I knew better than to go there at all."

"You did it for your sister," Juss said.

"And you did what you had to," Shenza said. "You protected me."

Juss didn't answer that, but he walked a little more easily.

They passed a foaming cascade where rainfall drained from the terrace above. Heavy mist hung in the air above the splash pool. It held a strange, ripe odor. It wasn't from the volcano, but the cloying scent made Shenza nervous. They crossed the drainage channel on a low stone bridge, and the street curved back to run between large houses nestled among trees and gardens. Faint lampglow reached them. Shenza envied the people who were warm and dry inside.

They had nearly reached the grand stair. Shenza asked, "We go up here?"

"Wait a bit." Juss motioned for her to stay back while he went to the stairs. He looked both ways, then suddenly jumped backward. "Get down!"

Juss grabbed Shenza and pushed her against the closest hedge. She tried not to resent the fresh shower that drenched her as droplets fell from the wet foliage. Even Juss' shoulder was chilly as they crouched together. The part of the stairway Shenza could see was empty except for sheets of water on the risers.

"What is it?" she whispered.

"Keep still," he hissed back.

Faintly at first, Shenza picked out the slap of sandals on the stairs. A group of people, moving fast. Shenza was surprised. Anyone with sense would stay out of the rain or had already fled from the volcano. Then she realized who was most likely to be ignoring the weather. She tried to make herself smaller against the dripping hedge. Juss' back was rigid with tension.

Gray shapes formed in the rain, a double line of men jogging up the stairs. They wore short mantles, a workman's plain brown made darker by moisture, but these were no dock workers. Spear points and shield rims gleamed in the dim light. These were mercenary fighters.

"They must have come under cover of the weather," Juss said in a low voice. "Someone's going to be in trouble for not watching the harbor."

"They're dressed like laborers," Shenza whispered back. "Lord Oriman and Lord Manseen must have been planning this for a long time. Who knows how long these men were hidden among us, working at the port and waiting for the signal."

His broad shoulders twitched in a shrug. Together, they watched as the armed column continued up the stairs and dissolved into the rain. Shenza counted at least thirty men, a significant force in a town as small as Chalsett.

"It looks like they're headed for Lord Aspace's estate," Juss said when the rain's rhythm was once again the only sound. "We were too slow."

Shenza laid a hand on his shoulder. "It isn't your fault."

He ignored her. "We can't go that way. What now?"

Shenza bent her head, thinking hard. There was only one gate into the first lord's estate, a basic security precaution. She hoped desperately that the guards had remained at their posts despite the miserable weather. Something nagged at her, though. She stared at the ground, barely seeing the runnels of water between the cobblestones. A moment later she had it.

"Do you remember when we investigated Lord Anges' murder? Makko went over the wall and down the slope."

He paused, then nodded. "Right. The men of the household chased him. We were looking at their tracks. What about it?"

"If Makko got down, maybe we can get up," Shenza said.

His expression brightened. "Where was that spot?"

"I think I can find it." Shenza closed her eyes, trying to remember how the gardens lay. "It's on the opposite side from the Sengools. We won't have to get past them."

"I like it even better." Juss stood, motioning Shenza to stay where she was. He sidled around the hedge and spent what seemed like a long time peering up and down the stairs. Finally he beckoned. "Quick, let's go."

* * *

"A body?" Lord Aspace demanded. He spoke in a taut voice that reminded Chimi of a stick bent in half, just about to break.

"My Lord is correct," Laraquies said. "One man and also several birds. Based on what Chimi told us, the birds must have been sacrificed to create the golems."

"Where's Shenza?" Chimi wailed.

"I don't know." Laraquies gave her a rueful smile. "Her mask protects her from scrying. We magisters don't like to be spied on. But Shenza is free. That's what matters."

Chimi nodded, trying to believe him.

"Who was the body?" Borleek cut in.

"I didn't recognize him, but he wore sorcerer's purple," Laraquies said.

"Then it's not Juss." Shamatt sounded relieved.

"Of course not," Borleek snapped, apparently irritated that anyone would think his men were so feeble.

"He and Shenza must have escaped together," Laraquies said.

"They saw Vesswan conjure the golems," Chimi said, doing her best to be logical. "If I know my sister, she's on her way here. Shenza will want to warn my Lord."

"She may have other information, as well," Laraquies agreed. "I'm sure she's doing all she can to bring us news."

"If Juss is with her, he'll do his best to get her here alive," Shamatt said.

"I said we won't abandon her," Lord Aspace said to Borleek and Shamatt. "I meant that. But until we know where she is, I can't send anyone to help her."

Shamatt bowed. "As my Lord says."

Turning to Chimi, Aspace went on, "Thank you for bringing me this warning. Now we can try to prepare for what they're bringing against us."

"It was only my duty," Chimi answered, but she broke off when he shook his head.

"Later, I'll think of some way to reward you," Aspace told her.

A day ago, his words would have filled Chimi's mind with visions of gems and silken clothing. Now she just hoped Aspace would survive to make good on his promise.

"As my Lord wishes," she said.

"Laraquies," Aspace went on crisply. "How do you plan to deal with these monsters my enemies have summoned?"

The old man hesitated. "Sadly, this wasn't a problem my Lord's servants had considered."

Behind him, Chimi heard murmurs from the other sorcerers. "If I had a few days for research," one said.

And another, "Who could have imagined?"

The sorceress who had made the pineapple barricade murmured, "They must have some weakness."

Lord Aspace watched them impatiently, while Borleek snorted with open disgust. Then everyone stopped talking as a horn call rang in the near distance. Its shrill tone came strangely muffled through the misty gardens. With a jolt, Chimi realized the Sengools must be at the gates. How could they be here so soon?

Silence followed the alarm, until Lord Aspace drily suggested, "You'd better think of something."

"Your servants will make every effort," Laraquies said. Alone among the sorcerers, he didn't seem frightened. They withdrew into their tight huddle again.

Borleek came around Lord Aspace's throne and made a curt bow. "Permit me to lead my Lord's defense."

"I'm counting on you," Aspace replied.

Chimi was surprised by Borleek's sincerity. He had always struck her as a bully, bellowing and bossing people around. Now he strode down the steps, calling the men into line behind the barricade. In this emergency, peace officers and guardsmen jumped at his command, not out of fear but with trust and determination. Then Chimi jumped, herself, as Sub-Chief Shamatt approached her.

"My Lord has honored me with the duty to safeguard Lady Izmay and the women of his household," he said. "I'm sure my Lady would welcome your company."

"All right... Oh." Chimi faltered. After several minutes of silence, Lelldour was back at her side.

"You should stay," he told her.

"Me?" Chimi squeaked. "I can't help here. I'll only get in their way."

If Shamatt was startled by Lelldour's sudden appearance, it didn't show. "This is no place for a young lady," he said.

Once again, Lelldour ignored everyone but Chimi. "You might," he said with his usual flat impatience, "but I do have something to offer: my skill and experience as a necromancer. If you leave, I cannot help to defend my Lord."

"You can't do anything," Chimi said, frowning. "You told me weeks ago. You're just a ghost."

"You're not," Lelldour said.

"No, no, no," Chimi stammered. "I can't. Not with you just telling me what to do. I need more time!"

"Chimi."

"Oh!" She jumped again as Master Laraquies came over. "What is it?"

"Master Lelldour is your teacher," the vizier said gently. "And you are his apprentice, correct?"

Chimi nodded warily.

"They you must follow his instructions. In addition," Laraquies gestured to take in the sorcerers, who had stopped talking to stare at Chimi, "none of us is a necromancer. We need Lelldour's advice if we're going to protect my Lord from Vesswan's creatures."

"But I don't know what I'm doing!" Chimi protested. She was acting like a child again, but she couldn't help it. Everyone was looking at her, and it just wasn't fair!

Lord Aspace had left his seat and was prowling restlessly along the edge of the pavilion again. "You've already helped," he tossed over his shoulder. "I'm sure you can do even more."

Chimi swallowed heavily. That was practically an order. She turned to Shamatt and spread her hands in helpless surrender. "I can't come with you."

"If that is my Lord's wish, you must obey." Shamatt bowed slightly and hurried out the far side of the pavilion.

Chimi watched, wishing she could go with him. She was surrounded by the noise of excited guards, magicians arguing and rain pouring endlessly down, and she had never felt so alone.

"Young lady," called one of the magicians, an older man who Chimi didn't know. "You must ask Master Lelldour to tell us what he plans to do. Find out how we can help."

Chimi turned to Lelldour, who had begun to fade into the rainy background.

"Oh, no, you don't," she told him with rising indignation. The necromancer's ghost became more solid as Chimi focused her will on him. "You're not leaving me here. Now tell us what you have in mind. I want to know, too."

* * *

"Are you sure this is the place?" Juss asked.

"No," Shenza admitted, "but we should be able to find it from here."

It was hard to recognize features of the landscape in the dull light. Still, the place did look familiar. A low retaining wall ran beside the street. The royal estate was on the hilltop above them. There should be a slightly lower section of wall just up the hill from here.

"All right." Juss swung a leg over the knee-height wall, wincing at the movement, and started to climb. He kept his knife ready. Shenza followed. The hillside was forested with a mixture of conifers and palm trees. The trees blocked what little daylight there was, so that they scrambled up the slope in near darkness.

It was almost as if nature itself resisted their coming. Chilly mud flowed into their sandals, grating between their toes. Hanging vines caught at their heads and the travel case in her hand. A treacherous layer of wet needles made them slip and slide backward as much as forward. Still, Shenza forced herself to keep climbing. Her heart pounded with urgency. Lord Aspace was in danger. She had to reach him.

"I see the wall," Juss grunted from farther up the slope.

Shenza grabbed a tree trunk so she wouldn't slide down the hill. A pale surface rose through the rain. While Juss roamed along the base of the wall, Shenza looked around. She spotted a branch with a familiar, twisted end.

"That's it," she said, pointing. There was a break in the hedge just across from that branch. Two months ago, Makko and his pursuers had cut through it and run down the hillside. Juss stumbled in that direction, but soon came back to her.

"We can't climb this," he said.

The wall was white marble, darkened a little by moss. It was seamless and slick with rain. The lowest point was at least eight feet above them, too far for Juss to reach even by jumping. Fortunately, Shenza hadn't been expecting to climb the wall. The tree she leaned on was festooned with tough vines.

"Grab some of these," she said.

Juss reached for the nearest dangling vine and tugged gently. Branches swayed above him, showering them both with water. Cursing under his breath, he pulled harder. With a snap, the vine slithered down around him.

"I don't know about this," he grumbled, kicking the wet stems away.

"We need one more to make a rope," Shenza said. "I know a charm to keep rope from breaking."

Juss looked skeptical, but he started yanking on the vines again. He soon presented Shenza with a second one. She leaned on her tree for balance and tossed the two vines to either side so they wouldn't get mixed up. Finally, she began to twist the two vines together into a crude rope.

She worked fast, with hasty jerks. She hated to take so much time on this when they didn't have a moment to spare. Yet she knew there was no other way to reach Lord Aspace without facing the Sengool forces—an encounter the two of them could never survive.

She twisted harder, trying to focus her will on the spell. Again, everything seemed to be against her. There hadn't been time to cut the leaves off the vines, so they stuck out and caught against each other. Her fingers were thick with cold. Shenza chanted the rhyme, but her tongue felt heavy and clumsy. Her head ached as she tried to summon her magic. The power just wouldn't flow into her hands, no matter how hard she tried. Some force in the air itself seemed to soak up her magic before she could bring it into focus.

Shenza stopped for a moment, shrugging her shoulders to release the tension. Maybe her idea wouldn't work. These were vines, not rope. She hadn't thought it would matter, but maybe it did. What could she do then?

Or maybe, she thought, it was the dark energy Lelldour had warned her and Chimi about. It certainly did seem like the weather was part of some destructive magic that leached all life from the world. For that matter, she didn't feel the volcano shaking the ground anymore. Maybe Vesswan had been right that the nature spirits couldn't come onto the island without a necromancer absorbing the dark energy.

"Don't give up," Juss said. "We have to do this."

"You're right," she murmured, though her throat felt tight with fear and cold. She thought of Lord Aspace facing the golems and heat surged in her chest. Shenza closed her eyes and bent over her work. She was a sorceress. She had trained for years. This was an easy spell. She wouldn't let her magic fail her.

She started again, working with all the concentration she could muster. Warmth flowed fitfully through her fingers. The cord she was creating gleamed faintly in the sight of her mask. Shenza focused on that small success, pushing aside her fear of how long this was taking to nurture that spark of faith in her own abilities. Beside her, Juss balanced on the hillside. He didn't speak, but gathered the rope as she made it. When the vines got twisted, he separated them for her.

After a while, he tapped her shoulder with fingers that felt as chilly as her own. "I think that's enough."

"I hope so." Shenza watched wearily as he slashed off the uneven ends of the vines and knotted the cord's end. She rolled her head from side to side, trying to loosen muscles that were stiff from her intense concentration. Her sodden headcloth threatened to slip off her head.

"Come on," Juss said. "I'll boost you up."

Shenza struggled up the last few feet of the muddy hillside. She would rather have sent Juss first, in case the Sengools had already penetrated the estate, but she knew he was right. Juss was strong enough to get Shenza over the wall. She couldn't do the same for him.

The peace officer knelt, cupping his hands at knee height. Shenza stepped into his hands and wobbled as Juss straightened, lifting her upward. As soon as the top was in reach, she swung her travel case over the edge and grabbed it with both hands.

"I've got it," she called in a low voice.

"Hold on," Juss said, grunting with effort.

The moss on top of the wall was slippery. Shenza teetered as he shifted his grip. Hard stone dug into her fingers. Then he pushed upward again. When the wall was at shoulder height, she managed to drag her upper body over the cold verge. Her travel case lay on wet grass, just at the level of the wall. She kicked her knees upward, fighting the drag of her saturated robe, and finally tumbled onto the firm ground of Lord Aspace's estate.

"I'm up." She crawled around to peer over the rim.

"Catch this!"

Juss flung the makeshift rope upward. It twisted in the air. Shenza leaned outward, grabbing wildly, and managed to snare it. She stumbled to a small tree near the edge of the wall and wrapped the rope twice around the trunk, making sure the loose end was tucked under. Holding tightly, so it wouldn't come loose, she leaned over the wall. Juss was below her, looking up anxiously. She waved him upward.

The small tree shuddered as the rope tightened. Shenza kept low, alert for any sign of discovery. The vines creaked with strain, but held long enough for Juss to reach the top. He rolled over the wall and came to a crouch. Shenza pulled the rest of the rope up after him. They both froze as a horn call sounded, shrill with urgency. Shenza glanced at her companion to see if he knew what it meant. Juss merely shook his head.

"Let me go first." His dagger was ready in his hand once more.

Shenza nodded. Juss moved off through the bushes, keeping as quiet as he could. At least the steady rain helped cover the sound of their footsteps. Shenza followed, hoping they weren't too late. She wouldn't feel comfortable until she saw Lord Aspace with her own eyes and knew he was still alive.

* * *

"Don't be afraid," Laraquies said. He patted Chimi's shoulder. His hand felt like the only bit of warmth left in a gray, dreary world.

"I'm not," Chimi said. It was only a little lie.

"You can do it." The old man smiled reassuringly, but he was already moving off. Since Master Lelldour had outlined his plan, the whole coven of sorcerers had gone into action. Laraquies went to join them. Chimi caught a dull golden glint as he put on his magister's mask. The rest of the coven were chanting and doing something with amulets all along the sides of the pavilion.

Chimi loitered nervously behind Lord Aspace's throne. There was nothing for her to do until Vesswan got closer. Lelldour had faded away, biding his time until he could act. Chimi didn't like his plan at all, but nobody had a better idea.

It was quiet except for an ominous murmur as trees stirred beneath the dank breath of the storm. Then came distant shouting and shrill, metallic clashing sounds. They must be fighting at the gate. Chimi tried to imagine what combat looked like, but nothing came to her. There had never been a battle in Chalsett-port during her whole life. She didn't like to think about it happening now. Or how soon the battle might reach the grass in front of them. Where could she hide then? How could she avoid the dreadful sight?

There was a faint creak and a swish as Lord Aspace stood up. Spear at his side, he resumed his restless pacing. His handsome face was almost a blank except for his eyes. Even in the lamp-lit pavilion, they blazed with emerald fire. Aspace stopped when he saw Chimi looking at him and turned abruptly, facing the sounds of combat.

Then he glanced back at her. Chimi had the feeling he wanted her to say something. She wished she knew what to say. If she was nervous, she knew Lord Aspace must be feeling worse. After all, the monsters were coming for him.

"My Lord?" she asked, ready to apologize if he didn't want her to talk to him.

Aspace looked away again, his lips tight. Then he said, "Shenza. You think she's all right?"

"It seems like it." Chimi was keenly aware that any answer she gave could be wrong. "Too bad we don't have a mind bond, like sisters do in the legends." She tried to laugh. It came out strange and hollow.

"Hmm," Aspace said, the barest acknowledgment of her words.

From the corner of her eye, Chimi caught a gleam as Laraquies looked in their direction. Could he hear what they were saying? She cleared her throat and hurried on, speaking more softly.

"I know she'll be here as soon as she can. Shenza would never turn her back on you."

"Really?" Aspace's gaze was sharper. "I've always had the impression she doesn't like me."

"Not like you?" Chimi felt her eyebrows rise in surprise. She stopped herself from saying any more. Just because she knew about Shenza's feelings didn't give her the right to meddle.

On the other hand, Shenza wasn't likely to speak up for herself, even if she had been there.

"Oh, you know her," Chimi fumbled, uncomfortably aware of Aspace's stare. "Well, maybe you don't. You're the first lord, so she would be loyal to you no matter what."

Aspace's face went rigid. "Of course," he muttered, and scowled at the empty air before him.

Watching his reaction, Chimi felt confused. Why was he so angry? Then she wondered if Shenza wasn't alone in her feelings.

"You don't have to worry." Chimi spoke quickly, before she lost her nerve. "She likes you."

If possible, Aspace frowned even more fiercely. "How can you tell? She's always wearing that mask."

"I know!" Chimi gave a breathy chuckle as she realized that she and Aspace shared the same frustration. "I think she feels safer wearing it, especially at a time like this. Or maybe..." She edged around the painful truth. "She just doesn't want to be disappointed. I mean, you know... Our father was just a fisherman. We don't have much to offer..."

"Besides loyalty and integrity?" Aspace interrupted.

His expression hadn't changed much, but there was a warmth beneath his sarcasm that Chimi had never heard before. She was suddenly jealous of Shenza. Aspace did like her, and he was so handsome. Shenza didn't know how lucky she was!

"Um, yes, besides that." Chimi tried to push the distracting thoughts away. "Nobody would accept it. The nobles—"

"They don't control me," Aspace answered at once. "A first lord gets what he wants."

There was his wry humor again, but Chimi didn't sense any pride in his words. It wasn't arrogance. He spoke the plain truth.

But before she could respond, they both heard a muffled roar and people screaming. A dull glow came through the fog about where the gate should be. Something was on fire.

"How can anything burn in all this rain?" Chimi asked nervously.

"See the color? It's magic fire." Aspace's voice was grim.

Chimi looked again. The glow was almost as much blue as red. Magic fire? Aspace's older brother, First Lord Anges, had been murdered with magic fire.

"Do you think so?" Chimi found herself edging backward. She tried to stand still. Lelldour's plan couldn't work without her. Anyway, there was nowhere for her to run.

"Somebody had to teach Makko that spell. Don't worry, we're safe behind the wards." Aspace tried to be casual, but he didn't sound as though he felt any safer than Chimi did.

"Oh, is that what they were doing?" Chimi asked, remembering the wizards' chanting. Looking carefully, she saw a row of amulets hanging in the air, and the faint glow of the magical wall the sorcerers had created.

"That's what they were doing," Aspace said. He added, "Thank you, little sister. I'm glad we talked."

The first lord went back to his throne, leaving Chimi tongue-tied. He had called her little sister, almost as if they were family. She could hardly believe it, but he really seemed serious. Chimi decided that if she and Shenza both survived, they were going to have a good long talk.

Chapter Twenty-Five

Battle Magic

On the grass before the pavilion, Borleek roared, "Get ready! Here they come!"

Peace officers in gold and Kesquin guards in magenta stood shoulder to shoulder in the rain. At the base of the steps, Laraquies and six other sorcerers gathered in a second line. Their purple robes were nearly black with moisture. Aspace stood surveying the scene. Chimi was slightly behind him, Lelldour's bone tight in her fist. She wished there was somewhere to hide.

Aspace slid into his chair, crossed his legs, and leaned to the side. His whole posture said that he wasn't a bit worried about the battle's outcome. A first lord had to play his part as much as anyone, Chimi guessed.

Everyone remained in place, poised, through a long silence. The air was heavy with fog and waiting, rain and fear. Then came a defiant yell from the soldiers at the pineapple wall. Chimi saw their shoulders work as they thrust with their spears.

"I don't care what they look like," Borleek hollered. "Get them! Beat them back!"

Chimi felt cold even beyond the chill that was coming to seem normal to her. She knew what was coming.

The soldiers tried hard, but she could see real fear in them. Shields rose a little higher, and their knees were bent to brace against a terrible blow. The thorny barrier shuddered and thrashed. Beyond it, Chimi saw a pulsing glow. The hedge started to steam. Despite themselves, the men staggered back.

An answering chant rose from the sorcerers before the pavilion. Wind blew a sheet of rain to douse the smoke. Desperate soldiers answered Borleek's roaring with redoubled efforts, but only for a moment. Again the barricade blazed with light. The team of magicians chanted on, and the flickering died away again.

To Chimi, watching from behind Lord Aspace's chair, it looked like a stalemate. She wondered how much longer the duel of spell against spell could go on. Then came a searing flash and a deafening roar as lightning snaked out of the clouds. With a shriek, Chimi ducked behind the throne.

It took a moment for her to realize that she wasn't hurt, only badly startled. Mortal shrieks barely penetrated the ringing in her ears. A black shape obscured her vision—the after-image of lightning. She straightened, blinking against the haze.

As her vision cleaned, she saw the barricade in flames. Wizards lay scattered before the pavilion like petals from a spent flower. Many of the fighters were also down. Some struggled to their feet, while others beat at robes that had caught fire.

The pineapple bushes burned with unnatural speed. The flames were a garish red and blue that clashed against each other instead of blending together. Then the barricade burst apart in sparks and flying debris. Rain quenched the smaller fires, but the main blaze kept burning. It lit the fog and smoke with an eerie glow.

First one, then three, then four gray shapes advanced through the fumes. They were huge, much bigger than Chimi had realized. Mismatched eyes shone scarlet from the wrong parts of their bodies. The hulking brutes didn't seem to notice the flames, nor the normal-sized warriors who swarmed past them. Some of the invaders wore Sengool orange, others a plain brown. All hurled themselves at the scattered defenders.

Chimi stood with her hands over her mouth, transfixed by horror. She wanted to look away, but she couldn't tear her eyes from the carnage before the pavilion. Everywhere, men struggled. She saw Borleek squaring off against three mercenaries. On the other side of the field, four Sengools attacked a man in magenta who might have been Winomi's brother, Radu. Blood seemed to be everywhere. It was simply grotesque.

The golems didn't so much walk as flow across the clearing, like enormous sea-creatures with multitudes of feet. Yet they were terribly quick to lash out with their massive arms. They didn't care who was on their side. Anyone who got too close was laid low and then crushed or smothered by the sand. Spears had no effect on them. They carried the weapons within their bodies as they ground ahead.

All too soon, Chimi saw only Sengool fighters in the clearing. The golems advanced on the pavilion. As the terrible creatures came on, someone stirred among the fallen wizards. Master Laraquies got up, moving with obvious effort. He straightened his shoulders and placed himself between Lord Aspace and the golems. His mask must have protected him from the worst of the lightning's effects, Chimi thought, but he still wasn't very steady on his feet.

"Oh, no," Chimi whimpered through her fingers. She couldn't bear to watch those monsters kill Master Laraquies, but there didn't seem to be any escape. She couldn't even see if Borleek was still alive. No one could help Laraquies.

"Stay out of sight," came a breath of sound in her ear. It was Lelldour. The red-robed spirit was only faintly visible. He cautioned, "Don't let Vesswan see you too soon."

Trust Lelldour to ignore the blood and focus on the practical, but Chimi was too sickened by the mayhem to argue about it. She crouched behind the throne and peered out, steeling herself for what she might see.

The golems converged on the lone sorcerer. Just as they came within striking distance, they stopped. Then they slid backward, clearing a path for someone behind them.

Two carrying chairs emerged from the trees, flanked by warriors in orange. A small procession of attendants followed, clutching umbrellas against the rain. This had to be the rebel lords, Oriman and Bosteel. Chimi was surprised to feel a flicker of outrage mingled with her panic. Palanquins? What a ridiculous vanity! Why should they be dry when everyone else was soaked to the skin?

Among the retinue, Chimi saw one older man wearing purple. He looked familiar. This must be the sorcerer who had called the lightning down. Beside him was a slimmer figure in crimson. Vesswan! The necromancer was too far away for Chimi to see her expression, but there was smug self-assurance in the angle of her umbrella over her shoulder. Several bone necklaces glimmered in the gloom.

"She has them," Chimi breathed to Lelldour. He nodded.

The palanquins stopped, and the bearers knelt to lower them to the ground. Two servants hurried forward with umbrellas on long poles. Everyone else waited as the draperies parted and the two lords stepped out of their chairs.

Lord Oriman looked like he was out for a stroll on a pleasant tropical evening. He strutted forward to gaze on the bloody work his servants had done with a satisfied grin. By contrast, Lord Manseen walked with a kind of deadly stillness. He had seemed nice enough at the feast, from what Chimi had seen, but now he looked like the spirit of darkness itself. His robe was a green so deep it was nearly black, sewn with pearls that gleamed like stars in the night.

Manseen had only a few retainers. Chimi recognized Hydara, Seelit's bodyguard, and the little man, Udama, who had been at Manseen's elbow during the feast. Unlike Oriman, Manseen had a dagger in a jeweled sheath. He held himself like one of the soldiers, poised to strike at any moment.

"Step aside, vizier," Oriman sneered as the two got closer to Laraquies.

"You know I can't do that," Laraquies replied. His voice was mild, almost as if he spoke to a child.

There was an angry rustle among the Sengools. Oriman stiffened, and his face darkened. However, Lord Aspace spoke before Orimon could respond.

"Why does my subject raise his hand against me? And why does my guest bring a military escort?" Aspace called with dry mockery. "Were the accommodations not to your liking?"

"I am your subject no longer!" Oriman shrieked, fairly spitting in his rage. "Your house was first to betray the bond between us. Now I shall take what is rightly..."

Manseen, who had never taken his eyes off Aspace, cut Oriman off with a curt gesture. As the Sengool lord sputtered into silence, he said grimly, "You know why it has come to this."

"You'll have to remind me," Aspace drawled lazily. "I have so much to keep track of, now that I'm a first lord."

He was goading them, Chimi thought, reminding them of his superior rank. Oriman was a clan lord, head of his own house, but Aspace was a ruler. Manseen was a first lord, too, but this wasn't his island, so he stood lower. Oriman's fists tightened with fury at the taunting, but it had no effect on Manseen.

"Rank is nothing," he replied. "It is a leaf falling from a tree. The wind brought it to you, and now the wind will snatch it away."

"More leaves fall when someone shakes the tree," Aspace responded with a hint of challenge in his tone. "Isn't that so?"

Chimi wondered how they could speak in metaphors at a time like this. She was sure Lord Aspace was hinting at something, but what?

"The fruit falls to whomever is bold enough to reach for it," Oriman interrupted, trying to reclaim everyone's attention. "Your brother understood that."

"Yes, my poor brother," Aspace said. "Was he just another leaf on the tree?"

Manseen shrugged. "To reach the fruit, it's sometimes necessary to cut a branch and cast it aside."

"Or maybe cut the whole tree and get all the fruit at once," Aspace suggested acidly.

"I see that we understand each other," Manseen said with somber menace.

Chimi shifted in her place behind the throne. It was hard to blame Lord Oriman for getting impatient. She wasn't sure what they were talking about. It seemed to be about Lord Anges' murder, but what did that have to do with Oriman's rebellion?

"If the tree is to be cut," Oriman interrupted, "permit me to strike the first blow." He didn't wait for Manseen's approval, but fixed his bitter gaze on Laraquies, who stood alone at the base of the steps. "I'll begin with you,

Vizier. You, who supplanted my brother in the first lord's esteem and then spoke against us at every council. Now you shall pay for your presumption."

"I am not afraid to die for the sake of my Lord," Laraquies answered, "but if you valued your position in the court of my Lord Anges, I marvel that you now ally yourself with the man who cut his rule short."

Chimi couldn't see Laraquies' face, but he sounded as serene as ever. She bit her lower lip. At least now she understood. Laraquies thought Lord Manseen had hired the man who killed Lord Anges. Lord Aspace must think so, too.

Oriman's face showed a war of feelings, frustration against pride and greed against fear. "That wasn't my choice," he spat, "but it's done. Now I do what I must for the sake of my house."

Manseen must have sent the assassin without telling Oriman, Chimi guessed. Once Lord Anges was dead, Oriman hadn't been able to get out of the scheme. His treachery had already been too great.

"Look to your own Lord for blame, Vizier," Manseen added. "His interference in other areas made it necessary to remove him from the capital. But we always knew his authority here would be a temporary obstacle."

"If you thought I was a nuisance in Porphery, only wait," Aspace said. "I won't apologize for speaking out when I scented treason in the high lord's court. I knew your boy Tenbei was up to something, although I must admit I underestimated your ambition. You're not just helping my resentful subject." Aspace made a negligent gesture that caused Oriman to grit his teeth with rage. "You plan to reach as far as the high lord's own chair. And you think these creatures will take you there."

"It seems to be successful." Manseen looked around deliberately, taking in the death and wreckage. "However, I did need a place to test the golems and make sure of their power. As my host, you were kind enough to provide for my needs." He gave a mocking half-bow.

"Anything for a guest," Aspace replied with equal irony. "You must have thought killing my brother, forcing me to come here and take his place, would prevent me from interfering anymore. Yet here I am, blocking your path again. Do you still think I'm a temporary obstacle?"

"I will when you're dead," Manseen replied. "I see you have wards up. They won't protect you for long." Turning to Oriman, he bowed again. "Would you care to finish this?"

Oriman had been standing in a sulk, irritated at having everyone talk around him. Now he straightened eagerly. A fiendish sneer twisted his lips as he looked up at Aspace.

"I know how fond you are of this old man," he said, pointing at Laraquies. "His magic may keep you safe, but he is all alone. Now watch as I crush him!"

Oriman beckoned to his entourage. Chimi wasn't surprised when Nurune and Vesswan stepped forward. Nurune stopped, hatred glaring from his eyes. Vesswan came a little farther forward, smiling like a vine snake that had scented a frog. Rage made a knot of cold fire in Chimi's chest. She looked forward to helping Lelldour make Vesswan's smug smile disappear.

"I humbly thank my Lords for this opportunity," Vesswan declared. Chimi wondered how she could be so beautiful and so ugly at the same time. "I, too, look forward to being free of interference from one who has intruded into my affairs too often."

"Farewell, Vizier," Nurune added with grim satisfaction. "We won't miss you."

Vesswan raised her hand in a theatrical gesture and commanded, "Kill him."

With a grinding hiss, the golems slid forward. Chimi watched them come with horror. One of the golems passed right over a sorcerer who lay unconscious after the lightning strike. It buried his face in a flow of sand. Chimi shuddered. If the lightning hadn't already killed him, the man would be smothered.

Laraquies stood facing the onslaught. He didn't seem to be frightened. Chimi saw one hand cupped behind his back, holding something. She couldn't tell what it was. Her throat tightened with fear. Someone had to save Master Laraquies!

"Are you ready?" a voice asked behind her. Lelldour! Chimi jumped. She had been distracted by the confrontation, but now she remembered Lelldour's plan. Maybe she could be the one to save Master Laraquies.

"Yes," she whispered back. "Possess me—quick!"

The next moment all sound caught in her throat. She struggled to breathe as Lelldour's ghostly presence closed around her. His spirit flowed in from everywhere at once, like sea water around a fish. It didn't hurt, but it was uncomfortable in a way she could never have put into words.

Then Lelldour was inside her, taking control. Chimi wanted to scream and fight, to make him get out of her body. Yet she had agreed to do this. She did her best to stay calm and let Lelldour do what he had come for.

"Stop!" Lelldour cried. He used Chimi's voice, and it came out coarse and alien. She felt him focus his will on the golems. The monstrous creatures were closing in on Master Laraquies, raising their misshapen hands to strike. They halted with a grinding sigh.

Lelldour stood her up and made her go to Lord Aspace's side. It was an eerie sensation to move without her will. She had the feeling the first lord looked at her in surprise, but she couldn't turn her head to see. Over the golems' heads, the attackers stared at Chimi.

"Isn't that the girl?" asked Lord Manseen. He sounded surprised, but not alarmed, by this deviation from his plan.

Lord Oriman fumed, "I thought you said she was out of this!"

"No matter," Nurune replied, soothing them. "Vesswan is more than a match for this child."

"You're too late, little fool," Vesswan said, smiling at Chimi with barbed sweetness. "I summoned these golems with blood and sorcery. If you couldn't bear the thought of touching a ghost, how can you hope to stop them?"

"You are the fool, if you don't know who I am," Lelldour answered through Chimi's mouth. If moving was strange, it was even weirder for Chimi to hear herself talk and not know what she was going to say.

A startled expression flashed over Vesswan's face. Eyes narrowed, she stared at Chimi. It was good to see Vesswan's composure shaken at last.

Master Laraquies seized the moment of confusion. He jumped forward, right between two of the golems, and threw what he had been holding behind his back. Something small gleamed in the air, then burst on the ground at Nurune's feet. All four of them, Vesswan, Nurune, Oriman and Manseen, vanished in a cloud of grayish vapors. Laraquies threw another, and most of the Sengool soldiers were enveloped as well.

Shrieks and coughing came from inside the clouds. Master Laraquies ducked backward, avoiding the golems, and dashed around the side of the pavilion. Chimi felt Master Lelldour holding the golems back from chasing him.

With an effort, she forced her own voice out of her lips. "What did he throw at them?"

"Black pepper," Aspace said. "We sometimes used it in Porphery to disable our enemies or interrogate prisoners."

"Oh," Chimi said.

Once, when she was a child, she had accidentally dropped a pepper grinder. She remembered how the dust had made her eyes and nose burn. With his magister's mask, Laraquies would have been protected from the effects, but Chimi could still hear coughing and cries of pain from inside the cloud. She hoped the Sengools would suffer for their betrayal.

"It won't last in this rain," Aspace went on, tense now. "Would you ask Master Lelldour to please continue?"

"As my Lord commands," Lelldour answered through Chimi's lips.

Even as Aspace spoke, the steady rain was beating the cloud of pepper dust from the air. Servants rushed forward to assist Lord Oriman. Udama did the same for Lord Manseen. With the edges of their soaked garments, they wiped pepper from the lords' faces. The common soldiers, including Hydara, leaned on each other, coughing violently and rubbing at eyes that streamed with tears.

Nurune and Vesswan had taken the worst of it, though. Nurune went on coughing, so hard that he couldn't even speak, while Vesswan's lovely face was twisted with rage. Her crimson robe had gray smears where she had cleaned the irritant off.

"What kind of trick was that?" she rasped. "It wasn't magic at all." Vesswan had to stop talking as a new fit of coughing overcame her.

"My foolish apprentice." Lelldour sounded almost sad. "You were always too ambitious. That is why you're no longer my student."

"Shut up, old man," Vesswan snarled, still rubbing her nose. "You and your preaching—I've heard enough of it. I found other masters who taught me better than you ever did. Let me show you what I've learned." She made a triumphant gesture. "Destroy them!"

The golems surged up the steps, coming straight for Lord Aspace's throne. Lelldour didn't try to stop them. Chimi guessed it was because Master Laraquies wasn't in danger any more. The golems struck the warding spell at the edge of the pavilion with a muffled roar. There was a dull flash, a wave of heat, and a crackle of power.

A normal person would have been thrown down the stairs, unconscious, but the golems didn't waver. They stood pounding at the magical barrier with their horrid, shapeless limbs. The warding spell snarled and popped, but the sorcerers' power held. For all their great strength, the golems couldn't penetrate it.

Beyond the golems, the rebels were recovering from their confusion. Chimi heard Oriman's braying voice and Manseen's cold one speak briefly. She couldn't understand them through the din.

The golems stopped a moment later. They stood in a line at the edge of the pavilion, clearly waiting for something. Chimi thought their silence was even more terrible than their violence. Then came chanting in what might have been Nurune's voice. A red and blue flicker followed, and hissing that started softly but grew steadily louder. Aspace looked up, a quick glance that betrayed his concern. Nurune was using magic fire on the pavilion's roof, and this time there were no loyal sorcerers to stop him.

* * *

"You're not going out there," Juss warned. His low voice was one with a growl of thunder from the sky.

"I know," Shenza answered, though it hurt her to say it when Chimi and Lord Aspace were in danger.

Shenza and Juss crouched beneath the trailing fronds of a young palm tree, where they had a view of the confrontation at the pavilion. Unfortunately, the small tree did nothing to shelter them from the incessant rain.

It hadn't been easy to find their way here. The first lord's estate had always been confusing, but today some force was actively trying to keep them away. Hedges that Shenza didn't remember appeared from the mist, blocking the path. Roots tangled their feet and cold air made their bodies feel like wood. The gray light and changeable landscape reminded Shenza of the spirit realm where she and Juss had accidentally strayed during their search for Lord Anges' killer—a brief visit that had left Juss scarred and limping.

Despite the fear her memory raised, Shenza had focused all her will on finding a way through, because she knew Lord Aspace needed her. Fierce concentration had brought them to the front gate. From there, it had been only too easy to follow the Sengools' trail of destruction.

Terror had been growing inside her since she saw the charred barricades and slaughtered guards. It seemed to squeeze the very breath from her lungs. Even with her mask's magic, Shenza couldn't make out most of what Oriman and Manseen were saying, but Vesswan's command came through clearly: "Destroy them!"

Shenza knotted her fingers in her wet robe as the golems started forward. Sengool and Manseen meant to kill Lord Aspace! Seeing Chimi with Aspace only made it worse. Shenza was delighted to see her sister alive, but Chimi was still in danger.

She didn't know which loss would be worse, her younger sister or the man she loved. But she couldn't deny it was Aspace's name that burned in her heart. If Chimi died, Shenza would miss her. If Aspace died, that would be unbearable.

Heat rose within her, power and fury enough to banish the chill from her bones. She didn't care what Juss said, or that her magic wasn't working well. If they hurt Aspace, she would punish them. Not as a magister, within the bounds of the law, but as a lover whose grief must be avenged at any cost.

Nor would Shenza hide, like a frightened child, while those traitors did whatever they wanted. She would stop them. For Aspace. She was at the point of leaping to her feet when Juss' whisper broke into her thoughts.

"Look at that. They can't get in."

Indeed, the golems had crashed into something at the top of the steps. Dull booming sounded as they pounded at the air. Over the distance, Shenza picked out the faint glimmer of magic.

"It's a ward," Shenza told him, "but it won't be enough."

"You mean," Juss said slowly, "they can't get in, but he can't get out, either."

Shenza answered with a curt nod. Juss was silent a moment longer. Then he said, "I have an idea."

Staying low, Juss started to crawl backward through the brush. Shenza stayed where she was. She had to know what happened to Lord Aspace.

Juss grabbed her ankle, rough with urgency. "I'm not leaving you here by yourself. Come on!"

"Stop it!" Shenza scowled at him, but then realized the futility of her defiance. She had her mask on. He couldn't see her face. Reluctantly, she eased back from the palm tree and followed as Juss set off in a direction that roughly paralleled the clearing's edge.

Even so, she clung to the anger in her heart. Just for that moment, when love and rage had filled her whole being, she had felt powerful and confident. Stronger than Vesswan and Nurune together. Transcendent, because of her love for Lord Aspace.

Whatever Juss had planned, she would need that strength to make it happen.

Chapter Twenty-Six

The Darkest Powers

Chimi sensed no concern in Master Lelldour as he walked her over to one side, where they could see better. Vesswan and Oriman watched Nurune eagerly. Only Lord Manseen remained alert, his hand ready on the hilt of his dagger.

"Vesswan," Lelldour called. Her head turned with an angry snap. "Your power has indeed grown. Yet it seems there is one more lesson I must teach you."

"Hah," Vesswan sneered.

Chimi felt Lelldour gather his will, though he didn't move or say anything else. It was a summons, she realized. Just as she had called Hawadi's spirit, Lelldour was calling for aid, but he was more powerful. He could invoke something bigger.

A shiver in the air that wasn't rain, and ghosts started to appear. First a few, then more, and suddenly dozens of spirits materialized in a ring with Vesswan at its center. Chimi saw men and women, young and old, some dressed in rags and others in fine robes. All had the patient, dead expression she knew so well.

From the gasps, not only the necromancers saw them. Soldiers scrambled back, then Nurune and the two clan lords. Chimi remembered how the supernatural cold had bothered her the first few times she felt it. No living person could stand to be near so many ghosts.

"What's this?" Vesswan laughed mockingly. "Ghosts? You know they can't hurt me."

"These are my allies," Lelldour replied. "All the ghosts I ever helped to find peace. All the bones in my necklaces, which you are wearing."

"I—" Vesswan faltered. "What are you talking about?"

"You have no necromancer's bones," Lelldour went on, relentless as the rain, "for you never helped a wandering spirit. Not in the way that matters. Yet how could you call yourself a necromancer when you had no bones? Even Nurune of Sengool wouldn't have hired you."

Lelldour paused. Chimi saw Nurune staring at Vesswan with a disdainful curl to his lip. He didn't seem so much shocked by the lie as irritated that Vesswan had been caught doing it.

"These are mine," Vesswan cried, shrill in the rainy air. "I earned them!"

Only if murder counted as work. Chimi wondered why Vesswan bothered to protest. Did Nurune's opinion mean that much to her?

"You sent the enchanted spider to bite me," Lelldour said. "You poisoned me to get my necklaces and teaching scrolls. Every day you pilfered my knowledge for your own profit, and wore my bones as a trophy. Did you think I wouldn't sense them? They are part of me. They cannot be hidden."

"The bones are nothing," Vesswan retorted, speaking more to Oriman and Nurune than to Lelldour. "A mere decoration, a symbol of my art. They have no other meaning."

"You say so because you don't understand their power," Lelldour answered. "Even if you did, you couldn't use it because the bones aren't yours. However, I can now demonstrate their usefulness."

All this while, the ghosts had been crowding close to Vesswan, isolating her as everyone else instinctively retreated from their frigid presence.

"Don't try to frighten me," came Vesswan's scornful reply. "They can't do anything!"

She pushed at the ghosts, but there were so many that new ones constantly pressed forward. The spirits weren't just milling around aimlessly, either. Their circle slowly expanded outward, forcing the two rebel lords and their retainers farther back. Even the heartless Lord Manseen was starting to look uneasy.

"It isn't the ghosts you need to fear," Lelldour said. "You have upset the balance of nature. The atmosphere of this island is saturated with negative energy, especially since you nearly killed my new apprentice. That must have made it easier to conjure your golems, but it also gave free passage to other things. Can't you sense them?"

A visible gap opened around Vesswan as the throng of ghosts continued to push outward. Threading through the ghosts were other creatures, things Chimi had never seen or imagined.

The entities were vaguely human in that they walked on two legs. They had sickly white skin with long, spidery limbs. Their hands were more like fins with savage talons on the fingertips. Naked of hair or clothing, they seemed to have no gender. Their mouths were too wide for a human face, full of jagged, sharklike teeth, and their eyes were mere dark slits. They even moved like sharks, with a darting, swaying motion.

Chimi felt a wave of nausea as two of the creatures circled the body of a fallen peace officer. She sensed they were about to pounce on it a moment before they did. One tore at the dead man's shoulder. The other raked bloody flesh from his leg. Chimi gave a strangled moan. She wanted to shut her eyes, but Lelldour was still in control. He didn't seem to feel any emotion as he watched the gory feast.

"What are these?" Lord Aspace asked tightly.

"Evil spirits," Lelldour explained through Chimi's lips. "The nature spirits we know draw their power from the positive energy of the elements: sea, sky and earth. Though sometimes cruel, they are still beings of light. Yet they have their opposites, corrupted spirits of madness and violence which can emerge in any village where there is no necromancer."

Those last words were aimed at her, Chimi knew. Lelldour had warned her about evil spirits back when she had said she didn't want to learn his trade.

"How long will they stay here?" was Aspace's next question.

"Once the balance is restored, they will not be able to linger," Lelldour said.

"I guess that's something," Aspace said.

The soldiers drew into a tight cluster around Lords Oriman and Manseen. Oriman, in particular, looked pale and sick. For once, Chimi didn't blame him. Vesswan, meanwhile, had been left in the center of an expanding circle.

"What about me?" she called out.

"What do you expect us to do?" Nurune called back with something like Lelldour's deadly rationality. Chimi liked it even less coming from him.

"I crave my Lord's mercy," Vesswan cried to Lord Manseen. "Haven't I done everything you asked?"

There was a murmured consultation between the two lords. Oriman showed a trace of sympathy, but Manseen was unmoved. The Sengool lord finally shouted back a weak excuse.

"You lied to us. A real necromancer wouldn't need help."

"You can't just leave me here!" Vesswan shrieked, close to hysteria. It wasn't as satisfying to watch as Chimi had expected.

Yelling wasn't a good idea, either. Across the widening gap, sharklike heads turned. The two who were tearing at the corpse went back to their grisly meal, but several others trotted toward Vesswan with unmistakable, predatory intent. The necromancer looked around desperately. Her eyes fastened on the pavilion.

"Come to me!" she cried. "Help me!"

Chimi wondered how Vesswan could dare ask for Lord Aspace's help after what she had done, but it was the golems she spoke to. The four monsters flowed down the steps in a sandy rush.

The first of the corrupted spirits had already reached Vesswan. It lunged at her, raking with its fin-hand.

"No!" Vesswan swung her umbrella. Wood splintered as the umbrella's thin ribs broke. The creature shook its head, an almost human gesture.

Then fabric tore as it lashed back.

Everything got confused as the golems and evil spirits converged on Vesswan. The golems battered the spirits, sometimes flinging them across the clearing and sometimes grinding over them. Spirits voiced eerie wails of rage and pain, but they seemed as immune to harm as the golems were. Sand flew as they turned on these new attackers. Neither side in the wild melee seemed to care that it couldn't hurt the other.

Vesswan's voice rose above the chaos. "Get away!" She kept flailing with her shattered umbrella, backing up until she reached the ghostly human chain. Rain drenched her, dripping from her many braids. Terror distorted her lovely face.

"Leave those!" she shrieked to the golems. "Come to me! Save me!"

One of the shark spirits finally caught the umbrella and wrenched it from her hand. In the same instant, a different spirit leaped on her from the other side.

"No!" Vesswan wailed, but the two evil spirits dragged her to the ground, tearing at her robes, jaws gaping wide. Chimi was deeply grateful when the golems' massive bodies blocked her view. On the other side of the ghosts, even Hydara and the mercenaries winced as Vesswan's screaming trailed off into silence.

Chimi felt a kind of sigh within herself. Lelldour wasn't exactly happy, but he seemed satisfied by Vesswan's fate. Chimi wondered if he had planned this revenge all along, or if events had gone beyond what anyone could control. She was afraid to ask him.

A moment later, she felt Lelldour release the ghosts he had summoned. One by one, the human spirits faded away. Only the darkest magic remained—golems and corrupted spirits. Without Vesswan's control, the golems ran berserk, attacking spirits and humans alike.

Somehow Lord Manseen's mercenaries kept their heads. They closed into a knot around their employer and moved off together, trying to get him away from the danger. The Sengools were left with only Nurune and a few house soldiers.

"Stop them!" Lord Oriman shrieked when he realized there was nothing between him and the monsters.

Nurune stood transfixed. "I can't," he said. "Only Vesswan could control them, and she..."

"Why didn't you say so, brother?" Oriman's voice was high with panic. "You should have thought of that!"

Someone else screamed, "Run!"

Lord Oriman and his followers scattered like a flock of birds before a falcon. At least one of the golems went flailing after them.

"Does my Lord wish me to stop them?" Lelldour inquired. He didn't sound like he cared whether the golems killed the renegade lords or not.

Lord Aspace cried, "Look out!" He grabbed Chimi's arm and yanked her back from her vantage point at the top of the stairs. "Don't stand there—pay attention to what's around you."

A stream of charcoal and sparks fell from above, just missing them both. Chimi sensed Lelldour's surprise. They had both been so caught up in the drama outside that they forgot Nurune had set the roof on fire. Now she could feel the blazing heat and see ominous wisps of smoke in the air.

"Master Lelldour," Chimi snapped, seizing the ghost's moment of confusion. "If you don't want to search for another apprentice, you'd better let me get out of here."

She felt a kind of shrug in her mind. Chimi ran after Aspace as another wave of fiery debris dropped toward them. Looking up, Chimi saw tongues of flame spreading through the pavilion's beautifully carved rafters. Painted designs blistered and scorched. Metal inlay ran down the spiral columns in burning rivulets. The fire's voice was a greedy hiss as the rain tried to quench it, but it took more than water to quench a magic fire. It took more magic, and all the sorcerers were dead or fled.

"Do you know how to put out magic fire?" she asked nervously.

"No," Aspace told her, "but I'm sure Laraquies does."

"He's not here. What should we do?" Chimi asked. She couldn't help rubbing her eyes, for the smoke was making them sting.

"We have to go." Aspace led Chimi toward the back of the pavilion. He added sarcastically, "At least Nurune got that much right. He's driven us out of our refuge."

They had reached the corner of the building farthest from the fire. Chimi felt a flutter of dismay as she saw the warding amulets still suspended in the air.

"The ward is still up," she cried. "We can't get out!"

"It's all right," Aspace reassured her. "I know this one."

He raised his hands, not quite touching the magical barrier, and shut his eyes in concentration. Chimi looked back. Lord Aspace's chair looked very small inside the grand pavilion. There was an alarming groan from up in the rafters. The chair vanished beneath a cascade of burning wood and roof tiles. Chimi gave a yip of fear.

Lord Aspace opened his eyes to frown at her. "I need to focus," he said.

Chimi nodded, pressing her hands to her mouth. She tried not to panic when she saw how far the flames had spread. She snatched up the trailing end of her robe and used it to cover her nose and mouth so the smoke wouldn't make her cough.

"It isn't working," Aspace murmured, frustrated. "Something is absorbing my magic."

Inside Chimi's mind, Lelldour reminded her that Vesswan had deliberately let negative energy build up in the atmosphere. Naturally, this interfered with the positive energy of normal magic.

"Oh, no." Chimi whispered behind her makeshift mask.

"What?" Aspace demanded.

Chimi quickly repeated what Lelldour had said. For the second time she asked, "What should we do?"

"I'll just have to try harder," Aspace replied, but Chimi saw a flash of worry in his eyes.

The first lord turned back to the amulet above him, frowning with concentration. Long moments passed. The smoke inside the pavilion was steadily getting thicker.

"Release," Aspace commanded, but nothing happened.

Through the smoke, Chimi glimpsed movement outside the pavilion. Someone in dark, full length robes. Not a soldier, then. It might be Master Laraquies. Or maybe it was Nurune of Sengool. She couldn't tell. Even though Lord Aspace had told her to stay quiet, Chimi started to yell.

"Help us! Please help us! We can't get out!"

Aspace scowled at her, but a voice from outside cried, "Dispel!"

The amulet Lord Aspace had been focused on suddenly fell. It clattered down the steps from the pavilion. Chimi and Aspace followed amid clouds of smoke that had been trapped behind the magical wall.

"Sister!" Chimi cried when she saw who was standing at the bottom of the stairs.

Shenza lowered her spell-breaker wand. Juss stood beside her, looking around warily. Both their robes were soaked and muddy to the knees. Shenza's headcloth would hardly stay on. Juss had bits of leaves all over his arms. But Chimi didn't care, because neither of them was hurt.

"Oh, you did get away! You're all right!" She flung herself at Shenza and hugged her, despite hearing a distinct squish as moisture from her sister's robes soaked into her own.

"I'm glad to see you," Shenza said. Chimi couldn't see her face beneath her mask, but her hug was real enough. "I was so worried about you, sister."

"Not so loud," Juss rumbled. "Someone else might hear you."

"I don't think anyone is left to hear us," Aspace answered, following Chimi down the steps, "but Juss is right. Let's be careful until we know where those golems went."

A kind of shock ran through Shenza. Chimi felt it in her sister's arms. Emerald eyes searched the golden mask, as if Aspace could see what lay behind it. The silence stretched between them, as thick with emotion as the rain in the air. Chimi edged backward, feeling like an intruder.

Released from her embrace, Shenza pressed both hands to her chest and bowed. "Forgive your servant for coming so late. I was..."

"I know," Aspace put in. His expression shifted rapidly from relief to annoyance to something else. A kind of joy, Chimi decided. "You couldn't help it. Chimi told me what happened. I would promise to punish Vesswan for striking out at my loyal servants, but she's already paid the price for her errors."

"My Lord?" Shenza straightened. She seemed to be struggling over what surprised her more. Finally she glanced at Chimi. "You knew?"

"Yes, uh..." Chimi paused, not sure how to explain all that had happened.

"Later, please," Aspace interrupted. "We need to get farther away from here." He gestured upward, and Chimi saw that the flames had spread to their end of the pavilion. The magic fire sent a column of bruised-looking smoke and steam roaring skyward. It also threatened to drop more roof tiles on them.

The four of them quickly walked away, but Chimi couldn't help quipping, "That's the warmest I've been all day."

Juss and Aspace chuckled, but Shenza looked back. "It was a beautiful building," she said.

"I'll build you a new one," Aspace replied. "First we need to know what's happening. He glanced at Juss, who immediately stepped forward.

"My Lord?"

"If you didn't know, the main battle was just on the other side there."

"We saw," Juss cut in. "You want me to scout for survivors?"

At any other time, it would have been unforgivable rudeness. Now, Aspace merely nodded. "Please."

"Right." Juss lifted his knife in salute and limped off, keeping a distance from the burning pavilion.

To Shenza, Aspace said, "Master Laraquies was here with me, but I seem to have lost track of him. You will stand at my side."

Shenza straightened slightly. "As my Lord commands."

Her voice seemed to hold some deeper meaning. Aspace must have heard it, too, for he paused, searching the inscrutable face of her mask, before he finally turned to Chimi.

"Little sister, if Master Lelldour is still with you, I'll need his power as well."

Chimi felt Lelldour's agreement. "He's ready."

Shenza looked at Chimi, curiosity plain in the tilt of her head. She must have been expecting to see Lelldour's ghost nearby. Chimi almost giggled. There was so much to explain.

There was no time for it, though. Juss ran toward them, bellowing, "They're right behind me—run!"

* * *

They were safe! Shenza's knees wobbled. She was so relieved, she hardly knew what to do. After a day of rain and fear, when she had thought she would lose both her love and her sister, Chimi and Aspace stood before her alive and well.

Chimi said something, and Juss, too, but their words were like the rain, noise without meaning. Lord Aspace was the only one who mattered. Shenza stood in silence, drinking in his presence. It had been less than a day since she saw him, yet she had forgotten how beautiful he was. She had forgotten, too, the power of her own feelings.

In folk tales, people lost all self-control when they fell in love. They were driven to the darkest crimes and the greatest sacrifices. Shenza had never liked those stories. She didn't believe in that kind of love. Not until now. As Aspace looked at her, saying nothing, new strength flowed through her. Shenza, who had never trusted her own abilities, felt suddenly powerful. She could do anything as long as Aspace was with her.

"You will stand at my side," he told her. That was where she wanted to be—at his side, always.

"As my Lord commands," Shenza replied. What else could she say?

He stared at her a moment longer, then turned to Chimi. "Little sister, if Master Lelldour is still with you, I'll need his power as well."

"He's ready," Chimi said.

Shenza glanced around. The first time she had gone to Lelldour's house with Chimi, her sister's powers had made the spirit visible right away. Why couldn't she see him now?

Before she could ask about it, she heard Juss' warning cry. "They're right behind me—run!"

Shenza stepped forward, putting herself between Lord Aspace and whatever Juss was running from.

"My Lord must go!" she said.

Aspace held his ground as Juss pounded back to them with only a slight hitch in his stride. The looming hulk of a sand golem was close behind. With almost malicious timing, the burning pavilion sagged toward them. It collapsed in a roaring billow of smoke and sparks.

"Juss!" Shenza cried as her friend vanished in the cloud. She felt a hand on her shoulder, holding her back.

"Stay here," Aspace ordered.

Despite the circumstances, Shenza felt a thrill of pleasure at his touch.

Aspace took his hand way as Juss broke out of the smoke. He coughed and his limp was worse, but he was alive.

"Hurry," Juss called. "You've got to get away!"

Still Aspace didn't move. Just as Juss reached the little group, Chimi stepped forward.

"That's not necessary," she said.

Juss skidded to a halt. "What?"

Shenza turned to stare, too. It was Chimi's voice, but it didn't sound anything like her. She used a queer, flat tone and her face wore a somber expression. Chimi had never been so calm in her life. She stood differently, too. Not straight, with her feet together, like a proper young lady. Her feet were braced, her chin held higher. In fact, she carried herself like a man.

"Chimi?" Shenza asked warily.

"No." The girl didn't even look at Shenza.

The golem appeared from the fumes of the collapsed pavilion. It rushed forward with deadly speed.

"Come on, we can't stay here." Juss jigged nervously. In another moment, Shenza thought, he would pick up Lord Aspace and carry him to safety, as he sometimes threatened to do with Shenza. For her part, Shenza tightened her fingers on the slim length of her spell-breaker. She didn't know if it would work on a creature like this, but it was all they had.

"It's all right," Aspace told them. "Just watch."

Chimi raised her hand, palm outward, as she confronted the golem. "Halt."

Vesswan's runaway atrocity slowed abruptly. It wavered, as if resisting Chimi's command. Shenza wasn't the only one to breathe more easily when the golem stood still at last. The four of them gazed up at the baleful creature with its ruby eyes and misshapen limbs. The only sound was the hiss of rain falling on the ever-burning magic fire.

"How did you do that?" Juss demanded.

"I am a necromancer," Chimi answered, as if that explained everything. Turning to Shenza, she continued in that strange, toneless voice, "To answer your previous question, Magister, I am Lelldour Mokseem of Salloo. Your sister has kindly allowed me to share her body for a time."

Both Shenza and Juss stood speechless. Then the peace officer edged away. "You're sharing her body?"

"We needed Master Lelldour's skill as a necromancer," Lord Aspace said. "He can't focus his power without a body."

"I suppose," Shenza murmured. She could hardly believe her sister had agreed to let a ghost possess her.

"It's a temporary measure, I assure you. I have no wish to relive my youth in the form of a female child," Chimi said with a hint of acid humor.

"Nevertheless, Magister, I must thank you and Officer Juss for taking the time to locate my skeleton. I appreciate it." Chimi pressed both hands to her chest and bowed.

Now Shenza was sure that Aspace was telling the truth. The Chimi she knew would never use such stiff, formal language. This had to be a different personality. Lord Aspace cut them off with a quick gesture.

"We'll have time for this later," he said. "Master Lelldour, can you control all four golems?"

"Of course," Chimi said.

"Then I want to make sure my guests don't leave without saying goodbye." Aspace smiled with his usual ironic quirk. "Juss, did you see where they were before the golem came after you?"

"I saw a lot of bodies," Juss replied. "It was hard to tell who was who. One golem was fighting with some kind of fish creatures." He shuddered at the memory. "I don't know what they were, but they were cannibalizing the corpses."

"Corrupted spirits," Chimi told him.

"Spirits?" Juss repeated. Then he shook his head. "Never mind. Two other golems were going out the other side of the clearing. They were chasing some of those mercenaries we saw coming up the stairs."

"That must have been Manseen's group." Aspace's eyes narrowed in thought.

"Should we follow the evil spirits?" Shenza asked. "My Lord might be in danger."

"I'm not letting Manseen get away after what he's done," Aspace snapped. He added, more quietly, "Besides, I'm not afraid of anything. I have Chimi, I have Juss... I have you." And he smiled in that way of his that filled Shenza with so much warmth that she didn't even feel the rain falling on her.

"As my Lord says," she whispered.

The others were watching them. Chimi had a glint of humor in her dark eyes. Juss raised his fist to his mouth and coughed dramatically.

"Show me which way they went," Aspace ordered.

"Right."

Juss led them in a half circle, keeping well away from the remains of the pavilion. An eerie silence lay over the battlefield. The slaughter was even worse than it had been at the gate. Bodies were scattered across the grass, all of them lying terribly still. Shenza didn't want to look at their gaping wounds and empty expressions, but she knew it was her duty.

Mostly she saw peace officers and Kesquin house guards, though a few of the hired soldiers had joined their foes in death. Directly before the burning pavilion, a handful of sorcerers lay together, struck down by some lethal spell. Shenza paused, heart pounding, but Master Laraquies wasn't among them.

She did see the spirits Juss had described: gangly, naked things, pale as deep sea squids. Another sand golem stood its ground there. It seemed to be protecting one of the bodies, for it whirled to charge whenever one of the evil spirits got too close. The slit-eyed monsters turned, eyeing the four humans.

"Stay close to me," Chimi said. Without a visible signal, the golem she controlled surged forward. The shark spirits reluctantly gave way. Chimi must have taken control of the second golem, too, for it moved aside to let them approach.

Vesswan of Zeell lay face down in grass and blood. Shenza had never liked the woman, but her stomach churned at the sight of her injuries. Flesh and fabric were savagely torn, and gore dyed her robes a deeper crimson. Only the color and the cluster of narrow braids on her head made her recognizable.

Chimi stood over the corpse. Shenza saw her throat move as she swallowed heavily, perhaps resisting Lelldour's compulsion, but then she bent to snatch at something. Vesswan's head lolled at an unnatural angle as Chimi tugged at two thick loops of white bones strung on red cords. Necromancer's necklaces.

"Do we have time to rob the dead?" Aspace inquired. He sounded so bored that Shenza knew he found the sight as disturbing as she did.

Chimi straightened. In a decisive gesture, she laid the bone necklaces around her own neck. "By now my Lord should realize the importance of the bones. I won't leave them here."

Shenza didn't know what to say to that, but she was interrupted by a startled cry from Juss.

"Chief!" The peace officer swerved toward a cluster of men's bodies, all of them clad in short, dark gold kilts. Juss knelt to lay his hand on one of the still backs. Aspace and Shenza hurried over, but Juss was already standing up.

Even in death, Borleek was unmistakable. The big man lay on his side. He had a deep puncture wound in the back of his right leg and several more in his back, sides and neck. Borleek's fists still clutched a broken spear shaft. The body of a man in Sengool colors showed that he had fought to the end.

"Too late." The muscles of Juss' jaw were clenched tight. "They must have brought him down with that slash on his leg, so they could come at him all at once."

Shenza hadn't liked Borleek of Bentei much more than she did Vesswan, but she was surprised to feel real sorrow at his death. With an effort, she found her voice. "I'm sorry, Juss."

"He died as he would have wished," Juss answered in an unusually quiet tone, "as a warrior, defending his Lord."

"With the golems and so many mercenaries, I couldn't have asked for more from him," Aspace answered.

Juss nodded, but Shenza saw his grim expression. Maybe Juss saw a shadow of himself lying among the fallen. If he hadn't come with her to Vesswan's, he would have been one of the defenders, either here or at the gate. In that case, he would certainly have died.

Nobody had told him to go with Shenza. He had simply appointed himself her bodyguard during Lord Anges' murder investigation. She wondered if he felt guilty for putting his first priority aside.

Before she could find the words to ask, a man's scream echoed from somewhere nearby. Everyone but the golems turned toward the noise.

"If you wish to help his spirit rest in peace, we should finish his work," Chimi said. Her voice sounded so mature that Shenza was sure Lelldour was still speaking through her. "We must bring down the traitors who dared attack my Lord."

"That's right." Juss bent over to pick up a spear that had been left on the grass.

Lord Aspace said, "We will."

Chapter Twenty-Seven

The Final Passage

The sand golems moved swiftly, with the humans following. Screams and cries came from behind a partly burned hibiscus hedge. Aspace and his companions moved toward the noise, passing yet more broken bodies. Among the dead were a man in gaudy orange robes, and another in purple robes studded with copper beads. Farther off, Shenza glimpsed Manseen's little aide, Udama, who would no longer smiled as he spied for his lord.

Shenza didn't stop, but looked on her enemies with deep anxiety as she passed. Oriman and Nurune were dead, too. It had started with the death of First Lord Anges, but now in this one terrible day, everything was changing. The leaders of her community were being swept away. Treachery had claimed Borleek, his chief peacekeeper, and Nurune, his vizier. Master Laraquies, the former magister, was the sole survivor of that era. Shenza had a sudden desire to see her old teacher and make sure he wasn't among the casualties.

Shenza asked Lord Aspace, "Where did my Lord say Master Laraquies had gone?"

"If he followed our plan, he went to join Shamatt, who has a small squad in the Pearl Court," Aspace said. "They're supposed to be protecting my mother and the other women."

"I see," Shenza said. If Lady Izmay was there, that was probably where Master Laraquies wanted to be, anyway.

"Laraquies should be scrying to see what happened," Aspace went on. "If they can, they'll attack the Sengool estate, since we assume that's where Seelit is."

"Sengool left no defenders?" Juss asked doubtfully.

Aspace shrugged. "Laraquies is supposed to find out. Shamatt will make the final decision whether to try it or not."

They had reached the scorched hedge at the border of the field. Heavy cloud cover muted the blossoms' vibrant colors. Petals fell as the golems forced their way through with much thrashing of branches. The monsters stood aside, holding the greenery back with their massive bodies. The smell of crushed leaves was thick in the air.

Chimi stepped through, carefully lifting her feet over the shattered stubs of hibiscus bushes. Juss followed, barring the gap with his spear so that Shenza and Aspace were kept on the outside. The thud of blows and grunts or gasps of pain were clearly audible from the other side.

"I appreciate your concern," Aspace said with a trace of humor, "but I need to see what's happening. Or must I command you to let me through?"

In answer, Juss lifted his spear. Aspace strode forward confidently, and Shenza followed, eager to get farther from the sand golems. Once they were through, the creatures released the hedge. It snapped back with another loud crackle. Shenza glimpsed one of the shark spirits on the other side. She hoped it wouldn't get angry after the branches hit it in the face.

She stopped worrying about that when she saw the remaining two golems. Shenza couldn't see who they were attacking because of their bulk, but she could guess. The golems drew back when Chimi got closer. One of them swayed violently, fighting Lelldour's power, but the necromancer won in the end. The golems slid backward to join the pair already under his control.

As she had expected, the golems had been after the mercenaries. Perhaps twenty remained of the force she and Juss had seen going up the stairs. Several had already fallen before the raging monsters. She saw one richer headcloth near the center of the group. Lord Manseen Bosteel of Bosteel was trapped by the very monsters he had helped create.

The sand golems spread out to surround the Bosteels. Aspace stopped, Shenza and Juss at his shoulders. No one spoke as he faced the man who had tried to kill him and seize his throne.

Lord Manseen stood proud and erect among his supporters. His dark eyes blazed with emotions Shenza could only guess at. His mind must be racing, trying to understand how victory had turned into disaster. Seeking, too, a way out of this trap. Shenza saw fear, but also desperate courage, in the eyes of the soldiers. She hadn't expected such loyalty from hired thugs.

"Oriman is dead. Nurune and Vesswan, too," Aspace finally told them. He spoke casually, yet soberly, not taunting his enemies as Shenza might have expected. "Your allies are broken."

"So are yours," Manseen bit out defiantly.

"I have the ones that matter," Aspace replied. His lips twitched in a mocking smile, but his green eyes held a stark light.

"Don't patronize me." Manseen tensed, unconsciously raising his dagger.

Juss took a step forward, spear poised.

"Try it," he growled. "It'll make this a lot easier."

Manseen's men crowded forward, too, but Manseen had already halted. Shenza watched pride and fear balance in his eyes.

Aspace tapped Juss on the shoulder. "You're in my way again."

Reluctantly, the peace officer moved aside.

Speaking to Manseen, Aspace went on, "I would rather not kill you."

The would-be high lord silently snarled with rage, though Shenza noticed he kept a wary eye on Juss.

"I don't need your pity," Manseen bit out.

"Are you sure?" Aspace retorted. "There are others who depend on you. What will happen to them if you die?"

"Seelit?" Manseen went rigid again. Dark color flooded his face. "How dare you threaten my daughter!"

"If you take her home with you," Aspace interrupted, "no one would be able to harm her."

"But he's the one who brought her here!" Chimi burst out, clearly speaking for herself again.

"Chimi," Shenza scolded, shocked by her younger sister's interruption.

"It's true!" Chimi whirled, fists clenched, to confront Lord Manseen. "You were just using her to get invited here. Then you made her give me that cursed bracelet. I don't think you care about Seelit at all. She would be safer if she stayed with us."

Manseen drew himself up, more affronted than before, if that was possible. The men around him muttered, offended by the boldness of such a young girl.

"I don't expect a child to understand affairs of state," Manseen sniffed.

"You might be surprised what a child understands," Chimi snapped back at him. "I think Seelit understands you very well. That's why she's afraid of you!"

"Sister, stop!" Shenza cried. She couldn't believe Chimi would speak up for Seelit after what the girl had done to her. Even so, that didn't give her the right to interfere when Lord Aspace was negotiating. "You're not part of my Lord's council."

"At this moment, the four of you are my council," Aspace corrected her mildly, with only a trace of sarcasm. "Counting Master Lelldour among the four, of course."

Shenza stood there, silenced as much as Lord Manseen. Juss, too, seemed startled. Shenza wondered how Lord Aspace could listen to any of them. They were all of low rank, except for Shenza, and even she was new to her position.

Lord Manseen sneered at their confusion. "You must be truly desperate."

Lord Aspace didn't answer him directly. "Well, Chimi, what do you think?" he asked pleasantly, indicating Manseen. "What should happen to a person like this?"

"I..." Chimi hesitated, perhaps realizing the responsibility she had taken upon herself. "I don't think you can trust him," she finally said. "He won't keep a promise."

"Master Lelldour?"

Chimi gave a kind of shudder, then bowed low. "It is an honor to serve my Lord," she said in a voice no longer her own. "My Lord must know that once this decision is made, it cannot be recalled. Death is death."

That was even less an answer than Chimi's, but Aspace didn't seem put off by the cryptic words. "Juss?"

"He attacked you," Juss answered bluntly. "You'd be within your rights to kill him. And," he hesitated before adding, "we might not have enough men left to guard all of them."

He gestured to take in the mercenaries, who shuffled their feet uneasily. None of them had spoken up, and Shenza didn't blame them. What was there to say, after all? Lord Manseen had gambled with their lives—and lost.

Still, Shenza wondered if Aspace could really order his prisoners killed. It was one thing if they died in battle. This would be different.

"Shenza?" Aspace asked.

At first, she had no idea what to say. She drew a deep breath.

"Lord Manseen did attack," Shenza said, "after my Lord had made him welcome with courtesy and hospitality." She couldn't bring herself to mention the bridal negotiations which had caused her so much torment. "He abused his status as a guest to support a rebellion against my Lord. He encouraged those who aroused the wrath of the spirits and summoned an abomination into my Lord's lands. Also, I heard Lord Manseen admit that he ordered the murder of my Lord's brother. Each of these crimes is enough to die for."

"You think I should kill him?" Aspace pressed.

Shenza nodded, hating what she had to say even as she knew she must speak the words. It was what Master Laraquies would have said if he had been there.

"My Lord must kill him," Shenza replied. "If he does all of this and my Lord permits him to live, then who would my Lord ever punish?"

After a moment, Aspace looked away.

Remembering something Chimi had said, Shenza continued softly, "A ruler cannot shrink from justice, but neither should my Lord condemn the innocent. My Lord must allow Lady Seelit to return her father's remains to Sardony, so that his family cannot call for vengeance."

A quick flash of sarcasm crossed Aspace's face, and Shenza knew what he must be thinking. Lord Manseen's son, Tenbei, had probably been a conspirator as well. He might still find some pretext for a blood feud.

"I can't argue with your logic," Aspace said. His eyes were fixed on the men trapped before him, but Shenza wasn't sure he really saw them.

"Oh, spare me the ceremony!" Lord Manseen erupted. It must have galled him to stand there, helpless, while they talked about him. "Is this some game, dangling your mercy before me? Do you think I'll crawl to you and beg to be spared?" His mouth worked, and for a moment Shenza thought he might spit at Lord Aspace.

"I'm glad we agree." Aspace spoke in clipped syllables. "As for the rest of you—" He looked to the men who surrounded Lord Manseen. "You're not the mercenaries you seem to be. You're soldiers of House Bosteel, come here on the orders of your Lord."

Shenza heard Juss suck in a breath. Now that Aspace said it, she knew he was right. Real mercenaries would have abandoned their employer when everything went wrong, yet these men stayed with Lord Manseen to the end. They must, indeed, come from House Bosteel.

"I can see that you're prepared to die along with him," Aspace went on. "I respect your courage and devotion. However, I cannot permit it."

For the first time, a murmur broke out among the Bosteel loyalists.

"You won't make us crawl, either!" one of them cried. Shenza recognized Manseen's bodyguard from the feast. Hydara, that was his name.

"You think not?" Aspace's sharp voice rang over the protests. "Remember who commands the golems. And remember this—there is still one who has a right to your loyalty. Your Lady Seelit needs you." The murmuring died away as Aspace said, "You came here with two large boats. Since I'm not a thief, they belong to Seelit now. It will take all of you to get them safely home, and her with them. For her sake, you must stand aside."

"This is my wish," Lord Manseen snapped. "Go."

Slowly his men shuffled away, the wounded supported by their fellows. Some, like Hydara, turned back to offer deep bows to their doomed lord. Others walked with shoulders hunched, looking away. There was shame on their faces, but also guilty relief. Loyal as they were, they didn't want to die.

Lord Manseen stood alone. He drew himself up with grim resolve. A long moment more, Aspace and his enemy locked eyes. Then the first lord said, "Master Lelldour?"

Chimi crossed her hands and bowed. Her face was still unnaturally calm. Three of the golems ground their way toward Manseen's men, pushing them farther from their lord. The fourth went for Manseen himself. It lashed out, swift as a serpent's strike. Shenza blinked, startled by its speed and violence. She heard a heavy blow, a muffled cry, then a grisly snap and the thud of Manseen's body falling.

Before Shenza could react, wails went up from the Bosteel men. The golems moved back except for the last one, the one that had struck Manseen down. It stayed, swaying like a tree in the high wind, while Chimi's face went pale and stern. Finally, slowly, it came back to her.

Manseen's men rushed to his body. They wept, their faces distorted with grief. They tore their clothes and smeared mud into their hair. For some, Shenza was sure, this was only ritual grieving. Still, she couldn't help wondering how many of them had truly believed in Lord Manseen's promise of conquest.

A new voice hailed them: "My Lord!"

Chimi continued to watch the mourners, but Shenza, Juss and Aspace turned. Men with spears and dark gold kilts were jogging along the path. At their head was Shamatt, Chief Borleek's second in command. Shenza felt a pang of disappointment that Master Laraquies wasn't with them.

"Sub-Chief!" Juss called as he hurried to meet them.

The peace officers seemed to relax as they saw Lord Aspace alive and well. The column slowed behind Juss and Shamatt as they approached, talking rapidly in low voices. Shenza caught the end of Juss' explanation just as the men reached them.

"I'm glad to see my Lord alive," Shamatt said, bowing low.

"So am I," Aspace said. "Lord Bosteel's men will require a litter. They can take his body to the Jade Court. Also, send your men to fetch Lady Seelit from Sengool House. She will stay in the Jade Court until tomorrow, no longer."

Shenza knew it was wrong of her, but she couldn't help being glad that Aspace was sending Seelit away.

"The other bodies we saw?" Shamatt asked.

"Sort them out as best you can," Aspace replied. "If anyone is still alive, send for the curomancers. Otherwise, send runners to notify the families of the dead when you can spare them. And—" his voice took on an edge "—as long as you're there, tell the Sengools they need to retrieve Lord Oriman's body and the rest. Say that I want to speak with their new clan lord, as soon as they choose one."

"As my Lord commands," Shamatt bowed again and turned away, preparing to pass the orders, but Aspace stopped him.

"One more thing. Juss must have told you that Chief Borleek fell in the battle." Shamatt nodded, and Aspace went on, "We'll have to wait for all the ceremonies, but from this moment you're my Chief Peacekeeper."

Shamatt bowed even lower than before. "It is my honor to serve my Lord."

Aspace merely nodded. "You have a lot to do."

* * *

"That one is going to be trouble," Lelldour whispered in Chimi's mind.

"What do you mean?" Chimi asked. She spoke aloud, but softly. The old necromancer would share her body until there was no chance he would need to control the golems. Even so, Chimi was aware of curious glances from Juss and Shenza.

Lelldour made Chimi look toward the main group of people. "The golem," he said.

The sand golems stood sentinel around the Bosteel fighters, who had lost all heart for battle. They had dropped their weapons to focus on mourning Lord Manseen, despite having no place to lay his body and no litter to move it with.

Shamatt had gone back to his men, who watched uncertainly. They obviously wanted to surround Hydara and the invaders, but didn't want to get close to the golems. Chimi felt the same way herself.

For the most part, the golems seemed content to obey Master Lelldour, but one of them rocked slightly as a prisoner passed near him. She could feel her teacher's concentration as he stopped the creature from lashing out.

Chimi focused her own fledgling powers to sense what Master Lelldour was feeling. The rogue golem's emotions washed over her like a wave of black, sticky mud. With a shudder, she broke contact.

"It's so angry," she murmured. Chimi rubbed her arms, but that did nothing to cleanse the psychic taint.

"The ghost inside it must have been a sorcerer," Lelldour said. "Its mind is strong and full of rage."

"Can you control it?" Chimi asked nervously. "You told my Lord—"

"I had forgotten something," Lelldour snapped, irritated by the reminder. "I don't need to rest, but I'm only borrowing your powers. You are still human. You have to sleep, and while you do, that golem could break away. Like the evil spirits, it is stronger in darkness."

Chimi glanced nervously at the sky. The clouds above the treetops were taking on a tawny hue. Somewhere beyond the rain, the sun was going down. And just hearing the word sleep brought on a wave of fatigue. She had been up really late, and then faced so much trauma in one day— trapped outside her body, forced to confront the worst in herself, now sharing her physical form with a ghost. Fatigue dragged on her shoulders, her head. Master Lelldour was right. She couldn't possibly stay awake to supervise the golems all night.

"What can we do?" she asked.

Before Lelldour could answer, Shenza put her hand on Chimi's shoulder. "Do about what, sister?"

"What's going on?" Juss demanded warily.

Everyone was looking at her—Aspace, Shamatt, Juss and Shenza, who understood her new powers, plus most of Lord Aspace's soldiers, who must have had no idea why she was talking to herself. Shamatt and his men were rested, but the others all looked as tired as Chimi felt. She hated to add to Lord Aspace's problems, but there was no way around it. Chimi explained Lelldour's concern about the rogue golem, and finished with his recommendation, "He thinks we should dispel the golem and release its spirit right away."

"Should we do that?" Juss asked. "We might not have enough men to guard them without the golems."

"We'd still have three of them," Chimi said.

Aspace was silent, his eyes narrowed in thought, until Shenza spoke up.

"This isn't the only problem," she said. "Have you noticed how quiet the volcano is?"

"I've been a little busy," Aspace answered drily.

"You're right, though." Juss frowned.

"I did notice," Shamatt said. "I just thought we were lucky it chose today to settle down."

His words were half a question, which Shenza answered with a shake of her head.

"It's not luck," she said. "When Vesswan held me prisoner, she told Nurune that the nature spirits couldn't interfere with her rituals because of how much negative energy had built up while Chimi was unconscious."

"And?" Lord Aspace prodded.

"I don't know if you'd heard, Chief Shamatt," Shenza went on, "but the spirits were angry because someone stole the sand from one of the sacred isles. I'm sure that's what Vesswan used to conjure the golems. The nature spirits created the volcano to punish us, but the negative energy must have forced them to leave it. That's why the earthquakes stopped."

"It also let the corrupted spirits come here," Lelldour said in Chimi's mind. She repeated this, and Shenza nodded.

"The nature spirits may even have sent the corrupted ones to punish us because we hadn't caught the thief," Shenza said. "Now that Chimi is awake, the negative energy should slowly disperse."

"But then the nature spirits can come back to the volcano?" Shamatt guessed.

"Correct," Shenza said. "It could still erupt if they aren't satisfied with what happened to Vesswan. Our best hope is to go to the shrine before they return to full power. If we make enough sacrifices and explain that she's dead—"

"If they're so powerful, wouldn't they already know?" Aspace asked in a stinging tone.

Shenza hesitated behind her mask, and then said gently, "I think they'll want to hear it from us. Especially from my Lord. Returning to the question of the golems, destroying one of them might be a very good sacrifice."

"But we may still need them," Juss repeated stubbornly.

"Even if it could run wild?" Chimi asked. Juss frowned at her.

"It would be ironic to survive a rebellion and then be wiped out anyway," Shamatt put in. Juss closed his mouth. "What would my Lord have us do?"

Aspace glanced at peace officers, and then at the Bosteel mourners. "Do you have enough men to keep them under control?"

"I believe so," Shamatt said.

"Then we'll go to the shrine," he decided. A sweep of his hand took in Shenza, Juss and Chimi. "You three, and if Chimi brings the golems, I'll be more than protected. Shamatt, you and your men can start moving bodies. Take Manseen to the Jade Court. Tell Vizier Laraquies to drag himself away from Mother and join you."

"As my Lord commands." Shamatt smiled slightly, and Chimi wondered why. Really, though, she was just glad Lord Aspace was willing to listen to Shenza and Lelldour.

* * *

There was a brief delay while Aspace and Shamatt made their arrangements. Shenza used the time to talk with Master Lelldour about how they would dispel the golems. Soon they set off together, Aspace leading Shenza, Chimi and Juss while the golems ground along behind them. One of the monsters kept lurching toward the humans until Chimi and Lelldour sent it to the back of the line. Shenza suspected that was the one that needed to be dispelled first. She could certainly see why.

The procession stopped at the burning pavilion so that Shenza could extinguish the magical fire, then went to the front gate. She put out that fire, too. The stench of charred greenery hung heavily in the air.

No one spoke as they passed the motionless bodies of the palace guards. Shenza guessed everyone had too much to think about for trifling conversation. From time to time, she caught Lord Aspace glancing in her direction. A rush of warmth went though her every time. No matter how difficult the circumstances, and how lucky they both were to have survived, she was glad to be with him.

As they reached the grand stair, the rain tapered off at last. It was a relief to start drying out, yet the absence of the rain's constant patter made the unnatural silence even more pronounced. Every footfall and rustle of damp clothing sounded loud. The harsh grating noise as the golems slid along seemed deafening.

Just as they glimpsed the shrine's tiled roof through the trees, the clouds parted. Shenza's mask protected her, but Chimi and Juss raised their hands to shield their eyes. The volcano's peak loomed across the harbor, a dark blotch against the sunset's angry glare. A trickle of smoke rose from its summit in silent warning of the disaster that could yet occur.

Nobody spoke, but they all quickened their steps. The lush forest surrounding the shrine gave way to intricately carved pillars, and then they saw a flash of sunlight from the pool at the center of the sacred place. Three bronze statues loomed on the far side of it. The dying sunlight struck fire from their jeweled eyes, while ruddy shadows gave the inhuman faces a severe appearance.

Everyone stopped at the edge of the courtyard. It looked deserted. Only the trees around the shrine whispered with movement, although Shenza felt no wind. She thought she glimpsed something pale moving in the shadows.

Turning to her, Aspace said, "Light the braziers."

"As my Lord wishes." Shenza bowed and hurried around the edge of the pool. She bowed even lower as she passed in front of the statues to reach a rack full of firewood. There was always fuel here at the shrine. People cut wood as penance, or to show their devotion.

She quickly filled her arms and returned to the statues. The nearest brazier held no trace of warmth as she lifted the grille. Shenza laid wood over the gray mass of spent coals and replaced the bars, then she extended her hand over the brazier and chanted a rhyme to start the fire. To her relief, the power flowed more quickly than it had earlier in the day. There was hissing, then a warm curl of smoke. Finally a flame sputtered to life. Shenza went on to the other two braziers.

"All right," Aspace called as soon as she had them lit.

Shenza bowed and stepped back to join Juss and Chimi, who had lined the four golems up as far from the statues as they could go without leaving the shrine. Juss held a basket of offerings that Aspace's staff had given him.

"All right," Aspace repeated. Shenza thought she saw a trace of doubt in his eyes, and her heart went out to him. When she had encountered the spirits, she had never felt prepared. She only hoped the spirits wouldn't reject their offerings as too little, too late.

Chapter Twenty-Eight

Truth Be Told

Whatever he was feeling, Aspace stepped up to the edge of the pool. Shenza watched, feeling a new tension in the air. Usually when a first lord came to the shrine there was a lot of ceremony—music, dancing, dozens of offerings. They had none of that today. Yet so much more was at stake.

"Lords of the Branches," Aspace said. His voice echoed in the shrine. "Lords of the Heavens, and great Lords of the Waves, I honor you as my ancestors."

Shenza was surprised that he said this. According to legend, Aspace's family did have spirit blood, but she knew he was uncomfortable with that.

Aspace went on, "I am lord of this island and its people, but you are the land on which we dwell. You are the clouds that give us rain. You are the sea that gives us food. You are the true lords of us all. I, who am only your servant, lead my people in honoring you."

He turned slightly. Juss stepped forward and bowed, awkwardly balancing his spear and the basket of tribute. Together they circled the pool. Aspace reached the first statue and held out his hand. Juss fished in the basket and passed him a bundle of cassia bark. With great ceremony, Aspace untied the ribbon that held it together and dropped a portion into each brazier. The flames burned higher than Shenza expected.

After the incense, Aspace added a handful of grapes to each one, then a portion of wine, and finally a set of silver bangles. The flames crackled and steamed, but didn't go out.

When Aspace was finished, he bowed again and stepped backward. Juss hurried back to join Shenza and Chimi, leaving their lord alone again.

"We give you these gifts to thank you," Aspace went on. "In your wisdom, you must know that we have been attacked. Our foes were defeated by your own kindred, whom you sent to aid us. For this, also, we thank you."

That was clever of him, Shenza realized. The corrupted spirits hadn't been sent to help them, and the outcome of the battle had probably been accidental, yet Aspace praised the spirits as if they had planned it all. She hoped they would like the flattery.

"I have heard of your anger," Aspace continued, "that a thief invaded your sacred isle and stole what you would have given freely if asked. I and my servants searched for that person. Vesswan Sanguri of Zeell was the guilty one. She was killed by your dark kindred. May her blood serve as an offering to satisfy your desire for justice."

Again, Shenza heard whispering in the trees around the shrine. She was afraid to look around and see if the evil spirits were creeping up on them.

"But the crime of Vesswan was even greater," Aspace said. "She abused your holy essence to create abominations, which she brought against us. These we have taken. We bring them to your shrine so that you may see how we destroy them, for they have no place among us who praise the mighty spirits."

Aspace beckoned to Shenza and Chimi. They both walked up beside him, where they were in clear view of the statues. A glance over her shoulder showed Shenza three golems standing obediently where Chimi had left them. With a scrape of sand over stone, the fourth one came to them. As it got closer, she could smell its dirty-beach odor.

Shenza knew her duty, but she still edged backward. The monster looked even bigger than it had when Vesswan summoned it. Its blank face glowered. The red bottle around its neck blazed in the half light. She felt for her spell-breaker wand, which she had tucked under her left arm.

Chimi stood alone, facing the sand golem. She looked tiny and frail beside its bulk. Her shoulders were rigid with concentration. Lelldour wouldn't help this time, Shenza knew. It was Chimi's task, a final test she had to complete on her own, just as Shenza had had to find Lord Anges' killer.

Distracted by her thoughts, Shenza barely saw a blur of movement. She ducked instinctively, and the golem's massive fist passed just above her head.

"Halt!" Chimi's hand rose in a firm gesture, forbidding the golem to move. Shenza stumbled backward on rubbery knees. Aspace was right at her side, and Juss arrived moments later. The golem rocked in place, its fist still raised in threat.

"What's wrong?" Shenza tried not to squeak with fear.

"It really doesn't like you!" Chimi cried. A sheen of sweat was on her face. "I'm in control, but get the necklace off it, quick."

Shenza struggled with her own fear. Like the golem, she didn't want to do what she was told. This creature had only existed for a few hours. How could it know who she was, let alone hold a grudge against her?

"Hurry up," Chimi snapped.

Every muscle in Shenza's body felt tight, but she stepped past her sister. The golem's stench was nauseating. The crimson bottle on its chest pulsed like an enraged heartbeat. Shenza seized it with her free hand, then gasped.

The bottle wasn't warm, as she had expected, but cold enough to numb her fingers. She dropped the glass and grabbed the cord instead. A shudder rolled through the golem. Loose grains of sand trickled down its sides. Shenza tried to lift the bottle over the golem's head, but she was too short.

"I can't reach," she said anxiously.

"Let me do it." Juss practically shoved her back toward Aspace.

"Hurry!" Chimi warned through gritted teeth. It looked like she might be losing the battle for control. One great fist twitched upward.

Even Juss was shorter than the golem. He grabbed the cord with both hands and flipped it upward. The line caught on the crown of its head, but he yanked it free in a spray of grit. Chimi didn't speak, but thrust out a hand, demanding. He passed her the bottle.

"Much better," Chimi sighed, relieved.

The golem no longer swayed in place. Shenza watched the ruddy light fade from its single eye. Only the bottle in her sister's hand continued to pulse wildly.

"Now?" Shenza asked.

"Yes."

Juss stepped back, and Shenza raised her spell-breaker. She focused through it, feeling how tired she was and how sluggishly her power still flowed. But she also knew that Chimi was just as tired, and she had managed to control the golem. If she had the strength of will, so did Shenza.

"Dispel," she commanded.

There was a brilliant flare of purple light, dazzling even through her mask. The husk of the golem collapsed with a dry sigh. Sand flowed outward, covering their feet.

Shenza watched the pool in case the Eleshouri chose to reappear. Instead, a sudden wind blasted into the courtyard. Flecks of dirt stung where they hit bare skin. The vortex spun over the fallen monster, sucking a plume of fine sand into the air. It shone white, eerie in the dusky shrine. Then it was gone. The spirits had reclaimed their own.

The wind died down as quickly as it had come. Nothing was left but a heap of sand mixed with bits of shell and other debris. They all stepped back, shaking the sharp grains out of their sandals.

Lord Aspace faced the three statues. "Great ones, you are wise, and you must know that I still have enemies who are my prisoners. I require the last three golems to subdue them." Once again, Shenza heard a susurrus in the forest around the shrine. Aspace ignored it. "You have seen that I keep my word. Before the sun rises again, my prisoners will be gone. I promise that my servants will bring the golems back to dispel them, just as this one was destroyed."

Silence fell. Even the air was still as they waited for a response. The faintest growl touched Shenza's ears. She looked through the trees, toward its source: the volcano, with its black wisps of steam against the sunset. A familiar shudder rolled beneath her feet.

For a moment Shenza thought all was lost, that the spirits were preparing to destroy Chalsett-port. She bowed to the statues and said, "I thank the mighty spirits for giving me the strength to destroy these creatures."

Chimi bowed, too. "I promise to always do my duty as a necromancer."

It was impossible to tell if their words had really won the spirits over, but the earth gave a final twitch and the steam dissipated from the tip of the volcano. With Lord Aspace in the lead, they walked out of the shrine. Even the golems seemed to scurry away, lest they annoy the spirits further.

In the street outside the shrine, Chimi spoke up. "I haven't really finished yet. Step back," she warned.

She raised the glowing red bottle over her head, then threw it violently to the ground. It shattered in a ruby flash.

"Careful," Juss protested. He jumped to protect Lord Aspace and Shenza from shards of flying glass.

"It's all right," Chimi assured him. The bottle had broken into a few large, curved fragments. "Now, let's see who this man was and why he's so mad at my sister."

Shenza wasn't sure what she expected to see, perhaps a shimmer in the air. With no fanfare, a figure appeared in front of Chimi.

He wasn't especially tall, but he held his head with enough arrogance to make even a first lord bow before him. His garb was a short mantle and kilt of bright blue, the color of Lord Aspace's own household.

"No!" Shenza gasped. There was no mistaking the narrow shoulders, so oddly matched with strong, muscular legs.

"Hey," Juss exclaimed. "That's him!"

"Who is it?" Chimi asked.

"Makko," Shenza choked.

"Makko?" Aspace demanded. He stared at the man who had murdered his older brother.

"Yes," Shenza said. She wasn't likely to forget Makko's scowling face. "We saw him die in the spirit realm. The roots dragged him down."

"Is this really him?" Chimi squeaked. "He was following me for days!"

"But you're in charge now," Juss said. "He's just a ghost, right?"

Chimi nodded, then added slowly, "Master Lelldour thinks that if he died in the spirit realm, no one could have held a funeral. That's why his spirit can't rest. I guess I'll have to take care of it," she added with a trace of the bitterness she had shown during the days when she tried to reject necromancy.

"I want him to answer some questions," Aspace said. "Can you force him to tell the truth?"

"I think so. What do you want to know?"

Everyone looked at Makko for a moment. The revenant stood with one hand on his hip, dark eyes brilliant with rage. His lip curled in a sneer, just as Shenza remembered. However, the man who had once tried to kill her didn't acknowledge her now. His blazing eyes focused on Chimi.

"Why do you hate Shenza?" Aspace asked him.

There was a pause, during which Makko stood and glowered at them. Finally Chimi repeated, "Why do you hate Shenza?"

"She trapped me here," he said with a savage glare. "I was hired to do a job. I did it. I gave her a perfectly logical explanation, but no—she ignored it. Because of her stubbornness, I got stuck here. And then I died. It's all her fault!"

Shenza felt her own anger rise. How could Makko be so indignant! The job he spoke of so casually had been murder. As magister, it had been her duty to investigate.

"What about Lord Manseen?" Aspace asked next. "Why were you so eager to kill him?"

When Chimi had repeated the question, Makko snapped, "It was his stupid idea. He was the one who hired me. Now, Vesswan—she was useful. We worked together on other things, before I got here. She gave me a body, and I could act again. She would have lost her concentration eventually, and I could have gotten back at both of them. Now you've taken that away from me. I'm trapped again."

Makko glowered as if he would have liked to tear Chimi's flesh the way the evil spirits had done to Vesswan.

"He was like this in life, too," Shenza told Lord Aspace. "Always blaming others for his crimes. It's no wonder he can't stay in his grave."

"Hm." Aspace barely acknowledged her words.

"Do you want to ask anything else?" Chimi inquired meekly.

"Manseen told me the rest," Aspace said. He glanced at Shenza, who also shook her head. A few months ago, it would have been really useful to have Chimi interrogate Makko's ghost. Now, she already knew everything he had to say.

"All right," Chimi said. She focused on Makko again. "What do you want? How can you rest in peace?"

Makko went on sneering, and Shenza felt a prickle of fear down her back. What could they do if Makko's rage was so powerful that Chimi couldn't get rid of him? Would this vicious killer continue to haunt Chalsett-port forever?

Chimi looked back at the ghost. She might have been forcing him to reply. Slowly the fury drained from his face. Makko stood before them with a terrible emptiness in his eyes. The killer Shenza had been so afraid of was a hollow shell, lost and bewildered.

"I want to get off this island," he whispered, as one with the wind still murmuring in the trees. "I want to escape."

That made perfect sense. During their last fight, Makko had been trying to make Shenza let him go free. The need to get away must be the only thing he remembered.

"That's easy," Juss muttered.

"Yes, fine," Aspace said. "Let him go."

Shenza felt a twinge of regret. She hadn't really brought Makko to justice, and now she never would. Soon he would be no more than a bad memory. She wondered if that was enough. Still, she had to admit there was little more anyone could do to punish him.

"Take him out in a boat," she suggested. "It sounds like he'll be able to rest once you get off the island."

"Okay," Chimi said She started to walk away, but then stopped. "Sister, we don't have a boat."

Aspace laughed briefly. "Just borrow one from the docks. Juss, go with her. She might need help to row if the golems have to ride along."

"As my Lord commands," Juss said. He looked slightly disappointed.

"When you're done, bring Chimi up to the palace. Then you can go home," Aspace concluded.

"Right." Juss looked much more cheerful.

Naturally, he wanted to make sure his wife was all right. Shenza felt a moment's guilt as Chimi and Juss walked away with the golems trailing after them. She hadn't even thought about her own family.

"I should go home, too," Shenza said. Mother must be frantic. She might not even know that Chimi had revived.

"Don't bother," Aspace shrugged.

"My Lord?" Shenza asked. She suddenly realized they were alone, although it wasn't so scandalous because they were in a public street. Even so, her heart skipped in her chest.

"There's no one there," Aspace explained. "Chimi convinced your mother and brother to leave with the elders when things got dangerous, and Laraquies is up at the estate with Mother."

"Oh," Shenza said, surprised.

"You might as well come back to the palace." Aspace spoke with a feigned boredom that told her he was irritated, although Shenza couldn't see why. The battle was over and he had won. Why should he be angry? Still, she would use any excuse to be with Aspace.

"Chief Shamatt would want me to escort you back safely," she replied.

Aspace smiled. Shenza's heart skipped again as they walked in silence. The sky was still overcast, with patches of fog lingering among the gardens as they passed, but hints of sunset fire reflected from roof tiles and treetops. She even felt a trace of humid warmth in the air. It felt like the weather was returning to normal.

The city was quiet, with a shattered calm that showed how stunned and exhausted even the victors were. She was glad to be with Lord Aspace. She didn't want to be alone on a day like this.

"I thought it would never stop raining," she said, timidly, in case Aspace didn't feel like talking.

He glanced at her, brow crimped with annoyance. She was ready to apologize when he abruptly said, "Shenza, will you please take off that mask? I can't talk to you."

"Oh." Was that was he was irritated about? Shenza fumbled self-consciously to open her travel case. She raised her free hand and willed her mask to come loose.

"That's better."

Aspace didn't say anything else, but the way he looked at Shenza made her cheeks burn. She quickly looked away.

Nothing more then, except for the shuffle of their feet over damp pavement. Far in the distance, she heard shrieks and wails rising on the air. Chief Shamatt must have started notifying families of the fallen. She felt her throat tighten. It was impossible to tell who the mourners were, Kesquin or Sengool or the lesser families of officers and guards. Their anonymity made their grief all the more compelling.

Aspace stopped. Shenza looked at him uncertainly. Golden sunset sketched his face in fine strokes against the leafy shadows behind him, turned his eyes pale as sea-foam. He was the most beautiful man she could imagine, even dressed as he was in plain clothing suitable for fighting. Shenza's heart grew tight with longing.

"Shenza..." Aspace stopped and cleared his throat. He turned to look through a gap in the trees, where they could see the harbor and the volcanic peak.

"My Lord?" Her words came in a whisper.

He asked, "Did I do the right thing?"

Shenza was sure what she had expected him to say, but this wasn't it.

"You mean, about Lord Bosteel?" she asked, trying to hide her chagrin. "I don't know that you had a choice under the law."

"The law is what I say it is," Aspace countered. His gaze seemed to be fixed on the looming volcano.

Shenza breathed deeply, controlling her disappointment. Aspace just wanted her opinion as magister. Maybe that was only natural. And maybe

Shenza had been wrong in what she thought Lady Izmay was telling her. Maybe Lord Aspace didn't want to be with her, not in the way she wanted to be with him.

"Did my Lord truly wish to let him live?" she asked. Aspace blinked, perhaps startled by her renewed formality.

"He lost. That's more of a punishment than death," he said. "But that isn't why." His fists clenched at his sides. "Between the golems and the spirits, I saw a lot of men die today. People I knew as a boy. They fell, while I sat safely behind wards." Aspace drew a breath that could almost have been a sob. "I just didn't want to watch one more person get killed."

"Of course not," Shenza murmured, ducking her head. It was selfish to focus on her own feelings, when so many others had died to prove their loyalty. She asked, "Do you expect any more trouble from Lord Bosteel's family?"

"Sardony's next first lord will come of another clan," Aspace predicted with great certainty. "High Lord Jerusha won't allow them to keep the honors after I report what Manseen did. Anyway, I thought every death would just make those evil spirits stronger."

Again, Shenza remembered how upset Aspace had been to learn that the blood of nature spirits flowed with his own line.

"You're not like them," she said, "feasting on the pain of others. And you're not like Manseen. He didn't care who got hurt because of his ambition."

Chimi's voice rang in her memory, scolding Lord Manseen for using his daughter in his schemes. However, the last thing Shenza wanted was to make Aspace think about Seelit. She stood beside her lord, staring at the volcano. Emotion swept over her. The volcano was there because of Vesswan, who had stolen the sand after Manseen demanded his "perfect soldiers." Aspace had been the target, but Manseen could have caused the destruction of Chalsett and everyone on it.

"I'm glad we stopped him," Shenza said fiercely.

Aspace watched her face. He asked softly, "What are you thinking?"

"He—" Shenza started to say that she couldn't forgive Manseen for almost killing her sister, but when she looked into Aspace's eyes, the words dried on her lips. If she told him she only cared about Chimi, it would be a lie. No matter how long they worked together as first lord and magister, every word she said would be tainted by that lie.

"I was thinking," she corrected in a trembling voice, "that if Manseen had hurt you, I was going to kill him myself."

The words fell like petals into the silence. Shenza waited, steeling herself for Aspace to step away and laugh at her confession. The sun's light glowed in his eyes, and he did laugh, but not in a mocking way.

"Well," he said quietly, "when Chimi told me they had captured you, I was thinking the same thing."

Shenza caught a breath of startled joy. "You were?"

"I knew the risk I was taking when I let Manseen come here, but I thought I was the only one who would be in danger." He stopped, then added bitterly, "I didn't expect him to stage an outright attack. I put everyone in town at risk. I don't know how I can ever make up for it."

Now it was Aspace who looked away, maybe waiting for Shenza to condemn his foolish mistakes. All she could think to say was, "Be a better first lord."

"I will." Aspace smiled at her again, his eyes bright. "I also didn't think he would strike at you. I'm sorry for that."

"It was just part of their plan," Shenza replied. "If they'd had a chance to get at Master Laraquies, they would have done it just as quickly."

"Maybe," Aspace said. "But they didn't know how I feel about you. And I didn't know how you felt about me."

Shenza felt giddy with combined exhaustion and relief. The way he felt about her? How she felt about him? All she could feel was the heat in her face, the radiant joy in her heart.

"I didn't think you could care about someone like me," she faltered. Then, with the force of her old pain, "How could you let me think you planned to marry her? Did you think how it would make me feel?"

"I never said I planned to marry Seelit. I just wanted to know what her father was up to." Aspace sounded a bit defensive, but he went on softly, "It must have been hard for you to watch us. I'm sorry for that, too. I don't want to keep secrets from you anymore. I love you."

Speechless, Shenza stared at him. The cold and doubting part of her insisted this couldn't be real. A first lord would never fall in love with a fisherman's daughter. It was like a story, one of those awful, wonderful fairy tales—no more than a dream.

"It doesn't change anything." Shenza forced out the hateful words. "You must marry someone of suitable rank, and I... I won't be just a concubine."

"You won't have to!" Aspace replied with quick indignation. Then he chuckled with sarcastic humor. "After seeing what came of my courting a suitable lady, I'm sure everyone will be glad to have a local girl whose loyalty is beyond question. Kesquin has shown himself to be a faithful ally, and if the Sengools know what's good for them, they won't say a word."

Shenza wasn't so sure of that. The Sengools didn't like to lose, and Innoshyra of Sengool had been trying very hard to get Aspace's attention. Mostly, though, Shenza could hardly believe they were having this conversation.

"Do you mean it?" she asked.

"If you want me."

"Of course," Shenza breathed.

Aspace raised his hand to brush a loose curl away from her face. Her skin burned where he touched her. Shenza's cheeks blazed with embarrassment, but she couldn't tear herself away. He was standing so close. Would he kiss her?

Her lips tingled with longing, but Aspace merely smiled into her eyes. A moment later, he stepped back and gestured onward, down the street.

"We should go. Shamatt will be wondering where we are."

"All right." Shenza ducked her head as they began to walk again. It was good that Aspace understood the need for decorum, but she couldn't help feeling a little disappointed.

"I was sure you were going to tell me we were in an improper situation," Aspace teased after a moment.

"You don't need me to tell you that," Shenza said. Aspace chuckled.

Mourning cries went on in the distance, but the street around them was still very quiet. Whichever way she looked, no one was walking. Instead of feeling eerie, the silence made Shenza feel close and special. She would be sorry to let it end.

Unaware of her thoughts, Aspace said. "We'll send someone to track your family down tomorrow. My mother will want to talk to your mother right away. About the real marriage negotiations, I mean."

Once again, Shenza could hardly breathe. Her mind whirled with questions, especially about how they would achieve a balance between their official duties and their private relationship. For the first time, she no longer felt that she needed her mask to hide behind. Perhaps if she wore her mask only when she was magister, and kept it off when she was wife, that would help distinguish between her roles.

Aspace angled a glance at her, perhaps concerned that she hadn't reacted when he mentioned marriage so casually.

"As...as my Lord wishes," she stammered. Marriage was more than she had hoped for, but it was exactly what she wanted.

"Stop saying that," Aspace began with an irritated sigh. "Just call me—"

"Beloved," Shenza whispered, trying out the word.

Aspace smiled. "That will do."

Chapter Twenty-Nine

Closing Circles

Chimi and Shenza spent that night in the Pearl Court, Izmay's private residence. It wasn't lavish hospitality, since Shenza went from one meeting to the next and Chimi had to stay outside the Jade Court monitoring the golems until late at night. Lelldour, still possessing her, felt free to comment on every thought she had. Even so, it was better to be with people than alone in a house that echoed with the absence of her family.

Chimi slept lightly, a part of her constantly alert for any change in the golems' silent vigil. It felt like the sisters had only been lying down for a moment when Tio came to wake them. Chimi blinked sleepily. Pale light crept through the window screens, and birds twittered in the trees outside.

"Is it morning already?" she mumbled as the maidservant slipped away.

Stretched out on a pallet beside Chimi's, Shenza said, "We have to see the Bosteels off." It sounded like she was trying to convince herself to get up as much as Chimi.

"And we have to dispel the golems," Chimi moaned. The ache of exhaustion still clung to her bones. She wished there was time for a long, hot bath. She felt grimy inside and out.

But Chimi felt Lelldour's impatience. "My Lord Aspace wants the invaders off the island by dawn," he reminded her.

"I know." She sat up, feeling too tired even to yawn. Comfort would have to wait.

Lamps glowed in the main room, where Lady Izmay and Master Laraquies sipped tea. A pair of cups steamed invitingly. Rubbing her eyes, Chimi mumbled a greeting and took one. The tea was harsh, not at all like the delicate brew Izmay had served at the feast.

"I thought we needed something stronger this morning," Izmay said, smiling at Chimi's startled expression.

"I guess I do," Chimi said.

Like Chimi, Laraquies and Izmay were wearing the same robes they had had on the day before. It made Chimi feel a little bit better to see them looking rumpled, too.

In addition to tea, the small table held a bowl of sliced pineapple and a tray of steamed breadfruit. Chimi helped herself to the breadfruit, but she couldn't make herself touch the pineapple. She would never look at pineapple the same way again.

"Good morning," Laraquies said as Shenza settled beside Chimi.

"Did you sleep well?" Izmay asked. She pushed the last cup of tea toward Shenza.

"As well as you could expect." Shenza took the cup with a shy smile. She sipped and said, "Thank you. This is wonderful."

Chimi ate more breadfruit to hide her smirk. Shenza was blushing. No, glowing with happiness. Chimi had never seen her somber big sister look this way before. She watched as Laraquies and Izmay pressed food on Shenza. For once, Shenza didn't try to avoid the attention.

Actually, everyone at the table was glowing the happiness. Shenza was in love, and of course Chimi was happy for her. Izmay was pleased with her future daughter-in-law. Chimi wondered what Laraquies was so happy about. Maybe he was just proud of Shenza, but it seemed like more than that.

"Chief Shamatt will be here soon, so try to eat," Izmay told Shenza. Then, to Chimi's surprise, the first lady turned to her. "I've been thinking about your situation. If you're going to be our necromancer, you need to look the part."

Embarrassed, Chimi said, "I do have more clothes at home. Not really the right kind, but until I earn some more money..."

"Your official debut is today," Izmay interrupted. "So you come with me, and we'll see what we can do."

"All right." Feeling a bit confused, Chimi stood up and followed Izmay. Inside, she sensed Lelldour's agreement, that she must wear a plain red robe.

"*Under the circumstances,*" Chimi silently asked, "*are clothes more important than results?*"

"*Yes. My Lady is correct,*" Lelldour insisted. "*You're young. You won't be taken seriously if you don't dress properly.*"

"*Yes, teacher.*" Chimi thought back at him.

Izmay's chamber was up a short flight of steps. A row of painted screens gave her privacy. Chimi noted a wide netting bed and tousled covers. A leather travel case was propped against one corner. A pair of women who had been tidying the chamber quickly bowed to Izmay. The first lady nodded in return.

She went to an open wardrobe, where exquisite fabrics hung, but the travel case nagged at Chimi. Its worn leather looked so familiar. After a moment, she realized that it was Laraquies' case! What was it doing beside Izmay's bed?

Chimi willed herself not to blush. Laraquies and Izmay were good friends, she knew, but it was none of her business where Laraquies slept.

He was a friend of her family, just like Byben. That made Chimi wonder about Byben and Grandmother. Was their friendship, too, more than it seemed? And if she knew the truth, would she respect her grandmother less, or more?

While her mind grappled with these concepts, Izmay sorted through the robes. "Let's take a look."

The words brought Chimi back to what she was doing. It was a privilege to choose from Izmay's wardrobe, and she knew Winomi would want to hear all about it later.

One by one, Izmay looked over the robes. Most she pushed aside because the colors were wrong, but once or twice she gently took an edge and pulled the fabric out to see it more clearly.

"Hold this one," she told Chimi.

Complying, Chimi said, "It's lovely."

The robe was pure silk, of course. It was deep red, the color of a plum, dressed up with a glittering spray of pearls.

"Too much decoration," Lelldour said in Chimi's mind.

Unaware of the necromancer's complaint, Izmay frowned as she looked from the robe to Chimi. "It might be too dark for you."

Moments later she offered another, pale green delicately painted with red hibiscus flowers.

"No flowers," Lelldour said.

"At least they're red," Chimi thought back at him. *"It's really nice of Izmay to give me a new robe. No matter what she chooses, I'm going to wear it and be proud."*

"How about this one?" Izmay showed her a brighter carmine robe with golden-orange streaks along the bottom that looked like seaweed. Tiny yellow leaf-dragons peered between the stems.

Chimi couldn't help smiling at the miniature world within the pattern. Sensing Lelldour's disapproval, she murmured, "Whatever you think is fine with me."

"But you've earned it," Izmay insisted with a kind light in her eyes. "Besides, I have more than I need." She stretched out the three robes together, plum and carmine and green. "Which will it be?"

"This one," Chimi said, stroking the robe with the leaf-dragons. Who could resist their cute little faces?

"Done. Let's try it on you."

A glance from Izmay brought the two maidservants scurrying. They swept off the pink and orange hemp robe. Tuseeva would have been shocked to see it so soot-stained and wrinkled.

"I still need that," Chimi said. She hadn't worn it often enough to part with it yet.

"We'll only wash it for you," Izmay assured her.

Under the robe, Chimi wore one of Grandmother's plain white sheaths. That was clean enough to keep wearing. Chimi shivered with delight as the maidservants wrapped her in her new robe. Pure silk! She had never thought she would have a robe like this. Izmay watched critically, reaching out once to make the fabric fold just so.

"Excellent," she declared. "You'll represent Chalsett-port very well."

Lelldour still disapproved of the leaf-dragons, but Chimi ignored him. "This is so nice of you," she said. "Thank you. I love it."

"A girl like you deserves pretty things," Izmay said.

Chimi stroked the silken fabric. "Just because I'm a necromancer doesn't mean I can't look nice. I think that's the only good thing I learned from Vesswan."

Again she felt the prickle of Lelldour's irritation, but Izmay nodded.

"You can't let others make your choices for you." Some deeper note in her voice made Chimi wonder if Izmay was only talking about clothes, but Laraquies called a greeting to someone down in the main room. A deeper voice replied, and then Shenza's soft response.

"Shamatt must be here," Chimi said, glancing at the doorway.

"Too bad," Izmay sighed. "I wanted to do something about your hair."

"Oh, you don't have to," Chimi said. "You've done so much for me already. Thank you, really. Thank you."

"It's nothing." Smiling, Izmay patted her shoulder. "Don't make them wait."

With a quick wave, Chimi jogged down the steps to the main area. Shenza was already up from the table, straightening her purple robe and picking up her travel case.

"Here's Chimi." Laraquies' dark eyes sparkled as he took in her changed appearance.

She smiled back at him, but hurried on through the room. Shamatt wore the same uniform Chimi remembered, a short mantle and kilt in dark gold, spear and shield in his hands. Yet he, too, sported new finery: a larger plume adorned the brooch on his headcloth. Seeing him in the Chief Peacekeeper's uniform wiped away Chimi's pleasure at her new clothes.

After brief farewells, Shamatt led them down the stairs. No one spoke as they walked. Chimi even felt Lelldour's presence fade for a moment as he reached away from her to check on the golems. The first lord's gardens were quiet, colors muted by the gray dawn light.

More soldiers waited outside the Jade Court. Having spent time there last night, Chimi knew the Jade Court was a pair of large cottages facing a shared courtyard. The bodies of Lord Manseen and his followers had been arranged in one of the buildings, while the survivors stayed in the other.

The golems stood in a line at the base of the steps, barring anyone from entering or leaving.

The soldiers, a mixture of peacekeepers and palace guards, clustered where the walkway led into the courtyard. They were all heavily armed and still keeping a careful distance from the golems. Chimi didn't blame them. The golems had a sinister presence even when they stood motionless.

As Shamatt, Shenza and Chimi approached, Juss limped out of the group and saluted everyone by tapping his fist on his chest.

"It's been quiet?" Shamatt asked.

"So far," Juss said. He took his place at Shenza's side.

Inside the cottage, the Bosteels were stirring. It looked like they were ready to leave as soon as the way was clear. Sensing Lelldour's query, Chimi asked Shamatt, "Should I let them out?"

"If you would."

Chimi focused her will. Within those monstrous forms she sensed the spirits she knew so well: Toothless, Scarface, the Drowned Girl. Helpless spirits, trapped between death and life, still waiting for her to help them. Well, it wouldn't be much longer. The golems moved as she told them, sliding to the side of the courtyard with a heavy rasp of sand over stone.

At once, the static scene burst into life. Aspace's guards jogged into the courtyard, still avoiding the golems. One of the Bosteels came to meet them. He moved warily, and spoke only to Shamatt. More men emerged at his signal. They crossed the courtyard to the other cottage and came back out with bodies on pallets. The corpses were shrouded in red cloth and bound with white bands. Lines of runes were sewn onto them.

"The runes will keep their spirits from bothering anyone on the voyage home," Lelldour explained in Chimi's mind. *"I will teach you how to read the runes and make those bands."*

"All right," Chimi said. His words no longer sounded like a deadly threat to her.

The Bosteels formed a procession, flanked by Chalsett soldiers. The pallets all looked the same to Chimi, but the Bosteels seemed to know who had higher rank. Meanwhile, a slender form appeared out of the cottage. Seelit was a childlike figure in her scarlet robes of mourning. Her great dark eyes were filled with shock and terror. Hydara and two others escorted her closely.

Chimi couldn't help feeling sorry for Seelit, despite all that had happened. It must be terrible to lose her father, even if he had abused her trust. Now she was alone in a strange place. Chimi wished she could say something to make her feel better.

There was really no point, though. She had never been Seelit's friend. She had just wanted to use Seelit, the way Panubi of Kesquin wanted to use her. And then she had let the golem kill Lord Manseen. How could Seelit forgive her for that?

Shamatt stepped forward to meet Seelit and Hydara as they came down the stairs. The procession moved out slowly. First Seelit and her guards, then the line of bodies. Chalsett guards walked on both sides. Chimi watched them pass. Seelit didn't look at anyone, but Hydara was proud and defiant despite his torn robes and the dried mud in his hair.

Chimi came last, with the golems. Chief Shamatt wanted her at the back, so if anyone tried to escape she could see it and respond. She did her best to watch carefully and not think about things that might have been.

Across the first lord's estate they went, and down through the town. The eastern horizon was brighter, but it was still dark in the streets. Chalsett-port was unusually quiet. Even the volcano hadn't been rumbling or shaking. Chimi wondered if the town was empty because people had fled its power, or if news of the fighting made them afraid to come out of their houses.

There were more people about in the market, though many stalls were empty. Tight groups stood whispering uneasily. Heads turned as the peacekeepers and their prisoners moved through. Angry voices rose from the onlookers. A few people started toward them, until Chimi sent one of the golems to that side of the procession. The intruders stopped, staring at the golems with instinctive revulsion. Glancing back at Chimi, Shamatt nodded approvingly.

This was the real reason Chimi and the officers had to be there, she realized. Without them, people might have attacked the Bosteels. From the way some of the peacekeepers scowled, they might even have joined in.

Moving faster, they swept down the steps to the first level. Just as in the market, there was more talk going on than work. A crowd of dock hands stared at the pier where Seelit's two ships were tied up. They muttered in dark and ugly voices. Half a dozen peace officers had lined up to block access.

With a bit of pushing and shoving, Shamatt and his men got the Bosteels to their ships without Chimi having to send the golems. Seelit disappeared into her ship's covered passenger area, while Hydara fastened the draperies to frustrate prying eyes. The servants took the bodies to the other ship. There was no farewell of any kind. Oarmen took their places and started rowing so quickly that Chimi wondered if all the bodies were tied down.

Onlookers yelled and jeered as the ships glided away from the pier. A few even threw things, though nothing came close to hitting the ships. Chimi stood with Shenza, Juss and Shamatt until the Bosteel ships were past the breakwater and into open seas.

"That's one down," Juss said.

"And the golems are next," Shenza said. She sounded relieved.

"Can we use the shrine?" Chimi asked.

She pointed, and they all looked across the harbor. A column of thick black smoke rose through the trees near the town shrine. Faint wailing carried across the water. Someone was holding a funeral.

"*The first of many,*" Lelldour observed to Chimi.

"Should we interrupt?" Juss asked doubtfully.

"Maybe somewhere along the beach would work," Chimi said.

"No, we need the shrine," Shenza said. "The spirits will expect us to bring the golems to them, not make them hunt all over the shore."

"That would be best," Shamatt agreed. "Let the people see you destroy the golems so that no one can say Lord Aspace approves of these monstrosities."

"I guess that settles it," Juss said with a shrug. He nodded toward the unruly crowd. "What about them?"

"We don't want this going on too long," Shamatt said. "If you don't need my men?"

Shenza and Juss both looked at Chimi. It still surprised her when they turned to her for instructions.

"The peacekeepers can't help us dispel the golems," she pointed out. "We only need me, Shenza and Juss."

"Excellent." Shamatt bowed to Shenza and went to join his officers. The peacekeepers fanned out and the crowded started to disperse. Chimi took one last look at the departing ships, and followed her sister toward the shrine.

* * *

All the way up the hill, Chimi was haunted by the sense that someone was watching her. She glanced left and right, thinking there might already be a new ghost who needed her, but didn't see anything. The gardens of Chalsett were wrapped in shadows, giving the golems' ruby eyes an eerie glow. Only the trees whispered restlessly. Dawn was coming fast, and she knew they had to hurry. They didn't dare break Lord Aspace's promise.

The funeral they had heard was going on just outside the shrine. They had to walk past it to enter. Chimi felt the pyre's heat on her face. The mourners had finished their formal grieving and were singing a song of farewell as they lined up to toss gifts into the fire. They seemed intent on their task until the golems came into sight.

"Excuse us." Shenza apologized as the song faltered. Juss and Chimi quickly bowed.

With her mind, Chimi hurried the three sand golems into the shrine.

The inner courtyard was brighter than the rest of the town. She couldn't tell where the light was coming from, but it lit the faces of the three statues and erased the glare of the golems' eyes. Even more than before, Chimi sensed a presence hanging over them. It felt impatient and demanding.

"We should hurry," Shenza said in a low voice.

At the same moment, Lelldour advised Chimi, *"Do not delay."*

Shenza and Juss were looking at Chimi again. "Go ahead," she told them.

Shenza faced the statues, as Aspace had done the day before. "Lords of the Sky, Lords of the Trees, and mighty Lords of the Waves," she called. Her voice was thin and nervous. "You know why we have come. Our enemies are gone from these shores. Now see how my Lord honors his agreement."

As Shenza spoke, Chimi called the three golems forward. Juss edged along behind them, grabbing cords and lifting bottles one by one. He stepped clear, holding the bottles away from himself with an expression of disgust. Shenza raised her spiral wand.

Three times she ordered, "Dispel!"

Just as before, the simulated humans slumped with rasping sighs. A sudden wind swept in, tossing tree branches and scouring away the pure white sand. Chimi thought the ceremony was over, but the water in the pool suddenly bubbled and swirled. It swished upward and coalesced into a humanlike form even more alien then the golems'.

A nature spirit! Juss stared, the glowing bottles forgotten in his hand. Chimi trembled until Master Lelldour made her bow low. Shenza also bowed in respect. She started to speak, but the Eleshouri cut her off.

"This is acceptable." Its gurgling voice was barely understandable. "But do not think we forget so easily. The volcano shall stay to remind you who is supreme."

With a final swoosh, it sank back into the pool and was gone.

Chimi stood frozen. Just as with the shark spirits, she could hardly believe what she had seen. Then she heard whispering and turned, startled. Mourners from the funeral stared from the shrine's entrance with wide eyes and open mouths.

"It's all right," Shenza called to them.

The mourners shuffled off, still murmuring. They were soon singing again, but Chimi guessed the deceased person's life was no longer the sole topic of conversation. Chimi, who loved to gossip, wondered how long it would take for their story to spread through the town.

"Here." Juss offered Chimi the three bottles, which still glowed faintly. She barely felt the cold as she took them.

"That's it, then?" Shenza asked nervously.

Chimi nodded. It seemed almost too easy. Yet she had sensed no protest as the golems' artificial bodies crumbled. Except for Makko, she didn't think the ghosts had liked being part of Vesswan's scheme. They could never have known peace while they were trapped that way. Now she held their spirits in her hands, like some kind of bizarre jewelry.

"Not yet, you silly girl," Lelldour inserted into her mind.

"Oh!" Chimi exclaimed. The necromancer's ghost was doing something weird.

"What's the matter?" Shenza demanded, but Chimi couldn't reply.

Invisible to the others, Lelldour released her from his control and dragged himself free of her body. She felt dizzy, as if she had been carrying something heavy and was finally allowed to put it down. Her hand jerked, making the glass bottles clink together. Juss grabbed her elbow, steadying her, but Chimi's head was already clearing.

"I'm fine," Chimi assured them.

"We both are," Lelldour corrected.

Shenza and Juss both jumped as the necromancer's ghost materialized beside Chimi. The sun was rising at last, though its radiance didn't touch him. Chimi gave a shaky laugh.

"Now we're really done," she said. With the golems destroyed, the spirits appeased, and Lelldour no longer possessing her, the emergency was truly over.

"Thank you for all your help," Shenza said, and she bowed to Lelldour.

He merely nodded at her words. Once again, his eyes focused on Chimi. There was still a lot to learn about necromancy, and she would have to put up with her ghostly mentor for months to come, but it felt so good to be alone in her body that Chimi didn't even mind.

"Master Lelldour, can I have the rest of the day off?" She bobbed a pert bow and wheedled, as she would with Byben. Lifting the three bottles, she said, "I know I have to help these ghosts, but there's something else I need to do first."

"Chimi!" Shenza started to lecture her.

But Lelldour nodded. "I, too, would like to refresh myself. It was unpleasant to be in someone else's body. Come to my house at dusk and we'll begin your training."

"I'll be there," Chimi promised. As the ghost faded away, she thought he looked at her with a little less disapproval.

They left the shrine, walking fast to avoid disrupting the funeral any more. Once they were in the street, Shenza tried again to scold Chimi.

"Sister, you shouldn't put off your responsibilities."

"Oh, let her alone," Juss countered. "After yesterday, we should take the day off, too."

Chimi laughed. She felt light and carefree, reveling in the sensation of privacy within her own body.

"Let's all take the day off!" she cried. With a smirk, she added, "Besides, I think Lady Izmay wanted to talk to you about a few things."

To her delight, Shenza actually blushed.

* * *

They returned to Lord Aspace's estate, where Shenza and Juss had to report their tasks accomplished. Chimi left the three red bottles in her temporary quarters at the Pearl Court. She still had one job left, and it might be the hardest one of all.

A short walk brought her to the Kesquin estate. Glancing seaward, she saw the volcano looming on the other side of a narrow channel. No fumes darkened the sky now, but Chimi still shivered when she looked at it. The new mountain was a very tangible reminder of how much things had changed.

The Kesquin household was in mourning. Strips of scarlet fabric draped the gate and were woven into the branches of nearby trees. Chimi hesitated when she heard keening inside the compound. She didn't see any smoke, but there might still be a funeral going on. She didn't want to interrupt another one.

The gate guard was an older man who usually tended the gardens. He must have been pressed into service after some of the trained fighters were killed. Catching Chimi's eye, he beckoned to her.

"I'm glad you're feeling better," he said. "We were worried yesterday."

"I'm sorry to be a bother," Chimi apologized. "Is the family receiving visitors?"

"We aren't ready for public viewings, but I know Lady Winomi would want to see you," he said. "Please come in."

"If you're sure," Chimi said. The latch was already lifting, and the gate swung inward to admit her.

Chimi knew the family wouldn't be relaxing under their arbor on a day like this, so she turned right, toward the living quarters. The cottages were clustered among a grove of small camphor trees. On her left, the family's private shrine stood on a low knoll open to the sky. Chimi glimpsed the usual three statues and a row of at least ten pallets. Some were still empty, while others held bodies shrouded in crimson.

One of these stood closer to the statues, raised slightly higher than the others. A woman knelt beside it, moaning wildly as she rocked back and forth. A large man sat nearby, shoulders heaving. With a shock, Chimi recognized Lord Fastu. The woman threw her head back and howled her grief. Chimi knew that voice. It was Lady Panubi.

Chimi's throat tightened. Whatever ill-will she felt toward Panubi evaporated like dew from the leaves. Lord Fastu had sent his own son to help Lord Aspace and lost him to the golems. It was something that went beyond mere politics.

Feeling like an intruder, she hurried up the path toward the camphor trees. A short flight of steps brought her to a landing of marble blocks.

"Excuse me," she called into the nearest cottage.

Just inside, she saw a central chamber. Pillows lay scattered around a table, which held a teapot and half-empty cups. Doorways led to the bedchambers of Winomi, her two sisters, and Azma. At the sound of her voice, there was a flurry of scuffling noises in one of them.

"Chimi?" Winomi darted out of Azma's room, clutching a scarlet robe, which she seemed to be trying on. "Oh, it is you! I was so worried!"

Winomi threw the trailing end of the robe over her shoulder and rushed to hug Chimi. Gratefully, Chimi hugged her back. All at once, she had the urge to cry.

Azma strolled into the room behind Winomi. She wore a mourning robe and her usual acid expression. Chimi's moment of self-pity vanished. Her own family was safe, but the Kesquins weren't so lucky. She drew back and looked at Winomi. From her puffy eyes and constant sniffle, her friend had already been crying.

"Are your brothers all right? Yassart and Radu? Tolari?" Chimi asked. "I know Miroth died. I saw him fighting. I'm so sorry."

"Radu is fine, but what do you mean, you saw?" Winomi asked.

For some reason, Azma was furious. "You were there? Impossible!"

"Yes, I was there." Chimi did her best to meet their eyes without either bragging or whining. "I'm a necromancer. I didn't want to tell anyone. I was afraid of what you would say, but I can't hide it anymore."

"That's true," Winomi added somberly.

"A necromancer?" Azma edged away, just as Shenza had the first time Chimi mentioned ghosts. "You don't know anything about necromancy."

"I'm going to learn," Chimi said ruefully. "Anyway, I had to be there. I was helping Master Lelldour help Lord Aspace."

"Who?" Azma interrupted.

"My teacher, Master Lelldour. He's a ghost. It's too complicated. I'll explain later." Chimi hugged Winomi again to ease the sting of her words. "But, Nomi, you don't know what it was like! When I got sick, my soul was trapped outside my body. I saw what was happening, but there was nothing I could do about it."

"It wasn't your fault," Winomi reassured her. Good old Winomi.

"I can see how upset you were," Azma snapped, recovering her bad humor. "It didn't stop you from buying a new robe, I see."

Chimi plucked at the folds of her new crimson robe. "This? It was a gift." She decided it would be better not to say who had given her the robe. Trying to reestablish some kind of friendship, she asked, "How about you? Are your father and brothers all right?"

"They're fine," Azma answered stiffly. Her mood seemed unusually sour. Was something else bothering her? Chimi caught her breath as she realized what it must be.

"Oh, no!" she cried. "Your parents haven't called off the wedding, have they? I know what that means to you."

"Did you come here to make fun of me?" Azma's voice was so shrill that Chimi knew she had guessed right.

"Cousin!" Winomi chided. To Chimi, she added, "They haven't said anything, but we have to wonder. Now that... I mean... The match might not be so good anymore."

But Chimi said, "No, Azma. I came to apologize. I haven't been a very good friend lately."

Azma stared at her suspiciously, while Winomi blurted, "*You* haven't been a good friend?"

"Not really." Chimi looked into Azma's sullen face. "All I could talk about was myself, even when I could tell it bothered you. So, I'm sorry."

She pressed both hands to her chest and bowed to Azma. Then she bowed to Winomi.

"Thanks for staying with me when I was sick. I never deserved to have a friend like you."

"You don't have to apologize," Winomi said.

"It's all right," Azma finally answered. Her expression softened for the first time in months.

Awkwardly, Chimi went on, "I know you have funerals, but maybe later on you can tell me about your wedding. I mean, if your parents decide to do it. I really want to hear it."

"Maybe," Azma said.

Chimi still felt a prickle of guilt inside, because she had a lot of choice gossip—Shenza and Aspace, Laraquies and Izmay—and she couldn't tell them. It would undercut her whole apology if she started preening again. Besides, she had promised Shenza she wouldn't blab.

Instead, she said, "My family left to get away from the volcano, so I should have a couple of days before I go back to work. Do you think we can get together and go shopping again?"

"What is there to buy?" Winomi asked.

"A red robe," Chimi said.

"But that one is so cute!" her friend cried.

"I know." Chimi couldn't resist twirling to show off the design. Then she explained, "Master Lelldour says it's too fancy. It has to be plain red."

"I guess we could help you out," Azma said. Chimi knew she wasn't totally forgiven, but it was a start.

"With Jeruki and Lukita, too?" Winomi asked. "That would be fun."

Chimi nodded. "We've all lost a lot, even those whose families got away safely. I don't want our friendship to be ruined, too."

"It won't be," Winomi promised.

Chimi felt a wave of hope and relief. Lord Manseen's ambitions had hit them all hard, but Chalsett-port survived. She still had her friends. Chimi remembered how Shenza and Izmay had been glowing this morning. At last, she felt like she had a reason to glow, too.

THE END

Breinigsville, PA USA
25 January 2010
231303BV00002B/3/P